URBAN QUEEN

JASON KEEBY

 iUniverse®

URBAN QUEEN

iUniverse books may be ordered through booksellers or by contacting:

iUniverse
1663 Liberty Drive
Bloomington, IN 47403
www.iuniverse.com
844-349-9409

ISBN: 978-1-6632-3197-0 (sc)
ISBN: 978-1-6632-3196-3 (e)

Library of Congress Control Number: 2021923213

Print information available on the last page.

iUniverse rev. date: 02/03/2022

CHAPTER 1

"Smile for the camera, Angelika! What's wrong?" Her mother, Felisha asked, holding her brand-new Dycam. Angelika's older brother, Andrew, was sitting on the couch, sipping on a small glass of Jack Daniel's, wearing a simple pair of blue Wrangler jeans and a white T-Shirt. He'd just quit his job at the Waste Management plant and was currently in between jobs. Constantly being gotten on by their mother.

Angelika and Stephan, were taking their first Senior Prom photos. He'd just slid the corsage, that he'd purchased from Safeway, over her caramel-colored wrist. The White Orchid complemented her solid black, waist-cinching dress. The dress was knee-length and flared out towards the bottom, with wide shoulder straps. Her Mary-Jane flats came with a white flower glued onto the toe. Her black shoulder-length hair curled out at the tips, and her straight bangs stopped right at the brow. Stephan had on a matching, all black tux, with a black button up and black patent leather Steve Maddens. His hair, pulled back into a tight ponytail.

Stephan has loved Angelika since the moment he first laid eyes on her their Junior year in High School. Angelika and her mom, Felisha, moved to Oakland, CA shortly after her father died. He was almost home from a business trip in Alabama, excited to see his wife and kids again, when Atlantic Airlines flight 2311 nose-dived, just 2 miles short of its final destination, Atlanta International airport.

The left propeller suddenly malfunctioned at the plane's peak height, causing the plane, and everyone on it, to fall to a fiery grave, his body being incinerated on impact. Despite her devastation, Felisha won a $2

Million settlement from the airline, which she then gave half of to his mother and father. She couldn't remain in the house that they raised a family in without him and headed to the Bay Area for a new start. Andrew, whom was only 6 when their father died, hated leaving his home. Angelika had just turned 2 the day before and didn't have many memories of him.

Stephan was in 6th period, 11th grade English, when he heard the commotion, from the classroom grow louder. He glanced upward, just as any normal person would, trying to locate the instant cause of disruption. He laid eyes on Angelika, immediately taken away by her beauty. His heart fluttered so fast, it almost seemed to stop right in his chest.

Angelika was petite, with shoulder-length hair and a caramel-chocolate complexion. She wore a black t-shirt, with the picture of Tupac's, All Eyez on Me album cover, under a pair of jean over-all's. She rolled them up to her ankles, showing off a pair of black Chuck Taylor Converse. She was obviously nervous as she held her orange and black textbook close to her chest.

"Attention, students!" Yelled the teacher, Ms. Jenny. She was a short, skinny, young Chinese lady with straight, black shoulder-length hair, that she often tucked behind her ears. "We have a new classmate! Welcome Angelika, everyone." She said, looking over her class schedule. She handed the paper back to Angelika and pointed to the empty seat next to Stephan. He felt like the luckiest guy in the world. He remembered his backpack was currently taking up the occupancy of the plastic chair, attached to the wooden table by large steel rods. He removed it, sliding the bag under the seat he was in.

"Hola. Mi llamo, Stephan." He said, introducing himself, extending his hand out to her. Angelika smiled, turning away, as she pushed a few fly away strands of hair, behind her ear. She looked over to her right, at a picture of different paragraph structures. Still smiling, anxiously, looking back to him. He still had his hand extended towards her, ready to be shook, which she grabbed, after a few moments.

"Hi, I don't know Spanish, but my names Angelika."

"How'd you know what I asked you?" He said flashing a million-dollar smile. Angelika was blinded by his manly beauty and soft to the touch, shoulder-length curls.

Stephan was built like a basketball player; tall for his age at 6', slim with an impressive muscle mass. He was fair skinned with hazel-green eyes.

"Really? That's one of the first things Spanish teachers teach you, is how to introduce yourself." She said smiling, becoming a little more comfortable, that the cutest boy in class talked to her on her first day. Her anxiety began to subside. After being kicked out of her last and 4th school for fighting, she hoped this school would bring about a pleasant change. Or it was off to job corps.

"I am smiling, mom." Angelika said while forcing a smile. She was ready to go and get her night started. Stephan was excited to finally have her to himself for an entire night. He was happy for the moment, even though he could tell something was eating at Angelika. Weighing heavily on her. She'd been acting strange, since last Saturday.

Felisha took a few more pictures, and allowed the teens to head to their car, parked right outside, a black, 1988 Lincoln Townecar.

"You guys be good. Have her back by midnight." Felisha said, watching as Stephan let Angelika into the limo first, then followed behind her. She continued taking pictures of the car that they were in. License plate included.

"You really let her go out in that short ass skirt?" Andrew chimed in, walking to the doorway, next to Felisha.

"Boy let her have fun. Yo' prom date wore something worse, remember?" Felisha replied, walking into the house as the limousine pulled away from the curb. Andrew watched the red lights stop at the stop sign and disappear after turning left.

"Whooo!" Stephan said excitedly. He couldn't wait to pull away from her mother's house, to open the sunroof and yell out into the quiet night sky. He plopped down into the leather seat, noticing Angelika staring out of the window. She had moved all the way over to the corner of the limousine, closest to the driver. Steph remained seated directly under the sunroof. "You ready to party tonight, baby?" He asked, shooting over to a seat next to her. He wrapped his arm around her shoulder, but he couldn't seem to get her to come closer to him. He knew in his heart something was wrong with her and he tried his best not to let the mood die down.

"Yeah…can't wait." She replied dryly, still never looking at him.

"Baby, what's wrong?" He asked her, just wanting to figure out what was going on with her.

She replied, "I'm fine, baby. Just ready to get there." She forced a smile and kissed him on the lips. He could tell she wasn't being real with him, but he let it go. For the next 15 minutes, until they made it to their prom, he went through his head all of the wrong things he could've done. He couldn't come up with more than 2, but they wouldn't have upset her to this degree. He held her hand, staring out of the window with her, not sure of what it was that could be bothering her.

They made it to Oakland High School. Prom night 1990, *Welcome to the '90's*. The limo driver rushed over to open their door, after pulling over behind a line of other limos. The two of them stepped out, feeling like movie stars, looking around as a lot of other students laid eyes on them, after being dropped off by their parents. They walked through the sea of students, passed the large blue, front gate. There was a security guard, directing kids to the large gym, through the quad. They weren't allowing anyone into the main building.

Hi-Five's, *I Like the Way* blasted through the speakers of the auditorium. The decorations bright and bold, with lots of bright purples, blues, and greens. The gym looked like an amazing trip to Miami's Ocean Drive. The room was littered with students dancing, with barely anyone holding the wall or staying seated. The atmosphere made those in attendance want to dance and feel free for a night of minimal supervision. Angelika even found herself bobbing to the music, though still plagued by the thoughts on her mind.

Stephan danced and sang to her, as they made it to their table, meeting his friends Johnathon and Liam, AKA Liam.

"Hey guys." Angelika said, once again dryly, sitting in the cushioned white chair Stephan held out for her.

"Damn, girl. What's up your snatch?" Liam asked. He was thin and not really the tallest amongst his peers, most of whom, especially his female counterparts, considered him soft, due to his flair for style and his soft-spoken tone. He had on a white button up, under a silver blazer, with a matching pair of silver slacks, and a pair of white loafers. He wore his hair like Prince in Purple Rain, his idol.

"Hey, Angie." Johnathon said, sitting next to Crystal, his girlfriend of 2 years now. Johnathon wore a white suit, with a pink tie and almost pink Hi-gloss Oxfords, paired with a nice, white button up. His hair cut into a high-top fade.

Crystal had smooth, brown skin. She wore a white, skin-tight, leather dress, with matching ankle-strapped pumps. Her long, black hair was done up into a bun, with a strand of hair hanging from each temple, showing off her beauty. She wore a gorgeous silver necklace which rested perfectly on her collar bone. Her diamond earrings making it pop.

"Los siento." Liam said, noticing Steph shoot him a death stare. He reached into his sliver blazer, pulling out an equally silver flask, decorated with the Oakland Raiders shield and one-eyed pirate.

Stephan and Johnathon have been friends since kids, growing up in the 65 village, otherwise known as the Lockwood Gardens. Like West Oakland's Acorn projects, housed many of East Oakland's impoverished, minority families. The area was gritty, not really safe for anyone not from there. Day or night. Many homeless and drug riddle individuals roamed the area. They caused trouble, robbing, or worse if they felt the need to.

Stephan was anything but a product of his environment. Between him and Johnathon, he was the more level-headed one. It took a lot of pushing, prodding, and poking to get him upset. But once he was there, his Puerto Rican blood always got the best of him. His yellow skin turning red, like the whites in his eyes, and his green pupils going hazel.

Johnathon was a hot head through and through, taking after his Dominican, jail-bird father. He liked to fight, finding the fun in it, like most of the area's youth. He walked down the street, looking for anyone to lay hands on. And he was damn good at it. Older than Stephan, by 3 months, he felt a sense of being an older brother. Though he'd lost his own big brother, to the gun violence in the streets when he was just 5 years old, contributing to his violent nature. His mother became extra protective over him. It was just them 2 now. Them and her newfound love for crack cocaine and heroin.

Stephan didn't like fighting much. His parents, mother especially, continued to drum into his head the dangers of it and the possible outcomes. His father agreed, but knew, just how everything couldn't be solved with violence, he also knew you couldn't walk away from everything either. Behind his wife's back, he trained Stephan with guns and fighting, until he ended up winning the sparring match. A few times.

Frick Middle just opened its doors for classes, after a 2-week winter vacation. Their parents had a good year and was able to buy the boys Jordan's for Christmas. The red and white Air Jordan OGs, which were released just a year prior, in 1983. They both got theirs to match, and came to school on the first day, styling on their classmates. 8th grader, Thomas Baker, walked up to them and said, "Not one, but two pairs of new shoes." They stood in the cafeteria, waiting to get their lunch. They looked at him, then at each other, not sure what he was talking about. "Your shoes. Give them to me." He ordered, serious as a stroke. The white kid had hit puberty early, growing up and out faster than his classmates, giving him the obvious advantage. This wasn't the first that the two of them had witnessed Thomas bullying someone at the school, they just never thought it'd happen to them personally. They burst out into loud, boisterous laughter.

"Nigga funny, bro." They ignored him and his request, as they followed the line, moving forward.

"Bitch, I'm not fuckin playing with you!" He yelled, grabbing Stephan by his left shoulder. He pulled Steph back so hard, that he fell to the ground. Stephan, realizing what happened, jumped up, getting ready to box. But, before he could get his feet firmly planted back on the ground, Johnathon was already swinging. He threw lefts and rights, into Thomas' face, not stopping until Thomas himself was on the floor, holding his now bloody nose. Stephan ran over and kicked Thomas in the side of his face, temporarily putting him to sleep.

"Still want our shoes, bitch?" Johnathon asked laughing. The two of them ran outside, to the courtyard, where many other students were hanging around. They did their best to blend into the sea of students on the blacktop.

It wasn't until later in the day that the principal called them into the office. Mrs. Baker, sat with her son in the row of seats, directly outside of Principal Dyson's office. She looked at them with a grimace on her face.

"Boo, bitch." Johnathon said, walking passed her.

"You ought to be ashamed of yourselves." She said.

"Teach your son to be ashamed of himself." Stephan shot back before entering the office and shutting the door.

"Have a seat, you two." Said Principal Dyson.

It was a few months later, the summer of '84 when Liam moved into the apartment complex. Stephan and Johnathon just barely beat the streetlights home, enjoying the warm, summer night air.

"Aye, check it out. New neighbors." Stephan said. They were stopped at the entrance of the parking lot, peeping out the U-Haul truck. There was a large man, carrying a two-seated couch into the empty apartment next to Johnathon's. He had on a tight, muscle-bound t-shirt, and a pair of black Dungarees. That's when they noticed a kid around their age, standing inside of the back of the truck. He had a basketball, bouncing it in the same spot over and over again.

"Is he slow?" Johnathon asked.

"Shut up, man." Stephan said, chuckling. "Let's go see." He said, riding his bike over to Liam. Johnathon followed.

"Liam!" A woman yelled. "Deja de remoter was pelota!" She yelled out of the kitchen window.

"Si, Miami!" He yelled back in response. He jumped down and continued to bounce the ball on the concrete.

"Hey, where you from?" Johnathon asked as they made it across the parking lot. The boy looked up, confused. He had on a green Oakland A's tee, a pair of grey cargo shorts and a pair of white Nikes that looked to be as old as he was.

"¿Que?" The boy responded, still wearing a confused expression.

"De donde eres? Where you from?" Stephan asked again, translating for Johnny.

"Ahhh, okay. Mejico. Ensenada."

"Oh, so ya'll illegal and shit, huh?" Johnathon asked.

Liam was confused again, "Que?", he simply repeated.

"Bro, shut up." Stephan chuckled.

Liam didn't take long, to show his new friends who he was. An asshole. He was the type of person to go out of his way to be an asshole, but he was always there for them. Stephan translated conversations between the three of them. It took Liam about a year to learn enough English to communicate on his own.

The three of them sat in Liam's living room, watching the brand-new show, MTV's Top 20 Countdown. Liam's mom had a simple sofa, directly placed on the other side of a glass-top coffee table with a charred-oak wooden frame. The walls were a boring off-white, which she decorated with generations of family pictures and religious wall art.

"Ustedes necesitan algo antes de que me vaya?" Liam's mom, Rosalita asked, throwing her keys into her brown, leather purse with a strap that went down to her upper thigh. She was headed out to her overnight stocking job at Walmart, over by the Oakland Coliseum.

"No, we don't need anything Ms. Hernandez. Thank you." Stephan said.

"No, mami. Gracias." Liam replied to his mother. She smiled and nodded, before heading out of the door to make it to her bus.

"So, ya'll came all this way, and didn't stop to learn English?" Johnathon asked, chuckling.

"Bro-"

"No, es bueno." Liam said, cutting Stephan off, mid-sentence. "I'm tired of this pendejo." He said, stunning both of them. They each leaned to the side shocked his English was so strong.

"Nigga, what the fuck you call me?" Johnathon asked, standing up, offended Liam just called him a dumbass. Liam stood up with him.

"Nigga you heard me. *PENDEJO. Fucking idiot*!" Liam yelled.

"Whoa, whoa." Stephan said, standing as well. He could feel the tension in the room starting to build. "What the fuck, ya'll?" He asked, trying to keep them away from each other.

"I'm tired of him, brother!" Said Liam.

"And nigga I'm tired of you. Do something, bruh!" Johnathon said, shoving Stephan out of the way. He didn't wait for a response before punching Liam in the face. He came back with a swift left swing, and a bear-hug, taking them both down to the floor. Stephan did his best to break them up, but Liam continued to throw punches while Johnathon was down. It was his first time ever seeing Johnathon on his back during a fight and it urged him to shove Liam halfway across the room.

It's been 6 years now, and so far, they've managed to keep their hands to themselves.

"Los siento, mami. Really. Just wanted to have some fun, cha-know?" He tossed his head back, taking a swig of his mother's Tequila.

"Dude, you trynna get us kicked the fuck out of prom?" Stephan asked, pushing the drink away from his lips, still upset about his comment to Angelika when they first walked in the room.

"Agh!!" He exclaimed in frustration. "Fine, I'm going to smoke. Ya'll taking me down." He whined, grabbing a joint out of the breast pocket of his button up.

"Now, that I can get with." Johnathon said, standing with Liam. Their girls followed. As did Stephan and Angelika. She held tightly onto his hand, as the six of them snuck into the boy's locker room, where the air was thick with must and cheap cologne. The bright blue paint on the lockers were chipping off, leaving them in desperate need of a touch-up. They hurried through, to the main building, as to not get caught by security or one of the chaperones. They were now inside the large cafeteria. The only light that shown in the large room, was the ambient moonlight through the window almost 2 stories up. It was spooky, being in the school at night, but also exciting. The group headed upstairs and made a left down the first hallway. They walked around, jiggling door handles to find an open classroom.

"Oh shit." John whispered loudly. "Aye, right here, ya'll." He slowly opened the door to his science teacher's classroom making sure no one was inside. Mr. Padilla was just downstairs, acting as one of the many chaperones.

"Bruh, what you doing? He's right downstairs." Stephan said, whispering loudly.

"Shit, estroy dentro." Liam said, walking right into the room. Johnathon and their girlfriends followed behind him. Stephan started to walk inside but stopped. Angelika held his hand, pulling him back into the hallway.

"What's up, baby?" He asked smiling, turning to her.

"I need to talk to you." She said shyly. She couldn't look him in his eyes. She, instead, stared down at the flowers on her shoes.

"What's going on?" He asked again. He lifted her chin to meet her gaze. Just then, he heard the squeak of large, heavy rubber boots, against the slick tile. "Fuck." He whispered. He could see the bright circle from a flashlight, coming down the intersecting hallway. He grabbed her hand, ducking into the classroom before the source of light could turn the corner and come down their hall, exposing them. Johnathon and Liam were standing by the open window, already smoking the joint.

"Aye, nigga, get down." Stephan warned.

"Nigga, what for?" Johnathon replied, blowing a cloud of smoke through the window.

"Security, bitch." He said, locking the door. They all suddenly scattered: Steph and Angelika took safety under Mr. Padilla's desk. Johnathon and his girlfriend Crystal hid under the large, 50-gallon tortoise tank, which was home to about 15-20 small turtles, while Liam and Esmeralda hid under the computer desks. Everyone's heart stopped as they watched the beam of light breach through the darkness of the room, through the door's glass window. They all held their breath as the light crossed over the computers. The door handle jiggled. Liam looked at the floor in front of him, noticing that he'd dropped the joint, and it was still lit. The beam of light was only inches away from the weed cigarette. Without hesitation or a second thought, he snatched it up. Rather being caught in the wrong area, than with weed. He was able to remain unseen. Everyone exhaled a sigh of relief as the security guard continued down the hallway.

"Fuck, that was too close." Crystal said, as they all came out of hiding, dusting themselves off. They all began laughing. All but Angelika. Something was still weighing heavily on her heart and mind.

"Joder, si." Liam replied, taking another swig of the flask. He held it out, offering anyone else a sip. They all took one, happy they remained undetected.

They continued smoking. Stephan never forgetting that Angelika wanted to talk. He knew she had some bad news to share. Doing his best not to let his anxiety show.

Suddenly they heard the door handle jiggle again, but before they were able to hide this time, the door flung open. "Whoa! What are you guys doing in here?" It was Mr. Padilla. He had come back to the classroom. Lord only knows for what.

Mr. Padilla was the definition of a hippie. He was a tall Italian man, with a chest-length beard, long blonde dreads, and a complete minimalist attitude. He wore a brown, plaid blazer over a similar button-up and brown slacks. "Is…is that weed I smell?" He zeroed in on Liam, who was trying to hold the lit joint behind his back. "Hand it over." He ordered. Liam did as he was told and handed over the burning joint. He looked at them disappointed, before putting the joint to his lips. After two long pulls, he passed it back to Liam.

"Whoa, really? Mr. P, you smoke?" Johnathon asked.

"I have a life outside of school, guys." He replied, walking over to his desk. He reached into the bottom drawer on the right and pulled out a half-drunken bottle of Jack Daniel's. Twisting off the top, he put the bottle to his lips. "No one's spiked the punch yet." He chuckled. The students were floored. Not sure how to process what was going on. He turned to leave, then stopped at the door, turning back around to face them. "Don't burn down my classroom, please. And also, this stays in this room." He finished before leaving. They were all silent for a few moments.

"Yo' knew I liked that nigga!" Johnathon said excitedly, breaking the silence.

"Right!? That could've ended in expulsion. Too close to graduation." Said Angelika.

"I'm glad he's cool, shit." Crystal added.

The group of teens headed back downstairs to join the party, only a few moments after finishing the weed. It was still lively, with students all on the floor. Angelika was reluctant to have some fun. Stephan didn't want her to break up with him, so he convinced her to dance with him. Hoping this could save the two of them, by at least taking her mind away from what was wrong.

Prom night was just about coming to an end. Liam and Johnathon had already gone home with their girlfriends. Angelika and Stephan sat at the table, eating on some of the deserts supplied by the school. He looked across the table at her. "You're really beautiful, you know that?"

"Thank you." She said, forcing a smile.

"It's almost midnight. You ready to head out of here?" He asked, standing, extending his hand out to help her. She grabbed his hand and stood.

They were now once again alone. Sitting in the back of the limousine, the atmosphere was thicker than before. He sat, looking out of the window, as the driver started the engine.

"Hey, Steph?" She called out to him.

"Well, this is it." He thought to himself. "What's up, baby?" He could feel his anxiety running rampant.

"I have to tell you something." She said, nervously. Her anxiety and fear of the unknown also getting the better of her, knowing she couldn't hold onto her secret any longer. It was starting to eat away at her like a virus.

"Y-y-y-yeah babe. What's on your mind?" He could feel his forehead getting warm.

"I don't even know how to say this…" She rolled the window down, allowing June's warm night air to rush through the interior of the car. Stephan watched her, wanting to tear up at her beauty, as the lights from the street hit her high cheek bones. He felt like God was staring down on her from above. He sat silent, with his hands folded into his lap, waiting for another girl to ruin his life. He twirled his thumbs, looking at the lint embedded into the dark grey carpeting, wondering what he could have done to lose her. He sat there, waiting for her to break his heart.

"I love you." He said through a lump in his throat. He was trying to hold on the best he could.

"I love you, too. But, you might not after I-." His sadness turned into confusion.

"Are you breaking up with me?" His psyche, and more importantly, his heart, couldn't sit in suspense any longer. That was the least of his worries, considering the thoughts that were racing through his mind now. "Did she fuck Liam, or worse Johnathon?" He continuously thought to himself, starting to get angry.

"What?" She looked at him with tears in her eyes. "No, I- I could never leave you." She admitted.

"Then what is it? Are you fucking one of my fr-", he couldn't bring himself to finish the sentence.

"No! Hell no! Babe, you're going to be a father." She said after grabbing his face with both hands. She repeated herself, "You're going to be a dad. I'm pregnant."

Stephan was speechless. He flashed back to a couple years ago, when Liam had his son, Phillippe. He remembered lecturing him about not using protection and how they were still kids themselves, when Esmeralda was pregnant. Not to mention the fact she comes from a crazy cartel family and wasn't all the way there, mentally, herself. She was older than him by 3 years. Her only redeeming qualities were that she was gorgeous and had long money.

But that wasn't their situation. Stephan and Angelika were broke. His heart sank into his stomach. He had no idea what to do, or what to say. He couldn't afford a baby, or an abortion for that matter. He then started to think about Andrew. "What if he tries to fight him?"

It's been a couple weeks since Angelika broke the news to Stephan. He was able to land a closing job, after school, at the McDonald's on 63rd and International, almost directly across from his home. His parents just assumed he was ready to start making his own money and thought nothing more of it. But it wasn't enough.

Stephan laid atop the messy covers, of his queen-sized bed. He'd just gotten off of work less than an hour ago, still wearing his full uniform. He was dog-tired, but his mind was racing, not allowing him to go to sleep. He stared at the rotating blades on the ceiling fan, trying to figure out what he was going to do.

TINK! TINK! TINK! He heard someone tapping on his window. He peeked through the curtains, seeing Johnathon and Liam holding their bikes.

"What's up with ya'll?" He asked, lifting up his window.

"Essie was able to get some shit from her dad's stash." Liam said, holding up a large black duffle bag. Stephan reached for it, interested in what was inside.

"The fuck?" He said, unzipping the bag. He found five bricks of what looked to be cocaine.

"I need money, bro. Not coke." He zipped up the bag and tossed it out of the window, onto the ground.

"Nigga, it's between $80,000 and $120,000 in this bag bruh." Johnathon said picking the bag up.

"How did she even get that? He ain't gone know it's gone?" Stephan asked.

"Bruh, he gave it to her to give to me. And I'm trynna help ya'll two." Liam said. "Come on, brother. Just take one or two bricks, we only need a couple to flip and pay her father back anyways."

Stephan stood there, looking between the bag and his two friends. He was starting to consider what life would be like, catching his reflection in the mirror of the sliding closet door. His heart sank to his stomach, thinking about how Angelika and their baby would eat if anything happened to him. All due to something he could've avoided.

"Yeah, nigga. Life can be all Gucci and Prada." Johnathon said, smiling, smoking on a joint.

"Oh, now ya'll niggas agree on something?" He chuckled.

"Eh," Liam hunched his shoulders, "when he's right, he's right."

"Nah, I think imma pass, bruh." Stephan said.

"Aight, man. Suit yourself. If you change your mind, just hit me, brother." Liam said as he mounted his bike.

"See you later, bruh." Johnathon said, doing the same. They rode away. Stephan watched, hoping the two hot heads didn't get into any trouble. He shut his window, taking off everything except his boxers. He laid down thinking back on what his friends were wearing. Liam's hair was freshly French braided. He had on an all-white FuBu tracksuit, and a pair of matching FuBu sneakers, and a brand-new silver watch, and diamond earrings. Johnathon wore a white wife-beater, a pair of brand new, black Levi's, with a pair of fresh Timberland boots. His hair was cut into a fresh, low fade.

Stephan was beginning to feel in over his head. There was no way he'd be able to support a baby on $4.25 an hour. He suddenly began to feel a pit in his stomach, as he thought about what it was that he had to do. He had to tell his parents. He sat up in bed, nervous, like someone was trying to break into the house and he was there alone.

"Fuck." He whispered. He stood up and threw his jeans back on, then opened his bedroom door. He could hear a soccer game playing loudly on the living room tv and could smell his mother's enchiladas cooking for tomorrow's dinner. He walked down the hall slowly not sure how he was even going to begin to tell his parents. His nerves grew with each step. "Can I...can I talk to you guys?" He asked, shyly.

"Que pasa, hijo?" Asked his mother, she had just gotten done washing and drying a few dishes, drying her hands with a black kitchen towel.

"Mi novia esta...novia esta..." He cleared his throat. He thought that he'd just spit it out, but when he actually saw his parents, he didn't know how to formulate his thoughts, let alone his words. "Mi novia esta-"

"Que?! Escupirlo. Spit it out kid!" His father exclaimed, shutting off the tv. He had a look in his eyes, like he'd already known what his son was going to say. His mom looked worried as she came into the living room.

"Just, tell us son." She said, placing a hand on his shoulder guiding him over to the couch to sit down.

"Está embarazada." He said. More nervous now than he was before. The room grew silent for all of about 20 seconds.

"Oh no." His mother whispered, covering her hand with her mouth. She tried to hide her disappointment, but it was too late. He'd already seen it.

"What are you talking about son? Are you telling me your girlfriend is fucking pregnant?" His dad asked, standing up and now in front of him. "Huh?! Is that what the fuck you are telling me?!" His dad yelled.

"Hey, hey, hey. Frank, calmate." His mother said, standing up between them.

"You go get your shit and get out of this fucking house." His father growled, grabbing his upper arm, and hoisting him up off of the couch and to his feet.

"But, dad-" Steph begged, with tears building up in his eyes.

"Salir ahora mismo!! Ahora!"

"Okay, bien esperar. Let's all just, calm down. Please we can talk about this." She could see Stephan was hurt.

"No, Talia, he has to go!" Franklin yelled.

"Dad, I can't do this by myself!" He yelled, full of frustration, anger and sadness.

"Raise your voice again, and I'll toss you out myself. You made the baby yourself, go out there and be a man. Take care of it."

"Frank-"

"No! My word is final." He said, back in his reclining chair, turning the tv back on.

Stephan ran back to his room, scared, sad and angry. He began to rip his posters off of the walls, yanked the tv off of the stand it was on and onto the floor. After punching a couple holes in the wall, he packed everything he could fit into a large blue Adidas duffle, then grabbed his bike. Through the walls, he could hear his parents arguing in Spanish about him. He wiped away the tears that fell from his eyes before he opened his bedroom door once more, this time to leave. They stopped arguing as he was walking through the hallway.

"We need to help him, Franklin!" Talia yelled.

"You remember when I got you pregnant? My father did the same. I had to grow up and so does he."

"Frank!-"

"Stop! No more!" He yelled. "I mean it Talia."

"Don't worry, mom. Dad doesn't give a fuck about anyone but himself."

"Perdón?" His father asked, getting in his face. Stephan sucked his teeth and attempted to brush passed his father. "No, say it again, you little shit. No sabes nada!! You know nothing!"

"I said, you don't give a fuck about me or mom-"He then felt a heavy fist come down on his left eye. Next thing he knew, he was sitting on the floor, looking up at his father, ready to strike again. Tears began to flow down his cheeks. He looked over at his mom, tears flowing down hers as well. She didn't do anything to stop him from picking him up and tossing him outside, followed by his bag and his bike.

"AHHHHH!!!!!!!!!!!!!!" He yelled out in anger on his knees, as his father shut and locked the door. He could hear dogs in the neighborhood, starting to bark. He grabbed his bag off of the ground, then mounted his bike. He thought about going to Liam or Johnathon's house, but then remembered they were going to sell off that cocaine. He rode down

International Blvd, starting the 40-minute ride to Angelika's house in Piedmont.

"You're wrong." Talia said, rushing to the bedroom, crying. Franklin sat on the couch, reminiscing about the past and how he felt when his father did the same thing to him.

Franklin Reyes grew up in Morovis, Puerto Rico. Parents, both Creole and Puerto Rican. He met Talia, when he was just a little younger than Stephan, about 16. They were the definition of High School sweethearts. They had the perfect relationship for about a year before he went to his father, telling him and his mother that his girlfriend was pregnant. His father wound up throwing him out of the house with nothing but the clothes on his back and the shoes on his feet. He walked 20 miles trying to make it to Talia's house. Going from corner to corner, neighborhood to neighborhood, scrapping up just enough to keep a little food in his stomach. One evening, looking into the sky, he sat on the curb, tears streaming down his face. He sat in front of a boutique, getting ready to close its doors.

"Aquí vas niño." He heard a female voice from behind him. He turned around, only to find that he was being handed a blanket, stitched into an American flag. He jumped up with the blanket, running to Talia's house. It took him an hour to get to her 2-bedroom home, where she lived with only her father. He ran around to the back of the house, the side her room is on. The sun had just gone down behind the mountains a few moments ago. He could see her bedroom light come on. He searched the ground, looking for little pebbles to toss at her window, tossing two before the window split open outward.

"¿Qué coño haces?!" It was Talia's father.

"Lo siento, señor. Es Talia Inicio?" He asked, wanting to know if she was home.

"No, she lives with her grandparents in the States. New York. Good luck finding her." He said, shutting the window, and turning out the bedroom lights. He was heartbroken that her father would ship her off like that, without even letting her say goodbye. He took it as a sign that the states were where he was meant to be.

Walking out of the backyard, he tripped over something, almost causing him to fall flat on his face, but he maintained his balance. It was a large rock, sitting directly in the middle of the paved walkway, about 20 feet from the rock garden that he knew it came from. There was a note attached to it.

East Harlem. 125th. That's all I remember. I'm sorry. I hope you get this.

There was a kiss mark on the note, in red lipstick. He felt a knot form in his throat as a tear hit the piece of paper. He folded it up and tucked it into his pocket, and from there he made the journey of a lifetime.

He snuck onto the docks, and onto a boat with the word Florida labeled on a bunch of the shipping containers. He hid inside of one, finding a nice spot behind a stack of boxes and a nice bucket to defecate in. He knew it wouldn't be an easy trip, but he had to make it to his love.

It took him 6 days to finally make it to New York, and another 4 months to find her.

Franklin was panhandling on the block of 125th street in Harlem, NY, waiting to run into Angelika. Every day for 3 months, he circled the area. Until one day, standing outside of Sunny's Liquor, he saw her. Her stomach had definitely gotten bigger. He was one of the happiest men alive, at that moment. He was stuck. So stuck he didn't even see the bus she was getting on, until she was already on it, and it was pulling away from the curb.

"Angelika! Angelika!" He screamed at the top of his lungs. "Angelika!" He sobbed, feeling his happiness slip away, just as quickly as it'd come. Suddenly, the bus pulled over at another stop just 2 blocks away. She got off, hearing his voice, and seeing him through the bus window. He ran to her hard and fast, tears blowing in the wind. She ran to him, as fast as she could in her condition.

"Franklin! Oh my, God. What…what are you doing here?" She asked, hugging him as he squeezed her.

"Finding you." He replied, kissing her all over her face.

Stephan finally made it to Angelika's. Adrenaline coming down. He'd rode all the way, non-stop. He struggled with walking up to her porch, but he was able to eventually gather the nerve to do so. His finger was inches away from the doorbell when the front door opened. It was Felisha, coming outside to enjoy a cigarette. She was wrapped in a navy-blue sweater, with her hair pulled back into a messy ponytail. She reached back to shut the door before any more of the beef stew aroma escaped the home.

"Whoa! Shit!" She exclaimed, startled. "Stephan, what's going on?" She said, chuckling, straightening herself up. The smile slowly faded away from her face, as she noticed the large bag strewn over his right shoulder, and then his bike. "What...what's going on?" She stopped herself from lighting her Virginia Slim. "Are you okay?" She asked. He dropped to the floor, sobbing, the word, "no."

"Oh, honey." She whispered holding onto him, as he cried into her shoulders.

"What's… going on?" Angelika asked, opening the door. She could see them on the porch, through the window panes in the front door and could tell Stephan was crying. He looked up at her. Angelika knew exactly what was going on and began to tear up.

"Can somebody talk to me, please?!" Felisha begged.

Felisha sat in the large brown recliner, smoking a cigarette, and sipping on a glass of whiskey. She looked between the both of them, not sure what to say next. She couldn't believe her 17-year-old daughter was already pregnant. Regret and silence permeated the air. The three of them, just sitting there.

"My baby's having a fucking baby." She forced out a little bit of a chuckle, shaking her head, still in disbelief. Stephan and Angelika held hands, as they awaited her mother's decision. He had nowhere else to go.

"When did u get pregnant? Where did you get pregnant? Was it here? On my couch? Did you guys fuck-excuse me, have sex in my house?" She asked, taking a shot of her whiskey. Suddenly, the front door swung open, then slammed shut. "Mama! Is there dinner?" Andrew called, walking passed the staircase, and into the living room. He stopped, seeing Stephan and Angelika on the couch, holding hands. "Ya'll having some type of meeting or something? Ya'll getting married?"

"That's a good question." Felisha said, turning away from Andrew, and looking back at her daughter and her boyfriend. "Are you?" She asked Stephan

"A…a…a…absolutely," he stuttered, "when the time's right. I love her more than my own self." He continued.

"It seems to me like the time is right."

"For what? Mom, what's going on.?"

"Boy, go get some food and leave us alone!" She snapped. "And you," she said, looking back at Angelika. "Go to your room, please."

"But-"

"Go..." She ordered, sternly. In a tone that let her know that she wasn't going to say it again. They cleared the room. It was just Felisha and Stephan now. She sat there, staring at him. The room refilled with that deafening silence. "You can stay, but you need to get a job."

"I have one. I work at McDonald's, across from my-my parent's house." He replied. There was a spare room, right off of the kitchen, that was mainly used for storage. It was hot in the summer's, and freezing in the winters, but he took it. "Thank you so much!"

"Don't thank me. It's for my grandchild. Both of you guys are still wrong. But I'm going to help you. I won't let that baby be in harm's way." She insisted. "Can't believe it. I'm a grandmother." She shot the rest of her drink back. "You can sleep on the couch until we get a mattress."

"I'm so sorry. I just want you to know I really-"

"Eh, eh, eh, eh. Stop. I get it. Have you ever heard of a condom?" She asked.

"We used protection every time. It broke." He admitted. The room filled with an awkward silence. Neither of them still not knowing what to say, but they knew the conversation was far from over.

"So, what are your plans?" She asked, sitting her empty glass down on the table next to her. She reached into her sweater and pulled out her pack of cigarettes.

"I have a few jobs lined up," he lied. Knowing a couple hours after school flipping burgers wouldn't do anything to put money in their pockets or food on the table. "The parents of a friend of mine, owns a liquor store over on MacArthur."

"Good. Now, she'll be 18 by the time the baby's due. I expect you guys would've been on your own feet by then?" Stephan nodded his head yes.

"Yes, yes, ma'am." He stammered, nervously. Happy she was letting him stay.

"I told you already, call me Felisha. Or mom, just not no damn ma'am. Shit makes me feel old." She said, taking a hit of her slim cigarette. She could see Stephan was still feeling a little tense. "Come here." She said standing, he did as well. He walked over to her and was welcomed a second time. "You two will be okay." She said before heading outside, to finish her smoke. "Oh," she said, stopping in her tracks. She looked at her watch, "no visits after 10. Its 9:45 now." She said before continuing outside.

Stephan stood there for a second, then ran up the stairs to share the news with Angelika.

The next day, Felisha took Angelika to their family doctor. She wanted to know for sure. After talking to her daughter, she realized that she'd missed her last 2 periods, which definitely is a sign that it could be positive.

"Mrs. William's?" The nurse called. She had on lavender, Scooby Doo scrubs. Her long blonde hair pulled into a loose ponytail.

"Come on, Angie." Felisha said, grabbing her purse and tapping Angelika on her shoulder. They followed the nurse back to the exam room, where, after another 5 minutes of waiting, Dr. Sheila was in to order her a urine test and a blood draw. Before leaving, she instructed them that she should have results no later than tomorrow morning.

Stephan sat at the house, on the couch, anxiously awaiting Felisha and Angelika's return. He stared out of the window. "The hell?" He whispered. He could see his mom's white, 10-year-old Toyota station wagon, pulling up to the curb, in front of the house. He jumped up and ran to the porch, as she walked around the front of the car. Stopping when she saw him standing there on the porch. "What are you doing here mom?"

"Quiero hablar contigo." She said, clutching her purse. He waved her inside.

"Would you like something to drink?" He asked as she sat on the couch.

"No, I can't stay. I have to get home with the groceries. This is a nice house." She said, looking around.

"What's going on, mom?" He asked.

"I just wanted to say, I'm so sorry about your father."

"Why? Why are you sorry, mami?" He said, sitting in the white recliner. "You didn't do anything to stop him from blackening my eye or kicking me out. Thank God for Ms. Felisha."

"I'm sorry, hijo." She said tearing up. "No sabía lo que debía hacer." She said, starting to cry. He started feeling sad again himself. Stephan hated seeing his mother cry. He moved in closer and put his arm around her shoulder.

"No es culpa tuya. Papá es un gilipollas." He said, chuckling.

She did as well, "Yeah, he is an asshole." She said, sniffling. "Take care of yourself. Okay, son. Call me if you need *anything*." She said standing. She kissed him on the forehead and walked out of the house. He fought the urge to cry as he watched her walk away and jump into the car.

CHAPTER 2

It's been 2 months since Angelika got the confirmation from the doctor, that she was a month into her pregnancy. Recent events have been hard on all three of them especially for Stephan. Only a week after he found out he was going to be a father, he lost his.

Franklin was out drinking at a bar in Downtown Oakland called The Disco. The Bartender ended up cutting him off at 3 am.

"Yo Frank, you got a ride or something buddy?" He asked.

"I'm…I'm going to taxi…I'm catchin' a cab." He slurred, as he stumbled out of the bar and made a left, towards the parking lot in the back. He pulled his keys out of his pocket and started up his old, red 1975 FORD truck. "I…I can do this." He said, backing out of the spot, and rolling into the street. It was only minutes before he made a wrong turn, down a one-way street, running head-first into an 18-wheeler truck. His seatbelt probably would've saved his life if he'd remembered to wear it.

The service wasn't much, held in a small church in his hometown of Morovis, where his parents were buried.

Stephan thought that once he made it back home from his father's funeral, that things would be better for him, but he still felt the guilt of not seeing, or saying anything to him since the night of the fight. Seeing him being lowered into the ground actually just made it worse.

Nevertheless, he had to grow up and take care of his own growing family. His cashier job allowed him to buy a few diapers and some baby food, but it wasn't enough. And the baby was closer to arriving with each passing day.

Stephan didn't have much time on his hands lately, but he needed to see his boys, just to get away from his reality. He got off of the number 12 bus, from Lake Merritt to Ashby BART station, walking through the station parking lot, until he made it to the main street walking down Prince, until he made it to the corner of King. There was a brand new, red 1990 Mustang parked out front, and a brand-new BMW parked in the driveway, of a beige, one story, 3-bedroom, 2-bathroom house. It was parked behind a ruby-red Mercedes. He scoffed, shaking his head as he walked up the four steps, to the porch. He could hear Easy-E blasting out of the house, through the black screen door. He knocked on the wooden frame that it was housed in.

"Aye, Liam! Johnny!!" He yelled over the music, knocking a second time, this time harder.

"Hold up." Liam yelled back. He appeared at the door, seconds later, with his son Phillippe on his hip and a blunt between his lips. He had on a pair of black sweats, and a pair of Gucci loafers. His chest was bare, with the exception of a heavy gold chain. "Oh, it's you. Hey brother." He said opening the door, letting him in.

"Hey, bro." He replied. "What's up, man?" He said, shaking Johnathon's hand.

"Oh shit! Look who's back from the fucking dead!" He said excitedly. He was sitting on the couch, smoking a blunt, counting out a lot of money, on the glass coffee table. He wore all white: a pair of St. Laurent jeans, a Hugo Boss button up, and a pair of Timberland boots. His bracelet, chains and Rolex watch were all gold. "This nigga finally convinced you to come to work?"

"Nah, it ain't like that, bruh." He responded, looking at the contents of the coffee table in front of him as he took a seat on the couch with Johnathon. There was a scale, currently filled with weed. There were also about 7 bricks of cocaine littered across the table as well. Liam handed him the blunt, then went over to go put his son in the walker. Steph sat back on the couch, almost choking on some of the strongest weed he's ever smoked. He could feel the underside of his tongue begin to tingle, as the smoke filled and scratched at his lungs.

"Hey, Stephan." Esmeralda said, coming down the hallway holding a black Jansport backpack. He waved at her hello. She had on black tube top, and a pair of Thierry Mugler jean short shorts. She handed Liam the bag, taking a large brick of cash from Johnathon, before walking over to pick the baby up. Disappearing down the hallway and into the bedroom.

"Shit!" Stephan said, coughing. Tasting blueberries on his tongue.

Liam began placing the bricks of coke on the table, into the backpack.

"You want one, bruh? It ain't too late to join us. Especially with Angelika giving birth in just a few months." Johnny said, holding out one of the bricks for Stephan to take.

"Nah, I'm straight. I just came to chill with my brothers." He said, handing the smoke back to Johnny. They chilled for a few hours, before Johnathon tried to again convince Steph to work.

"Man, you need to get in on this. McDonald's ain't taking care of ya'll or that baby." Johnathon said, looking him square in the eye. Liam handed Johnathon the bag once he filled it up.

"Nah, I'm cool. For real." He said, taking the blunt from Liam. Johnathon sucked his teeth.

"Aight, nigga, here. Take this as a gift." Johnathon said standing. He wrapped a wad of cash into a rubber band and tossed it into Stephan's lap.

He picked it up, studying it. "H-h-how much...how much is in here?"

"Don't trip, just make sure you buy your baby something nice."

"Nah, bruh. I can't take this." He responded, holding out the money to take. Johnathon looked over at Liam in disbelief.

"Nah, nigga, take that shit. It's yours. I get you don't wanna be a dope boy, but I wanna help my brother out." He said, hoisting his bag over his shoulder. "Imma hit you when we ready to go this Friday." Johnathon said, turning to Liam, who was lining up some coke to snort. He had a $100 bill all ready to go.

"Here, man. I can't take this." Stephan repeated, still trying to hand over the cash.

"Then give it to Liam, or to a charity or some shit." He said, heading to the front door.

More time had passed than Stephan realized. He looked at his watch, noticing it was almost 1:00 am. "Hey, bruh, you mind dropping me off?" He stood up, shoving the wad of cash into his jean pocket.

"Yeah, let's rock."

"Alright, brother. Never forget we got your back, *whenever* you change your mind." Liam said. He and Stephan shook hands and hugged before parting ways for the night.

He slid into the passenger side of Johnathon's red Mustang Gt. The bucket leather seats were soft and almost seemed to swallow him in. Tupac's, *Static*, began to play through the speakers, as Johnathon started the engine.

"Whooo! This shit nice, boy." Stephan said, rubbing the wooden interior on the upper part of the door. The car still had that new smell, like he'd just picked it up from the dealer that day. He could feel himself getting a little jealous.

"Thanks, man." He said, pulling away from the curb. "I got a house out in Richmond, too. I gotta keep my work life and my home life separate." Johnathon said. "Welcome to the Daddy club, bruh." He added, chuckling, just recently finding out that Crystal herself is almost 4 months pregnant.

"Man, lifetime membership." Stephan responded. They both shared a chuckle. Deep in the back of his mind, he doubted himself. Beginning to wonder if he was making the right choice for his new family, by living by the rules of society. He could be ruining their lives everyday he decides not to get into business with Liam and Johnathon. Liam and Esmeralda looked more than happy, and Phillippe was extremely spoiled. With his Gucci onesie and his Louis Viton pacifiers.

Johnathon was obviously doing pretty well for himself, too. New house, clothes, shoes, jewelry. His brothers had the life, and he was starting to want in on it, too.

"Bruh, so you ain't scared to be selling this shit?"

"Hell nah, ain't shit to be scared of. All I know is, I got something everybody want. And I'm gone be the one to give it to 'em. Either they gone get it from me or another nigga on the streets. Plus, once I make enough, I can pay niggas to do this shit for me."

"I feel that. I just don't want to get them caught up in all of this shit." He could feel his jeans pressing against the wad of money in his pocket.

Andrew was sitting on the porch smoking a cigarette. They caught his attention as they were pulling up. He did his best to see who was in the car, but all he could see was Stephan in the passenger seat.

"Thank you for the dough, bruh." He said, before opening the door. "Thanks for the ride, too."

"Don't mention it, man. Just remember, we got you if you need us. We ain't forgot about you." They shook hands, before Stephan shut the car door. He walked up the steps.

"Who the fuck was that? You sellin' drugs now?" Andrew asked, as Stephan walked up the steps.

"No, I ain't selling no drugs, Drew."

"Well, you better be selling *something*. Ain't no sister of mine gone be with no broke, bum nigga." Andrew replied, just as Stephan was shutting the front door behind him. He dragged his feet, through the kitchen, and into his bedroom. He walked through the door and turned left to hang up his coat. Stepping back a couple of inches, he plopped down onto his air-mattress, which rested on the wooden floor beneath it. He got up and walked around the bed to open up his window, allowing some of that warm August air to fill his room. He turned to his right, to the 6-drawer dresser that was right next to the window. After tucking the money into a clean pair of folded socks, he reached up and turned on the small radio that was on top. *Poison* by Bell Biv Devoe, filled the room. Walking back over to the bed, he plopped down, looking at the ceiling, something he's always done to help him think. He thought about going upstairs to kiss Angelika's stomach, but Felisha's curfew was like an electric fence around the staircase.

He started thinking about school. Thinking about how he didn't go to college after graduation, so that he could work more. He knew if he started working with his brothers, that he would be able to work and go to school. He thought back to how drastically his life changed, when just two months ago his girlfriend told him she was a month pregnant. He missed his father and wished he could just say hi to him one more time. Tell him he loved him.

Stephan jumped back to his feet and went over to grab the wad of cash. He engaged the lock on his bedroom door, and sat on the windowsill as he removed the rubber band.

"1,2,3,4,5…10,11…16,18,19…24,25." He counted out loud. He couldn't believe it. He counted the money again. His first count was correct. "$2,500." He whispered to himself. He chuckled, looking at the money. After placing the cash back into the stock drawer, he flopped back down onto the bed, staring at the ceiling again. But, this time, all he could see were dollar signs.

The sound of shuffling noises greeted Stephan into the next morning. The sun flooded the room, filling it with heat. The shuffling noises continued from the kitchen, the indication that Felisha was headed out to her job as an RN at Highland Hospital. He grabbed the alarm clock that sat on the floor, next to his mattress. It read 7:28. He smiled, thinking about the dreams he had last night, considering working with his brothers. He looked up at the ceiling, wondering if Angelika was awake yet. He looked down between his legs, realizing he needed her help with something. Before heading up stairs, he waited a few minutes after Felisha's car pulled out and drove away.

"…are you going to be a boy or a girl?" He heard Angelika's voice through the crack in the door, as he was just about to walk in. She was lying in bed, on her back with her pink shirt lifted over her stomach. Stephan's heart began to warm. He smiled as he opened the door, walking into the room.

"I kinda want a little boy." He whispered.

"Good morning." She said smiling, from ear to ear. He crawled in between her legs, laying his head right underneath her belly.

"Hey, baby." He said smiling, holding her. She ran her fingers through his soft, curly hair.

"Are you okay?" She asked, sensing something was wrong with him.

"Nah, and honestly you shouldn't be either." He said, looking up at her.

"What do you mean?" She asked confused. "Why shouldn't I be okay?" She started to wonder if he was having second thoughts about the baby. But he'd just said he wanted a boy.

"How would you feel if I… if… I went into business with Johnathon and Liam?" She grew silent, biting her bottom lip, rubbing her belly as her wheels began to turn.

"I…how much money would you be able to make doing it?" She asked.

"Be right back." He said, running downstairs to grab his stash. Just holding it made him smile. He ran back upstairs, skipping steps. "Look at this shit, baby." He said, tossing the money on the bed next to her. "$2,500. All large bills. We could be millionaires baby!" He said, excited. He was all but jumping up and down. She picked it up, unable to believe how much money she was holding. It was more money than either of them had at one time, ever.

"Where…how did you get this??!"

"Johnny gave it to me…for the baby. Said to buy something nice for it-for him." He corrected himself. He was excited to actually be doing something out of his realm of comfort.

Angelika sat there for a second, wondering if she should say yes to this.

"Say 'yes'! It's about time he's being a man!" Andrew yelled from his bedroom. She shook her head as she smiled.

"Let's do it. But once we have enough money, we're out." She said. "My mom cannot know though." She continued.

"Of course not." He replied, going up to meet her for a kiss. Which reminded him of the second reason he was up there in the first place. He shut and locked her bedroom door.

Stephan zapped all of Angelika's energy and took it for himself. She was stone cold when he crept down the stairs to grab the house phone from the kitchen to page Liam. The phone began to ring less than a minute later.

"Hello?" He answered

"Oh, hey what's up, bro?!" Liam asked. Stephan thought hard about his next words.

"Hola hermano, I want in."

"Say no more. We're on our way." Liam said before hanging up the phone. Stephan's anxiety began to grow out of control. He ran into his room and went into his weed stash. It wasn't as strong as the weed he'd soon be smoking, but it managed to get the job done when needed. He sat on the front porch, smoking his blunt, waiting for Liam to show up.

It was less than 45 minutes later, when that Red BMW pulled up and stopped in front of the house. Liam and Johnathon both hopped out, each carrying 2 large, black duffle bags.

"Hey, how ya'll niggas doing?" Steph said, hugging his friends. Johnathon was dressed down in a black sweat fit, with black Adidas. Around his neck was a large gold chain and hanging from it was a large 'J' medallion. On his ears, was a pair of diamond studs, and his wrists were flossed out with gold bangles. Liam wore a pair of baggy Levi jeans, a black cashmere pull-over sweater, and a pair of black Timberland boots. His ears were decorated by the same size diamonds as Johnathon's. On his left wrist was a big-faced Rolex. Stephan's eyes grew wide, as he thought about all of the money he'd be touching. "Follow me." He said, they followed him into his room.

"Ugh nigga, this your bed?" Johnathon asked, flopping down on Stephan's bed, noticing the lack in bounce.

"Where's everything? Nigga all your clothes in these drawers?" Liam asked, heading to the dresser, after noticing nothing was hanging in the closet.

"He, he, he." He fake-laughed. "Fuck both of ya'll niggas, man." Johnathon and Liam took a couple brief moments, to laugh at their friend's expense. But he wasn't worried. He knew he and Angelika's situation was only temporary.

Stephan sat on the bed, going through the bags he'd been brought. Two of them filled with bricks of marijuana, the others with bricks of cocaine and $10,000. What really caught his attention was the large, silver six-shot revolver. Holding the gun in his hand, made him flash back to the days when he was just a little boy. His father teaching him how to shoot at a young age, about 4 and 5. Giving him an extensive knowledge, that boys his current age, probably wouldn't...or shouldn't know.

"2 keys of coke will pay back Essie's dad. Pocket the rest." Johnathon said. "Simple right?"

"We all split 18 bricks of hard, and 24 bricks of purple."

Stephan thought about the set up. It didn't sound bad, for the time being, though he could already see himself wanting to make more than that. Already thinking of ways to do so, too.

CHAPTER 3

V alentine's Day, of 1991 came around faster than Stephan or Angelika could've imagined. The couple just signed the lease for their first home; a 2-bedroom, 1 bath apartment located right off of MacArthur Blvd. Stephan's bed now in the master bedroom of his own apartment. Angelika sat on the bed, going through one of her boxes, from home. Stephan was in the kitchen, cooking up some Mac and Cheese and baked chicken. It wasn't much, but to them it was everything.

"Uhm, babe!" She called out to him.

"Hey, I'm coming, baby." Stephan said, walking in with her plate of food. "I know you're hung-." He stood in the doorway, caught off guard. Angelika was standing in a puddle of liquid, jeans soaked. "Oh, God. Oh, my God. Is that…? Is it time?" He asked, dropping her plate. She smiled, tears filling her eyes. She nodded her head up and down, unable to make words. Seeing the fear in her eyes, he rushed to the kitchen and grabbed the house phone, calling her mom then his. After grabbing her baby bag out of the closet, they shot out of the door. The sky was cloudy, with just a peak of sunlight trying to break through. He helped her into the front seat of his black 1988, 2-door BMW. He sped all the way to the hospital, running lights and stop signs, not caring about cutting people off. He wanted to be sure his girl got the help she needed, excited to finally be meeting his child.

Their gift to each other, was a beautiful, healthy baby girl. She was welcomed into the world by her parents, with help of Talia, Felisha, and Andrew. Johnathon and Liam were also in attendance with their wives

Crystal and Esmeralda. They made it to the hospital, not too long after she'd given birth. They even brought Johnny Jr. and Sean-Phillippe. Johnny Jr. was just born a couple months ago in December.

"What should we name her?" Asked Stephan. He stood by the hospital bed, caressing Angelika's hair. He couldn't handle how beautiful she looked, holding his daughter. He could barely take his off of the newborn. She was light-skinned, with a full head of curly hair and large, round green eyes, her father's identical twin.

"Liyah. Liyah Angel Reyes." Angelika whispered, staring down at the baby. She looked up at them, smiling, eyes wide.

"My, God. I can't believe I'm a grandmother." Felisha said, tearing up. Chuckling as she and Talia helped each other through the shock.

"Oh, gosh, same here." Talia said, tearing up as well.

"She's beautiful, just like her mom." Stephan said, leaning down, kissing her on the forehead. "I have something to ask you." He reached into his pocket. Felisha, knowing what was happening, walked over to grab the baby. Angelika was confused, she didn't want to give her up. "Angelika Marie William's. The last year really showed me who I am… as a person, and I want to spend my life with you two. Will you please spend yours with me?" He asked, sitting on the edge of the bed, her left hand in his right palm. Tears began to stream down her face.

"Yes! Yes, I would love to marry you!" She exclaimed, excited. Tears of joy pouring from her brown, almond-shaped eyes.

The wedding took about 2 years to complete. The couple did their best to maintain a low profile, and that meant making sacrifices. The lovebirds said their vows on a beautiful, white-sandy beach in Lake Tahoe, during the peak of the summer of 1993.

The year 1994 rolled around like the blink of an eye, only 3 years since Liyah was born. The money Steph was making was too large for their small apartment. He'd been scoping out houses and found the perfect one to raise his family. He was able to buy a 6-bedroom, 7-bathroom mini-mansion, and a white Ferrari for Angelika, all for about $1.2 million. It was everything they had, but he wasn't worried, knowing that the money was about to start flowing like water. He was done working for Caesar, Esmeralda's father. He'd just hoped his wife agreed with his purchase, or he'd just spent a mill on a doghouse. But what woman wouldn't love a luxury mansion and matching vehicle.

Angelika was standing at the stove, of their small apartment, frying chicken with a side of rice and greens. Liyah sat on the floor of the living room, watching The Little Mermaid, singing every song, word for word, for the sixth time today. Angelika loved it and sang along with her. Andrew sat on the couch, watching the movies as well.

"Aight, baby," Stephan said, coming into the kitchen from the bedroom. He wrapped his arm around Angelika's waist and kissed her on the cheek. "I'm headed out." Andrew stood, throwing his leather coat on. Stephan was reluctant to bring his brother-in-law, but to keep the lifestyle away from Felisha, He needed to be included.

"Be safe, please." She said reluctantly, kissing Stephan. She watched as he ran into the living room, Liyah's giggle filling the room and her heart as he spun her in circles over his head. He kissed her on her face repeatedly before heading out of the house, smile beaming from ear to ear. They trotted down the stairs to meet Liam and Johnathon in Liam's, all black Chevy Tahoe. He opened the driver's side back door and was greeted by a large cloud of purple haze.

"What's up with, bruh." Johnathon said, passing him a blunt and lighter. He sparked it, relaxing in the leather seats, letting his high ease its way in. "Did she like the house?" He asked, turning all the way around in his seat. His gold top and bottom grills catching all of the light coming into the vehicle. They were the new trend for niggas who had enough money to melt gold or platinum over their teeth.

"Man, I haven't told her yet." He responded, before taking another pull from the blunt.

"That's cus she gone beat yo' ass!" Liam laughed. Johnny and Steph both joining in.

Stephan and Johnathon came up with the idea to start knocking off trap houses. The goal was to sneak in, take everything that they could see and move on, doubling as a way to knock down some of their competitors. They started with a rundown, 2-bedroom house on the 64th block of East Oakland, making a left on Majestic Ave, lights off.

There were two guys, both wearing puff coats, one with cornrows, sitting on the porch of the house. They shared a blunt while having a conversation. Liam cut the lights, then pulled over about 3 houses down, in front of a run-down house that's been forgotten about by the city for almost over a decade.

"You sure these niggas got what we're looking for? They don't look like much." Andrew said, peeking through the windshield.

"I know these fools. They always buy big around this time from us. I'll take care of them. Ya'll run around back and let me in through the front when it's good."

"Bet." Johnathon said, screwing on his silencer to his semiautomatic 9mm pistol. He, Andrew, and Stephan, lowered their beanies over their faces, before quietly getting out of the vehicle. Liam grabbed a warm beer out of the center console, opened it and spilled a little over himself, then acted like he'd been drinking it, as he stumbled towards the two men.

"Bruh, you should've seen how her sister looked when she walked in. I had that bitch feet on the wall- Hold up, whose this nigga?" One of them asked. He chuckled, "Look at this bum-ass nigga, bruh."

"Let me grab a smoke, por favor." Liam said, stumbling closer to them. He tripped himself, causing him to fall over one of the guys. He was surprised the men didn't recognize him.

"Aye, back the fuck up, dude!" The other man yelled, pushing Liam into a car parked on the curb. He grabbed his pistol from him waistband, aiming it directly at them.

"Say anything and I'll blow your fucking face off." Liam said, grinning ear to ear.

Stephan, Andrew, and Johnathon, went around the back of the house, through the side. The side of the house was filled with garbage of all kinds, accompanied by the type of smell that invaded their senses. They stepped through the rubble, careful not to make much noise. They made it to the back yard, which was just as messy and trashy as the side of the house. The back door was wide open, only secured with a black, mesh screen door. The door let them into the kitchen where a pot of water was boiling. The house smelled of ammonia and weed and was eerily quiet. They expected more guys to be here. "Let's get this and be out. I don't like-."

"Nah, nigga. The shit is still here waiting to be-oh, shit!" Said a heavy-set guy, coming into the kitchen. Caught off guard, he dropped his phone to the floor, and went falling backwards with it. They all had their guns drawn. "Aye, ya'll niggas -." Andrew put two bullets into his chest, trying to stop him from calling for help, but it was too late. The three of them rushed into the living room, stepping over his dead body. There were stacks of kilos of cocaine, sitting on the large, wooden coffee table. In a cardboard box, there were little sandwich bags filled with glass vials of a white, rocky substance. Just then they heard heavy footsteps coming downstairs.

BAH! BAH! BAH! BAH!

Gunshots began to ring out around them. Adrenaline fueling the fire, they ducked, behind anything they could. The small space proved to be a little difficult to hide in. Johnathon and Stephan began shooting, hitting 3 of their targets. One more was still on the steps shooting at them, using the wall as coverage. He was in the perfect position, able to see them, but they would have to expose themselves to get to him. He took advantage of it, keeping them in their hiding spots.

"We gotta get the fuck out of here!" Johnathon yelled, keeping his head low.

"Not without everything in this muhfucka!" Stephan growled. He ran out of his spot, heading straight for the stairs, dodging 2 bullets before he was face to face with the shooter. Two bullets in his face and he was done for, tumbling down the stairs towards Stephan. "Let Liam in." He ordered, continuing up the stairs, gun drawn.

"What the fuck took ya'll so long. I had to drop those two fools outside." He stopped speaking eyeing the coffee table.

"Jackpot, bitches!!" Stephan yelled from upstairs. He darted back down the stairs, with a few bags. He tossed one to Andrew. "Grab all that shit, bro. I need help up here, too." Liam and Johnathon followed him upstairs to the lit bedroom. There was a large, king-sized bed, completely covered in stacks of cash and more heroine with a little bit of coke. He gave Liam and Johnathon a duffle bag, like the one he tossed to Andrew. He only had two more, that he found, moving through the second bedroom, hoping to fill them up. There wasn't much in the second room, just a mattress, laying on the floor, with no types of bedding. A large sawed-off shotgun, instead rested on top of the bed.

Stephan grabbed it and went back in to meet Johnathon and Liam. They had gotten the contents off the bed and was starting to head downstairs.

"Let's go, ya'll!" Liam said as they ran downstairs. Andrew had cleared the coffee table and flipped over the couch cushions, finding a rifle, two shotguns and 6 police issued 9mm pistols. Liam wasted no time getting the hell out of dodge once they made it back to the truck. The adrenaline still hadn't subsided as they got closer to their side of town. Cars honking and swerving out of the way. He ran a few lights as they made it to downtown. Stephan had to have Liam slow down so that they wouldn't get pulled over.

"Whoo!" Stephan yelled out in excitement. "Did we really just do that shit and get away?!"

"We did that shit, bruh!" Johnathon replied to Stephan with a handshake.

They sat in Liam's living room, dividing their take by 4; 20 kilos of cocaine, 16 bricks of marijuana, 100 vials of meth and about $250,000 in hard cash. It was like Christmas had just begun. "We need more." Stephan said. He was excited about their success, but he wanted more. And that's excitedly what they did. Andrew had become part of the crew. The four of them spent the next couple of months, planning and plotting on their next come up. They even managed to add a few more guys to the team. Making the hits much easier. Their names were Marcus and Frank. Stephan was taken aback with the name reminding him of his father, feeling like he met him for a reason. They instantly got along and bonded as boys when they first met.

Marcus was big, buff and mean. He was used as the muscle for the team, not the brains per se. He stood 6'8, 380 pounds. His head was bald, and he had a salt and pepper goatee. He was the strong, silent type. Franklin was small; only 5'9, weighing 165 pounds, and light on his feet. He was a hot head who was extremely good with his hands, and he knew a shit load about guns.

The team got word on a dope house, just blocks away from San Francisco's Tenderloin district. They purchased a black van, and spray painted the windows white.

It was almost 2 in the morning and the streets were dead. They rode down Pine St., passed a set of bricked apartments, just built a short 6 years ago and home to 6 families, before the gangs took it over. The police, unable to bring them down, eventually joined their payroll. They rode passed the apartment on the main street to get a quick, better idea of the security detail they had. There were guys sitting outside shooting dominoes, directly in front of the entrance. One of them stood watch, looking out at the street behind them, holding a half-empty Seagram's Gin bottle.

They parked the van directly around the corner from the entrance. After screwing on their silencers, they pulled down their ski masks, ready for war.

"We go in hard, we go in fast, and we leave the same way." Liam said, before they all exited the van, through the double doors located right behind the passenger's seat. Frank stayed behind, acting as the groups getaway driver, leaving the engine running.

Marcus, using the element of surprise, threw himself into the 3 men, acting as a human wrecking ball. He crushed two of them between himself and the wall, allowing the group to take down the other one for good. He grabbed the two that were pinned down by their heads, mashing them together like rocks, cracking their skulls, killing them almost instantly. They dragged the bodies into the building's lobby, making sure to stay as quiet as possible. Marcus stayed out front, watching the building with an AR-15 assault rifle, equipped with armor piercing rounds.

The four of them walked inside, suddenly hit in the face with an indescribable stench. They smelled chemicals, mixed with human feces, accompanied by the unmistakable scent of death. The main hallway lobby was littered with debris; garbage, newspapers and food bags. There was a young, black woman sitting on the steps. She was passed out, high, leaning against the wall. She had on a pink tank top and blue jean shorts. She sweat profusely, to spite the cool conditions outside.

"Damn, is this what our customers end up like?" Stephan asked himself, aloud. He could feel himself starting to feel guilty for be a part of the reason this drug was introduced to his people.

"Spread out, then we go upstairs." Liam whispered, looking at the three units downstairs. Johnny took the apartment at the end to the right. Stephan and Andrew, took the one directly across. Liam took the apartment near the entrance. He walked in, shutting the door behind him. The apartment was empty. Nothing but small pieces of debris littered the brown, dirty carpet. He walked through to the bedroom.

"Fuck!" He yelled out in frustration, realizing this apartment was, in fact completely empty.

Stephan was one of the lucky ones. The apartment he walked into; the door was wide open. There was a man asleep on the sofa, next to the door. He had on a grey wife beater, a pair of black basketball shorts, and a pair of NIKE slip on's, with a black wave cap. Stephan quickly grabbed his pistol off of the coffee table, which was sitting next to 5 bundled stacks of $100 bills.

PEW!! PEW!!

Stephan shot his attention towards the apartment door. Liam stood there, smoking pistol aimed at the sleeping man. His eyes quickly shot open, then closed back slowly.

"What you are doing, brother?" Liam asked. He didn't wait for a response before shutting the door and running through the house. They split up and checked every dark corner of the apartment. The kitchen proved to be very lucrative. The freezer was filled with money. Stacks of 100s and 50s. Stephan wasted no time emptying out the freezer and drugs out the cabinets.

"Whoo! Yes! Come to papa." Liam yelled out in excitement. Stephan ran to the bedroom to remind Liam to keep it down and that they had no idea who was still upstairs. His words left him when he saw that there were bricks of weed, stacked almost as tall as a grown man.

"Bruh, that gotta be at least 40, 50 pounds." Stephan said ready to stuff his bags.

Johnathon walked into his unit and felt as if he hit his own jackpot. He immediately commenced to cleaning off the contents of the coffee table; 4 kilos of cocaine and two pistols. He moved through the apartment, hitting the first bedroom, finding 30 pounds of marijuana in the closet, wrapped and bound by layers of cling wrap. His face sparkled as he grabbed everything he could. He was on his way out, when he suddenly felt an intense pressure, accompanied by a searing heat, radiating from the back of his left shoulder. He looked down, seeing a puddle of blood beginning to pull into the fabric of his blue

Fendi sweater. He had no idea that someone was in the unit, until it was too late. He collapsed, unable to remain strong enough to continue standing.

Stephan and Liam were stuffing everything they could, when they suddenly heard a loud, pop. His heart dropped, knowing they always used silencers. Marcus heard the shot and immediately ran inside of the building.

BAH! BAH! BAH!

Liam and Stephan ran out into the hallway of the apartment, by a stunned Andrew. He was hiding on the side of the fridge, pistol at the ready. They opened the apartments main door, peeking into the hallway. Marcus lay in the doorway, on his back, in a pool of his own blood. He'd been shot twice in his chest, and once in his neck. They then heard movement coming from their left. They saw Johnathon laying on his stomach. He then seen a thug come out of the apartment and stand over him, ready to put a bullet in the back of his head. Stephan shot off two bullets before the guy had the chance to do anything. They heard someone rushing down from upstairs. Stephan and Liam quickly ran into the unit that Johnathon was going through, dragging him inside and shutting the door. All Johnathon could think about was his wife and son. He was terrified imagining them at his funeral and not growing old with him. He let a tear fall from his eye as he held his chest, not ready to let go, though he could feel his life slipping away with each passing moment.

BAH! BAH!

The gunman came down and dragged Marcus' body into the lobby, before placing another 2 bullets right between his eyes. Finishing the job for sure.

"Fuck, bruh we're two down." Stephan said, as they ducked behind the unit's kitchen/dining area.

"We gotta fight our way out." Liam said, cocking his pistol after checking for ammo. Johnathon was sitting next to them, fighting to stay awake.

They suddenly heard the door being kicked open, then heavy footsteps against the laminated wood floor.

"Shh," Stephan motioned to them. Andrew looked terrified. He waited right at the corner of the kitchen entrance, waiting for someone to cross his line of sight. Once the gunmen finally did, he wasted no time, placing three bullets in the shooter's side. Right into his heart. Liam ran over and stopped him from hitting the ground, alerting anyone who could be outside. Johnathon began coughing up blood all over his sweater.

"We gotta get him outta here." Andrew said, sitting by his side applying pressure to the wound.

"We will. Get him up." Stephan said, helping Andrew stand Johnathon to his feet. He groaned in pain. They could tell he didn't have much time left and needed to get him to a hospital immediately.

"Vamos." Liam said, standing near the coffee table, gun ready. Andrew and Stephan had a grip on Johnathon, walking him out of the apartment. The hallway was pretty quiet, they thought that maybe everyone that was in the 2-story complex, was gone. Andrew and Stephan led the way, trying to get Johnathon out the door as quick as possible.

BAH! BAH! BAH! BAH! BAH!

Johnathon suddenly got extremely heavy. Stephan looked to his right, to see Andrew falling face-first to the concrete tiles. He was barely able to drop Johnathon onto Marcus' dead corpse, before taking cover for himself, barely missing a bullet to his head.

BAH! BAH! BAH! BAH! BAH! BAH!

Stephan shot until the gun was out of bullets. Once, he was done, he seen a flash of light coming from upstairs, then a dark figure coming out from behind it, seeing the man raise his gun. He darted to the left, before the guy had the chance to shoot a bullet, exactly where he was. Liam came from around the corner that Stephan ducked behind and let off a couple of fatal shots into the man's torso. They heard running around upstairs, as the man's body tumbled down the stairs to the first floor.

"After you." Liam said, waving his gun towards the rickety staircase. Stephan forced a chuckle and headed upstairs. Guns drawn. They made it to the second floor, suddenly being met with a wall of gun fire. They jumped to the left, into one of the empty apartments, dodging the bullets. There were six guys upstairs, waiting for them to come up.

Stephan and Liam were in the living room of the apartment trying not to get hit by bullets. Stephan sat against the wall of the entry door, wondering what the fuck he'd gotten himself into. He looked over at Liam, sitting next to him, shooting back. He crawled over to him and was struck by the sight of a young woman, not much older than them, peeking out into the hallway. She looked scared, wondering what was going on. He peeked into the hallway and could see two men coming directly at them. He shot off four rounds, killing them both. Liam heard the gun fire subside and busted out, shooting another 3 of them. The dust and gun fire settled again. Stephan looked over at Liam for confirmation the coast was clear, who was nursing a shoulder graze, held up by the apartment's entrance. He stuck his head out to see the location of the shooter.

BAH! BAH! BAH! BAH!

He was shot at but wasn't hit. It was enough to tell the shooter was alone, and where he was. They had one more person to get through before leaving with the riches they found. Liam nodded his head and stood up, ready to finish this. Stephan had his back. Guns drawn, they entered the hallway. No shots fired. Liam was headed in the direction the earlier shots came from.

They walked down the hallway, and into the last apartment to the left, around the dead thugs. Liam made a signal, letting Stephan know that someone was still in here. They walked into the apartment.

BAH!

A bullet flew right by Stephan's head, too fast for him to react. He saw a body run down the hallway of the apartment, banking a left into the dirty unit. They walked through the drug riddled living room. The two couldn't wait to snatch up everything they could and get their partner to the hospital. Stephan remembered looking down at Andrew as he lay flat on top of Marcus. Blood poured from his mouth and his eyes were wide open.

Liam and Stephan crouched, walking down the hallway. The shooter bent his arm around the corner and squeezed the trigger until his gun clicked. Liam and Stephan laid flat on the floor, covering their heads. Once they heard the gun click, they jumped up and rushed to where he was hiding. They caught him trying to escape out of the window, but his time was up. They let off rounds into his back, dropping him to the floor.

"I'm gone take shit to the van." Liam said, hurrying downstairs. He thought for sure Johnathon was dead, along with Andrew, until he began coughing. "Fuck, brother. You're still alive!" Liam rushed to his side. He grabbed him with all his strength, taking him to the van to rest.

"Watch him. Me and Steph will be right back." Liam said before shutting the door. Frank's eyes bulged out of his head as he ripped his seat belt off, jumping into the back of the van

"Oh, my God. Oh, my God..." He repeated continuously. "Stay awake, man."

Liam ran back in the building, moving as fast as he could to empty out everything he could. Stephan was up and down the stairs doing to same. He entered the last apartment to the right, it looked seemingly empty until he continued through the bedrooms. He reached the master bedroom and looked in the closet. There was a large, black Honeywell safe. It was closed just barely; the lock wasn't even engaged. Next to it was a large, green plastic bin, filled with guns and rifles of all types.

"Bruh! Get in here, quick!" Stephan yelled, eyes wide. He couldn't believe what it was he looking at.

"We gotta hurry up and get this shit. Get Johnny to the hospital."

"Look at this shit, bruh." He said, pointing to the closet. Liam turned the corner to see what it was Stephan was looking at.

"Adios mio." He said shocked and surprised. "Bro, we gotta get all this shit out of here."

"Go get Frank. We're going to need his help getting this shit." Stephan said. Liam took everything he had on him and ran out to the van. Stephan opened the safe up all the way and was floored by the contents of the two-level safe. The upper part was stuffed with cash. Stacks of 100s. The lower level was filled with weed and cocaine. Frank ran into the room, followed by Liam, just a few minutes later.

"John's not looking so good." Liam said as they emptied the contents of the safe into their bags. Stephan saw a piece of paper in the upper-level portion, once the money was taken away. He examined it. Seeing the name Sandra, scribbled messily on the paper. After stuffing the paper into his jean pockets, they opened the door to leave. It was now almost 2:30 am. Stephan expected to be met by a wall of cops, responding to the hail of gunfire as they exited the apartment complex. They stepped over Marcus and Andrew, making it to the van before they did start hearing the sirens. With not a lot of time to fully clean out the apartment building, they had to leave with what they had, or they wouldn't have left at all.

"Ahhh, fuck!" Johnathon cried as they sped to the hospital. He was okay until the van began to move. The bumps caused his gunshot wound to throb. His friends could see him sweating, and his breathing becoming labored. He was terrified but starting to accept the fact he was dying. His wife, Crystal popped into his head. Their son, Johnny Jr, just turning 3. He thought about her smile and that kept him strong. But, he knew, that this was it. "We had a good run, boys." He said, forcing a chuckle, but it only caused him to cough up more blood. Stephan could feel his heart beating into his throat as he watched his brother bleed out.

"Yeah, and we got a hell of a lot more to go." Stephan said, holding back tears. Johnathon closed his eyes and rested his back. "Aye, nigga! Johnny! Wake up, bruh!" Frank said. Liam sped down Stanyan St, trying to get to St. Mary's as quick as possible.

They made it to the Emergency room, carrying Johnathon inside. He was still fighting for every breath, not willing to go out that easily. Two nurses rushed over with a gurney.

"What happened?" One of them asked.

"Bitch, he was shot. Look at him." Liam said. The nurses got him on the gurney, checking his pupils with a flashlight.

"He's slipping away." She said to the other nurse. "Please go to the waiting room, the police will have questions." She said, turning to them, before they rushed him inside.

"We gotta get this van out of here." Liam whispered to Stephan.

"Frank, wait here. Just tell them somebody shot up a party in the heights." Stephan said. He and Liam hopped into the van and were off.

It took them about 45 minutes to get back to Liam's house. He waited a few hours before grabbing the house phone and heading to the garage. He sat on the washing machine, staring at the piece of paper in his hand, debating if he should call. They needed their own connections, so he dialed the number, hoping Sandra would be their golden ticket. It was almost 8 in the morning when Frank came back, updating them on Johnny's condition. They were able to stabilize him, but he wasn't out of the woods just yet.

"This is Sandra." She answered on the first ring. Stephan sat silent for a second. He could hear a door open and shut on her end. "You got my shit, Henry?" She asked.

"Henry got smoked." Stephan responded, not entirely sure who Henry even was.

"Who…who is this?" Stephan could hear the suspicion in her voice.

"That's not important. What was your relationship with Hector?" He asked.

"I…I can't disclose that information." She said, forcing herself to chuckle.

"Why? He's dead." He responded. She sat quietly on the phone, not sure exactly how to combat his point. He sat there quiet, waiting for her to respond. She reached over and powered on her computer. He could hear her typing as she pulled up Henry's account. Being the owner of a large metropolitan bank, surely had its perks.

"I own the bank he stores his money in, as long as he gives me 25% of his profits. I'm assuming that information helps you somewhat?"

"Not really. But you giving up who he buys from will. And you just keep the money in Henry's account." She burst out into laughter, whole heartedly laughing in Stephan's ear.

"Are you fucking thwacked, bro?" She laughed. "You think I'm going to roll over them for someone I've never even laid eyes on? I own the bank, little boy. This money was mine the moment you called me. You're sitting on $16 Million worth of guns and drugs. No one's just going to let that go."

"Okay, pay your connects back with that money sitting in Henry's account. Though that doesn't even come close to what it was I got from you…" He hung up the phone before she had the chance to respond, hoping she'd call back. She did, within only a few seconds.

"Alright. Let's do this. How about you be the new Henry? You get the money and the name of the connect to buy from. We're both winners."

"Fuck Henry. I'm me. Meet me at the Oil Changers, by Oakland High. Midnight. And we can do 10, fuck that 25%. We ain't no dumb niggas over here."

"You got yourself a deal." She said, hanging up the line. Stephan smiled, feeling accomplished. He couldn't wait to see the payout. He jumped off of the washing machine and rushed back into the house. Frank and Liam sat on the couch, smoking a blunt as they thumbed through all the cash they stole.

"Alright, ya'll, so tonight. She gone drop 16 mill on us, we give her the guns and drugs."

"Guns, too, bruh? What if we kept a few for ourselves?" Frank asked, handing Stephan the blunt. He reached into his pocket and grabbed a pack of Marlboro reds out of his pocket.

"Nah, what if they got a inventory or some shit? Think smart man. We get this right, we ain't never gotta hit traps again." The two of them looked at each other, thinking about what Stephan was proposing. "And I say we get some soldiers on our team, take down them other connects."

"Nigga, what!? You think you Al Pacino?" Frank asked, grabbing his glass of vodka off the wooden coffee table. He wasn't too happy with the idea.

"That's exactly what the fuck I'm saying. I want this fuckin money." Stephan said with passion. He stood in front of them, from the other side of the coffee table. He could tell they weren't really sold.

"Bruh…" Liam sighed.

"We already started. We just made $16 million-fuckin' dollars, bro."

"We got lucky. Super lucky. What about Marcus and Andrew… Johnathon's laid up in the ICU right now." Frank exclaimed.

"Then why ain't you stay with him?" Liam asked.

"Bruh, you know I can't do no hospital for too long. Plus, he up there resting."

"We should go up there and see what's going on with him." Stephan said. "But, as far as this money goes…I'm making the deal with or without ya'll. You gone get yo' cut, but I really don't care about the opinions. We're doing it." Stephan said, taking the blunt from Frank. "We gone become the connects."

"And you think it's going to be that easy?" Asked Esmeralda, walking down the hallway.

"Morning, baby." Liam said.

"Nah, ain't nobody said shit was gone be easy. But it's for real gone be worth it." Stephan said.

"Steph, we can't afford to lose Liam. Me and Phil need him. Isn't the 16 enough?" She asked, sitting on the couch next to Liam.

"Hell, nah." Stephan said. "Ask Andrew if it was enough. I have no idea how I'm going..." He began feeling a large lump form in his throat. "to tell Angel her brother's fucking gone."

"I'll ask my dad if he can dispose of any foot soldiers from Mexico..." She said.

"Thank you. Somebody with an actual fucking idea." He said, clapping his hands, pointing at her.

Stephan fell asleep in the middle of the floor, with money on his mind. He was flat on his stomach, arms folded for neck support. Franklin was stretched out on the couch, in a deep alcohol induced coma. Liam couldn't sleep. Esmeralda was too busy making him worry about the path he was about to go down.

"Babe, I don't know if we should do this."

"Why not?" They were laying down in bed. They'd just sent Sean-Phillippe to school on the school bus.

"I don't think it's safe. My father's rich. We're not needing for money." She said pointing between them.

"Baby, your papa has all the money. We don't got shit." Liam responded. He looked Esmeralda dead in the eyes. She looked away, out the bedroom window. "I got this, love. If it gets too crazy, I promise, I'm out." He said. She looked at him for a second, smiling, unable to deny his hustle. She jumped over him, kissing him. He removed her fluffy pink, Versace robe, exposing her naked body.

Stephan woke up, to the sound of a fire engine, speeding passed the front of the house. Drool covering the back of his hand. He looked up to see Frank still on the couch, asleep. He grabbed one of his cigarettes and then the house phone. Stretching the cord, he took it back out to the garage. He sat on the washing machine, dialing the phone to his house.

"Hello?" Answered Angelika quickly, like she'd been waiting by the phone. She sounded worried.

The conversation was hard to have and lasted for what seemed to be hours. He didn't know the right words to say to her, so he just told her what happened. The truth, which was almost just as difficult to spit out. He couldn't stand to hear the sounds of her sobbing, and him feeling responsible for it.

"I'm on my way home." He said, hanging up the phone.

By the time he had gotten there, Felisha's car was sitting out front of the house. He parked behind her in the U-shaped driveway before he anxiously walked into the house. It was still, quiet. He heard Felisha sobbing in the living room. He walked in slowly as Angelika was consoling her mother. The floorboards creaked, getting both of their attention.

"No." Felisha said, face drenched with sorrow and pain. She stood. "You get out of here!" She yelled, walking towards him. "This is your fault!" She cried, poking him in his chest. It escalated to her punching him in his chest.

"Mom, mom. Stop." Angelika said, holding her mother back. "Baby, just go." She pleaded. Tears running down his face, he backed out slowly, exiting the house. He reached his car, slamming his hands against the roof. Folding his arms, he cried, resting his head on his arms. He heard the heavy, glass front door open, then shut behind him. He turned around, looking back at Angelika. He rushed over to hug her, dropping to her knees.

"I'm so sorry, babe!" He cried, sobbing. He grabbed her body and cried into her stomach. She grabbed his head, pulling him closer into her. Crying, thinking about how today has been an emotional rollercoaster, for her and her family. Earlier this morning, she found out that she was 12 weeks pregnant. And now, before the sun even had the chance to set, she's finding out her brother was murdered, and that her mom blames Stephan for it. Andrew knew the consequences and possibilities of this line of work. But it didn't absolve him of his guilt.

"I know, baby." She said, crying with him. "My mom's just hurt right now. I know she doesn't really blame you for what happened." She fought with whether now was a good time to share the news, feeling like he needed it. "I have something to tell you." She grabbed his chin and tilted his face upwards. His eyes were bloodshot.

"Is everything okay?" He asked, standing to his feet. He was confused when he noticed a smile break through her pain. She quickly nodded her head, up and down, rubbing her stomach. He still didn't understand, and then it clicked. "Wait…baby, are you…?" He asked. She continued to nod her head. "Oh my, God." He sighed, laughing. He swept her off of her feet, kissing her, twirling her around in circles.

Stephan went back to Liam's house, on cloud nine, Andrew's death was still fresh on his mind, but he found a reason to begin to forgive himself. He should've known Andrew wasn't built for this life.

Liam, Steph, and Frank, parked at the Oil Changers on the corner of MacArthur and Park Blvd, with the guns and drugs. Neither of them wanted to show it, but they could all feel the nervousness creeping through their guts. The parking lot was silent, empty. The bright moon overhead casting a light down upon them. The harsh smell of chemicals making their anxiety grow. They looked at their surroundings. Across MacArthur, between them and the 580 freeway, was a thick row of trees. And on the opposite side of the lot, on the other side of a brown fence, were some houses. This gave Steph a card to play, if needed. He refocused his attention to the two entrances. He hoped this deal with Sandra goes through, so that he could set his family up nice and get out. He'd accomplished what he started for initially, but it was time to recoup the money for the mansion he'd just purchased.

At exactly midnight, they seen a pair of bright headlights, enter the parking lot. The white BMW parked directly in front of the van as they jumped out and stood in front. The lights from the BMW, blinding their ability to see the occupants of the vehicle. Suddenly, two doors swung open. They were both large Samoans, each carrying large assault rifles. The driver stood in front of the car, eyeing the boys, daring them to try anything. The passenger went to the back door and an older white woman stepped out and walked to the front of the car, standing between her two guards. She looked highly successful, and only in her mid-30's.

"Hmmm. You are a little boy." She said smiling. She leaned against the car, hands in her knee-length, beige trench coat pockets, ankles crossed. "What's to stop me from just taking the package, and killing the three of you?" She asked. Her blonde hair, long and flowing. She looked serious, scaring the boys even more.

"For the simple fact, that there's 8 niggas, surrounding us all. If you, or I, shoot even one bullet, all three of ya'll are dead." Stephan said, courage never faltering.

"Chance you feel like taking tonight?" Liam added, backing his bluff.

"Yeah, we could just…kill you and take the cash and the drugs." Stephan said. He held his pistol in the air. Her security aimed their guns directly at them as she looked around, wondering if he was bluffing or not. She looked back at him, smiling, deciding not to take the chance, but admiring his courage.

"Get the cash." She ordered, admiring the size of their balls, still not sure if they were bluffing or not. The man to her left, the driver, went to the trunk. He grabbed three large duffle bags and tossed them into the beam of light that met between them.

"Liam, get the shit, bruh. Frank, help him." He ordered. He reached down and grabbed the bags, as Liam and Frank came around with the tub of guns and drugs. They kept everything else that they found in the complex. Totaling almost $70,000 in cash. Even split four ways, they were off to a good start before the meet. "So, what's next?" He asked as her thugs grabbed the loot.

"Well, that's up to you. Let me know when u take down Spider, and we can talk." She replied, walking back to the open back door. "Oh, and please, preferably before I have to pay him for this shit." She smiled sliding into the seat. She knew there was no one around, but she appreciated how tough the little boy was. They had more heart than half the full-grown men she knew.

They watched as the car turned left in front of them, then as the red lights faded away into the darkness, they exhaled. A strong sigh of relief.

"That's a bad bitch." Frank said, breaking the tension. They all shared a laughed, taking a breath, realizing that they were all now rich, officially.

Let's go, bruh." Stephan said, laughing, slapping him in the chest. They jumped back into the van, silent for a while, looking around at each other.

"Whooooooo!!!!" Liam yelled. Frank and Stephan joined in.

"We're fucking rich!!" Stephan yelled out. He started the engine as Frank and Liam lit blunts. "We gotta get a bottle and go see Johnny." He said, heading to a familiar liquor store. One that stayed open like 7-11. They had a classmate whose parents owned the store, making alcohol trips a breeze for them. They grabbed a bottle of Belvedere and hit the freeway. Barely able to contain their excitement, they popped the bottle.

They made it back to Liam's house close to 2 in the morning. Literally swimming in cash, their lives were starting to take a turn, for riches and gold.

"Aye, who the fuck is that?" Stephan asked, staring at the porch. He seen a hooded figure standing next to a child, sitting on the steps.

"I don't know. Wait…that's one of my corner boys." He responded, cocking his pistol.

"Put this in the garage." Steph said to Frank, cocking his pistol as well. They jumped out and approached the front porch.

"What's going on, Moe?" Liam asked. Moe was 4 years younger than them. At 16, he was one of Liam's youngest foot soldiers. He was slim, dark, and tall. He always wore a black windbreaker with the hood cinched tightly around his face. He had on a pair of black jeans, with a pair of black and red Air Jordans.

"Lil dude said he was looking for some shit…for his mom."

"Okay…and why is *he* here?" Steph asked, not sure why he didn't just sell it to him. He looked at the kid and slowly began to understand.

"I didn't feel right selling to him. I know ya'll want ya'll money. He only five. I wasn't sure what to do."

"I'm 6!" The little kid yelled out.

"What's your name, lil man?" Steph asked kneeling down to his eye-level. "I'm Stephan."

"Demetrius." The little boy responded timidly. Never looking up.

"Nice to meet you, Demetrius. Let's…head inside." Steph said, looking around to be sure this wasn't a set up. Moe was sent back to work.

"Who the fuck…?" Frank asked, smoking a cigarette, and drinking a glass of the Belvedere.

Demetrius explained to them, that the man he thought was his father, took his older brother and left their mother alone with him and his baby brother, James.

Frank went with Steph and Liam to take Demetrius to his apartment on the corner of 55th and Adeline, after tossing his 5-speed bicycle into the back of Liam's Yukon.

"Damn, yo moms made you ride all this way just for some fuckin dope?" Steph asked. "You sure this ain't for you?" He continued, turning around in the passenger seat to face the little kid. He was surprised by his resolve and how he wasn't even the least bit afraid.

"No, sir. My mom used to send my big brother, Rod. But when he left a few weeks ago, she started making me go. It was that or my brother, and he's only 3. And I…if I didn't go, she'd make us sleep on the back porch until she got back with her own stuff. Usually, a day or two later." He said, looking around at the crew. The car grew silent. No one able to believe what they'd just heard.

They walked into the dark home, after Demetrius. The smell that hit them almost knocked them off of their heels. It was kin to the combination of human faces mixed with ammonia, vomit, and urine.

"Baby, is that you?" Cried a weak, female voice from the rear of the apartment home.

"Yeah, mama, it's me." Demetrius responded. Steph reluctantly handed him an 8-ball, to give to her.

After taking her poison, Steph made the decision to take the kids out of that situation and take them back to his home. Angelika was accepting and more than willing to set up one of their plural spare bedrooms for them. The next morning, over breakfast, Angelika and Stephan sat him down, alone and asked about his home left. He started with the day his father left him.

Demetrius and James, sat in the bedroom playing with Pokémon cards, waiting for Rodney, their eldest brother to return. He did his best to keep their mother's drug habit away from them, but Demetrius was smart. It didn't take him too long to catch on. And she was about to confirm it.

"Stop, Reginald! Give it back!" She yelled running up to him to snatch the little baggy, filled with a white powdery substance out of his hand. Rodney sat in the corner, crying, trying to stay out of the way. Reginald pushed her off of him, and to the floor.

"What the fuck is *this* shit, bitch?! You got my son getting yo shit for you?!!" Demetrius heard his father yelling from the living room. He and James looked at each other, then back at the door, before they walked over, peeking their heads out, giving them a perfect view of the action.

"Please, baby! I need it! You know it make me *feel good*." His mother begged, hanging off of his father's work overalls. Her pink slip, hanging off of her left shoulder. Her short, matted hair, riddled with debris from the living room carpet. She dropped to her knees, clawing at his legs.

"Get the *fuck* off of me." Reginald growled, kicking her off, narrowly missing her jaw.

"Please, you can have the boys." She cried. Reginald's head cracked back, eyes locking onto Demetrius and James.

"Rodney's my only child." He said, grabbing 13-year-old Rodney to his feet, by his wrist. He tossed the bag into the corner, watching as she dove for it, head-first. He'll never forget the day he watched his father walk out of his life. He quickly understood why, though and it took no time for he and James to want to follow in his footsteps. Their mother didn't blink an eye when Rodney was taken to New York with Reginald. His responsibility simply fell onto Demetrius.

CHAPTER 4

Working with Sandra was one of the best things they've could have done. They decided to help her get rid of Spider, a low-level street thug, like them, trying to come up in the game. With the help of her men, and the guns, they were even able to get some more guns from him. A crate full of AK-47s. Taking him out for good in the process. Whoever fronted him the goods would be pissed but wouldn't know who to look for until it's too late.

Sandra gave Stephan and Johnathon a place to store their millions, a mass of about $8 or $9 Million for them both. She also got them a way to clean their money; a rundown night club in the heart of San Francisco. It took almost a year for renovations to complete: and $3.9 million split between the brothers. It was called Déjà vu. The entrance floor was a full-on two-story night club. The floor below was a nude, gentlemen's club. It was a place that where, whatever a customer was willing to pay for, short of abuse of any kind, they got it. The dancers were previous prostitutes who felt safer doing their jobs there, than on the streets. Plus, they got paid almost 10 times more on a nightly basis. The boys quickly turned into men, growing up fast in this game. And only at the tender ages of 20 for Stephan and Johnathon. Liam was only 19 years old.

December 18th of 1994 brought the couple, Angelika and Stephan, two more gifts of joy in the form of male twins, Malakhi and Malik. Their early Christmas presents from God. Liyah was already in love with her little brothers. Angelika breast fed them while Liyah lay on the side of her, their first night in the hospital.

"Are you crying?" Angelika asked, seeing tears swell up in Stephan's eyes. He leaned in and kissed all four of them on the forehead. He couldn't hold back how happy of a man he was.

"I love you so much." He said, kissing her on the lips. He wished his mother could be there, but just a month ago, she'd lost her battle to a very aggressive lung cancer. Angelika felt sad that her own mother disowned her for remaining married to the man she thought responsible for her son's death. To keep her hurt buried deep, she dreamed her mother dead. If anyone was to ask her, someone broke into her home. Killing Felisha and her brother, Andrew.

New Year's Eve celebrated more than just a new year for the team. They were on the way to becoming Urban Kings, and they celebrated as such. They threw a party at their club, in the player's skybox where they could see the entire club and all of the action. On a normal night, customer had to pay $100 an hour to enjoy their party here.

"Aye! Aye! Aye!" Liam screamed, shooting his P90x into the ceiling. The music was too loud for the people downstairs to notice, but some did begin to look around. With DMX playing, they just assumed it was part of the song.

With his now, small fortune of a combined wealth, with his wife, of $26.5 million, he began to act extremely reckless, resorting back to his childish ways. And with the business that they worked in, it could spell danger for every single one of them and their families.

"Aye! Dude, what the fuck are you doing?!" Johnathon yelled, looking over at his wife, Crystal. She was sitting down at the bar, looking freaked out with her cocktail in hand.

"Dude, you're fucking tripping!" Stephan yelled, snatching the gun away. Esmeralda sat in the back, smoking a long cigar, watching the scene unfold.

"Can you take him home, Essie? Get your fuckin husband, dude." Crystal said.

"Oh, so I'm getting kicked....out now?" Liam slurred, holding a bottle of Rum in his hands. Holding it by the neck, he took another swig.

"Nigga, you need to go." Stephan said, aiming his hand to the door. He was in Liam's face, Johnathon stood behind, to the side of him.

"Go get some rest. You been snorting lines all night." Johnathon added.

"I'm a grown ass man, bro." Liam said, face stern. He wasn't backing down. Instead, he stepped up closer, challenging Stephan.

"Okay, that's enough, baby. Let's just go home. I'm ready to fuck." Esmeralda said, getting between them. She kissed him, distracting him from the confrontation.

"Nah, this dude is being a fuckin asshole." He said, nudging her out of the way.

"Liam, don't call me no asshole. You finna get us all locked the fucked up…or killed." Stephan said, pushing Liam out of his face. He stumbled backwards, onto the couch behind him. Surprisingly not dropping the bottle. The room grew silent, with the exception of the hard beats of Nas. There was enough tension in the room to suck the air out of their lungs. Liam stood up; chest puffed out. Suddenly, he relaxed and broke out in laughter.

"I'm just playing with you, brother." He chuckled, gripping onto Stephan's left shoulder.

"Let's go, Liam." Esmeralda ordered, handing him his leather jacket. "It's almost 4 in the morning." She grabbed him by the arm and guided him out of the skybox. A few moments later, they watched them leaving the club. Liam looked back up at them, and made direct eye contact, through the one-way glass.

"What the fuck was that?" Crystal said, walking up to Johnathon and wrapping her arm around his waist. He placed his arm around her shoulders.

"We gone have to watch him, man. I heard he was the one who killed that lil kid on 62nd last week. He too hot, bruh." Frank said, sparking a blunt. His words permeated Stephan's thoughts like a virus. "I can get more solid information by the morning."

"Yeah, we can do that tomorrow. Tonight, we celebrate." Stephan said smiling. He felt Liam was going to become a problem. And soon.

He stumbled into the house, a quarter to 5, barely beating the sun home. Not wanting to disturb his wife, he flopped down on the couch and flipped on the local channel 2 News.

He remembered feeling afraid and angry. Johnathon couldn't help him. His family was in trouble, and there was nothing he could do to help. He was sinking in sand, fast. He could feel his breath being held in his lungs, jarring him from his sleep. He sat up, catching a whiff of bacon and sausage in the air. He dragged his feet into the kitchen, following the heavenly scent. Angelika was in the large kitchen, walking over to Liyah's kid table, handing her a plate of food.

"Hey baby." She said smiling at him. She placed the food on the table, then walked over and hugged Stephan. "How was the party?" She asked after kissing him.

"It was cool until the ball dropped, Liam acting like a fool and shit." Stephan said, sitting down at the table. He started describing the night, including how close he was to fighting him. Angelika wasn't entirely surprised by the antics of their partner. It hadn't even been 2 months since he first put them all in jeopardy.

It was the Saturday just after Thanksgiving. Angelika couldn't do much on a daily basis but count down her days until the pregnancy was over. Liam had just robbed a house with a few of Esmeralda's brothers. They didn't really like Stephan and Johnathon for deciding to go into business for themselves, but since Liam was Esmeralda's husband, they had no problem staying close to *him*.

Liam got split up from them and found himself in Stephan's neighborhood. Only it was Angelika and the kids, who were home alone. He showed up at the back door, sweaty and out of breath.

"Liam, what's up? Everything okay?" She asked, opening the door, letting him in. He rushed in, looking through the curtains like someone was after him. They were. Liam and his brothers-in-law, tripped the silent alarm. If they didn't get out when they did, they wouldn't have had time to get away. With or without the loot. Liam was explaining the situation to her when they heard a heavy pounding on the front door. Both their hearts sank into their chairs. He looked at her, shaking his head.

"Don't answer that." He whispered, jumping to his feet.

"If I don't, they're going to come back with a warrant, and if they find you my whole house goes down." She whispered back. She slid her feet into her pink Versace house shoes, and walked into the foyer, through the split-staircase, to the front of the house. As she walked, through the glass in the doors she could see three men in OPD uniforms, standing on her porch.

"Hi, how can I help you?" She asked, smiling, yet wore a confused look on her face.

"Yes, ma'am there was a robbery in the area, and we believe the suspect may still be around. We caught one of his accomplices over your neighbor's fence, next door."

"No one's here but me and my children." She said, opening the door wider so they could get a peek into the house. "My husband should be here soon, though." They looked behind her, into the foyer, through the two sets of staircases. Then to her right, into the sitting room.

"House clear." Said the first officer into the walkie-talkie, clipped to his shoulder." Sorry to bother you ma'am. Thanks for your time." He said, before the three of them turned and walked away, back down the long driveway.

Stephan sat at the table, eating, and talking to Angelika, when they heard Johnathon come in. "Hey, where ya'll at?" He asked, coming down the hallway, and into the kitchen. Johnathon wasted no time, getting the information that they needed. He couldn't rest on it.

"Hey, bro. What's going on? You hungry?" Angelika asked, standing up from the kitchen table, and turning to head back to the stove.

"Nah, I'm okay, sis. Thank you." He replied, sitting down at the table.

"What's going on, Johnny?" Stephan asked, motioning for Angelika to take Liyah out of the room. She did, and headed upstairs to check on the twins, and Demetrius and James.

"He fuckin did it, bruh. And what's worse, that nigga's running around with them Mexicans that don't even fuck with us. Word on the street is, them niggas dying to set us up. But they can't, you feel me? I'm still waiting on some calls, but I heard he been fuckin' around with our enemies, too. Nigga playing both sides."

Stephan chuckled. "You playing, right?" The smile faded from his face. He thought back on the conversation he'd had with Liam, when he brought heat to his home, with his pregnant wife and little kids. He felt his blood boiling as he bit down on his back teeth.

BAM!!!

"Fuck, bruh!" He slammed both fists on the large wooden table. He stood up and walked over to the alcohol cabinet and pulled down a bottle of Patron and two crystal glasses. It was only 7:45 in the morning, but a drink was needed. A strong one.

"What you wanna do?" Johnathon asked, taking the cup of liquor from Stephan. He stood, looking out of the patio door onto his perfectly manicured backyard. He didn't know how they were going to handle the issue with Liam, but he knew his kids would never feel the heat from his mistakes. He was ready to give his life for that.

"I'll go talk to him, again. See what he tries to tell me."

"Maybe, ya'll should go together." Angelika said as she fixed a plate of food for Johnathon as well.

"Nah, he'll know something going on."

Later that night he headed to Liam's Berkeley mansion, on San Antonio Blvd., in the Hills. He reached the gate and hit the call button. There was a long buzzing sound, followed by a short beep, and the gate slowly swung open, allowing him to ride up the narrow, bricked driveway. He parked directly in front of the door and was shutting off the Ferrari's engine, when Liam was coming outside to meet him. He wore a gold and black, Versace robe, with golden Gucci flip flops.

"Brother! To what do I owe the visit? Is this about last night?" He asked as they walked into the house.

"Yes and no. We gotta talk, bro." Stephan responded.

"Follow me." Liam said, leading the way passed the water fountain, that was housed in the middle of the heated, white marble tile floor. He followed him to his first-floor office, right off the foyer, closing the wooden, glass-paned door behind him.

The office was decorated in classic Liam fashion; expensive. He had a large wooden desk, completely covered in Aztec carvings. The window adjacent to the door gave a gorgeous view of the backyard, even at night do the area lamps Liam had built into his trees. The pool also helped to illuminate the gorgeous space.

"Siéntate, hermano." Liam sat in his large, black leather seat, at the oak desk. After turning on the fireplace, he reached onto his desk, and into a wooden box, with a crystal window in the center of the lid, displaying the contents of the box, full of Cuban cigars. He pulled out a silver cutter, and a box of matches. Stephan looked around at the paintings on the walls. He felt like Jesus and the Virgin Mary were staring straight at him, disappointed.

"What's going on with you, dude?" Stephan asked, straight out.

"Los siento, mi hermano. I'm not sure what you are talking about." He said, striking a match and lighting the cigar.

Stephan wiped his face in a downward motion with both hands. "You don't know what the fuck I'm talking about?"

"No, I'm not sure what it is you speak of-"

"Nigga, you out here breaking into houses, working with niggas that wouldn't blink an eye if me or Johnny took a bullet." Stephan said, fuming, trying not to yell. He knew Liam and Essie just had another little boy; Edwardo, just 4 short weeks ago.

Liam chuckled as he puffed on his cigar. "Don't be so dramatic, brother." He blew the smoke near Stephan's direction. He wasn't sure if Liam was trying to be disrespectful, but it did cross his mind.

"Bruh, you out here...!" He realized he was starting to yell, as he stood, slamming his flat hands against the wooden desktop. "You're out here killing kids, my nigga? And working with the opps? Really?"

"Look, brother, there are casualties of war. You know that just like I do. ¿Recuerdas al hermano de tu esposa?" Liam responded, standing, and walking out from his desk. "I need more territory man." He walked over to a large mostly colored map of the bay area that hung over the couch next to the door. He noticed East Oakland and West Oakland was blacked out. The color key said the black meant off limits. Those were also Stephan and John's territories. He appreciated the fact those parts were off limits. Other parts were colored red, and the rest blue. The red Berkeley, next door to North Oakland, which was Liam's. A lot of red covered San Francisco as well. And Vacaville was in the blue. The red meant it was almost under his control, and that the blue meant they were next to be under his control. "It's not enough man."

"What the fuck you mean? *It's not enough.*" Steph asked, arms spread out, looking around the very room they stood in. "Nigga, your wife has more money than the three of us combined, but that still ain't enough for you? I just had twins and my daughter turns four next month. I took in two kids that ain't even mine. You're starting to make shit hotter than it needs to be, bruh."

"Well, you know me. I like *wonderful* things, brother." He said, sitting in the large sofa, under his territory map. He crossed his legs. "I like a lavish lifestyle."

Stephan chuckled out of frustration. He could tell nothing was going to get through to him. "Bruh, if your *'lavish style's'* consequence's, come to my front door again, we're going to have a fucking problem. *Me and you.*"

Liam stood, heading towards his bar, which sat under the large window. "Well, luckily for you…and me, I tie *all* of my loose ends." Liam said, standing next to Stephan, facing the opposite direction. He chuckled and continue walking.

"If that's the case, then how'd Johnny find out that you out here shooting low-level niggas? Acting just like the niggas you out here trynna take over…"

"That little snitch…" Liam said. "Let me change. I have some *loose ends* to tie." He said, downing the drink he'd just poured. He hurried to the door, swinging it open, then running out of the room and up the stairs.

"The fuck is you up to now?" Stephan asked himself. He sat down on the couch, in disbelief, after he went over to the bar and poured himself a large drink. Gulping it down, in 3 and half shots. He felt the effects after about 3 minutes, just as Liam was coming back down the stairs.

"¿Listo para ir?" Liam asked. He had on all black; a beanie, a pair of black jeans and a pair of blood red Adidas sneakers, with matching leather gloves. In his right hand, he held a large hunting knife. The knife had a gold, 10" blade, and a black pearl handle. In the other hand, was an AR-22 rifle, with an extended clip.

"Si." Stephan sighed, following him through the hallway, through the large kitchen and to the garage. They got into Liam's black 1994 Navigator truck and raced down the hill. Stephan noticed that Liam had a little, white powdery residue, around his right nostril. "Liam, where we going, bruh?"

"I told you, 'To tie up a loose end'. Don't worry, you'll be home safe. I promise." He didn't trust that. Though every bone in his body told him to make Liam turn around, he couldn't leave him alone to tie up those *loose ends*. "Here, put these on." He said reaching into the back and pulling out a similar outfit.

"Why do you keep a set of clothes in your truck?" He asked, changing his shirt, pants, and shoes.

"In case I'm ever in your position. Get that semi out the glove box." He reached in and grabbed the silver, semi-automatic 9mm Luger. He checked the clip; It was fully loaded.

"Thanks, brother." He said, just as they pulled over in a neighborhood in West Oakland. Liam pulled his beanie down, over his face and led the way as Steph did the same. He put up his finger, signaling for Stephan to stop, as he checked their surroundings. He led them through the side gate, of a burgundy duplex apartment. The backyard was sizable, all concrete with a white, wooden shed tucked in the back left corner.

Stephan suddenly began smelling a horrible stench. He looked around and quickly found the source. The entire back staircase was encumbered with garbage, in and out of bags. His heart sank when he noticed Liam was leading him directly through them.

"Shit. For real bro?" He said, tucking his gun back into his Jeans. He needed both hands to stabilize himself.

"Shhhh." Liam said. They finally made it up to the back porch. The kitchen light was on. There was a strong smell of fried chicken wafting through the fabricated screen door. They noticed a large, white woman, standing at the stove. She had on a purple night gown, with a black floral pattern, and black house shoes. Her blonde hair was pinned up into a messy ponytail, but still touching the middle of her shoulders. There was a lot of commotion coming from inside of the house, like someone was watching a sports game that they bet money on.

Liam quietly opened the door and Stephan followed. Liam ran up on the lady, hitting her in the back of her head, with the butt of his knife, giving as much strength as he could muster. She immediately fell to the floor. Stephan caught her before she had the chance to fall and make any noise. Guns drawn, they crept down the hallway, following the commotion. Liam peeked around the corner. It was just Dashon, his loose end, watching a football game, with the volume up on high. The 4 empty beers next to him explained a lot about that. He was in a white Che Guevara T-Shirt and a pair of black, fleece pajama pants. He was covered up with a black and silver robe, with brown, leather Louboutin loafers.

"Sup', Dashon?" Liam said, pistol aimed at his head. He looked up at them, eyes wide.

"Hey, Liam. What are you - what's going on?" He asked, chuckling nervously. He saw their guns and immediately threw his hands in the air.

"We're about to take a little ride, you and me." Liam said walking up to him. His lit cigar dropped into his lap, as Liam grabbed him by his arm, yanking him to his feet.

"Whoa! What's going on? Where's Gelisa?" He asked, looking for his girlfriend.

"Oh, you want to see your little bitch?" Liam asked. Stephan watched as Liam dragged him by his feet, and into the kitchen where he seen a black pistol tucked into Dashon's waistband. Liam missed it. Dashon shot Stephan an evil look as he snatched it.

"You won't be needing this." Stephan said, tucking the gun into his pocket. They walked into the kitchen, where Gelisa still laid unconscious, in the same place that they left her. The fried chicken was starting to burn, filling the kitchen with smoke. Liam allowed Dashon to rush over to his girlfriend's side. His eyes grew blood-shot red, filling up with tears. "Don't worry, bruh. She's still alive-" Stephan said, just before Liam put three bullets into her upper back. No doubt, aiming for her heart. Dashon jumped back, eyes wide.

"Nooooo!!" He screamed. He was hurt and in shock.

"Won't be needing her anymore either." Liam said, he yanked Dashon towards the backdoor. "Go!" He ordered. Once through the door, Dashon pushed off of Liam, causing him to fall against the wall. Dashon, literally threw himself down the stairs, saved by the cushioning of the trash pile. Liam and Stephan looked at each other in disbelief.

"Get that nigga, man!" Liam yelled. They did exactly what Dashon did, catching up to him at the street.

BAH!

Liam shot a bullet, catching him in the back of his thigh.

"Ahhhh!!! Fuck!!" Dashon yelled out in pain, falling to his stomach.

"Come on, man, don't do this. Please." Dashon begged, flipping around on his back. He scooted away from them, trying to keep as much distance as he could.

"Get his bitch ass up." Liam ordered as they yanked him up to his feet.

"Help!!" He started screaming. "He-" Stephan hit Dashon in the back of the head, almost knocking him out.

"Drive." Liam said tossing Stephan the keys to the truck. "I'm going to show this dude how to keep his mouth shut." Liam said, pulling out his hunting knife. He tossed Dashon into the backseat, jumping in, and shutting the door behind him.

"I'm sorry, man. I'm so sorry." Dashon cried, looking at the knife. His gut was full of fear, as he slowly began to realize his life was no longer his own.

"I don't give a fuck. Stick your tongue out."

"What??" Asked Dashon. Liam was done asking. He used the knife handle to knock out his top, front four teeth, and the bottom two. Liam reached into his mouth, gripping his tongue between his thumb and forefinger. Dashon begged and pleaded to be let go. His spit running down Liam's wrist and arm. In one clean motion, he sliced his tongue clean out of his mouth

"Ahhh!!!" He screamed gagging and throwing up blood all over the back seat.

"Ew, bitch!" Liam yelled. After tossing the knife onto the floor of the truck, he started swinging his fists, connecting blow after blow. As Stephan watched through the rearview mirror, he could hear Dashon's face bones cracking and breaking. Once barely breathing, he grabbed the knife, stabbing Dashon in the chest over 6 times, then placing two bullets into his right temple, with his own gun. Liam placed his tongue back into his mouth as they rode down West Frontage; a sliver of 2-lane highway between the Bay and I-580. Stephan continued to watch in horror as Liam opened the door and pushed him out of the moving vehicle. The cars that followed behind them, rolled over Dashon like a speed bump, before slamming onto their breaks.

CHAPTER 5

Stephan's seen enough. It was the beginning of December in the year 1998, just four years since the murder of Dashon and his girlfriend. Stephan, after that night, knew his friend was becoming unhinged. He made the choice to protect his family, at all costs, without any harm coming to Liam. He hired Ramon, a petite private investigator from Portugal to follow Liam around the world for the last 4 years, to make sure he wasn't doing anything to harm the family. He watched as Liam continued to work with people whom they've tried to stay away from, for the sole purpose of them being competitors. And worse, enemies. It was all about trust and Steph couldn't trust the competition and his partner was crossing over the line to competitor.

It was almost 2 in the morning, when Stephan received a frantic call from Ramon.

"Hey, Steph, I think they maybe on to me. I'll drop the photos off in the mailbox. But I can't work for you anymore. I'm sorry." He said, before hanging up the phone. Stephan called back immediately.

"*The person you are trying to reach, cannot accept calls at this time...*" said the automated voice message. Stephan placed the burner phone back into his desk, after removing the battery.

The next morning, his body was found floating in Lake Merritt, with a whopping 49 stab wounds, done by what looked like to be more than 8 different knives. Luckily, for Stephan, he'd made it to the mailbox, before his killers made it to him. He waited a couple years before picking up the Manila envelope, just in case Ramon's killers followed him there before killing him.

Waiting until the house was quiet, when he could look through the envelop, without being interrupted, he sat on the couch in his personal office, the last check he wrote to Ramon for $100,000, sat in his hands. He ripped it up into little pieces and tossed the shreds into a glass ashtray. Before opening the envelope, he calmed his nerves by rolling up a nice blunt, setting fire to the shredded check once the weed was lit.

Stephan studied the photos, unable to believe it was one of his brothers on the other side of the film. There were pictures of him, standing and laughing at tied up women and children, beaten and bloody, then slaughtered like cattle. There was another photo, which jarred him more than the last, few. It was a photo of Esmeralda's parents, hog tied with a red bandana in their mouths. Esmeralda sat on top of her father, knees in his back with a sawed-off shotgun pressed to the back of his temple. Stephan wasn't sure how the PI got a picture of them after death; throats slashed ear-to-ear. But that wasn't the straw that broke his back. A few of their high rolling connects, were bound, and gagged, then murdered, by Andrew. The brother of Angelika, whom they thought was shot dead. He placed the photos back into the envelop and stored it under the couch cushion, burying his secret about Andrew being alive. He knew he had to come up with a plan to save his family, before shit started to hit the fan, knowing it was only a matter of time.

He grabbed the phone off of his glass, office table, fighting back tears of anger, sadness, and betrayal.

"Yo, what's up, bruh?" Johnathon answered. He looked at the digital clock on his nightstand. It was almost 3:45 am. "Everything alright?" He asked once Stephan didn't immediately answer his question. He sat up in bed.

"Nah, not at all. Liam gotta go, bruh." He responded. "Meet me at my house." Stephan said before hanging up. Johnathon took almost 20 minutes to get down there. Stephan was sitting on the front porch, smoking a second blunt, when Johnathon's red Range Rover pulled up in front of him.

"What's up, bruh? What happened?" Johnathon asked, jumping down from the vehicle. Stephan motioned for Johnny to follow him. He watched his face sink lower and lower with each photo. "Wait, Drew's alive?"

"Apparently. Bruh, I don't know what the fuck going on, be we gotta put a stop to that shit...before that shit put a stop to us. Johnathon's wife, Crystal, graduated from the police academy right out of High School. She kept a blind eye to what her husband and brothers were up to, supplying them with a few cop buddies to help them get out of jams for the last 4 years. Liam was putting that in jeopardy as well, with his recklessness, making it easier for them to put him away. Crystal was able to get a search warrant, taking copies of the photos and showing them to her sergeant. When asked how she obtained this evidence, she said it was left alone on her desk. That she'd checked for fingerprints but found none. The judge granted them a search warrant right away, and that's what they did. She stayed away during the raid on Liam's estate, knowing Liam's men wouldn't hesitate to point her out.

The police aimed for Liam, Esmeralda and Andrew, but were only able to find Liam. He was asleep in his large throne-like bed, with 5 half-naked strippers.

His brothers-in-arms, went to his trial to show him support, and to be sure he was convicted. Liam was confused at why he was the only one being thrown behind bars, but he decided to take his sentencing, knowing he's been doing some wild stuff as well lately. He knew he wasn't a saint and just felt like his demons were finally catching up with him. It took Stephan and Johnathon 6 years to get over their guilt. They decided to stop putting money on his books and let his wife or Andrew handle it, wherever they might be. It didn't take Liam and Esmeralda long to figure out why he was the only one behind bars. All his people needed, was for someone to go up to that mailbox, to find out who hired the PI. They immediately got the information and proof to Liam. He was furious looking at a picture of Stephan, removing the envelope from the mailbox. He knew Johnathan and Stephan were only sending 'stay strong' and 'stay up' letters and well wishes for the first two years he was locked up.

Andrew and Esmeralda executed a plan, before getting Liam out of prison after only 6 years of being incarcerated. He was now out and ready for blood, spending the next 3 years concocting a plan to get back at his 'Brothers'.

CHAPTER 6

I twirled around in the office chair, staring at the phone number in my hand. I was starting to think today was going to be one of those days. As soon as I pulled up to work, there was a line of people, waiting for me and Ashley to open the store. I always hated the first two weeks of the month at California Check Cashing on the corner of 51st and Telegraph. Everybody who needed loans, checks cashed, or just anyone without a bank account littered our lobby. And it lasted all day.

When I seen one customer though, Sean, all of that went out of the window. I wouldn't care if the quantity doubled in size, this boy was so fine! Tall, light-skinned, hazel eyes and corn rolls, every time I seen him. He was slim, yet muscular, stood a tall, 6'2", and had a voice that I could listen to for hours on end. Just hearing him say my name got my panties moist. For the last six months, every two weeks I have cashed this man's checks, waiting. Waiting for him to show me more attention than the infrequent flirt. And he did it. He finally slid his number under the teller window, in just enough time. Today's my last day here before I go to UCLA to earn a degree in Theater, to be more than just daddy's little rich girl. I want to be the next great black actress, like Taraji Henson or Halle.

"Liyah! Girl, we need you up here." I heard my coworker, Ashley, yell from the front of the store, snapping me out of my thoughts. "Did you call him?" She asked once I made it to my window and called the next customer up. My father's worth $100 Million, from owning a couple of different clubs in San Francisco, selling them before I was old enough to remember. Now he owns buildings all over the city, renting them out. And I'm standing here asking, *"How can I help you?"* Real humbling, right?

"No, not yet. Imma text him later." I said. "How can I help you?" I called the next customer to my window.

"Yeah, you don't want to seem too thirsty." She chuckled. "Let me know what happens with his fine ass."

"Girl bet. I will." I said, unable to wipe my smile away.

"Good, don't forget about me when you make it big." She said and we shared a chuckle.

The two of us finally closed the store down at 15 until 10. I couldn't wait to sink into my soft leather seats, reach into my ash tray and finish that blunt I had on my lunch break.

I made it home about 30 minutes later, deciding to shoot Sean a text once I was lying in bed, ready to fall asleep. That way I won't seem too thirsty when I respond sometime the next morning.

I walked into my personal palace, my bedroom. It was the size of a normal one-bedroom apartment, with a private balcony, sitting just beyond the large windows. I placed my bed against them so that the sun wouldn't bother me when it rose. I kicked off my red Versace pumps, feeling elated when my toes sunk into my fuchsia shag carpet, matching my Chloe Queen comforter. I flopped down onto my king-sized bed, body sinking into the cloud-like mattress.

"Hey, It's Liyah." I texted. To my surprise, he responded. Almost immediately.

"Hey beautiful." He said. "I was starting to think you wasn't going to hit me up."

"LOL. Nah, I was just busy. Just really got comfortable."

"Oh, okay. You mind if I call you?" He asked. I waited a couple of minutes before responding, feeling anxious. "Texts just seem so … impersonal."

"Yeah, that's fine." I replied. I turned into a ball of nerves.

It was hard to bottle the specific emotion I felt, watching his name and number flash across my screen. I've had a crush on this man for the last few months, and it was finally happening. He was finally calling me. I was anxious, nervous, and excited all at the same time. I could feel the butterflies fluttering around in my stomach as I answered, "Hello?"

"Hey, this Liyah?" A deep baritone voice rang through the phone. Like a vibration through a small, hollow tube, he sent chills, through each of the 206 bones in my body. I felt the universe was trying to show me who was boss, and I was ready to submit to him. I began to feel my body clench and tighten.

I didn't realize how long we'd been talking until the sky began to turn blue again. Today's my 19th birthday, and some sleep is to be had if I was going to do anything today. But I couldn't seem to bring myself to hang up with him. I heard my mom get up and start moving through the house. Burying myself under a mountain of pillows and blankets, so that she wouldn't hear me through the door if she walked passed.

I woke up later in the afternoon, grabbing my phone from the nightstand to check the time. "Fuck." I said, reading the time at 12:30. I called my best friend, Tracey, to let her know I was going to be late to our strip class that she'd set up. I jumped into the shower, unable to stop thinking about Sean. I began to feel a tickle between my thighs. I chuckled a little, shutting off the water and grabbing my towel off from the glass shower door. I towel dried my hair, before sliding into my Nike leggings and sports bra set.

"Where you headed to?" My dad asked as I came down the front steps. He was sitting on the couch, with his feet on the coffee table and his MacBook in his lap. He wore black Gucci robe over a burgundy wife beater and a pair of Gucci pajama pants. My mom sat in the reclining chair to the left of him, on her laptop as well, having an iced coffee. When I looked at my dad I saw the epitome of a man. His strong demeanor demanded respect when he entered the room. And at 6'3 220 pounds of muscle, he had no trouble obtaining it from those who tried and cross him. He loved his family, and his family loved him back.

I headed outside with my Louis Vuitton gym bag. It was a little warm for a Valentine's Day. I hurried to my coke-white, 2010 Tesla Roadster, rushing to start the engine and get the AC on. I made it to Atomic Allure, in Oakland's Downtown district, less than 20 minutes later. I walked in and saw Tracey starting to climb the pole. I almost busted my own ass laughing when she lost her grip and slid to the floor.

Me and Tracey have been friends for as long as I can remember. She was my height, 5'5, and weighed about 140. Stacked, tits and ass for days. Like me as well, she was Puerto Rican and Black. She wore a red PUMA workout bra, with matching leggings, and a pair of clear platform heels.

"Fuck you, bitch!" She laughed, coming over to hug me. "It's like extra slippery or some shit. I wanna see you get up there and do that shit."

"Don't you do this for like…a living?" I asked, chuckling.

"Nope, don't ask questions." She laughed. "How you been girl?" She asked as we walked over to the poles.

"Shit, still working. Dad's been making me pay off my credit cards since that weekend in Cabo." I said. Madame Shirl had us do some stretches before we got to our class.

"Right! Graduation weekend!" She said, stretching, laughing, reminiscing about the fun we had. Daddy was not happy that I ran up his card $110,000. But going into to college may get him to let me off the hook.

I was up first. I had no idea how Tracey, and countless other women, did this on a nightly to semi-nightly basis. Madame Shirl has us do some sexy moves for our men. I was already thinking about dancing for Sean the whole time.

We'd been dancing for two hours, and were reaching the end of our class, when the instructor had to step away to take a phone call. "So, I met this guy, right?" I said, plopping down on the waxed, wooden floor.

"Oh, really? Do tell, bitch." She said, as we stretched and drank a bit of water to regroup.

"His name is Sean. Fine as fuck, bitch. Like, I want his babies." I whined.

She laughed, unable to believe what she'd just heard. "You want this nigga's babies? Shit you should just invite him out tonight."

"Hey ladies. I'm sooo sorry." Madame Shirl said, coming back into the room after a few moments. I was playing around on the pole after catching my second wind, trying to do some of the moves I've seen the professionals do in the movies. That did *not* work out to my favor.

"Oh, girl, don't even trip. We were damn near done anyways." Tracey said taking to her feet. She walked over to her PINK Victoria's

Secret gym bag and hoisted what seemed to be 20 pounds over her shoulders.

"I have a question for you girls." She asked, almost as we were closing the door to the studio behind us. We looked at each other, wondering what she could possibly want to ask us. "Would you guys like to dance tonight...like at a club?" We paused for a second.

"Like at a *club*?" I asked.

"Like at a club." She smiled.

"What, is it like amateur night or some shit?" Tracey asked.

"No," she laughed. "There's some real money to be made. One of the girls couldn't make it. Long story. But I can get both you girls to dance tonight. My boss asked if I could, but I'm here for the next couple of nights." Me and Tracey looked at each other again.

"Hell yeah. We'll do it!" We said, excited. "Let me make some money on my motherfuckin' birthday, bitch!" I said, doing a little twerk.

"Really? How old are you?" Madame Shirl asked.

"I...I just turned 19 today." She got silent for a few seconds, looking me up and down. I was starting to think I just hurt my chances to make some money.

"Shit, you 21 today. Can you make it to San Fran by 8 tonight?" She asked, biting the tip of her pointer finger.

"Hell yeah." Tracey said. "We were already going out there." She added.

"Good. I'll text you guys the address." She said pulling out her phone. Tracey's iPhone 3g chimed only seconds later. "Thank you, girls. And most importantly, have fucking fun." She said, holding her hands up for us to give her five. Me and Tracey grabbed our stuff and headed downstairs, to our cars. I was so excited to go out dancing, once outside, I found a street sign and imitated some moves. Cars honked as I grabbed their attention.

"Bitch, go home and get dressed. We need to find some shit to wear to this mufuhckin' club. We 'finna turn San Fran the fuck out!"

"Bitch, you already fuckin' know!" I said excitedly. I could hardly contain my excitement.

I walked through the front door, just making it home, leaving my car in front of the porch. Dad hated when I did that, because when he would have client meetings, they would all line up right there, but I didn't plan on being here for that long. I checked my phone for any messages or calls from Sean. But none.

"Li, what you doing tonight?!" Malakhi, one of my brothers asked. Yes, there's two of them. They just turned 16, the day after Christmas of '09. They share the same cocoa brown skin, honey almond eyes, full lips and muscular figures. The only telling them apart was their hair. Other than that, they were the same person.

Malakhi and Malik are my heart. Though sometimes I want to snatch theirs out, I'd do any and everything for those assholes. Damn any bitch that tried to wrong them.

Malik is a sweetheart, not a mean bone in his body. He always made sure his hair was cut into a nice fade every two weeks and always made sure he helped mom and dad around the house. He's been a sweet little, seductive charmer ever since he was able to smile, birth. Once he flashed that smile, he could get anything he wanted. Then he learned to talk. Me, being his big sister, I was able to see through his tricks the first time he made the move. I was upset I didn't come up with it first. But, how was I supposed to know my parents planned on fucking still after making me. I should've been enough.

Malakhi, that boy's a whole different story. I'd call him a trouble maker, but that'd imply that he was sometimes not in it. He wore his hair dreaded, down his back. Begged mommy to let him do it since he was 5 years old. He wanted to stand out and look different than his twin brother. He was very militant. Got into many fights and couldn't stay out of people's faces if you paid him. Nevertheless, I loved them the same. They both were already 6' tall and lean, built like basketball players.

I ignored Malakhi as I headed up the staircase.

"Li!" Malik yelled after me. I ran faster into my room, not wanting to be bothered by, *whatever* it was they wanted at the moment. I could hardly contain my excitement as I walked into my closet and pulled out a pair of 7 Jeans, and a black Chanel sweater. After grabbing some panties and a bra, I plugged my iPhone 3G into my computer speakers and blared Jason Derulo's *Watcha Say*, as loud as I could, before hopping into the shower. I stepped out after a while and put on my under clothes.

KNOCK! KNOCK! KNOCK!

"What?!" I asked, now annoyed that they haven't gotten the message.

"Liyah, who you talking to?" My mom asked. "Open this door right now."

"Fuck." I whispered. "Sorry, mom." I wrapped a towel around my breast and opened the door. Her long, black and grey hair was pulled into a slick ponytail. She wore a white linen shirt, with spaghetti straps, and a pair of matching, loose fitting pants. She accessorized with gold bangles on her wrists, and a gold Patek watch on her left, and diamond-encrusted, gold hoop earrings with a pair of Fendi sandals.

"Aww, my baby is so grown up." She said hugging me. I struggled to keep the towel up. "Your father wanted me to give you this." She said, handing me one of those little black Rush Cards.

"What's this for?" I asked.

"Shit, it's $15,000 on there. It could be for whatever you want." She smiled. "Now don't go spending it all in one place." She said before coughing up the word Cabo.

"Thank you, mommy." I said hugging her. "Love you." I said as she headed downstairs, Botega Veneta perfume following her down the hall.

I shut the door and continued getting dressed.

KNOCK! KNOCK! KNOCK!

"What?" I asked, opening the door a second time. This time, being sure it was my little brothers.

"Can we get some weed?" Malakhi asked.

"Is he serious?" I asked, looking over at Malik.

"Sis, we need to smoke. Coach has been riding our asses lately." He said. I rolled my eyes.

"Give me a minute." I said, closing the door. I went into my closet and into one of the shoeboxes closest to the floor. I put a hefty amount into a honey Backwood and rolled it together into a blunt, ripping it in half so they won't fight over who's smoking more.

I opened the bedroom door, after rolling a couple for myself. "If mom or dad ever fucking finds out-"

"They won't, Li. I'll make sure he shuts the fuck up." Malik said.

"Whatever, nigga." Malakhi interjected.

"They better not or Imma beat both ya'll asses." I said, smiling. I shut the door then headed out to my terrace, looking out onto the perfectly manicured back yard, full of lush green grass, surrounded by trees and sculpted bushes. There was a pool area to the far side of the yard. Complete with a swim up bar, a grotto, and a waterslide. My favorite place in the world to be during the summer. I sat on my patio couch, kicking my feet up on the coffee table, enjoying the sun, smoking a blunt as I watched the trees sway in the wind.

I was about to start going through my phones internet browser, when I saw Sean's name come across my screen. "Hello?" I answered, trying not to sound like I was too eager to talk to him, even though there was nothing else that I wanted to do at the moment.

"Hey, beautiful." His sexy voice came through the phone. I bit my lip, feeling vibrations between my legs. "What you up to?"

"Shit, gettin' ready to head out to the City in a bit."

"What's going on? You having a little birthday party or something?" He asked.

I chuckled, "Nothing I do is little." I continued, "But I was invited to dance at Déjà vu'."

"Mm, okay, Miss Two Jobs." He said excitedly. I never really thought about being a stripper before today. I mean, Tracey does it and makes a damn shiny coin doing it.

"Nah, I've never done it. But depending on how much I make tonight, shit...I might."

"I know a few dancers that make pretty good money doing what they do."

"Oh, do you really? You fuckin' a stripper?" I asked.

"I don't know. Am I?" He asked, it seemed like his voice got deeper, making my panties a little moist. I didn't know what to say in response to that. He had me excited.

BEEP! BEEP!

Saved by the bell. It was Tracey trying to get through on the other line.

"Hold on really quick."

"Yup." He said before I clicked over.

"Girl meet me at my house. I gotta take Casey to my mom's."

"Aight. I should be there in an hour."

"Okay, see you soon." She said, then hung up.

I clicked back over to Sean. "Hey, I'm sorry. I'm back.

"It's cool. Can I come through tonight?" He asked. I could hear the sex dripping off of his voice.

"Yeah, come through. We going out after and I wouldn't mind kicking with you."

"Aight, bet. If I don't make your dance, I'll catch you later?"

"That works for me." I smiled.

"Okay. I'll see you later." He said before hanging up with me.

It took me another hour and a half to finish getting ready, and walk out of the door, to head to Tracey's house in West Oakland. She lived in an old fashioned, 2 story, 3-bedroom 3 bath Victorian home. The house was dark brown, surrounded by a black, iron fence. Her house was peaceful, despite being right across the street from West Oakland BART. She shared the house with her baby's father, Clarence, and their 3-year-old daughter Casey. I call him her baby daddy due to the constant state of ups and down they go through, but they'll never separate.

I parked my coupe behind Clarence's old modeled, candy-painted, souped-up 1992 Chevy Camaro. He was on the front porch, smoking a Newport 100.

"What's good witchu', Liyah?" He asked. I tried to dodge the smoke's toxic fumes.

"Shit, you coming out tonight?" I asked, looking at his wife-beater, grey sweats and Timberlands. He didn't seem close to being ready.

"You damn right. I heard what the fuck ya'll gone be up to. Ya'll must think we stupid." He said following me into the house, flicking his cigarette into the bushes.

"Boy, bye. Where my sister at?" I asked, headed straight to her liquor cabinet, pouring me a double shot of Ciroc Red Berry.

"She was dropping Casey off at her mom's. Should be back in a minute or two."

"Damn, still?" I said, sitting down on the couch, writing her a text message. "Hey bitch I'm at ur house." Send. She called me not long after I sent the message. "Hey, Girl. I'm at yo' house. Where you at?"

"Picking up my dumbass sister. Her fucking dude got her car took."

"Damn, is she even coming? If I was Kareena I'd be ready to go to jail." I laughed as I took a sip of my drink.

"You know this bitch ain't missing a turn up." She laughed. "We'll be there in 'bout 20 minutes. Bitch! Wait until you see this fucking suite!"

"Yes! I'm too juiced." I said, barely able to contain myself.

"So, you talk to yo' girl?" Clarence asked.

"Yeah they on their way now." I sank into the couch watching as my bitch, Nicki Minaj performed *Beez In the Trap* on BET. Clarence went and sat down on the couch adjacent from me.

"Nah, bout me being in the dog house."

"Hell nah. I would've put yo' ass out. She being nice. You was damn near fuckin with one of her co-workers."

"*Flirting*, not fuckin'. And the bitch tricked me, bruh." He said trying to plead a case.

"Nigga, ain't nobody trick you" I laughed. "You just a hoe."

Clarence is big, but he's far from being an ugly dude. He stands a solid 6'5, 280 pounds of muscle. His eyes were dark brown and he had long, brown dread locks that flowed down his back. I was looking at my phone, when 30 minutes later, Tracey and her little sister, Kareena walked into the house.

Me and Tracey met back in Frick Middle school. She was an eighth grader and I was only in 6th. But she took me under her wing, and we've been inseparable since. I met Kareena my first trip to her house. Yvette, their mother, immediately took me under her wing as a third daughter of hers, telling me I fit right in with her beautiful girls.

I remember, it was lunch time and I sat in the cafeteria, twirling my fork around in what they wanted me to believe was spaghetti.

"What's it taste like?" I looked up, pulled away from my thoughts. Even at the age of 12, I didn't care about having friends. It was the first day, of my second week at school. I was home-schooled up until this point, me and my little brothers were. So, the concept of socializing was a little jarring to me. I guess you could say I was a bit of a dork.

"I'm actually not sure. I'm playing with it because the lunch lady freaks me out." We both shared a chuckle.

"I'm Tracey." She said, holding her hand out. It took a second to remember what to do in these situations. I smiled and shook her hand.

"Hey, I'm Liyah. Nice to meet you."

"You, too. Me and my sister are about to head home for lunch. You should come. My mom makes a delicious BBQ chicken sandwich." I looked down at, what was supposed to be spaghetti.

"You know what," I chuckled standing up leaving the plate where it was. "I'll take you up on that."

"Happy birthday, bitch!" I heard Tracey yell as she walked in through the front door. I jumped up excitedly, eager to meet her and Kareena. Two of the baddest bitches I knew.

Kareena was like her mini-me. They looked just alike and wore the same sizes in everything, only a little lighter in her complexion. And much less of a firecracker than her bigger sister. Her hair was shoulder-length and curly.

"Oh, so you just gone start the party without me?" She asked, grabbing the bottle and a few more glasses. I laughed.

"Yes, bitch, ya'll took forever." I chuckled, taking another sip. "Plus, it's my birthday."

"Mm-Hmm. Blame that one." She replied, pointing to Kareena, then pouring them a drink.

"Bruh, it was not my fault." She said, defending herself, taking the glass from her sister.

"You still fucking with that lean head, Jovonnie? You good?" I asked, snickering.

"No, but that fucking dick is." She sang. We all shared a chuckle.

"Aight, babe, Imma go meet up with the fellas." Clarence said, wrapping his arm around Tracey's waist. "It's too much estrogen in this mothafucka."

"Yeah, see you later." She responded, rolling her eyes.

"I'll see ya'll later, man." He said, sucking his teeth, then leaving. I grabbed my phone and car keys from the couch.

"We should probably get going, too."

The ride to The City took a little over an hour, due to traffic. We took Tracey's white Audi. Our first stop was Nordstrom's in San Francisco's Westgate Mall. One of my favorites. Most of what I bought, had nothing to do with me dancing tonight, but I didn't care, it was worth it. Got a few pairs of True Religion and Balmain jeans. Some Gucci pieces and a leather Prada Jacket or two. Our next stop was Victoria's Secret, then Bloomingdale's and Hugo Boss. I couldn't manage to keep my mind off Sean. I decided not to send him sexy pics as I tried on lingerie, though it was very difficult abstaining from a little tease.

My imagination went wild with options. I couldn't decide what to buy, so I decided to get a few different ones, in assorted colors and sexy styles. Sheikhs offered a lot of different options in terms of clear-soled heels on 7" stilettos. Last, but not least, off to Sephora to get our faces beat, with only 3 hours to go.

We made it to San Francisco's Suites, on Nob Hill, and checked into our room. From the outside, it just looked like a normal hotel. The lobby was nothing special, with just a bell hop and a receptionist directly at the entrance. To the right of the entrance looked to be a quaint café. Stepping onto the black and white, checkered-tile floor, the smell of coffee made itself known as you walked into the building.

"Hi! Welcome to San Francisco Suites." The lady asked. She was super chipper and excited, with her short brown hair, pulled back into a loose ponytail. Her uniform looked like it belonged to a butler; black, with a white button up shirt underneath a black double-breasted blazer. "Checking in?" She asked.

"Yes please." Tracey said, putting her ID down on the counter. She gave us all a key and showed us down the hall, to the old-schooled elevator. The kind that opened like a closet door, with a drop and lift gate behind it. I was surprised there wasn't someone on there to manually operate it by rope or levee. We got off on the top floor, walking down the hall a couple doors, and into the suite. The inside of the Suite looked like the inside of a celebrity's Manhattan, New York condo. The entrance was brightly lit, walls painted white, with black marble floors, complete with tiny gold flakes. We passed the entrance to the kitchen, and a stair case, leading up to the bedrooms, into the beautifully decorated living room/dining area.

There was large sectional couch, in the corner, against a brick wall and under a window, looking over the street below. In front of the sectional was a large fireplace, with a large 60" Sony plasma, housed above it. Tracey grabbed a remote off of the coffee table and turned it on, along with the fireplace.

"This place is fucking sick." I said, as we headed up stairs.

"Your room is down the hall. It's the master." Tracey said, stopping off at one of the rooms. I walked into mine. It was decorated with a blueish turquoise theme. The bed was lifted, queen sized with a thousand and one blue and green throw pillows. The duvet was thick, and a pretty, metallic turquoise, with little, gold-stitched flowers throughout. There was an old-fashioned, turquoise, love seat at the foot of the bed, which was sat in front of a fireplace, and a mounted plasma. The loveseat matched the sofa exactly. The fireplace doubled for the bathroom behind it which was equally as gorgeous. There was a black claw foot tub, with gold feet positioned in the middle of the bathroom. The shower had a stone floor and walls and was big enough to fit 8 and a half people comfortably. The bathroom came equipped with a double sink. The black bowls of the sink looked to be just placed onto the counters. Behind them were large mirrors, framed in antiqued gold.

Even with all the things I just bought, I was still having a demanding time finding something to wear. I decided to go with the black lingerie set; a bustier, encrusted with silver studs, and a matching black thong, under black mesh stockings. I coupled the outfit with a pair of thigh high, black leather boots, and a trench coat, that barely draped over my ass. I twirled around in the mirror, loving my reflection. Before getting dressed, I platted my hair into tight braids, dipping them into a cup of hot, boiling water. Taking them out gave me the perfect crinkles.

"What ya'll think?" I asked, walking down the stairs, into a cloud of smoke.

"Bitch, you look like the Angel of Death." Tracey said, handing me the blunt.

"That's 'cus we out here killin' these bitches!" I said taking a long drag.

"Bitch, I know that's fuckin' right!" Kareena said, taking a swig from the bottle.

When I said we was killing these bitches, *WE* were killing all these bitches. Kareena had on a red, strapless, body fitting romper, that hugged around her thighs. Her shoes were a black, patent leather,

Louboutin pump, and she wore her hair slicked back, still down her back.

Tracey had on an all-white lingerie outfit. A little similar to mines. But instead, her bustier was not studded, but laced everywhere but the nipples. Her thongs matched, laced everywhere but the place these niggas really wanted to see. Her white leather coat draped to her knees. And her heels were an all-white Louboutin pump, patent leather as well.

KNOCK! KNOCK! KNOCK!

I opened the door and in walks Clarence. I was just about to close the door, when I felt some resistance. It was my ex-boyfriend Johnathon, Jr. for short.

"Whoa, you ain't gone let me in?" He asked, holding a baby-blue gift bag.

"I don't know. Depends on what you got in the bag." I said, reluctantly stepping to the side, letting him in. He handed me the bag before picking me up swirling me around, kissing me on the forehead. "Let me down, nigga." I ordered.

"Ya'll ready to turn the fuck up?" He said excitedly, pulling a small bottle of Patron Silver out of his black peacoat.

There was a point in time when I used to think Johnathon and I were soul mates. We grew up together, his birthday being only a couple months before mine, in December. Our fathers are like brothers. Johnathon used to be on the track to be a professional basketball player. He has the tall statute; about 6'5 and had a slim, muscular build. He had milk-chocolate, brown skin and deep brown eyes, with a wavy fade. The owner of a smile to make Shemar Moore jealous. The man was fine, and loyal to a fault. His only issue was that he got extremely mean and distant when he drank, every time he drank. And he love himself some Patron, every night.

I peeked into the bag and saw two light-blue boxes from Tiffany & Co. The first one was an 18 Karat Gold, wrap necklace, and the other was the matching bracelet. The entire gift had to be worth about $18,000.

"Damn, nigga. You wasn't playing." Clarence said, as Johnathon stood there, looking proud of himself.

"Gotta keep my baby in the best."

"I'm not yo' baby, nigga." I said. Seeing his reaction, I kissed him on the lips. "But thanks for the gift." I ran back upstairs to put the gifts away. "Ya'll ready?" I asked coming back down the stairs. It was going on 7:30, and Candice, AKA Madam Shirl, needed us at Déjà vu before 8. Luckily, the club wasn't far from the hotel at all. Maybe about 10 minutes, 15 maximum. We even had enough time to stop and pick up some more Backwoods.

"Oooh, I wanna sit on his face." Kareena said, looking at the bouncer, at the door checking IDs. He was big, full of muscle. Light skinned with a full beard.

"Hi, Candice sent us." I said, excitedly, holding onto Tracey's hand.

"Go ahead, ya'll." He said, letting the five of us through into the club.

The atmosphere made me want to dance as Young Money's *Bedrock* blasted through the speakers. The space was large, filled with booths and very soft-looking sofa chairs. The room was dark, lit up by only purple lighting, coming from the front and back of the bar, the main stage and also underneath the seats in the VIP section. The long stage, extended into the middle of the room. I looked over at the bar, realizing I was going to definitely need a drink before I did this. I was starting to feel like that scared little girl back in 6th grade. The place was packed with customers of all kinds; young, old, male, and female. We walked to the bar, where there were three girls, all running around, busy. One was cleaning the bar, one was counting money, and the other was taking orders and dishing them out at high speeds. I was impressed.

"Hi, I'm looking for Trixie." Tracey said, looking at a small piece of paper.

"Hey! That's me." One of the girls said, shoving a white towel in the back pocket of her LEVI jeans. She was younger-looking than I expected her to be. She was a short Asian girl, maybe about 5'2 with long black and purple hair that flowed just below her ass, stopping just above her knees. She wore a white tank top and a simple pair of hoop earrings.

"You must be, Liyah and Tracey." She said. She looked to one of her girls, snapping her finger to signal her to watch the bar as she walked out to meet us. "Candice told me you were coming down tonight. Nice to meet you girls, I'm Trixie."

"Thanks. Likewise." I said, shaking her hand before introducing her to Kareena.

"You dancing, too, sweetie?" She asked Kareena.

"Oh, no!" She laughed. "I'm just the support crew."

"No worries. Let me grab you girls some drinks, and I'll show you ladies around." She looked behind us at Johnathon and Clarence. "They gotta stay up here and pay for drinks though." She added.

"Shit, that's fine." We both said together. She whipped us up some Incredible Hulks, with an extra couple shots of Jamaican rum on the side.

"Alright ladies let me show you around." She said, motioning for us to follow her. We walked through the crowd of customers and lap dances, to a curtain on the side of the stage, and down a couple steps into the dressing room. The air immediately got thicker passing over the threshold. I felt like a rookie in a sea of vets, and I'm sure my feelings were displayed across my face.

"...that's because they can't get e-fuckin-nough! Lookit, lookit, lookit." Said one of the girls, she wore a black leather thong and a red bra, with a pair of 6" stilettoes, that wrapped up to her knees with a silver strap. "Bam, bitch!" She said as she hit a split and bounced. Swinging her long blonde wig in a circle. Her skill was absolutely intimidating. A few of the other girls cheered her on while the other girls moved around the dressing room, socializing and getting dressed for their performances, or to go home.

"Ladies, we got some new talent in the building for you." Trixie said, introducing us.

"Ohh, some new booty." The girl that perfected the split, said coming up to us. Her energy felt off. Not sure exactly what it was at the time, but I was sure I'd find out soon. She was 5'8, with D-Cup breasts, a slim waist and a large round butt. She wore a flashy 2-Piece, silver outfit. Her bustier top and thong bottoms had long, silver tassels attached to them.

"Sorry. Strictly dickly." Tracey said, joking. Or lying, depending on the bitch that was asking.

"Chill out, Zipporah." Said Trixie. "Make them feel welcome. By the way you're late this month." She said with her hand out. Zipporah walked away, switching her large butt as she headed for one of the purple lockers. "Are you thinking of working here? Or just covering for tonight?" She asked as Zipporah came back with a bundle of cash and handed it to her.

"I work at the Pink Monkey, in Oakland." Tracey said.

"Oh, okay, Cheyenne's your boss, huh?"

"Yeah, she is. You know her?"

"I divorced her." She said, laughing.

"Oop." Kareena said, laughing as well.

"Let's head upstairs." Trixie chuckled. We followed her out of the dressing room and back onto the main floor. The guys got us a booth, right in front of the stage. There were already bottles of Remy, Bacardi and Patron on the white, large table, sitting in purple buckets of ice. Glasses with lemons on the rims, sat next to the bucket, waiting to be filled.

"Where ya'll going?" Johnathon said as we passed them.

"Upstairs. She's taking us to see the private rooms." I replied.

"The hell!" Clarence said.

"Boy, bye. We'll be back in a minute." Tracey said, waving him off.

The three of us followed Trixie up a wide set of clear steps with silver, wired guard rails. There was a set of couches at the top of the landing. White, plush expensive couches, like the ones downstairs. We turned right and down a long hallway.

"All right ladies, these doors to your left are the private rooms. $250 an hour, 400 for every two. And that's per guy." She added walking down the hall. "I'm looking for one that's not occupied." I liked how the entire right wall of the hallway was all glass, giving you a clear view of the stage. The bar was directly below us. "Ahh, feast your eyes on this." She said, opening one of the doors and flipping on a switch. A pink light shot on, illuminating the room, and the decorations on the walls. There was a sign, that read, *Bring Your Own Toys.* I chuckled at the thought.

The walls were pink and fuzzy, matching the carpet. There was a large, high-backed couch against the far wall. Both walls on either end, hung whips, chains, hand cuffs and other BDSM like items.

"Do people *fuck* in here?" Kareena asked, noticing a box of condoms on the table, directly by the door.

"Well, it's not advised, but if the girls want to make a little extra money, then that's on them. Just don't tell me, because I won't jeopardize my business if you get caught."

"Okay! Girl, I heard the fuck out of that!" Kareena said. She grabbed a few condoms and put them in her purse. "Aw, and they say Déjà vu. That's dope."

"Just ghetto." Tracey chuckled, before turning back to Trixie.

"How much do the girls pay you?" Tracey asked. She began to let us know how business is broken down. $1,500 for the girls just starting. But, the longer you're dancing, the more money you'll make, so that then goes up to $3,000…and that's per girl. Anything made on your first night is yours, but after that, rent kicks in.

"Sounds good to me, shit! Can I dance too?" Kareena asked, finally giving in.

"Sure, let me get you queued up. I'm sure I have space on stage for you." Trixie said, heading out of the room. Kareena began clapping, while jumping up and down.

"I could see myself making some money here." I said, playing with one of the tassels that hung on the wall.

"Alright ladies. Kareena you're all set." She said, coming back into the private room.

"I got something for you, sis. It's still new. The tags are still on." Tracey said. Kareena was like a kid in a candy store as we headed back down stairs and to the dressing room, so she could get changed into her lingerie. Tracey gave her a lacey, one-piece La Perla lingerie set, complete with the see-through, silk robe, red garter and kitty-heels.

"Bitch, I am ready to shake my ass." Kareena said, opening up the one of the lockers to put her clothes into. We headed back out to the table, where the guys were.

"How was the Grande Tour?" Clarence asked, taking a sip of his drink.

"It was amazing actually." Tracey replied, sarcastically.

"Damn, it's some fine ass dudes in here." Kareena said, looking around.

Reality sat in as I watched the other girls dancing and doing moves I'm sure took a while to perfect. I was beginning to feel really inadequate. All of the other girls, even Tracey and Kareena, had bodies for this. The curves, the height and not to mention the moves. I was a more...petite figured, standing 5'5 with a C-cup breast, a slim waist and a round, perky but. I was looking at girls with large D-cups and fat, jiggly asses. My anxiety really began to take a toll on me. Johnathon poured me a drink to calm my nerves: a straight shot of Remy Martin. I took another to take the edge off. My left leg began to start shaking. I looked over at Clarence and Johnathon, having the time of their lives paying rents and mortgages. I began to wonder why I was even here. My dad is a successful businessman with, no doubt, clients from here to the East Coast, and probably South as often as he and my mom were taking trips to Atlanta.

Both Kareena and Tracey did the damn thing, and it was now my turn. "Welcome to the stage, ladies and gentlemen," The DJ yelled into the mic. I could feel my heart beating in my fingers, I was so nervous. "another new-comer tonight. Show some love for Miss Liyah!" I walked around to the steps, nervously climbing each one, trying to be as sexy as I could. I could feel my heartbeat in each step as Beyoncé's *Ego,* began to play. That's when I remembered, that I'm doing this for me. Yeah, my father has money, but I want my own. I can't depend on him for the rest of my life. So, let's woman up and see what this is really all about.

I got a big ego.

As my eyes scanned the lustful faces around, I started really getting into it. Grabbing onto the pole, all of my fears seemed to fade away. I did my best to recreate the moves Miss Shirl taught us. Even some I remembered Tracey doing a few times. Johnathon was standing right in front of me, making it rain. I decided to focus on him and use him as my muse and anchor for my nerves. He stood there licking his lips, trying to peak between my legs. I flashed him a peak, moving my thong to the side a little bit. The alcohol was really starting to take effect, making me feel invincible. "Why haven't I been doing this?" I asked myself, taking off my coat, letting it hit the floor. Money seemed to flow from the ceiling.

"Whoop! Whoop! Whoop!" I heard yells of approval coming from the audience, as the lights dimmed down. Tracey was already below me with a large garbage bag, picking up my money as it fell. I grabbed my coat and hurried my naked ass off of the stage as my inhibitions came rushing back.

"You go, bitch!" Tracey exclaimed, giving me a high-five. I felt exhilarated, taking a couple more shots before finally sitting down. I went through the bag and grabbed each bill. The stack was about 6" thick, full of $20s, $50s, and mostly $100s. I was ecstatic, stuffing the money into my black, clutch Celine purse. "Bitch, I see you. You a fuckin natural!"

"I started, and it was like…"

"You was on top of the world?" Kareena said.

"Yass. Exactly!" I said, lighting a blunt, kicking back.

"Damn, baby, you looked good up there." Johnathon said, plopping down next to me. I caught a whiff of his cologne and felt butterflies in my stomach. "Ya'll ready to get out of here?"

"Right, I got us a VIP table. Let's head out." Tracey said.

"I'll be back. I need to go talk to Trixie." I slid out of the booth and headed for the bartender. "Hi!" I yelled over the loud music. She was cleaning glasses and putting them away.

"Hi!" She smiled, "Need a drink?"

"No, I was wondering if you've seen Trixie?"

"Oh, yes. She's upstairs in her office."

"Thank you." I said smiling, turning to leave.

"Great job tonight. Hope to see more of you."

"Thank you," I laughed. "You just might." I headed upstairs, almost running into one of the dancers near the private rooms, holding up a customer with her small frame. He looked like he drank 3 too many glasses of champagne and it put him on his ass.

"Sorry." She said in passing.

KNOCK! KNOCK! KNOCK! I made it passed the private rooms and to a large wooden door, with a large piece of frosted glass right in the middle. Her name was printed all over the glass, in several types of whimsical fonts, all with the same lavender color.

"Come in!" She yelled. I walked in, the door was heavy, with a short, low creaking noise.

Trixie's office was huge, seemingly pulled straight out of a burlesque show. To the left of her desk, was a large window, that gave a magnificent view of the stage, with two purple, leather high backed throne chairs across from her. The gold frame, that they were housed in, made them glisten in the light. I was impressed by the number of books on her bookshelf, which made up the entire wall behind her. The walls were a dark purple, with the same artwork as her door. "This bitch love herself." I thought to myself as I walked over and sat at one of those chairs. She was sitting at her desk, counting money. She had a stack in each denomination, lined out in front of her. Each stack was the same size as mine or bigger. Zipporah was sitting on the large, white, sectional couch, that was located to the right of the office door, legs crossed smoking a Newport Platinum Smooth. She wore a black leather jacket over her bra and underwear. "Oh, hey, Liyah! Did you have fun? You looked good up there."

"Thank you. I'm glad you liked it. I want to work for you." She put the stack down that she was counting.

"Zippy, I'll talk to you more about that later." She said, waving Zipporah towards the door. She walked by me, not making eye contact, but I could tell something was wrong. "You want to work for me, huh? How much did you make tonight?" She asked, leaning back in her seat.

"Almost 3…thousand." I said, shyly.

"Don't be shy. Think about how much it would be if you lost the lingerie. You can get full-nakes if you want to." She said pointing to me. "Most nude clubs don't serve alcohol so that customers have more to spend. But we do, so they *do* spend more. Why you think I got ATMs lined up at the entrance?" She said, laughing. "Don't worry about being uncomfortable. You got a nice little body. I wouldn't have minded seeing it."

"So how much do I pay you?" I asked, changing the subject.

"Just $1,500 a month. And that's whether u dance or not, if you want to still work for me, that is. I ain't gone gouge you." She said, holding both hands out to her sides.

"I believe you." I said chuckling.

"Good. Nice to have you on the team." She held out her hand, and we shook. I was on my way out of her office when she stopped me. "Just watch out for some of these bitches. Not everybody who's friendly, is your friend." She said, picking her money back up off of the large desk calendar.

"Oh, that's life. Thank you for looking out."

"Have a good night." She said, going back to counting her, money as I closed the office door.

It was going on 11 O'clock as we headed back to the hotel suite, to get ready to go back out to another club, one with less poles. I checked my phone, looking for any missed calls or texts from Sean. None.

"I'm thinking about switching clubs. The whole vibe here is better. And I made more fucking money!" Tracey exclaimed, flashing around a portion of her profits, as we made it into the suite.

"You should. Come with me. How much did you make tonight?" I asked. "I pulled in about 3 racks." I admitted.

"Shit I got in almost two. What about you K?"

"I got 2, too." She said. "Now I see why Tracey wants to dance, but why you, Liyah. You're fucking rich...like literally."

"Correction, my parents are rich. I don't have shit. 19 with nothing but my High School Diploma."

"Right and what the hell you mean, 'you can see why I wanna dance'? The fuck that mean?" Tracey said, throwing one of the throw pillows at her.

"Bitch, because you broke." Kareena laughed.

It was just the 3 of us in the suite. Clarence and Johnathon had a few grams of coke to get off, so they headed over to the Tenderloin District, where they were bound to be able to sell them quickly.

KNOCK! KNOCK! KNOCK!

As Tracey got up to open the door, the three of us all popped 2 X-Pills for the night. Me and Kareena watches from the couch as Lamarr walked in, followed by our other best friend, Lamarr's girlfriend of 6 years, Monica.

Johnathon and Clarence have been friends for the last 3 years, meeting through me and Tracey, at my sweet 16th, being inseparable ever since. Clarence and Lamarr are cousins, though they didn't always know that they were related. Finding out when they were only 16. Almost 8 years ago. Back then, Lamarr was the fat, chubby friend. All throughout

Middle school, he was slightly larger than the rest of his class. Lamarr's parents were shot and killed one night, on the intersection of High St and International, when a man decided he was going to take their car. Lamarr's father gave in, but the man still chose to take more than the car that night.

Lamarr's 24, the same age as Clarence, 6'2 tall, and a strong, muscular build. His complexion was dark, with dark almond shaped eyes. His hairs been dreaded since he was only a 7-year-old boy. Now, they were long and flowing down his back like Damien Marley

Monica was closer to our age, just a year older. She'd just turned 20 a few months ago. She was 5'8, light skinned, with long curly hair. She had C-cup breasts, and due to their new daughter, Kamiyah, she now had a full, curvy figure.

"Oh my, God!" I screamed, rushing to hug them. I haven't seen them in months, since Monica's baby shower, right after Halloween.

Monica found out that she was pregnant, shortly after New Year's. It was actually during my 18th birthday last year.

We were on vacation in the Bahamas, with all of our men on a daddy-paid trip, dive-bar hopping. Me and Tracy couldn't help but notice she'd only had one Corona, and tons of water that night. Not to mention she was running back to the ladies room every ten minutes.

"Moe, why you ain't drinking?" Tracey asked. Once we made it back to our suite.

"Girl you know I ain't a drinker like that." Monica replied.

"So, why you ain't smoking?" I asked, trying to pull the answer out of her before Johnny, Clarence and Lamarr came back, with more alcohol and party favors.

"Damn, bitch." She laughed. "If you must know, I missed my period this month...and last." She admitted.

"Oh my, God. Are you fucking serious?!" I yelled screaming up and down.

"Shh, shh yeah. Lamarr doesn't know about it. I haven't taken the test." She smiled, looking up at all of us.

"You don't seem to happy about it." Kareena said, taking a sip of her vodka and OJ.

"I don't know. There's so much that I want to do. But I know I can't get rid of it…if there's an *it* in there." She said, starting to tear up while smiling.

It wasn't until March, the month after, that she'd finally decided to tell Lamarr and take the test. It turned out to be positive. That one, followed by the next 9 tests that she took as well. She was terrified but had grown to love the idea of being a mother, especially when she found out she was having a baby girl.

I was so happy to see her I didn't know what to do. The three of us crowded her with love and hugs. Tracey, Kareena and I were still in our lingerie, finishing off the blunt. Monica and Lamarr were already dressed and ready to go out.

Monica wore an off the shoulder, white, Gucci sweater, with a pair of distressed blue skinny jeans. She stepped out in a pair of white, Jimmy Choo, patent leather pumps and wore her hair in a low, right-sided ponytail. Lamarr wore a black, Armani blazer with pink and white rose designs, stitched using gold thread. He paired it with some nice black Levi Jeans and a pair of Louboutin loafers. He wore his dreads French braided into a long, ponytail, dipped fire engine red at the tips.

"Ahh, shit ladies. All three of these niggas together!" Tracey said.

"How you doing Trace?" Lamarr said, hugging her.

"I'm good, bruh. Long time."

"I know, I know." He laughed.

"Kamiyah is a handful, ya'll." Monica said as Kareena handed her and Lamarr a shot.

"Girl, we know. We're glad ya'll could come out tonight though." Tracey said. After looking at her Rolex watch, she exclaimed. "Fuck, guys, we need to get dressed." She said, grabbing me and Kareena's hands.

I made it to my room and went through the shopping bags, looking for the black, long-sleeved, off-the-shoulder dress I found at BEBE's, that stopped mid-thigh. I also set aside a pair of black, Fendi ankle-boots. The heels were thick and striped; black and white. I checked my phone for a sign from Sean. It was getting pretty late and still no word from him. I was starting to think he was trying to stand me up.

After sliding on one of the hotel's long, white, fluffy robes, I headed downstairs for another shot. I was just about to head back to my room to get into the shower when I heard a knock at the door. "Who is it?" I asked.

"It's Johnny. Open the door." I opened the door, watching him look me up and down, as I waited for him to speak. He was undressing me with his eyes, and I wasn't totally upset. His eyes started at my thighs, then worked their way up. I could see in his face, he was getting a little turned on and it was making me want to be nasty. He started to bite his bottom lip. I grabbed him by his hand, dragging him into the room like my sex slave. I slammed and locked the door behind him.

"You for real?" He whispered, smiling, flashing his platinum grill.

"Shh." I said, stepping back, dropping the robe completely. He hoisted me into the air. I kissed him, wrapping my legs around his waist, as he carried me to the dresser. I felt a shock, once my ass hit the cold, laminated wood.

He bent down, kissing on my inner-thigh. I wanted him to make me cum so bad. I didn't realize how horny I was until he started blowing a stream of air right onto my pussy. I grabbed the back of his head and moved his face to the middle. "Mm." I moaned, grabbing my breasts as he tasted me, lapping me up like a dog at his water bowl. As I rested my head against the mirror, he wrapped his strong arms around my thighs, pulling me deeper into his grips. "Yes!" I yelled out in ecstasy, grabbing the back of his head, getting ready to fill his mouth with my juices. He stopped, standing straight up, removing his shirt. I forgot how beautiful he looked. That sculpted body covered in tattoos. He dropped his pants. His dick looked like it wanted to break free from his Armani boxers. He slid his middle finger, in and out of my core, fondling me, as he dropped them next. His dick sprung into position, like a missile, staring right at me. I felt myself get more excited, but a little nervous. "Ooh, shit!" I yelled out, feeling myself stretch and open, to acclimate him. I wanted it so bad. I wrapped my legs around his waist as he filled me up. I could barely contain my screams, as he stroked every inch of me. "Fuck!" I screamed out. He was working on nut number 3 and we barely even started. "Yes, nigga! Fuck!"

"Dick good, ain't it, bitch?" He asked. I felt myself come again, hearing the sternness in his voice and feeling the passion in his eyes. Fuck he knows I love that shit. I could barely get my mind straight enough to answer him. "Do you … hear me?" He asked pounding into me.

"Fuck! Yes, daddy! That dick is so good!" I screamed out. He pulled out of me slowly. I looked down at the white juices that connected us. It felt like his dick was never-ending. He looked me in the face, grinning as he went back down to get his face wet. "OH MY GOD…!" I moaned. He made me come a few times, then collected his shirt, still smiling. He blew me a kiss, then left me on the vanity, still soaking wet. Once I was able to get my thoughts and legs together, I jumped in the shower, using the jet-setting, while thinking about him, to get another nut out, though it wasn't the same.

I had to admit, that once I was out of the shower, I felt a million times less tense.

RING! RING! RING!

I was sitting on the couch, zipping up my boots.

"Hello?" I answered, placing the phone between my neck and shoulder.

"Hey you. How you doing?" It was Sean. I found myself getting excited, then immediately guilty about letting Johnny fuck me.

"I'm good. We're getting ready to head to the club now. You still coming out?" I asked. I stopped what I was doing, anticipating his answer. I kind of hoped he'd stay away since Johnny's around.

"I'm sorry, love, I can't. I got to work tonight. But can I make it up to you tomorrow? I have a pretty good imagination and I've been told I'm pretty romantic." He replied.

"Okay, I'll take you up on that offer." I said smiling, happy that I can keep these two men away from each other. I didn't want *any* drama on my night.

"Okay. I'll talk to you tomorrow. Have fun tonight, 'cus tomorrow you are all mine." He said before dropping the line. I couldn't help but smile as I finished getting dressed, letting my natural hair and face shine, as my outfit did all of the talking.

I walked downstairs, securing my bracelet. I looked over at Johnathon. He was now wearing a white blazer, a pair of all white True Religion jeans, and a pair of white Gucci Loafers. I kept my thighs closed, trying not to end up in a puddle of myself looking at him. Those pills were really starting to take effect. I started to think about Sean, and walked over to Tracey, asking her to put on my necklace.

We made it to the club close to 12. There was still a lengthy line, wrapping around the block, and it looked like the bouncer was turning people away.

"I'm not standing in line, in these heels." Kareena said.

"You don't have to. I got us a table." Tracey said as we walked passed the line, and straight to the bouncer. Tracey showed him something, and he let all 7 of us into the dark, packed club. The DJ had the club shaking to Lil Wayne's *Every Girl*.

I like a long-haired, thick red bone…

I sang and danced along as we followed Tracey to our VIP table, right next to the DJ booth. We had a perfect view of the entire club. Of everybody with their hands in the air and having a good time. I couldn't stop myself from searching the club for Sean, even though I knew he wasn't coming.

"Hi, can I take your drink orders please?" The bottle girl asked, pen and pad in hand. She wore her dirty blonde hair around her shoulders. She looked like she had to be no older than 19 years old, little white girl with freckles and light brown eyes. Her smile was sweet and innocent. I almost asked her what she was doing here. She looked out of place. Like she should've been partying instead of working.

"Yeah, I want an Incredible Hulk, two bottles of Goose and a bottle of Remy, please. For the table." I said walking over to Johnathon, changing my seat. She left after taking everyone's drink orders, and I grabbed Johnny's hand, saying "I want to dance", figuring I had at least one song before she came back. But we fell into the same trap that we've always fell into: the inability to pull away. The DJ began to mix in Ludacris' *'How Low Can You Go'*, I could feel the bass pumping through my body as I found myself grinding against Johnathon. Good thing the bottle girl had no trouble getting our drinks to us.

CHAPTER 7

I woke up the next morning, feeling sore. Literally, from head to toe. I had a migraine, the size of Texas. The sun was shining throughout the room, not making it any better. My feet throbbed, most likely due to wearing those heels and dancing all night. My pussy was sore as hell. Like a train of big-dicked niggas ran through me. I rolled over, to get the blaring sun out of my face, and remembered the nigga that ran through me last night was Johnathon. "Fuck! Shit!" I whispered to myself, getting out of bed, barely able to move my jelly-filled legs. The insides of both of my thighs felt sticky as I struggled through clothes, and shoes, almost tripping over his size 13s. I ran to the bathroom and scooped the robe from the floor, before heading downstairs to nurse this hang over and get away from this mess.

Tracey was sitting at the dining table, counting her money from last night, with a fat ass blunt in between her lips. Kareena, was still passed out on the sofa.

"Hey, boo. How you feeling?" She asked, looking at me like she knew something. She handed me the blunt as I sat at the table with her. I sat on my ankle, so I wouldn't feel the throbbing.

"Bitch, my fucking shit is sore as fuck." I said, pouring a double shot, for the pain.

"I fuckin' bet. Sounded like that nigga fucked you out yo' mind and yo' fuckin soul." She said laughing.

"Shit, he did." I said, reminiscing, biting on my lip.

"It looks like it was good." She chuckled, pointing to her neck.

"Sex with him is always good." I said pouring up another shot. "Where's Clarence?"

"Oh, he slumped. Didn't go to sleep until almost an hour ago. He got jealous and felt like he should be getting some pussy, too. And bitch them pills had my pussy fuckin numb, but so sensitive."

"Bitch, no for real." I said, laughing. I reached over and grabbed her smoke box; a small, cherry-wood, jewelry box, full of her weed and all her weed accessories. I grabbed a Dutch and started rolling another blunt for us. "I'll be back. Let me go kick this nigga out really quick." I stood up and headed upstairs, after handing Tracey the weed.

I entered the room. Johnathon was sitting on the edge of the bed, face buried into his phone, chin resting on his palm. He looked worried and it made me a little nervous.

"Hey good morning. Are you okay?" I asked, sitting on the bed next to him. I went to rub his back, but he jumped up.

"No, you need to call your pops, boo. My mom just called and told me the police raided our shit, threatened to take both her and my dad, to jail. She didn't tell me why. The phone hung up and…I tried to call her back…" He looked like he was on the verge of tears as he went around the room picking stuff up. "I love you." He said kissing me, on the lips, then flying out of the door.

"What the fuck?" I asked myself, stunned and confused. I ran over to the side of the bed to grab my phone, realizing I left it downstairs on the table.

"What happened to him?" Kareena asked. Her and Tracey sat at the table, eating a slice of leftover pizza.

"Let me see." I grabbed my phone from between them and turned the power on. "Jesus…" I said. My phone was vibrating non-stop in my hands. I had missed calls from everyone. My mom, dad and two brothers. "What the fuck?" I asked myself as I opened a string of messages from my little brother Malik. There were pictures taken from the front of our estate. Men in what seemed to be workout fits, sweats and sweaters, and Federal Marshal medallions, moving all of our stuff onto one of six large moving trucks. The very last picture was of my dad being arrested in our driveway, in front of his black, vintage Rolls. They had him laying down on his stomach, 4 men holding him down, knees in his back. I called Malik, but the phone immediately went to voicemail. The same when I called my dad and other brother Malakhi. No answer. I called my mom, while heading upstairs to get dressed. She picked up on the first ring.

"Oh my, God! Liyah, they took everything!" She answered, screaming. She sounded hysterical, unable to stop crying. "They…they arrested your father. He was trying to fight the fuckin cops. Fuck!" She yelled, shortly before I heard something in her background shatter. I threw on a pair of black sweats, a green tank top and my Js.

"Mom! Please!" I cried, feeling a knot in my throat. I've never heard my mom cry and it was starting to tear me apart. "Mom, it's okay. I'm on my way home, now." I ran outside of the suite and down the hall after tossing on my black leather coat.

"Liyah! What's going on?" I heard Tracey and Kareena yell after me. I ignored them, keys and wallet in hand, as I made a bee-line for the elevators.

"Liyah, don't come home. They seized everything. House, money, cars, accounts. It's…all gone." She began to sob. "We should've, just…", she continued inaudibly.

"Mommy stop for a second." I said, interrupting her. "Where are you guys?" I asked. I finally made it to my car, but it was going to be at least another hour and a half to get to our part of Oakland.

"We're at the Harris motel…off Macarthur. They barely let us keep the cash we had on us. Almost took me too." I finally made it to my mommy as fast as I could, frantic and confused. I pulled into the parking lot, seeing her on the second story balcony, smoking a cigarette and speaking to someone over her cell phone. I looked around for my mother's black Porsche 911. It was nowhere to be found. I pulled in between a silver Corolla and an old modeled Lexus, taking a second before getting out of the car. The blunt I smoked on the way there did nothing to calm my nerves. But I had to get up there and figure out what the fuck was going on.

I walked up the steps and as soon as I saw the top of her head I asked, "Mom, why is all of our stuff being taken?"

"I got to go. She's here, D." She said, hanging up with whomever it was that she was talking to on her cell phone. "Hey, baby." She said hugging me. "We have a lot to talk about." She said, left arm around my neck, guiding me into the room. She continuously wiped the tears from her face as they fell. She smelled like copious amounts of beer, weed and some other scent I couldn't really put my finger on. Her long black and grey hair, which she usually kept decent, was a mess. I remember last night, right before my mom and dad went out on their Valentine's Date, my mom sent me a picture of the stunning Alexander McQueen dress she had just bought. It was sleeveless, blood-red and flared at the knee, with little darker red roses printed within the dress. The room was still clean, minus the bottle of Jamaican beer. I realized my brothers were nowhere to be found.

She sat on the bed, lighting a Newport cigarette. "Have a seat, sweetie." She said, motioning for me to sit on the bed next to her. The story she proceeded to tell me was unfathomable.

She began to tell me, that by the time I was 3, my dad, and his friends, Johnathon and Liam, ran Oakland. They were the sole distributors of weed, coke and heroin to the streets of Oakland. They made a fortune off of the backs of young dope dealers, and the addicts. They were like Kings to everyone who bought or sold their products. The city watched as they threw wild parties at their clubs, to clean their money. It was nothing to see them in matching Bentleys and Ferraris, Benzes galore. Liam started to get a little wild, so my dad had to do something to keep us all safe from him and the law. Liam was put away for 20 counts of murder one and drug, and gun trafficking. My dad left the drug game alone and stuck to putting all his money into his clubs, cleaning it all. Too bad Liam re-emerged, with enough of something up his sleeves, to trade himself for my father and Johnny Sr., and got out. Working with the feds to free himself.

I couldn't believe what it was that I was hearing. I asked, "So...they took everything? We have *no* money?" I asked.

"Just the $2500 I have in my purse." She said handing it to me. "Take this. I need you to be strong." She added. "Everything your father's name is on....gone."

"Mom..." I said, tearing up as she pushed the money into my bra. She began to push me up and towards the door, out the room.

"Go. You have to go." She said sternly.

"Mommy…" I said. Tears fell down my cheeks. I still didn't understand. Words couldn't express the sadness I felt, looking into my mother's eyes, waiting for her to tell me this was some type of joke. Or, at least, what we planned on doing to get back to the top. "Mom, what are we supposed to do?" I asked as she just reached into her purse and grabbed another cigarette. I was desperate for an answer and starting to feel afraid. Truly afraid, for the first time in my life. I noticed my mother falling asleep, while standing. She was just about to fall. "Mom!" I cried out, stopping her from falling onto me.

"I'm fine, girl! Go on, now! Keep your brothers safe!" She yelled, with one final shove I was out onto the patio. My back hit the banister, making me think for a second, I was falling over. I managed to catch my balance, but not before my mother slammed the door shut, locking it behind her.

"Mom!" I yelled. Pounding on the door with both of my fists. "Mama open the door! Please!" I screamed, pleaded and cried. No response. "Mommy, please!" I cried, still banging on the door. I began to feel weak, defeated. Why is this happening? My hurt turned into anger, just like it has all of my life. "Fuck this!!" I screamed, with one last bang on the door. I made it to my car, sobbing uncontrollably onto my steering wheel. My heart swelled at the thought of what my family was going through, and it looked like my mom was currently on whatever it is my family was selling.

I put the car into gear and slowly began to back out. I stopped abruptly, seeing a bright red figure fall directly behind me from the hotel balcony, flying to the ground and making the most horrific crunching sound I've ever heard. It was like someone slammed a bag of rocks against a brick wall. I jumped out of the car. My mother was lying on the pavement, in a pool of her own blood, neck twisted backwards. She reached out for help. I felt my knees caved in as I tried to rush to her. My link to this world was fading away. "Oh my, God. Mommy!!" I screamed at the top of my lungs, rushing over to her side. There weren't many people outside until now. A couple of guys rushed by her side. I pushed them out of my way and knelt down next to her.

I've never cried like that before. I could feel myself spiraling into a nothingness, a dark abyss of…pain. By the time I had gotten to her, she was gone. "Mommy." I sobbed, crying into her dress. My mind couldn't comprehend what just happened, even though I knew in complete clarity what had just transpired. I've never known such sorrow. She didn't even smell the same anymore. "Aaaaaaaaaahhhhhhhh!!!!!!!!!!!!!!!" I cried out in anguish. I'd rather be stabbed a million times, than to go through this once. I felt like I couldn't cry hard enough. And the more I cried, the more I hurt. "Someone call somebody, please!" I screamed.

"Hey sweetie, I'm calling the cops now." I turned behind me, there was a slim older white woman, with blonde and grey hair, standing at the hotel's office door.

"Liyah?" I heard a voice call from behind me. I turned to see Malakhi and Malik, holding McDonald's bags. They were standing at the end of the driveway, not looking at me, but at our mom. "Is that… is that mom?" Malik asked, dropping his bag, not needing an answer. They ran towards me, eyes wide like saucers. Their faces were struck with shock, fear and hurt.

My brothers, all but jumped me, trying to get to mom. They were a lot stronger than I thought as I tried to keep them turned away from her. I failed. As soon as I was able to get them into the car, I did, locking them in. But it was too late. They'd already seen her.

"Wait, you can't leave, Miss!" Yelled the hotel manager. I ignored her, throwing the car into gear. I sped off, down MacArthur Blvd, almost hitting a guy on a bike, as I sped out of the hotel parking lot.

"Go back, Liyah!" Malik yelled, pounding on the back of my seat. But, I couldn't. I looked at them, through the rearview, and saw that they were both staring out of the back window. "Liyah, please!" Malakhi begged. I could hear the tears in his voice. I wanted to go back, but we couldn't be around the police right now. They would split us all up for sure and throw them in the system.

Tracey and Kareena had been blowing up my phone since I left the hotel. I had no idea what to say or even where to start, but I couldn't leave them hanging like that, worrying. I called, unprepared, hoping they haven't checked out the room. I headed back to San Francisco, swerving through traffic, eyes full of tears.

"Bitch…are you okay?" Tracey exclaimed.

"No…not at all." I sobbed, trying to keep my vision as clear as possible. "Put ya'll seatbelt on!" I yelled to my brothers, cutting off cars, heading back to the city. I tried to stay strong for the twins and keep from breaking down, but I could barely keep it together for myself. "Are…are…you guys…still at the room?" It was hard for me to even speak. "I need to stop this car." I thought to myself.

"Yeah…yeah we booked it until tomorrow. What the fuck is going on, sis?" She asked.

"I'll tell you when I get there. Bruh…shit hit the fan."

"Okay, we'll be here." Tracey said, I hung up, trying to stay focused and didn't want to give the police any reason to pull us over, taking us another 45 minutes before we made it back to the suite. The twins hung their heads low, sobbing silently. Kareena, Tracey and Clarence were all sitting on the couch when me and the twins walked through. "Go upstairs." I ordered the twins. "The room at the end of the hall is mine." Surprisingly, they did exactly what I asked. I was frozen as I listened to their footsteps run up the stairs. I heard a door open, then slam shut. I couldn't cry in front of them.

The three of them, Tracey, Kareena and Clarence, jumped up, surrounding me. I couldn't hold back anymore. I missed my mom greatly. Seeing her all twisted up will never leave me, and it broke me down. My neck felt like it was about to pop as I screamed out in agony, "Mommy!!" I wanted her to hear me, so I screamed louder, to the top of my lungs, until my voice became a squeal. "Maaa'mmaaaa!!!!!!! Come back!! Please!!" I screamed. They just held me, the three of them, consoling me. Flashes of my mother was all that I saw. I remember her dressing me up in little Gucci dresses with flowers in my curly, kinky hair. She bought me my first pair of heels at age 14. A pair of black Prada pumps, and then taught me how to walk in them. Making sure I didn't break my ankle, or my neck as we played Debutante, on the grand staircase in our foyer. I remember, just last year, her taking pictures for my Senior prom. I couldn't believe she was gone, and I had no way of calling my dad. It was like my chest was caving, caving, caving. The more it hurt, the more I cried, and the more I cried the more I hurt.

I could no longer find the strength to keep standing. I felt myself fall to the floor and curl into a little ball.

"Oh, shit!" I heard Clarence cry out. The three of them helped me onto the couch, where I just laid down and cried.

"Is there anything we can do?" Kareena asked.

"I just need to be alone." I replied, rolling over on the couch. Facing the back, I buried my face in the pillows.

"Liyah!" I heard my mom, yelling my name.

"Mommy? Where are you?" I asked, pleading. I found myself in a dank, dark forest, with no recollection of how I ended up there. The moon bright over-head, crickets fighting each other for attention. It was too loud for me to think.

"Liyah, come here, honey." I heard her again, this time clear as day. My feet were sinking into the muddy forest floor.

"Ahhh!" I screamed, falling into a dark pit of...nothing. I suddenly felt a strong and forceful, yet soft and serine, grasp on my right wrist, keeping me from falling too deep. "Mommy?" I looked into her deep brown eyes. She wore a white, never-ending, long sleeved dress. Her hair flowed longer than the Nile and her skin was bright and vibrant. She had on peach lipstick, and her nails were done; a simple French manicure. She looked stunning.

"Mommy, why?" I asked, confused.

I woke up on the couch, in the semi-dark living room of the suite. I sat up, head kin to a searing pain. The room spun like I was hung over. I felt I was the only one there. It was too quiet. I stood and looked outside and onto the city below. The sun had just begun its decent, to provide light and warmth to the rest of the world.

I reached for my phone to call Tracey, see where everybody was. She let me know that the three of them took the twins to get dinner and was currently on their way back. I flopped down, back on the couch, flipping on the TV with the remote. My next thought was to go to an ATM and try to get any money I could. I found the strength to get up and stand again.

I made it to the 7-11 in less than 15 minutes, located on the corner of Market and 2nd street, next to a Starbucks. The parking lot was empty, with the exception of three cars, parked sporadically across the lot. I parked directly in front of the double glass doors, lights on so that I could keep an eye on it and went inside with an empty make up bag. I had a total of 3 cards. The first one I tried was daddies AmEx. Unlimited balance. I bent it in half, out of frustration, reading the message to contact my bank, flash across the ATM screen. I then tried my mom's Bank of America card, and her AmEx card. Nothing. I was surprised, the only card I was able to get money from was the one I started for Direct Deposit with my job at California Check Cashing. I was kicking myself for blowing that whole $15,000.

I rushed back to the car, slamming the door as I sat down. I locked the door, before resting my head on my steering wheel, sobbing until my head hurt, and my vision was blurry. "Oh, God! Aaaahhhhhhh!!!!!!!" I screamed out as loud as I could causing me to sob more. "Fuck…" I whispered to myself. I backed out of the parking lot, heading back to the hotel.

Before I could fully get out of the parking space…

BLURRP! BLURRP!

"Are you fucking serious?!" I yelled out. I couldn't believe it. Behind me was a pair of red and blue lights. I didn't even see a police officer in the parking lot. He must've came after me using my parents' cards. "Fuck!!" I screamed out, flustered and frustrated. I fought the urge to step on the gas and push this car's engine. I sat there, for a few moments. Watching through my side view mirror, as the officer exited his vehicle. Once he had finally made it close to the trunk, the urge won. I couldn't help it. Fuck 'em. Fuck 'em all.

I sped out of the parking lot, the nose of my car scraping against the pavement of the street. Sirens wailing behind me, I sped up Harrison street, trying to lose the police officer on I-80, before he had the chance to call for back up. I dove in and out of traffic, the cop unable to keep up. I cut my lights, before exiting on Treasure Island Rd. I checked in my rear view, seeing the flashing lights continue off the freeway, right behind me. My nerves were starting to get the best of me.

I made a hard right down 9th street, then a quick right down Avenue B. From the corner of 12th and Ave. D, I could see the police officer keep down 9th street. I sped back to the direction I came from, hitting Treasure Island Rd like a bat out of hell. I was careful to keep an eye on my rear-view mirrors, making sure I wasn't being followed. I didn't stop, for anything short of a red light, until I made it back to the underground garage. And, even then, I was still terrified.

I hurried back upstairs to the suite. Malik and Malakhi were sitting at the table, eating Chinese take-out. As soon as they laid eyes on me, they broke free from the table and rushed over to me, jumping on me. The three of us fell to the floor as they cried into my t-shirt.

"It's going to be okay. We're going to be okay." I said, rubbing their shoulders. "I got ya'll." Tracey and Kareena looked like they wanted to cry as well.

The twins went to bed just a couple hours later. I sat down at the table with Clarence and my girls, and told them everything that was going on in full detail. They started tearing up, hearing me talk about it. Especially after I told them that I witnessed my mother kill herself. I still didn't know whether to be pissed off at her for giving up so easily or follow in her footsteps. I thought about my brothers, feeling like she was extremely selfish for what it was that she did to us. But, God, I missed her.

"Why the fuck is this shit happening to me?! Like, what the fuck!" I tried to roll a blunt, but my hands were so shaky, that the weed kept falling out of the ends of the Dutch. Kareena took everything and rolled the blunt for me. After she lit it, she handed it to me, then rolled another one for her and Tracey. "She just...jumped, bruh." I cried. Flashes of her body laying there, neck mangled, flooded my consciousness. I wanted to climb to the top of the highest building in The City and do just what she did. Thinking about my brothers again, I couldn't do that to them. They deserve someone to be able to fight for them.

I sent them all home, against their will. They wanted to stay with me to keep an eye out, but I needed to be alone for a while. Alone with my thoughts, to try and figure out exactly what my next steps would be.

Later that night, I went down to the front desk to extend the stay. I had $8,000 on me. Some from my birthday dance, $4,000 and the other half from what my mother gave to me. The next three nights took all of that away.

I needed more money, if for nothing but food. I headed back upstairs and threw on my black, two-piece Chanel bathing suit. The silk fabric was lacey, with small, geometric cut-outs, showing off skin. I slid my feet into my black boots and tossed on my white, leather jacket. I did my make-up, natural tones, with a black eyeshadow and cat-eye. The twins were in the other two rooms, sleeping, by the time I was finished getting dressed. I snuck out and headed to Déjà vu, hoping things would be popping on a Sunday night.

I walked in and was severely underwhelmed. The club was empty, giving off ghost town vibes. There was only one girl on stage at the time, collecting what she could from the little audience there was. There were also a few girls, working the floor. I peeked over to the VIP section me and my girls occupied last night. Just a janitor sweeping with a black garbage bag tied to the belt loop in his black Wranglers.

"Oh, hey, Liyah. I didn't expect to see you in here tonight." Trixie said, walking into the club behind me.

"Hey, yeah," I smiled, "I had a family emergency. I need to make some fast money but…" I said, trailing off, looking around the club. The men in here didn't look like much and I was starting to think tonight would be an immense waste of time.

"Don't let the appearances fool you. These men could be some of your best customers. A lot of the wealthy ones don't really like the party vibe, so they go to the rooms, or come when its not so busy. Get to work, you'll see. Is everything okay at home?" She asked. I could see she was genuinely concerned.

"No, but we will be, soon."

"Well, good luck. Knock 'em dead." She said smacking my ass before continuing in front of me. I was shocked, causing me to stand still in place for a few moments, trying to process what just happened. I shook it off and headed to the dressing room to finish getting ready.

I was feeling a different feeling than last night. The vibe wasn't the same. Last night, I was putting on a show. Dancing for my friends. Last night was my birthday, and I was having fun. But not tonight. Tonight, I'm working and I don't have a choice. All I do have, is three mouths to feed.

I stepped into the dressing room, praying for a miracle. I tried my best not to let my mood or what was currently going on in my life, affect me, or my money.

There were a few girls back there. Zipporah was telling the other two, about how she beat her baby daddy's, girlfriend's ass. I looked over at them and smiled as eye contact was made. I sat down at a bench looking for a locker to put my stuff into.

"Hold on, hold on, hold on. You got a problem, bitch?" I heard her ask. "Oh, she wanna act like she don't hear me. You! Bitch!" I turned to look at her, to find out who she was talking to. "You, bitch. Yes, do you have a fuckin' problem?" To my surprise, she was looking directly at me.

"Girl, what the fuck are you talking about, bruh?" I asked, confused. She began walking over, prompting me to stand up.

"You're looking at me like you got a problem." She said, getting in my face. I snapped, pushing her into the girls she was just talking to.

"Bitch, I will beat yo' fuckin' ass!" I yelled. "Do not fuck with me today!" I always kept some sort of blade, mace, or both on me. Tonight, she was lucky I forgot my switchable at the suite. She was a good 2 inches taller than me, and almost an extra 60 pounds, but I didn't give a fuck. I needed to release some stress. I reached down into my open bag and pulled out my pepper spray, hitting her right in the face and got ready to start climbing her like a fuckin tree. "You fuckin bitch!" She screamed out in pain.

"Ladies, ladies, ladies." Trixie said, rushing into the dressing room. She must've heard the commotion from the main floor. There wasn't much else going on out there. "What the fuck, Zipporah?"

"What makes you think it was me?" She asked, vigorously rubbing her eyes, sobbing.

"Because, it's always you. Now what the fuck?" She asked, more sternly than the first time.

"Bitch was looking like she got a problem."

"Keep calling me a bitch and I'll show you how many problems I got, hoe!" I was starting to see red, and all I wanted to do was rip her throat out with my $1200 manicure. Trixie was small, but she was effective with keeping me away from Zipporah.

"Ok, ok, ok, ok, Zipporah…meet me in my office. Destiny, Macey, c'mon. I'm sure there's a dance on the floor for you, two. Go find it, please." She ordered. Zipporah scoffed, rushing into the restroom to rinse her eyes. "Everything okay?" She asked as we walked over to the same bench Zipporah and her girls were just sitting at. I couldn't hold it in and began crying uncontrollably. "It's okay, doll. You're going to be okay." She said, rubbing my shoulder as I cried into hers. "What's going on? I remember you saying that you had a family emergency earlier. Do you want to talk about it?" She asked. I sat up, wiping my eyes on my jacket. I already showed her too much.

"No, I don't." I stood up, straightening myself up. "Please, keep that bitch away from me. I will really fuckin' kill her. Not a threat, juts a promise." I said, walking back to my stuff, to secure it into a locker and to redo my makeup, before heading out to the stage.

"You got it." She said, before leaving and returning back to the front.

I stepped out onto the stage, not feeling as sexy as I know I looked. OJ Da Juiceman's *Make The Trap Say Aye*, began playing on the speakers, as the lights dimmed. I first felt awkward, like I was taking a shower in front of a ton of people. I could feel their eyes on me, rushing me to remove more and more clothing. I had no choice. Suddenly, I realized, that this is all a show. These men wanted what they couldn't have; or what they didn't know they could have. I began to feel like Lisa Raye in *The Player's Club*. I twerked and shook the little ass I had, the entire song and raked in a little under $600. Trixie was right. I decided to jump off of the stage and work the crowd. See what a private dance could rake in really quick. I stopped for an old white man. He was heavy-set and wore a black Adidas track suit, pants and jacket.

"Hey, sexy. Why not come show me your moves."

"Okay, honey." I responded. I turned, facing the stage, and gave him a quick little lap-dance to Ginuwine's *Pony*. He slid a few bills into my waist band by the end of the song.

I seen a couple of guys by the bar, who caught my eye. One of them was white and slim, tall, maybe 175. I could tell by the length of his legs that he had to stand at least 6'4. His hair was a dirty blonde, sides cut low, like a Mohawk, with the rest pulled back into a man bun. He had on a black, Northface vest and a pair of grey sweats. The other was Spanish, maybe Dominican or El Salvadorian. Heavier, about my height; 5'5 and about 220-230, but he carried it in muscle. I could see his biceps ready to rip through his Eagle Outfitters T-Shirt. The two of them looked a little out of place, but so did everyone else there who was not dancing. I thought nothing more of it as I walked over to them. "Would either of you handsome men like a dance?" I asked, getting chills seeing their FBI badges hanging from their necks. Everything in my body wanted to back off. Immediately regretting the decision to walk over.

"No, we're fine." One of them said. He didn't even look in my direction. Just stirred the ice around in his drink with his straw. I was relieved, thinking at first, maybe they were here for me.

"Actually, beautiful, I would love one. Drink with me first." The other said. He flagged down the bartender. "What'll it be, gorgeous?" He asked, looking at me. I did my best to remain normal and keep my nerves hidden.

"Ill have some Patron." I replied nervously. I ended up taking 4 shots, to take the edge off.

"Can we go upstairs, to one of those little private rooms? I got cash." He added. He had a strong jaw-line and a few muscles of his own, protruding through the sleeves of his white thermal shirt. He dug into his puff-vest pockets, pulling out a gold money clip, stuffed with mixed bills. I took it out of his hands, tossing the clip into his lap. I took $800 in large bills, and gave him the rest.

"Let's go." I said, grabbing his hand. He towered over me, standing close enough to seduce me with his Burberry cologne. He was actually kind of sexy. I held his hand as we passed the bar, heading up the stairs to the private rooms.

"Start the timer." He said once we made it to the room, snatching off his vest, showing off his muscular physique. "I'm Jacob." He said, holding out his hand.

"Nice to meet you. I'm Sade." I replied.

"That's not your real name." He said chuckling. There was a metal coat rack, just behind the door. As he tossed his vest onto the hook, I noticed the pistol on his hip. I still couldn't get over that badge. "It's okay, sexy. I'm off duty." He smiled, placing his gun and badge onto the glass table, next to the couch. He sat down, arms spread wide against the back of the couch. I walked over to the stereo and hit play. Aaliyah's *Rock The Boat* began through the surrounding speakers. I began to feel a little more relaxed.

"It's a strip club, who uses their real names?" I asked, starting to dance for him. I felt stiff, out of place. All I could think to myself was, "Just do It. Just fucking dance." I was beginning to really feel myself. Those 4 shots of Patron starting to assist in the fluidity of my moves.

"Imma cop, it's what I do." He said. I felt the mood start to die a little bit. I'm sure he felt it, too. "Don't worry, baby. Remember, I'm off duty. *Whatever* happens here, stays here, with me." He said, pulling a blunt out of the pocket of his grey sweats, and sparking it. "Call me Vegas." He continued, obviously trying to lighten the mood. Make it less awkward.

"Okay, Vegas, you want a fast or a slow dance?" I said, standing before him, swaying my hips to the rhythm.

"Dealers choice." He said, leaning back and getting comfortable, with his hand behind his head. I put on a smile and went to work.

I danced in his lap for about half an hour, grinding my ass against his dick. I turned around and straddled him, wrapping my arms around his neck we made eye contact, and for a moment I felt a strong chemistry between us. His lips were soft, as they pressed against mine. His tongue, massaging mine. I pulled back, feeling like I could get carried away. By the time he was done, an hour later, I was done and ready to go home. He gave me a few more bills, half of what was left in his stack.

"Hey, Sade, you do parties?" He asked, trying to hide his large bulge, standing with his jacket over his crotch.

"I can." I replied, chuckling as I followed him downstairs, heading back to the dressing room to count the money I made tonight.

"Give me a call when you get a chance." He said, handing me a business card. "I'll get you set up nice, with yo sexy ass." He said, smiling. I watched as he banked a left and went to the restroom by the bar, probably to go beat his dick. Apart of me wanted to follow him and help him out, but that just wasn't in my character. At least, yet.

I checked my phone, shortly after making it back to the dressing room. I didn't feel the time until realizing it was going on 4AM. Regretting not bringing a pair of flats to change into, I gathered my stuff, then headed back to the suite.

I sat at the table, money laid out in front of me, stacked by denomination. Although the 1's were stacked higher, almost $2100 in one night felt like a good start. Too bad this was only the beginning. I grabbed the box of weed Tracey left for me, and headed back upstairs, to secure the money in the safe that the hotel provides in the closets. It's small, white and dead bolted to the floor. After I rolled a nice fatty, I curled up under the covers, listening to KMEL in the dark and allowed the purple haze to rock me to sleep.

"Dude, give it back before I slap the shit out of you!" I heard, waking up.

"Do it and watch me beat yo' ass, bitch!"

"What the *fuck* is going on?" I said to myself, rushing downstairs, after grabbing my robe.

CRASH!!!

"Yo! Yo! What the fuck are ya'll doing?!" I yelled, running into the kitchen, to see glass strewn across the linoleum floor, between the twins.

"It was his fault!" They both yelled, literally pointing their fingers at each other.

"Just...go upstairs!" I sighed, grabbing the broom from aside the fridge. My phone rang as I was placing the glass into the garbage can. "Oh, fuck!" I yelled out in frustration, stepping on an unchecked shard.

"What?!" I answered, immensely upset. The number started with '510', but unsaved. "I'm sorry, hello." I repeated, checking my attitude.

"Hello, this is sergeant Morris, with the Oakland Police Department. I'm over at the coroner's office. Is this Liyah Reyes?" He asked.

"This is she." I replied. He gave me his condolences, and then went on to tell me that my mother passed, and that they needed me to come down and view the body, to identify it. Said that since my father was arrested, I was the only next of kin. "I can be down there in an hour.

I was anxious the entire drive to go and identify my mother's body. I smoked a blunt, attempting to relax my nerves the best that I could. I already knew she was dead, and now I had to act surprised. I sat in the parking lot of the Sheriff's building, staring at the front door. I watched as men and women, some police officers, other civilians, walk in and out of the building. I had to have been sitting there forever, only time didn't keep up. I finally gathered the courage to get out of the car and walk into the building, after 10 minutes of stalling.

After signing in, I sat in the lobby, in the sea of hard, blue plastic chairs.

"Ms. Reyes?" I looked up and was met by an older black, heavy-set, man. He wore a cheap grey suit and a matching tie, with black patent leather shoes.

"Yes." I said standing. I followed him down a long hallway, until we made it to a small room, with nothing inside but a tattered, brown leather cushion chair, next to a small box of lavender scented Kleenex, and an old, brown lamp sitting on the end table. The officer pointed to a medium sized window. He yanked the blinds up with the thin white chord. The coroner was on the other side, in the morgue, ready to remove the sheet from her face. It felt like losing her all over again. There was no need to *act* surprised. The detective gave the signal to remove the tarp from her body. I nodded, acknowledging that was in fact my mother. My broken heart still had smaller pieces to crack, and I felt every shard as the tears swelled in my eyes. I felt myself collapsing into the chair, sobbing into my hands.

"I'm so sorry for your loss." He said, reaching down, grabbing a bag from the floor. "Here are her effects." He said. He forced a smile. "I'll give you a few moments." He added, and left me to be alone with her.

"Why did you do this? Why couldn't you and dad just…" I asked her aloud. I stopped, noticing that she wasn't going to turn and respond. As bad as I wanted her to get up and walk away from that table, I knew it wasn't possible. But, I wasn't ready to let go. I couldn't.

I made it back to the car, tossing the bag of her stuff onto the passenger's seat. I stared at it a while before I started the engine. Before putting the car in drive, I decided to go through it really quickly; inside it contained the jewelry she had on, her wallet and her cell phone. Remembering that she was on the phone with someone that morning, I turned it on, met by the lock screen. "Fuck." I sighed out of frustration, tossing it into the glove box. After quickly rolling a blunt, aided by my tints, I tossed the bag into the back seat and sped out of the parking lot onto 14th, towards Lake Merritt Blvd.

I called Sean, trying to take my mind off of…everything. "Hey, I thought you was mad at me." He answered the phone, voice soothing.

"No, I'm not mad. How's your Monday morning going?"

"Not bad. Better now that I hear your voice. I'm off today, so just running errands."

"Oh, are you busy?" I asked, hoping he'd say he was free.

"Nah, I'm done for the most part. Can I see you today? Maybe in about an hour or so."

"Make it 2 and you got a date."

"Bet, meet me at the Taqueria on 39th and foothill?"

"Sure thing. See you then." I said, hanging up. I grabbed the half smoked blunt out of my car's ashtray as I headed into the hills. The drive took me about 20 minutes. I parked across the street from the house that I grew up in. The house that destroyed and tore my family apart, forever. I watched as FBI agents combed through our house, dumping furniture and other personal effects, onto the driveway. Breaking all of our shit like we weren't people, too. Just average, everyday criminals. It made my blood boil. I couldn't take it anymore, starting the engine and heading to Sean before I decided to mow down as many of them as I could. I couldn't shake the images of them disrespecting my family. I wanted to turn around and carry out my revenge, but I decided against it.

While pulling into the parking lot of Taqueria Durango, I saw Sean getting out of his brand new, black Jaguar, on black 20" rims. I parked next to him, checking to see if he had a child's seat in the back. Nope. There was a man, sitting against the outside wall of the restaurant. I dug into my purse, and grabbed a handful of change, to toss into his cup before I walked inside, looking for Sean. He was at the counter, looking to see what he was going to order. He had on a black t-shirt, a pair of red and black Jordan, basketball shorts, and a pair of red Jordan flip-flops. His black, Raiders fitted was tilted to the side. His hair was pulled back, into a tight ponytail.

"Hey, you." I said poking him in his side. He looked at me, licking his lips. Then smiled.

"Hey, boo." He hugged me, burying me into his chest. His Clive Christian cologne, filling my nostrils and flooding my senses. "God, I want this man so bad." I thought to myself, not wanting to stop hugging him. "How are you?" He asked.

"I've been better." I said, forcing a smile, trying not to break down.

"Well…I got us 20 tacos. Chicken and steak. You want to talk about it at the Marina?" He asked as we walked outside. "Here you go, bruh." Sean said, handing the homeless man a $100 bill. I felt my heart warm up a bit.

"God bless you two." The homeless man said.

"Yeah, let's do that." I responded. "Let me move my car to the street." He nodded his head. After parking curbside, so that my car wouldn't get locked in the gate or towed, I got into the car with him. Praying to God nothing happened to my car on the street.

Once we pulled away, for a moment, all of my problems did as well.

It was crazy how comfortable I was with him. Enough to be a little vulnerable.

It was already going on 3 O'clock in the afternoon. The over casted weather had most people in the house, in fear of the rain. I didn't mind it. The weather was almost a visual representation of how I felt inside. I was a bit nervous during the car ride, not sure what to say. He asked me about my family and I froze up, not knowing how to answer his question.

"My father owns…owned a few business buildings." I lied grabbing one of the loaded chicken tacos out of the cardboard box. I hoped he wasn't one of those guys that likes prissy women, because I was starved and I had no plans of being neat with these tacos. "What about your family?"

"I've never met my father. My mom is a business woman. It's hard to pinpoint exactly what she does, but she's good at it." He said, smiling. He grew quiet for a moment, looking at me.

"What?" I asked, chuckling.

"You are really beautiful. You know that?" He said. I was too shy to return his gaze, with a mouthful of food.

"Thank you." I replied with a smile, simply taking another bite of my taco. I finally got the courage to look up at him, feeling like a nervous little school girl, as his brown eyes seemed to just look right through me. He smiled, a perfect row of white teeth, behind pink medium-sized, soft, kissable lips. I noticed him staring at my lips, moving in slowly. I leaned in as well. But just before our lips could meet…

RING! RING! RING!

I looked at my caller I.D. It was Malik. My heart began to race, thinking they may be in some sort of trouble.

"Hey, 'Lik, ya'll good?" I answered.

"Yeah, we hungry. You left this morning and ain't been back."

"I've only been gone a couple hours." I chuckled a little. I looked at the clock on the dash and realized it has been a little while. I left San Francisco at 11 this AM when the detective called.

"When are you coming back?" Malakhi asked in the background.

"Tell him I said a little later. I gotta go. I'll be back soon." I said, hanging up the phone.

"Kids?" He asked.

I laughed, "Oh God, no." Shaking my head, "They're my little brothers...give me one second." I said while dialing Domino's Pizza, ordering two large pepperonis to the suite. "My dad was locked up recently and my mom's...passed away." I said taking another bite of a taco, trying to swallow the lump that was in my throat. But it was no use, the more I tried to ignore it, the more prominent it became. Until tears were flowing down my cheeks. I held back the full details, feeling like that would kill the vibe, even though I was doing a very good job at it myself. He held me, allowing me to cry into his shoulder.

"When did she pass?" He asked. I sat up, wiping my eyes, trying to rein in the tears.

"The day after my dad got snatched. Now I have to be a mother while learning how to be an adult. Its not fair." I said, sobbing into the sleeves of my sweater. He reached over, pulling me back into him.

I needed some air, so we decided to get out of the car and walk over to a bench, just at the edge of the water. I watched as the waves jumped up, smashing against the rocks. It was beautiful and relaxing. He grabbed some items to roll a blunt from his back pack, which he pulled from his backseat.

The two of us watched the sky go dark laughing and talking about each other's past. His mother's an heiress. He mentioned his regret not knowing his father.

I laid against his shoulder, listening to the waves and the crickets chirping. My feet kicked up on the bench, legs curled underneath. He periodically kissed my forehead.

"What do you have planned for tomorrow? Can I see you again?" He asked, cutting off the engine. We were double parked, next to my car. "I kinda don't wanna leave yo' side just yet, to be honest." He chuckled. "Would you mind if I kept you company? No funny shit I promise." He chuckled. I thought about it for a second, and how my brothers would feel about it. But I really needed some one-on-one intimacy.

"That would be really nice actually. Just follow me." I said, opening the door.

"I'll follow you anywhere." He said, smiling. I jumped into my car, really happy that nothing happened to it, and led the way. I smiled, looking at him keep up with me as we rode down the freeway. I suddenly began to feel guilty for smiling. I felt like I didn't deserve it. At least, yet.

"Nope." I said shaking away the tears. I kept the car steady with my knees, rolling a blunt as we crossed the brightly lit bridge, to get to the other side of the bay.

When Sean and I finally made it back to the suite, It was going on 10:30. I could feel butterflies partying around in my stomach as we made it to the door. All I heard, approaching the door, was Tupac. Probably being played as loud as possible. I was afraid to twist the doorknob and allow the music to escape into the hallway. But, I had to. We needed to get inside.

"Seriously? Why is this music so fuckin loud?!" I yelled, walking into the suite.

The suite was fitted with Bluetooth speakers, throughout the entire space. They can all be synced to play from the same device, or each play a separate device on its on. Currently they had every speaker playing *Thug Life*, at the maximum volume. Malik was kicked back on the couch, smoking a blunt, playing a video game. Malakhi was laying on his stomach, eating the pizza that I had ordered for them a few hours ago. I walked over to the stereo and unplugged the power cord turning off the TV as well. My senses thanked me for the immediate stillness.

"Aye, we was listening to that!" Malik yelled, as I walked over to him, snatching the blunt out of his lips.

"Go to bed. It's hella late. I gotta find ya'll a school to go to." I said, stepping over a brand new Xbox 360. I didn't even want to know where they got it from. I was so frustrated I put the blunt down on the dining table.

"Come on, Li." Malik begged. "We're Juniors and the years almost over anyways" He twisted his face up, looking behind me. "Who's the dude?" He asked. Malakhi looked up. Apparently, they hadn't noticed him before now.

"He's-" I began to introduce him.

"My names Sean." He said smiling, holding his hand out for them to shake.

"I'm Malik. That's my brother, Malakhi." He said standing up and shaking his hand.

"'Sup, bruh." Said Malakhi, nodding his head. He walked over to the table and grabbed the blunt, before heading upstairs. Malik followed him, with the box of pizza.

"Rude ass." I said.

"I'm not changing schools." Malakhi responded.

"If you can get to Oakland everyday, back and forth, then that's fine."

"That's fine, then." He replied, before slamming the bedroom door shut. I wanted to go up there and throw him back down the stairs, but I just figured he was grieving, and decided to leave it be.

Sean and I were in my room, smoking another blunt, chilling on the bed. He had on his jeans and a wife beater as we talked. Flashes of me and Johnathon making love all over the room, began to play in my head like scenes from a movie, and was hard to stop or even pause. It was hard to shake, but Sean's presence made it easier.

"The hardest part of my parents not being here is being the head of household. How do I even get custody over them?" I asked, not really searching for an answer, just venting. He wrapped his left arm around my shoulders.

"I got a home girl that work for CPS. She can help you get legal custody over your brothers." He went through his phone, then sent a text message. "I'll let you know what she tells me."

"Thank you so much." I said, smiling at him. He looked at me smiling, before grabbing my chin. He lifted up to meet me. His lips were so soft, and he was pretty good with them, too.

As bad as I wanted to hop on top of him and take out all of my frustrations with him, I couldn't do that. I was content with falling asleep in his strong arms.

***********************URBAN QUEEN***********************

The last two weeks has been trying, to say the least. I've never had to organize a funeral, let alone a loved one's. Sean offered to help, but I'd rather have it done on my own. I didn't have any money to buy my mom a casket, or even enough to dig her a hole to drop it into. Thankfully, the church she attended since she was 14, offered to throw her a service. It was a small church and they couldn't do much. But, the service was still beautiful. In attendance was myself, my brothers and my best friends. And also some of the churches congregation. My mother had been cremated a few days after I was called down to I.D. her body. I was able to track down my grandmother, Felisha. She lived surprisingly close; in a 4-bedroom condo in the suburbs of Martinez. I remembered my mother telling me and my brothers growing up they used to be close. She never explained to us why they fell off, only that it had something to do with her and my dad's lifestyles. I never understood what she meant, until now.

I parked my car in front of a complex of light brown condos on Mill Rd. My stomach jumped into my throat, as my nerves began to take over. I stared at the back of an old AMPM receipt, with her address scribbled on the back. The longer I stared, the more my anxiety grabbed a hold of me. I took a deep breath, before stepping out of the car and walking around to the sidewalk.

I paused before tapping on the large gold knocker that hung from the heavy wooden door. She came to the door and I was taken back by how similar my mother looked to her mom. She wore a beige, silk pant-suit, with a gold bracelet and 3 small matching chains. Her hair was down, gray, parted down the middle and passing her shoulders.

"Granny?" I asked, trying not to cry and wanting to just jump into her arms. Without response, the door suddenly slammed in my face and her gorgeous smile faded. I stood there, stunned as the locks were engaged. I could feel another piece of my soul dying as she didn't reopen the door, realizing her mistake.

"Wh…what?" I whispered. I stood there a few moments before somberly walking back to my car. I couldn't help but break down behind the steering wheel.

Karma caught up with her only a month later, taking her out by cardiac arrest at the age of 76. Maybe it was heart attack, caused by her guilt.

Sean helped me track down my dad. They had him locked up in Sacramento. I was able to write him a letter and let him know what happened, and to make sure he gets a temporary release to say goodbye to his wife. He couldn't come to both, the service and releasing of her ashes.

The pastor met us at Alameda Beach, to release my mother into the bay. When the paddy wagon pulled up and parked on the street behind us, with an escort fit for the president himself, my excitement grew 10-fold.

"Told you he was going to make it." Malik said, slapping Malakhi's chest.

"Yeah, it's the least he can fuckin do."

"Stop it. This could be the only time we see him without a damn glass between us." I said as I started walking towards him and the 6 C.O.s that accompanied him.

"Don't approach the prisoner, ma'am." One of them stated, left hand on his pistol holster, and the other strong arming me.

My father looked defeated. His beard had quickly grown grey and unkempt, over his swollen face. I could tell he'd been fighting. I wanted nothing more than to just hug him. I missed my father more now than ever. He's right here in front of me and I can't get within 10 feet of him.

Me and my brothers each scattered a pinch of our mother's ashes into the sand, where the waves were coming in at our feet. I motioned for the CO to hand my father her urn, so that he could finish the job, they agreed. I was in fear they would be dicks and not let him scatter the rest of her ashes, but they did, allowing us *all* to properly say goodbye to my mother.

CHAPTER 8

I was amazed and felt blessed to make it to April with my brothers, safe and healthy. I had to maintain a roof and at least 2 square meals a day, for all three of us. I had my girls, Tracey and Kareena, and my baby, Sean in my corner making everything that much easier. They helped me with buying us groceries by dropping off checks every now and then. I sold my car for close to $70,000 and bought an all-black '99 Chevy Tahoe, used, for only $20,800. I, then, found a house to rent in deep East Oakland; 2 bedrooms, 2 baths, near the AmPm on Park Blvd, next to Oakland High School. They loved living so close to school, though I hated the traffic it created every morning. It just sucks that they can't even go, or they run the risk of being snatched up by CPS, while losing out on their education.

Becoming a mother to two 16-year-old boys overnight taught me a lot about my strengths and my weaknesses. Not once have I seen them breakdown or cry. I was worried that if they continued to bottle up their emotions, that it may begin to affect them mentally, emotionally and physically. I had no idea what to do. I just hoped they knew I was here, if they needed me.

I've spent most of my time at Déjà vu and I couldn't believe this didn't always used to be a strip club. One of the girls showed me pictures from back in the day. The club used to be 3 levels. The entrance level was a regular nightclub. Upstairs where the private rooms are, was a large skybox. Downstairs, which is now the basement, and where Trixie keeps her liquor, was the strip club. Girls did more than get naked. They played with themselves and even the patrons. There were private rooms, where the customers would be able to live out their fantasies of sleeping with one of the dancers. The city got wind and threatened to shut down the entire building for prostitution. The private owners came in and completely rebuilt the spaces almost 7 years ago, leaving the old stage standing, minus the poles.

It was a task, trying to build up my clientele with the customers. Luckily, sexy ass Officer Jacob quickly became one of my regulars.

I was finishing up my 6th stage dance for the night, when I seen Jacob sitting at the bar, watching the show. He lifted his glass to me, once we made eye contact. I was tired, but I couldn't let him go unnoticed.

"This is almost your second home." I said smiling, walking up to him.

"I wouldn't be here so much, if you'd just let me take yo' ass home with me." He growled, hugging me, gripping my entire right ass cheek in his hand.

"You ready to head upstairs?" I whispered in his ear.

"Fuck, yeah." He said standing. I led him by the hand, to the very same private room, just like I've always done in the last two months. I locked the door, dimming the lights right after the slow music began to play. Egyptian Ember incense filled the room, giving it a sexy scent. He took out his money clip, removing 8 large bills from it's grasp, and placing them on the night stand, next to the large box of condoms. He grabbed one. I couldn't believe my life has sunken this low. I felt more like a prostitute, than cheater, though I knew I was fully both. I was at least happy he was a cute white boy.

"Ooh, look at that big dick." I whispered, getting on my knees, taking him into my mouth.

I sucked until my jaws were sore, then climbing on top of him. I grabbed the condom out of his hand, opening it with my teeth, acting excited. I slid down onto him. Gripping his shaft with my walls as I slowly rode up and down. "Mmmmm." I moaned, going faster.

"Shit, girl. That pussy tight." He moaned thrusting deeper into me, kissing me to stifle my screams as I felt myself climax.

"Fuck! YES!" I screamed out. I kissed him as I grinded on him slowly.

"Whew!" He exhaled. Exhausted after busting a fat nut into the

Magnum. I rolled over and off of him, feeling exhausted myself. I wanted nothing more than to go home and shower this night away.

Jacob stood up, pulling his pants up with him. He dug into his pockets, pulling out another five bills, just as he's always done. I sat there silent. "I need you and another girl for a party this Saturday. $3,000 for the both, plus whatever ya'll make in the tips." He said. After kissing me goodbye, he walked out of the room, closing the door behind him. I sat there for a second, silent and confused, not knowing what was wrong with him. He seemed tense, like he was having a bad day, or a bad couple of days.

I snatched the $13,000 off of the table and pulled up my panties, before hurrying back to the dressing room to get ready to go back home. I passed by Zipporah on my way out. She looked at me up and down chuckling. It took a lot in me not to drop my bag, and punch her in her fucking eye, but I thought about my brothers. I can't fight for them in jail, or prison like my father. I thought about the fact, that with everything that's going on, I haven't even had time to go see him.

I finally made it to my car and rolled a little blunt before starting the engine. KMEL was playing Nelly and Kelly Rowland's *Dilemma*.

I parked the car in the drive way, making it home at almost 3 in the morning, killing the engine. I sat there, looking at the messy lawn and the black sheets, covering the insides of all the windows. I got out of the car, looking around the neighborhood, watching out for any suspicious looking undercover Fed cars. I did my best to quickly hurry into the house, engaging all the locks.

I lay in bed, thinking about how long the twins have been out of school. One day, just a couple weeks ago, they where in class, and CPS was sent to pick them up. Malik seen them while at P.E., running the mile. He noticed an old, black Ford Taurus pull up. Two white men got out in cheap, black suits. He panicked, running into the locker room, to grab his phone, sending a quick text message to Malakhi. He knew in his spirit that they were there for them.

"CPS. GET TF OUT OF THERE!" Malakhi checked it, then asked his teacher to go to the restroom, leaving his back pack there to remain inconspicuous.

Running full speed once hitting the street, they fled the school. We only lived a few minutes away walking, but they were too afraid to go home. I told Sean what happened, and he immediately set up a meeting for me, with Rebecca, who had to clear some space in her calendar.

I was up bright and early the next morning, so I decided to make breakfast for Sean and the Twins; Cream of Wheat, eggs and a ton of bacon.

"Hell you doing?" 'Khi asked, dreads messy and out of place. He was rubbing his eyes as he walked into the kitchen.

"I have a meeting with a social worker. I have to become your legal guardian to keep you out of the system." I handed him two plates of food. "Wake up Lik and give him this." I turned back to make me and Sean's plates.

Walking back into the bedroom, I realized Sean was awake, flipping through channels and had already made up the bed. He was wearing black sweats, a white t-shirt and black socks as he rested against the headboard. His hair was out, wild like a lion's mane.

"Good morning, babe." He said, tossing the remote onto the end table. He sat up straight as I handed him his plate.

"You sure you don't need me to come with you today?" He asked, digging in immediately.

"Yeah, I'm sure. I have a few other things to handle." I replied. I was really starting to like him a lot and its only been almost two months. He's spent countless nights at my house and we still haven't had sex. That could be partially due to how often Jacob filled me up, or the guilt attached to it.

I sat in the Social Services office, waiting for 1:00 to finally come around. I've been here since 12, not wanting to take any chances on being late and looking unfit or unprofessional, in any way. I looked around the brightly lit office. Mostly young mothers, with their energetic children, and some single men with their children, also filled the building. I noticed there were two security guards, at the ends of each wall, and one at every entrance, whether it was the bathroom, or an office.

"Liyah Reyes! Window 12! Liyah Reyes, window 12!" I heard over the loud speakers. I quickly searched the wooden planked walls, for the number, then walked up to the window. I could tell the woman sitting on the other side, wanted nothing more to do with today. Her desk plaque read *Sharonda Miller.* She was a thin, dark-skinned woman, with a blonde, bob weave. She had on a beige leather crop-jacket, with a black and brown blouse underneath.

"Hi, I'm here to see–"

"Yeah, Ms. Rebecca?" She said, phone to her ear, looking right at me, but looking right at me. "I have your 1:00 appointment here. Sure." She said, before hanging up the office phone. "She'll be with you shortly. May I see your I.D., please. We need to get you put into the system." She said, holding out her ashy manicure. Her hands looked shiny, yet leathery. I grabbed my license out of my wallet, handing it to her. Standing there, I scrolled through social media, for a couple of minutes as she added me into the computer. "Here, you are." She said, handing me my license. I looked behind her, seeing a tall slender black woman, in a grey Armani pants suit and matching Stacey Adams pumps, walking up in our direction. She had a short brown afro, with dark chocolate skin and almond brown eyes. She carried herself well. Her presence exuding poise and grace.

"Hi, you must be Liyah." She said, walking up to me, holding out her hand.

"Hi, Rebecca. Nice to meet you." I said, as we shook.

"Follow me." We walked passed other waiting people, down a wide hallway, full of other offices. Her office was a little small, with no more room to fit anything other than her desk and the two of us. I sat down, as she shut the door. "I'm sorry that I couldn't get you in sooner. It's been a little crazy around here lately." She said, getting comfortable in her chair. "I must say, when I spoke to you over the phone a couple weeks ago, it broke my heart. And like I said, if you ever need someone to talk to like a grievance counselor…or anything. Just let me know." She said leaning in on the desk.

"Thank you…I…I really appreciate it." I responded, trying not to tear up again at the situation.

"Okay, now tell me everything again. Leave nothing that you know out." She said digging into one of her desk drawers. She pulled out a little red tape recorder and placed it on the desk in front of me. I only told her the surface details, like I did with Sean, not wanting to be too open. But I needed her help.

I decided to give her everything I knew. The reasons behind my father being arrested, leading to the reason my mother took her own life. I could see in her face that she was becoming disturbed and uncomfortable. I went on to tell her that I was a dancer. That it was new, but it's the fastest way to put food on the table. She didn't really enjoy that part. The late and wild nights. The fear of my personal well being, and the fact that I wasn't guaranteed a single dollar when I went to work. If for some reason we didn't have any customers, I just wouldn't make money that night. There wasn't a real guarantee that there would be food on the table every night. She brought up a lot of good points, things I've never really thought about before, like health insurance and college tuitions for the twins. There was no way I'd be able to afford all of that on a dancers salary.

Everything came rushing in at once. I haven't started a single thing and I was already becoming overwhelmed. I never thought about what being a parent would entail. All of the work that really goes into raising a child. And I had two teenage boys on my hands, while still growing myself. I rested my elbow on the arm rest, placing my palm against my right eye. I could feel a migraine, and the very strong need for a fat blunt coming on.

Though she was really sweet and helpful. Leaving Rebecca's office, gave me more questions than answers. She agreed to help me with as much as she possibly could, advising the first thing I need to do, get them back into school. Then, she could have more foundation, to push the judge to grant me at least temporary custody. I was stupid for even taking them out of school in the first place. But, after what happened, I was scared I would lose them. They turn 18 in just a little under 2 years. Why couldn't they just leave them be?

I'd just made it back to my truck, when my phone started to ring. It was Tracey.

"Hey, girl. What's going on-" I paused, noticing she was sniffling. "What's wrong?" I asked.

"They killed him." She sobbed. "Li, they killed Johnny."

I started the engine, confused, filling with sadness. "What? Who?! I...I'm on my way. I'll be there in like 15 minutes." I said hanging up the phone and tossing it into the empty passenger seat. Lamarr was sitting on the porch, smoking a Black-N-Mild cigar when I pulled up. He looked up at me as I walked up to the steps, my heart pounding like a marching band on their drums.

"Hey, Liyah." He said, standing. He had on a black, pullover hoody, a pair of black sweats and some classic Timbs. His dreads were wild and fell randomly across his shoulders. His eyes were bloodshot red like he'd been crying.

"Hey, Marr." I said, stepping in closer to hug him.

"Everybody's inside. Clarence found him. He was going crazy, bruh."

We walked into the house, by the kitchen and the second story staircase. The living room was a mess. Everything was everywhere, strewn across the floor. The large 60 inch plasma lay face down, half on the table and the top resting on the floor. I could see that it was bent, slightly in half. Tracey sat on the couch, next to Clarence holding him, trying to console him. He was smoking a cigarette, face in hand. I sat down, quiet, as the reality began to set in.

"What happened?" I asked finally, breaking the silence, doing my best to keep it together. I missed Johnny already.

"We don't really know." Lamarr replied.

"I went over to his spot this morning. Figure out why we ain't heard from him since ya'll parents got locked up." Clarence said, thinking back on his morning.

*********************♛URBAN QUEEN♛*********************

Clarence woke up this morning with Johnathon heavily on his mind. It's been 9 weeks since anyone's heard from him, and for the last couple days, Clarence has been feeling like something was wrong. I started feeling a ton of guilt, myself. Me and Johnny got so used to going weeks even months without speaking since we broke up, that when it happened, I thought nothing of it. And dealing with my family, he was the farthest from my mind. It never occurred to me that, his family was ripped apart just as mine was.

Clarence pulled up to Johnathon's 4-bedroom, 3-bathroom townhouse in Berkeley, off of Shattuck Ave. He couldn't explain why, but he was anxious the entire ride over there. His stomach felt like he was falling down a large, endless hole. Hands clammy as he gripped onto the steering wheel. All types of thoughts began to run through his head. What if he started using drugs? Johnathon's never had to work a day in his life, and his only lifeline dried up without him having a chance to save himself. What if he killed himself? All of these feelings flooded Clarence with emotion, which only intensified, when he killed the engine, sitting in the port outside of the town homes.

Johnathon wanted to have nice things and cars, but houses were never his cup of tea. He never cared for the space, and was at home in this 6-unit, apartment complex. He did, though, have it decked out with the highest-end furniture, and a few mid-century sculptures. The 6 burgundy-painted, 3 story homes sat right behind the parking lot, which was secured behind a large iron fence, housed in brick pillars. He dialed Johnathon's phone number, twice going straight to voicemail. He looked at Johnathon's ruby red Mercedes, sitting in the same spot it always had. He called again getting the same result.

"Fuck." He said, getting out of his Camaro and walking up the stairs to Johnny's unit. He stood on the first to top step and knocked on the black screen door.

"Aye! John, bruh! Open up!" He yelled, after noticing that the window next to the door was cracked open. "John, come on, bruh." He twisted the knob, realizing the screen door was unlocked. He was shocked to find the wooden door behind it was cracked open. "Johnny! Where you at, bruh!" Clarence yelled, first noticing an indescribable scent. It invaded his senses, almost forcing him to back out of the unit. Gagging, he covered his nose with the neck of his shirt. His Jean Paul Gauthier cologne doing little to block the stench as he continued through Johnathon's home.

The living room was open to the kitchen, which shared a space with the dining room. The house was still, filled with an eerie silence. He continued up the stairs, the smell only getting stronger as he made it into Johnny's bedroom. He recognized the evidence of a struggle. That's when he saw Johnny's feet, laying over the threshold of his bathroom door. "Fuck! Johnny!" He screamed running up to him. He was horrified, looking down at his best friend's dead body. There was a large gash in his throat, making the bone underneath, clearly visible. His eyes were wide open, staring straight up at the ceiling. He was beaten and looked terrified. The blood running to and staining the beige carpet before it dried. "Fuck, bruh." He sobbed, dropping down to his knees. There was a picture laying on his chest. It was of his and Liyah's parents, in front of what looked to be a night club, holding them as babies. All of their faces were ex'd out in black pen, except Liyah's. "Fuck, fuck, fuck." He sobbed, falling back into the wall behind him. He sat there for a while, staring at his friend's dead body, wondering what the photo had to do with Johnathon being murdered, especially in that way.

The smell began to overcome him again. He hurried to stand, almost tripping over his own feet as he ran down the stairs. Before running outside, he used Johnny's house phone to dial 911. He hit the call button and ran as fast as he could to his car, tires screeching as he sped back home.

************************👑URBAN QUEEN👑************************

My heart felt like it was going to burst, right outside of my chest. It was difficult to sit there listening to Clarence, without breaking down. The guilt was really starting to overwhelm me.

"Aaaaaahh!!!!!" I screamed, beginning to sob, thinking it would release some of the tension in my chest. I should've known by now that wouldn't work. My head was beginning to hurt, as my heart began to flood with sorrow. I felt bad for keeping him at arm's length all this time. I felt stupid. What he did wasn't even that bad. I didn't realize how much I truly missed him until now. How much I still loved him. "Oh, God!" I sobbed, burying my face into my hands. I wasn't sure how much more loss I could take. I just wanted to escape forever.

"I found this on him." Clarence said. I looked up and he was handing me an old photograph.

"Wh-I...It's a picture of us with our parents." I said, confused, looking up at him. It was an old, black and white Polaroid. Our parents, then, couldn't have been much older than we are now. "Where'd you get this-?" I asked, realizing they were standing outside of the club I now work at. Small worlds only get smaller.

"I told you, I found it laying on his chest. Why was it there, is the question" He said, studying me for an answer. "Flip it over." He ordered. I found a dollar sign written in, what I could only suspect to be Johnathon's blood. I was suddenly short of breath, like I was beginning to have a panic attack. "5 down..." I read the message under the dollar sign out loud. It seemed like everyone in the room sat there, waiting for me to explain everything that was going on, but I knew just as much as they did. "None of this makes any sense. I-I need some air." I said, rushing up to head outside tears streaming down my face. I dropped the photo on the carpet as I was headed to my car, realizing I left my purse inside the house. I stopped to turn around, and my legs gave out from under me. I held onto the railing for support as I sobbed uncontrollably, suddenly feeling arms around me.

"It's okay, sis." Tracey said. I grabbed onto her, sobbing into her chest. As hard as I tried, I couldn't stop. It just made it worse.

"I don't understand! Why is this happening!!?" I sobbed.

"Li, you don't know anything?" She asked. I shook my head, sitting up straight.

"No, I haven't been to see my dad and my mom couldn't even tell me that much before killing herself." I said, wiping my face.

"What does your daddy have to do with this?" Lamarr asked, standing at the doorway. I stood up, regaining my composure. I walked back inside, craving a drink. I went over to Tracey's bar and poured myself a triple shot of vodka. Downing it, I poured another one.

I sat down and explained to them, what my mother told me, before she killed herself. I was starting to get angry at her, and my dad all over again. The more I repeated to them what she told me, the more abandoned I was starting to feel. I felt pissed off, hurt, sad, mad. It was hard to fathom that my parents could put their children through...all of this.

"Bruh, so you mean to fuckin' tell me that my best friend was slaughtered, because ya'll parents were a bunch of fuckin' snakes? So, what his old school potnahs gone come after you next?" Clarence asked, almost accusing me of my parent's mistakes.

"I don't know! I don't know, Clarence. You know as much as I do." I stood up again, walking over to the fireplace, I needed to get away from the…just the area I was in. It was starting to feel a little tense. I calmed down a bit, turning around to everyone else in the room. "I don't know guys. Yeah, they did some snake shit. I have no idea who this friend of their's was, or even what the fuck he *looks* like." I sat on the floor, where I stood. I downed my third drink. "How am I supposed to deal with this shit?" I was on the verge of another breakdown.

"Just like you said. Talk to your dad." Clarence said, heading upstairs.

"Cuzzo, wait up!" Lamarr said, chasing after Clarence.

"Let me know if you need me to ride with you, sis." Tracey said, coming over and sitting down next me.

"I will." I hugged her before standing and grabbing my purse, "Tell Clarence that I am so sorry, but I may need his help with all of this. I might need all of ya'll.

"Girl, you got it. And don't worry about him. He's hurting. None of this your fault." She said, hugging me again. "Are you okay to drive?"

"I'll find out. I need to get home and lay down. This is too much." I said, heading out of the house. My pain turned numb for a moment. I felt nothing. And I liked it. Then suddenly, at a red light Downtown, I began to break down again.

BEEP!! BEEP!! BEEP!!

There was a car behind me, urging me to get through the green light, while we still had the chance.

I finally made it home, scared and watching my back. Making sure that no one followed me. I felt a small sense of paranoia fill my gut, not knowing if all of the cars on my street belonged there, I hurried inside of the house, closing the living room sheets once inside. I noticed the house was quiet. My brothers weren't there, and it was starting to make me feel a little worried. I headed to the hallway to go to my room, hearing a sudden knock at the front door, almost jumping out of skin. I rushed back over to the living room curtain, peering through it enough just to see. My heart pounded as I waited to see who it was, calming when I seen Sean's black Jaguar in my driveway, parked behind me.

"Thank God." I whispered, feeling better that I had a man in the house with me. I opened the door, forcing a smile. "Hey, baby." I said, letting him in.

"Hey, boo. What's wrong?" He asked kissing me on the forehead. I wanted so bad to lie to him and tell him that I was fine, and to just let him know about my meeting with Rebecca. But I couldn't. All I could think about was running away. The tears began to flow once more. "Baby…what's going on?" He asked, holding onto me as I cried into him. He held me tight, making me feel like I could never fall again. I felt safe. "Baby," he said pulling away, hands on my shoulders, he looked me square in my eyes, sad for me, like he wanted to break down and cry with me. I looked down at our feet, watching my tears hit the carpet below us. I told him everything I knew, everything my mother told me. We sat down and I explained to him, that on top of fighting for custody of my brothers, that I may even have to make sure no one tries and slits their throats like they did Johnny.

"Maybe we should just leave." I suggested, looking to him to tell me that it was a good idea. He looked at me, face full of pity. I looked away from his gaze, and around the barely furnished living room.

"Nah, baby. You can't run. The three of ya'll would be running for the rest of your lives, looking over your shoulder. You don't want that… for them *or* for you." He said.

"I know. I just-"

"I'll help you. Whatever you need. I'm here for you."

"You don't have to do that. Sean, you barely even know me."

"Fuck all that, boo. I got you." He said reaching into the inside of his Nike backpack, and pulling out a big silver pistol. A .380.

"I don't know how to-"

"It's simple. Safety off, aim and shoot. Like a camera." He said, smiling. He looked at me, licking his soft lips. He kissed me as he laid me down on the couch. He went from my lips to my neck, to unbuttoning my jeans. I lifted my hips, allowing him to pull them down easier.

"Mmm…" I moaned, as he kissed my inner thigh, only inches from my sweet center. I fought the urge to grab his head, pushing him closer to where it really counted.

"Where yo' brothers at?" He asked, as if it mattered now.

"I think they're at a friends' house." I replied passively. He smiled and began licking on my rose pedals. Flicking, licking, and sucking on my button ever so often. "Shit." I moaned, sinking down into the couch, and more into his mouth. He entangled his arms around my thighs, locking me into position, pulling me in closer.

Once we were done, my head went back to spinning again. Johnny began to creep back into my mind, along with the guilt.

"You gotta work tonight?" Sean asked, slowly standing up, putting his weapon back into its holster.

"Yeah," I said, sitting up. "Speaking of, I should probably get ready. She wants me there to open at 8."

"Ugh, really?" He asked, helping me stand up. My legs felt wobbly, but I managed to balance. He followed me into my bedroom, smacking my ass as we made it through my bedroom door.

"That pussy was built for gods." He whispered, wrapping his arms around my waist, as I started the shower. I could feel a hot spot on my back. That was when I realized, his dick was getting hard again, pressing against me. "Get in." He ordered, smacking my ass again as I took off my shirt and bra, and undid my hair tie. He jumped in, right behind me, pinning me against the wall for another round. Then silent, like a thief in the night, he jumped out of the shower.

"I'm thinking 'bout staying here tonight. I'll watch the twins for you." He said, as I sat on the edge of the bed, packing my outfits for tonight after throwing on my pink Nike track suit.

I turned around, looking at him lying on the bed, naked, left leg perched up while he flipped channels. "Really? O…Okay, thank you." I said, zipping up my bag. I had on a pair of black yoga-pants, and a red training bra, under one of Sean's large black hoodies. I took it from him a month ago, and I only give it back when I wash it, so that it'll smell like him again. I crawled between his legs and kissed him. "I'll see you later tonight?"

"For sho. You better get outta here before you get fucked up again." He warned.

"Bye, babe." I said chuckling, scooping up the bag before leaving the room. I walked down the hall to Malik's room, where the twins were chilling. They'd gotten home sometime while me and Sean were in the shower. I opened the door, and a cloud of smoke blew right passed me and into the hallway. "I'm about to go to work. Sean's gonna be here."

"What? Hell no. We don't fuckin' know him." Malakhi rejected, pausing his Mortal Kombat game, looking up at me from the floor. Malik was sitting on his bed, with the other controller in his hands and a blunt in his mouth.

"Well, stop being such a bitch and come out the room when he's here, and you'll *get* to know him."

"We don't want to." He replied, getting up and closing the door in my face. I wanted to burst it open and beat his ass, but I let it ride, grabbing a blunt out of my purse, as I walked to my truck.

I felt lucky that Sean came into my life when he did. It's literally only been 2 months since we met and already, I felt like I've known him my whole life. He's already proven to be the best I've shared myself with. And he looks like a fuckin' model, covered in tats with a rough, yet sweet boy attitude to match. If I didn't know any better, I'd think he was trying to get me to fall in love with him on purpose. I craved him every minute I was away. And the best feeling of all, was that he's all mine.

I made it to Déjà vu a little late, around 8:45 due to traffic. I was excited to work tonight. Friday nights, the majority of ballers came out to play, although it was still early, and the real money didn't come in until around 12-1. I rushed to the dressing room, trying to keep my mind off of Johnathon, even though every time I thought of him, my heart ached. I shook it off, changing into my black leather one-piece body suit, which zipped right down the middle in front, shaped like a bathing suit. The middle was cut out into different sized weed leaf layers. I paired it with a tall, 7" stiletto and a high slicked back ponytail. I was ready for war. J. Holiday's new single, *It's Yours,* began to play throughout the club. I rushed to center stage before the first verse could start. The bassline began to flow through my body, my moves seemingly choreographed. I had all eyes on me.

Grab my body, baby. Hold my heart, don't break it! And it's yours! ...

I thought about Sean as I moved against the pole, grinding for the audience. I Had the club screaming as I slid down the pole, upside down twerking. The money looked as if it was coming up from my feet. I was feeling the moment, like it was my birthday all over again. I could see the horny faces in the crowd. Men and women lusting after me as I got rid of the body suit, exposing underneath a clear bra and panty set.

I was now on stage alone. The other two girls who started with me, had gone off to do private dances. I danced a few more songs before Shayla, the big-booty'd stud who collected the dancer's money, helped me off of the stage, before handing me my large black garbage bag, full of cash.

"Good job, sis." She said, looking me up and down. "You finna fuck around and take Zip spot." I continued to ignore her flirting, hoping one day she'd get the hint. After securing my money in my car, fuck a locker, I hit the floor to get a few more dances in before calling it a night. Walking back into the building, I noticed Officer Jacob had come to visit. He smiled watching me as I approached the bar.

"Can I get 2 doubles of Henn?" I asked the bartender.

"Damn like that?" Officer Jacob asked.

"Like what?" I turned to him, leaning my elbow against the bar.

"Oh, I see. You mad at me?" He asked standing up, trying to put his arms around me. I pushed him back.

"Here you go, Li. You okay?" Asked Lexie, Trixie's kid sister.

"Yeah I'm good." I said, grabbing the shots. I took one. "And, no, I'm not mad. I have a boyfriend." I said, taking the other one.

"He a stupid mothafucka to let yo' fine ass work here. Let me get one last *dance*." He said, with a subtle pelvic thrust. After today, my first time with Sean, I wasn't even tempted by Jacob anymore. I shook my head, no, answering his question. He turned, grabbing his drink from the dimly lit bar. I could see the disappointment in his sip. "You still dancing at the party?" He asked. I was still reeling from the last party I danced for. I made the mistake of coming alone, trying to hog all of the money to myself, soon realizing I didn't like having all of the attention on me in such a closed space. I felt like I was setting myself for something to happen if I hadn't of left when I did.

"I'm gone always be where the money is." I said, walking away with a wink.

"Hey," I felt a strong hand on my right forearm, stopping me in my tracks. "you gone let me get a dance, lil' baby?" I looked down at the man, attached to the hand. He was sitting down in one of the plush white lounge chairs, next to a few of his home boys. I wanted to throw up both shots I had just taken. He was definitely a few times overweight, night black with a bald head, wearing a red, FUBU track suit. I tried my best to not let it show on my face by smiling. I wanted nothing more than to get back on stage.

"Of course, baby." I said as I began to work his lap. I imagined I was dancing for Sean, starting to regret not giving Jacob this dance. The only thing about this job is that if you want money, you can't cherry-pick. Meaning you can't choose who's going to pay you that night. Everybody is equal. At least until you see who's really cashing out.

I looked over at Jacob. He lifted his drink to me with a smile. I watched as he chugged it down and left the building. I continued to dance, going into my zone. That was before he had the nerve to grab my waist. "Oh, hell nah!" I exclaimed, standing up. Larry, Mark and Trent, the buildings security, immediately walked over.

"Whoa, whoa, whoa, nah, sweetheart. It ain't even like that." He said, standing. "I just got a little excited."

"Pay the woman, bruh. $400 a hand." Trent said.

"Damn, like that?" He said, chuckling. "Maaaan," He dug into his grey sweatpants, pulling out a wad of cash. He handed me $800 in large bills.

"Now let's go." The three of them grabbed him, assisting him towards the exit.

"Wait! Hold the fuck up, bruh!!" He yelled. "Bruh, I'll kill that bitch-" … was the last thing I heard before seeing the front doors slam shut. I was terrified as I hurried to the bar and ordered a tall shot of Hennessy. No ice, no chase. I took it back to the dressing room, pulling off my heels and grabbed my bag out of the locker. In my bag, I grabbed a pre-rolled blunt and sparked it.

Sitting in the corner, getting as faded as I could, I watched as girls zoom in and out, and around the dressing room. It was like someone had hit the fast forward button on my life. Before I Knew it, it was just me in there. I had finally decided to call it a night and take off my lingerie. The same one I wore on my birthday. I squeezed back into my leggings and had just put back on my training bra, when I shut my locker, noticing a large figure standing to my right, near the door to the dressing room. I jumped, startled, wondering why a large, man was in here. My first thought was that he was a crazy fan. He looked to be about 6 foot and 280 pounds of muscle. He wore a pair of army fatigue pants, a pair of army-like boots, and a black bomber jacket. His face was covered with large black shades and a big black Oakley hat.

"Uhm…sir, you're not supposed to be back here." I said, afraid, looking around for something to defend myself with. But, unless I could overpower him, the only thing I could use would be these benches. "Sir, if you want a dance, you're going to have to wait out front like everyone else!" I yelled, hoping someone would hear me. I backed into the corner, surrounded by purple, chipped lockers. He just stood there looking at me. "Dude, you're not supposed to be fucking back here!!" I yelled louder. He started towards me. "Help!!!" I screamed. He ran, grabbing me by the throat, pinning me against the locker. My head slammed against the thin metal, as he lifted me off of my feet. "He-" I tried to speak but he only gripped harder. I could hear the leather in his gloves crinkling against my skin. I tried to scratch, kick and punch. Nothing was working. In the struggle, all I managed to do was knock off his glasses and dig my manicured nail into his left eye. I noticed a large scar running down the right side of his face.

"Ahhhh!! Bitch!" He growled, dropping me. I gasped for air, but it wasn't coming in soon enough. I tried crawling away from him while he recovered. "Come here, you little bitch." He growled, grabbing me by my legs, pulling me closer to him. I glanced up towards the door, maybe hoping to see someone coming in to save me.

"No!!!! Get off of me!!!" I cried, fighting to get out of his grasp. He ended up on top of me, punching me. While continuing to choke me, he punched me a few more times.

"Blame your daddy, little princess." He mashed my back against the tiled floor. I couldn't fight anymore, barely able to move.

"Heeeeyy!!! Help!!! Get off of her!!!!" I heard a voice yell. It was like a movie and I was watching the scene from a third-person view, sitting next to myself. The last thing I remember, was his large black boot directly to my face.

CHAPTER 9

I laid in a cloud, surrounded by family; my mom, my dad, my brothers and all of my friends. I could hear Johnathon telling me I'd be okay and that I should wake up. I didn't understand what it was he was talking about. I could see Trixie, zipping around, behind the bar, making the drink. She was crying, trying not to bawl. I could see Sean, motioning for me to follow him, but I couldn't see down the tunnel he led me through. I just knew that I wanted to go with him.

Sean led me to a beach, where the weather was perfect, and the water was warm. Clear with a nice turquoise tint. He sat in the sand, watching me play in the waves with a large blue drink in his hand. I motioned for him to join me. He tossed his drink to the side, literally into the sand, then stood and walked towards me. He wrapped me up in his arms, pulling my hair, yanking my face upwards towards the sky. He kissed me, holding me tight. He had just ripped off my bikini top, when I began to hear this incessant, rhythmic beeping noise.

"What is that?" I asked, looking around, trying to figure out what it could be, thinking he had an alarm set on his phone.

"Don't worry about it." He said, grabbing my chin, forcing me to kiss him. The noise got louder and louder. I couldn't ignore it. It made my head hurt. Not the normal, kind of annoying headache that you'd get every once in a while. This felt like a group of horses just finished trampling me.

"Ahhh!" I screamed, falling into the water. I looked up into the sun, feeling completely dry. The blue sky turning white and pale. The beeping continued as my eyes began to focus on the ceiling above me. I curled my toes, just to be sure I could still feel them. Same with my fingers. I was barely able ball a weak fist. I looked around, realizing I had no vision in my right eye, and that it hurt, excruciatingly. My head and throat began to throb all at once. I couldn't take it. I attempted sitting up, but it only made my head throb more.

"Hey, Liyah. Just relax." I turned my head more to my right. Trixie was helping me lay back down, coming over to my good side. I immediately began to sob. She rushed to hug me. "It's okay. We're going to find the sick bastard that did this." She said, hugging me.

"W...where...are-" I tried to speak, but my words felt like razor blades.

"San Francisco General. I'm so sorry that happened to you. I really am. I have no idea where my security was. If you need anything. I mean, *anything*, please let me know. I put my thumb to my ear and my pinkie to my lips, motioning to use her phone, or to give me mine. "Right! She said, reaching into her back pocket, unlocking and handing me her iPhone. "Here you go."

"H-hello?" Sean answered, confused. I was happy I was able to remember his number correctly.

"Babe." I whispered as loud as I could.

"Hello? Liyah, is that you? I can't hear you." Trixie took the phone from me, and put it to her ear.

"Hey this is Trixie, Liyah's boss. There was...Liyah, she...she was attacked tonight. No, no, no she's fine. A little banged up but we got ourselves a little fighter here. Okay." She said, going to speaker phone. "Go ahead."

"Hey, baby. I'm on my way now. Don't worry, okay." He said. I began to cry again. I didn't want him to see me like this. All bruised and beat up. Sean released the line after Trixie gave him our location.

"Uh, oh." She said, returning the phone to her back pocket. I followed her gaze, to the room door. I saw the doctor, a younger Indian, lady with a long, messy ponytail. She looked like she was in her 20th hour, of a 12-hour shift. She was standing outside of the large window, talking to two police officers; Jacob and his partner. "What is he doing here?" I thought to myself. The doctor looked as if she didn't want the police to come inside. I know I didn't. I just wanted to be left alone. I was starting to get angry, instead of sad, like I've been. Not only has everything been taken away from me, but now I get attacked at my place of work. "Thank your daddy, little princess." My attackers husky voice rang through my ears, on a continuous loop.

"Hey, Liyah? I have SFPD here, they would like to speak with you about what happened? Are you up to it?" She asked, escorting the police in. Jacob couldn't take his eyes off of me. I could see in his face, he was genuinely concerned. "She can't *talk*. Her throats still way too swollen."

"Maybe we can get her to write out her statement?" Asked Jacob. The sooner we get this son of a bitch, the better. He could be out doing worse to someone right now."

"Please, ma'am, help us help you." Jacobs partner said, laying a notepad and pen on my bed, near my left thigh. He was a lot more helpful than the first time we met. I pushed the pen and notepad onto the floor. "Please, Liyah. I know you're in no condition right now-"

"Then, why are you here?" The sound that came out of me was guttural and unfamiliar. It hurt.

"Do you, by any chance, remember what he looked like?" Asked Jacob. I shook my head, no. Grabbing the remote, attached to the bed, flipping on the small 12" television that hung from the wall.

"Please, Ms. Reyes, anything. Black, white, Mexican?" Asked Jacob's partner.

"I said, no." I said growled. Not wanting to say anything else.

"Liyah, please." Jacob asked again, this time begging me to tell him. He held out the notepad when I didn't answer right away. Wanting them to just leave me the fuck alone, I snatched it out of his hand, writing down what it was that I *could* remember. Including his scar. Crooked ass PD is the reason I'm here, sitting in a hospital bed, and my mother is laid up 6' deep, while my father fought probably every day in prison.

"Thank you so much. If there's anything else that you can think of, just, please let us know." Jacob's partner said, handing me his business card, as I handed him the notepad.

"How are you?" The Dr. asked. She grabbed her small flashlight, checking the pupil in my good eye.

"Like I want to throw up and my head is still throbbing. Can I please go home?" I asked in a whisper.

"Absolutely not. You could have a possible concussion. I want to keep you at least overnight. Make sure everything is normal for you." I sighed, looking back at the ceiling, angry that I wanted to keep crying. "Do you need anything, honey?" She asked, resting her hand on my left forearm. I shook my head no. "Alright, you ladies have a good night." She said, smiling before leaving the room. She flipped off the major lights, leaving only ambient lighting on.

"Why didn't you want to help them?" Trixie asked.

"Because police ain't shit."

She chuckled, shaking her head. "You want me to get you anything?"

"Yeah, actually. Can you grab my duffle bag from my locker, please? And maybe have someone bring my truck. All the money I made tonight is in there. The keys are in my locker."

"Sure, what's your combo?" She asked. I typed it into a memo on her phone.

"Thank you so much." I said.

She gave me a hug. "Be right back." She said, before walking out of the room.

I looked back at the TV. One of those late-night, sex operator commercials played. One of those commercials that made you feel bad for staying up passed 2 AM, watching TV. I flipped through the channels until something caught my eye. It was him, the man that attacked me tonight. I turned up the volume, sitting up in bed, careful not to move too fast. It was really him. I watched as the news crew went live. They took the world into the dark alley his body was found in. Only a few blocks away from Déjà vu. My heart sank and the sound began to fade, as the description of the man, that I gave to Jacob and his partner, flashed as a list on the right side of the screen, with his mugshot from a previous arrest, on the left. He was shot in the head, execution style.

"Son of a bitch!" I yelled, feeling angry, forgetting that my throat was shredded. I grabbed for my neck while reaching for the small pink pitcher of ice water the hospital staff left for me.

"Authorities are saying, that this violent crime, could be connected to the violent beating of an exotic dancer, just hours ago." I began feeling sick to my stomach, leaning over the bed, I threw up all over the floor to the left of me.

"Fuck!" I exclaimed, realizing what I'd just done. I threw my legs over the edge to go and find something to clean the mess up with. They felt a little tingly, but I was able to get enough balance to walk to the bathroom, grabbing a wad of paper towels to clean up the mess. The longer I stayed upright, the more my head began to pound. I couldn't clean up the mess quick enough, before I was rushed to flop back down onto the bed and rest my noggin.

Trixie came back with my bag within only 45 minutes of her leaving. The thought of counting my money was definitely making my feelings lift. "They fuckin' found him."

"What?!" She said, smiling excitedly. "That was fucking fast!" She placed my bags at my feet, sitting on the end of my bed. She looked up at the TV, wanting more of the story.

"No, Trix, they fucking *found* him, in the alley. Half of his fucking head missing." I said, angry. I tossed the remote at the TV, but it was tethered to the bed. It bounced back, almost swelling my left eye as well.

"Somebody *killed* him?" She asked for clarification.

"Yes, and this is breaking news, at 4:38. This happened minutes ago!"

"It's okay. It's okay. At least he can't do it to-"

"Anyone else. Right." I said, rolling my good eye, scoffing. She looked back at me, over her shoulder. I could see the pity in her face.

"You okay, baby girl?" She asked, hand on my right shin.

"Yeah, I just need some time alone. Sean should be hear soon." About an hour after I said that…

"Baby." It was him, I looked towards the door. Sean was running in towards me, my brothers behind him, shocked at what I looked like. Tears began to flow down my cheeks again, hugging him.

"I don't want them to see me like this." I sobbed, holding him tightly, burying my face into his leather coat.

"Hey, you guys wanna do me a favor?" He asked turning around to them.

"Nah, nigga. We heard what she said. We want to see our sister." Malik said.

I smiled, "Let them in." I ripped the Band-Aid off, as they say, and looked in their direction as they walked closer. "Hey, guys." I said. They both rushed and hugged me.

"You know who did this?" Malik asked Sean.

"Nah, but we gone find out-"

"Don't bother. They found him in an alley, only blocks away from the club."

"Who are you?" Malakhi asked.

"This my boss, Trixie." I said introducing her to my family.

"When you coming home?" Malik asked, sitting on the edge of my bed. God, I wish I knew the answer to that question. I wanted nothing more to go home and have a smoke session with my brothers and my man.

I simply replied, "Hopefully tomorrow."

"Well look at what I brought." Malik said, pulling out a deck of playing cards, from the inside of his leather jacket.

"Oh, you ain't trynna get whooped in some speed!" I said. Speed is a card game the three of us used to play as kids. The object of the game was to get rid of all of your cards first. The rules of how depended on who you played with.

"I'm going to head home and get some sleep. The sun's getting ready to come up." She said, pointing to the window, looking at me. She hugged me. "It was nice meeting you all." She said, smiling, before she turned and walked out of the room.

After almost half an hour of playing cards, I was starting to feel sleepy mysef. Not a regular type of sleepy, but a type where I felt like I would've died without it. I floated in and out of consciousness for what felt like a few hours as the twins continued to play cards without me. I remember waking up for a little bit. Malik was asleep on Sean's shoulder, and Malakhi was knocked out across 2 of the four chairs they accompanied. My heart smiled for a moment, knowing that they were well cared for.

As I drifted off back to sleep, I began to hear rustling, but I was too tired to try and investigate. I forced my eyes to pop open, and saw Sean standing over the twins, with a scalpel. Immediately, I shot up in bed. Sean was still knocked out in the chair. Malik was asleep on the wall next to him, and Malakhi was still stretched across the other two chairs. The beeping from the EKG machine, began to go crazy. The three of them woke up, just as a team of nurses stormed into the room. It had to have been about 6 of them.

"I'm sorry, guys. I-I just had a bad dream." I said as they surrounded me. They made sure that everything was okay, clearing the room, after a few tense moments.

"Are you okay, baby?" Sean asked. I couldn't help but to feel apprehensive as he walked to my bedside. The twins looked scared and worried.

"Guys, I'm fine, I really am. It's okay." I said forcing a chuckle. I looked over at Sean, I could see in his face that he could tell something was wrong. I laid back down into the soft cotton pillow, trying to shake the creepiness of that dream.

"Are you hungry?" Sean asked, sighing. "I can run down to the cafeteria." The moment he mentioned it, my stomach began to growl. I hadn't eaten anything yesterday and it was now going on 1:30 pm. I nodded my head. "Come on, ya'll. I might need your help."

"Thank you, babe." I said forcing a smile as they walked out of the room. I tried my best to shake the dream, by flipping through channels and looking for something fun and upbeat. But even an episode of SpongeBob wasn't enough to lift my spirits. All I really wanted to do was go home and smoke a fat blunt laced with a little bit of codeine and knock the fuck out.

I looked around the room, thinking about how eerily real that dream was. Everything looked the same, down to the denim curtains being drawn back only slightly.

I woke back up without even knowing I had fallen asleep. Sean was holding onto me tightly. I peeked down a little and realized he still had his Timbs on. I grabbed his arm, pulling him around me tighter. I could smell food in the room, but I had lost my appetite and wanted to do nothing more than sleep.

I woke up the next morning, feeling more rested than ever before. I looked around realizing I was alone, and also that my phone was ringing.

"Oh my, God. Tre', Hi! I'm so sorry sis I hella meant to call you."

"Finally, bitch. Where have you been?!" She asked.

"I'm in the hospital." Forcing myself to smile. I should've known, that once I told her about the attack at the club, that she'd raise hell. I honestly expected nothing less. It was one of the things I loved about both, her and her sister Kareena.

"Sis, we're on our way to you now. I just got in the car." She said. I could hear her, and a couple other car doors slam shut, after I told her what hospital I was in.

"Hey, baby." Sean said, the three of them walked in with tons of food from iHop. Me and Tracey said our goodbyes as Sean came over and kissed me on the forehead, before helping me sit up to eat.

"How you feeling, sis?" Asked Malik, pouring syrup over his entire stack of pancakes, sausages, eggs and potatoes. Malakhi and I had the same.

"Shit, a lot-fuckin' better than yesterday." I replied.

"You look good, too. The swelling looks like it went down a little bit." Malakhi said, standing next to Sean. Who was still getting my plate together in my lap.

"Well, thanks bro."

"I can take some pictures on my phone for you." Malik said, putting his plate to the side.

"You sure you ready for that, baby?"

"I kinda wanna see." I took the bandage off and allowed him to take a picture. But, as soon as the moment was captured, I changed my mind.

Tracey, Kareena, Clarence, Lamarr and Monica, walked into the hospital room looking ready to fight, like the guy who attacked me was going to be in the hospital room with me, in the corner, checking his phone, on Facebook or some shit.

"Oh, God." Tracey said, rushing over to hug me. Kareena and Monica followed suit. They looked as terrified as I felt.

"Are you okay?" Kareena asked. Her and Tracey crawled up onto the bed with me. Lamarr and Clarence were introducing themselves to Sean. If I didn't know any better, I'd say they were sizing him up.

"Is that...?" Monica asked, looking over at Sean. I nodded my head yes. "Ooh, okay." She said, before the girls introduced themselves.

"Well, there sure is a lot of love in this room." Dr. Bakhal said, walking in. "How are you feeling?" She asked, coming to the side of the bed. I forced myself to smile.

"I'm okay. I really want to just go home."

"Is it okay for us to take her, Doc?" Asked, Sean.

"Let's run a few tests and see what the results are looking like, and we'll see."

An hour later, the doctor came back. I was so excited when she said there was no internal bleeding and that she was going to order my immediate release. Though there was no concussion, she still wanted me to keep it low-key for a few days. She said that there's a small chance I could get a huge, debilitating migraine, and if that happened, to give her a call. She gave me her card, before waving goodbye to everyone in the room.

"Oh my, God. Fucking finally." I whispered. My voice was still at a 15%...at best.

I was released within the hour, and happy as hell to be breathing fresh air. Sean wheeled me to his car in one of those hospital wheelchairs, even though I insisted on walking. Malik and Malakhi were in the back seat. I reached up and grabbed the sun visor, ready to finally look at myself. Sean grabbed my hand, stopping me.

"Are you sure, babe?"

"Yeah, I have to see it." I replied. He dropped his hand so that I can lower the visor and open the mirror. I could barely recognize the woman staring back at me. I wanted to cry. I could feel the lump growing in my throat. I sucked it up and remained calm.

My right eye was still swollen shut for the most part, surrounded by a large, purple and blue bruise, which covered the area of the right side of my forehead, down to my right cheek. The right side of my upper lip was almost 2 times its size, and normal pink color. There was a cut on my left cheek, where he kicked me down. I looked at my neck. Truly amazed I was able to fight him off for as long as I did. I counted 8, dark bruises on my neck, where he attempted to strangle me. I slammed the visor shut, finished with examining myself.

Sean reached into his glove box and grabbed a pre-rolled blunt.

"You think your throat can handle..."

"We gone find out." I said, taking it from him with a black BIC lighter. My eyes all but sparkled as I put the blunt to my lips. I inhaled the smoke, and sat back rested, as it filled my lungs, and tickled the underside of my tongue. The smoke scratched at my throat with every inhale and exhale, even made me cough a little bit. I'm sure damaging it that much more, but I didn't care. I had to heal anyway.

It was almost 2 hours later before making it back to my house. 7 O'clock traffic had the bridge backed up bumper-to-bumper. The first thing I did was shower. I wanted to fully examine myself. I realized I had a large bruise going up and down my right side, contributing to my back pain. I sobbed, sitting on the shower floor, with the bathroom door locked for privacy. I couldn't hold back the tears as I sat there, knees into my chest.

After my long shower, I walked into the kitchen, grabbed a bottle of Hennessey off of the shelf and went into my room, laying on the bed. My own bed. I missed my silk sheets. I wrapped myself up in them, trying to feel normal again.

CHAPTER 10

fter the twins got out of school Friday, I dropped them off at Tracey's house, then headed back home to meet Sean. If my attack had anything to do with my father and his old friends, I didn't want them to be left alone. He was sitting in his car when I pulled into the driveway. Getting out of his car as I got out of mine.

"Hey, baby. Let me run in and grab some stuff and we can head out." I said. He nodded in agreement, opening the passenger door and sitting down, feet planted firmly on the ground, face buried into his phone. I reemerged from the house, duffle bag in hand, and locked up the house. Sean got into the driver's side of his black AMG, as I walked down the bricked path, and entered the vehicle. It took two weeks for the swelling to subside enough, for me to go into public.

"You know what you're going to ask him?" Sean asked. We we're passing through Concord, going down 680.

"Everything. I know my mom left some shit out and I couldn't really talk to him at the funeral." I reached into my purse and grabbed a red BIC, lighting a blunt. "Like, why they fucked over their friends. And maybe how I can find him." I said before taking a long drag. He placed his hand on my thigh, stealing my attention away from the cars and buildings as they hurried by the window.

"I got a surprise for you when we leave the prison."

"What is it?" I asked.

"A *surprise*." He responded sarcastically, smiling.

The two of us made it to the Hampton Inn, almost 2 hours later.

The clock on the car's dashboard read 6:30 PM. I couldn't wait to get out of the car and stretch my legs.

He pulled the car in front of the main entrance. "I'll get the bags. Go check us in real quick. I gotta make a call." He said before getting out.

"Okay babe. I'll see you upstairs." I said as I stepped out of the car and stretched a bit, before walking inside the hotel. I was relieved to see that there was no line.

"Hi! Welcome to the Hampton. Checking in or out?" Asked the overly-chipper concierge. She was a tiny little white girl, with dark brown hair, tied into a low side pony. She had freckles on her cheeks and wore a pair of black-framed glasses. They matched the black, almost tuxedo-like uniform.

"Hi, checking in please." I said. "Two keys." She asked me for the name on the reservation. I told her Sean Rodriguez. I headed to the elevator, then texted Sean the suite number. I walked into the room, heels clapping against the shiny wood floor, as I passed by the kitchenette. The walls, were painted a calming green. The 3 large windows allowed the light to fill the rom. I walked in between two white, 3-person couches, separated by a glass coffee table, with golden U-shaped legs. The center piece was a bouquet of white roses, in a white vase, with a thick, gold strip around the rim I grabbed one, senses awakened by the aroma as I buried my face into the bud. I rested my hands on the center window's sill, noticing a small little balcony, looking out over the river.

I watched the water ripple, thinking of my mother. I began to think about my dad, feeling anxious about seeing him since the funeral and Johnathon's death. After flipping on the mounted 60" Sony, I poured myself a 5-shot glass of Whiskey, before I flopped down on the large, plush Cali King. I kicked off my black pumps and unbuttoned my skinny jeans, taking a sip of the drink. After placing the rose in my hair, I walked into the bathroom and started to fill up the 4-person spa bath. Slipping out of all of my clothes and replaced them with the fluffy, soft white robe, that the hotel provided. I walked back into the room and grabbed the hotel phone.

"Hello, front desk." Said the same chipper voice, I'd heard earlier. I ordered the two of us their largest bacon cheeseburger with a side of fries. She gave me about an hour until the food would be ready. I walked over to the door, cracking it a little bit to let Sean in. The hotel also provided a small bottle of lavender bubbles, that I used the entire bottle of. I began to feel my entire body starting to relax, from the moment my toes dipped into the hot water. I tossed the robe onto the floor, near the tub, and sank my body into the bubbly water.

"Baby!" I heard Sean call out. "Where you at?"

"In the tub!" I yelled back.

I watched as he turned the corner and smiled. "Oh okay. Can I join you?" He asked, removing his shirt. He flexed his abs as he lifted it over his head. How could I possibly say no.

I sat up, giving him room to slide in behind me after he tied his wild hair into a loose pony. Once he was settled and comfortable, I rested my head against his chest. The smell of the lavender bubble bath, mixed with his Versace cologne, sent my senses into overdrive. I arched my back a little, to turn around and kiss him. Sucking on his bottom lip, wishing it was another piece of him. I flipped my body around to face him. He smiled, biting his lip as I started kissing and sucking on the lip tattoo on his neck.

"Mm," He moaned softly as I slid my tongue down from his neck and down his collar bone. I held my breath as I gripped his meaty piece and took it into my mouth. I felt him scoot back, giving me more of himself. I used my foot to raise the drain stop. It was controlled by a switch under the nozzle, similar to a light switch. I could now stay down there for longer, having a little fun. "Fuck, baby." He moaned. He grabbed my messy ponytail, guiding my head up and down his. "You know I like that shit." He whispered. I put both of his balls in my mouth as I stroked his dick slowly. I sat up as his breathing became more labored. I sat on my ankles, watching his dick throb just above the surface of the water. He looked at me, still biting his lip. I crawled on top of him, slowly sliding all the way down his large shaft. He gripped each of my ass cheeks, squeezing them with all his might as he guided himself into me. I wrapped my arms around his shoulders, standing on the balls of my feet. I bounced up and down, squeezing him within my walls, gripping him tight. The water began splashing out and around the tub.

KNOCK! KNOCK! KNOCK! "Hello, room service."

"Leave it by the door." He yelled towards the door. "Shit, I'm already eating." He chuckled and went back down for some more.

"Ooohhhh, fuck!" I screamed out, legs shaking as I came again. He popped back up a few seconds later, face drenched with me. I grabbed his face, pulling him closer to me, kissing his soft lips. My eyes began rolling back as he slid into me, starting slowly. He wrapped my legs around his strong arms, and pinned me down by my shoulders, stopping me from putting my legs down. I couldn't run away as he dug me out. The room was filled was smacks, the squishy sounds of my water faucet leaking and our moans of pleasure. "Shit! I'm about to come!" I screamed out. As he leaned in to kiss me, I wrapped my arms around him

"Me too, baby. Me too." He whined, whispering in my ear, just before I felt his seed shoot up into me. He kept stroking me, slowly as he kissed me softly on my lips, chin and neck. "You love me?" He asked.

"I love you." I replied with a wide smile, wiping my juices from his chin.

"I love you, too." He whispered, smiling. He stood up, letting my legs fall freely onto the bed. "I'm hungry as fuck now, though." He said, booty jiggling walked over to the door. I watched him peek into the hallway, looking both ways before stepping out to grab our food. I was amazed at how quickly that hour flew by.

We spent the rest of the evening in the room, naked. Smoking and watching Pay-per-view movies. I felt better about seeing my dad and introducing them to each other. Sean's always done a great job at keeping my stress and anxiety levels down, just by holding me.

"You really ready for me to meet yo pops?" He asked, I sat between his legs, head resting against his chest. I wore one of the hotels robes, eating a piece of turtle cheesecake, sent up with our second order of room service. Sean only wore a towel, wrapped around his waist. His hair out and wild.

"Yeah, I meed you to come with me and twins aren't really feeling him right now."

I woke up the next morning, a bit earlier than usual; about 6:45. I realized Sean holding onto me a little tighter than normal. I laid there enjoying the tenderness of the moment, hearing early birds chirping through the open window.

"Nah, just five more minutes." He whispered groggily, squeezing me tighter as I attempted to peel his arm away from me. I chuckled, scooting back closer to him.

A few more moments passed, before we were finally able to pull ourselves out of the fluffy bed. The sky outside barely blue yet. I stretched as my toes settled into the plush carpet. I chuckled as he scratched his right ass cheek, walking into the bathroom. I went over to my suitcase and grabbed out something to wear, after rolling me a little blunt to get the day started. I picked out a black, long-sleeved Helmut Lang sweater, that rested just off of the shoulder, and paired it with some black jeans. I also put aside a black Chanel leather coat for warmth. Satisfied with my look for the day, I put my weed out and joined him in the shower for a little morning loving.

I sat on the edge of the bed, sliding my feet into my pumps. My anxiety began to arise seemingly out of nowhere. I didn't know exactly what it was that I was afraid of. If anyone alive has answers for me, he surely did. I looked up, seeing Sean standing at the mirror trying to fix his tie. He tucked in his black Armani button up, into a pair of blue Balmain jeans.

"You think he knows who killed your *friend*?" He asked as I walked over to help.

"I surely fucking hope so." I said, forcing a chuckle, tightening his tie around his neck.

"I think I'm a little nervous meeting your pops, real talk."

"Babe, he's not that bad." I said laughing a little. We continued to get dressed. Sliding on our black leather jackets, he grabbed the keys to the car and we were off.

My nerves began to settle a bit once we hit the freeway. I reached into my purse and grabbed one of the pre-rolled blunts we prepared, before leaving the bay. This is the first time I've seen him in 2 month and 19 days, since my mother's funeral. I could feel my stomach starting to cramp up. Guilt starting to build. I should've reached out to him sooner. But, at the same time I was still angry. Pissed off even. Pissed off at him for not doing a better job at keeping his family safe and at my mom for being so selfish and abandoning us.

We pulled off of Highway 50, onto Folsom Blvd, the prison still

20 minutes away. I wanted to cry, walking through the double doors of the prison. Sean must've felt my anxiety, because he wrapped his arm around my waist in an attempt to calm me.

The screening process was more than just a little rigorous. After walking through a set of metal detectors, they made us remove our shoes, jackets and even made us undo our ponytails. They then had us write down all of our information. License and plate information. Address and phone numbers, too. We turned in the paperwork and sat, waiting, amongst the other visitors, after they gave us our name tags, with my last name written on it in black Sharpie.

It was about another hour before a black, female CO emerged through a set of double doors with a clipboard in her hand. She yelled out the names of the inmates and their visitors stood to follow her. About 20 minutes later, she came back. My father's last name was the 4th one she called out. Sean stood and extended his hand to help me to my feet, my palms sweating as I grabbed his hand. We followed her through a set of steel doors then another set of metal detectors, and through a large steel door that swung open towards us. Another group of CO's came to see us to our table, based on our name tags. The room was big and cold. Loneliness, filled with 8 steel tables, attached to a cement floor. There were six steel saucers, attached to the tables, by steel pipes, thick as legs. The tables were split, four against a grey, brick wall, with only narrow slivers of glass, that only allowed light to come through. The other four were against the adjacent wall, right in line with the CO's watch station, against a set of checkered windows. The room was filled with a stale scent, like a basket of dirty laundry. The correctional officer scanned the room as the visitors sat down, looking all of us square in the eyes.

The two of us sat in our chairs. I was beginning to get excited about seeing my daddy. I rested my head on Sean's shoulder and closed my eyes for a quick second. Suddenly there was an uproar of excitement.

The room filled with, "Daddy! Daddy! Daddy! Oh, my God! Look at him!" I looked towards the wall behind the CO's station and seen a line of prisoners, wearing orange jumpsuits. My eyes locked onto my father almost immediately. Though, it was hard to recognize him. His hair and his beard had both grown full and grey. Tears filled my eyes and fell down my face as he walked over to us, shoulders straight, even with the weight of his world resting on them. How 3 months can change a lot.

"Hi, daddy." I said as he sat down. I noticed he had a cut on his bottom lip and above his right eyebrow. It was obvious he'd been in a fight or two. He looked emotionally worn down. "How are you doing?" I was so used to seeing my father a certain way. Dapper, clean shaven and in control. Today, it seemed like there was a completely different man sitting across the table from us.

"Been better, baby girl. Who's this?" He asked, nodding his head towards Sean. His voice sounded rough, gravely.

"My name is Sean, sir."

"Nice to meet you, young man. I'm Stephan, Liyah's father. I'd shake your hand, but…" He said forcing out a chuckle. He squinted his eyes for a second. "Do I know you from somewhere?" My dad asked him. He looked as though he was trying to see through to his soul.

"No, sir. Not that I know of."

"Hmm, I feel like I know you, just can't put my finger on it. But, what's up with the shades?" He asked, hands folded, resting strongly on the steel table. My heart sank. I almost forgot I had them on. The swelling in my right eye hasn't gone all of the way down, since the attack. Removing my shades, I could see the devil himself pass through my father as he laid eyes on me. My father jumped up ready to extend his sentence. "Whoa! Bruh, did you-"

"Reyes!" Yelled one of the six stationed guards.

"No, no, no, dad. It wasn't him!" I said standing, holding my arm out. I looked around the room at the guards, hands on their utility belts, ready to grab their batons. "It wasn't him." I pleaded repeatedly. He slowly sat back down, not wanting to take his glare off of Sean. "That's what I wanted to talk to you about." He shifted his gaze over to me. His evil glare now filled with confusion. "The person that did it was found in an alley hours later, a bullet in the back of his head." I said, holding back tears, as flashes from the event flooded my consciousness. "He told me to thank you, before knocking me out." Sean rubbed my shoulder, keeping me grounded and my eyes dry.

"Why would I-" He paused mid-sentence.

"And Johnathon was found dead. Murdered in his fucking apartment." I said, feeling myself getting angry. There was something he was holding back, and I intended to get it out of him. "Before mommy… died, she was talking to someone, said somebody named Liam could be responsible for it." He took both of his hands and rubbed his face, stopping over his mouth.

"Fuck." He whispered.

"What is it?!" I exclaimed. He began to tell me how he and Johnathon Sr. were locked up together, and how, the very day of my mother's funeral, Johnathon Sr. was jumped, stabbed in his chest and in his gut over 20 times. The attack was gruesome and unwarranted. Locked in his cell, waiting to be escorted to my mother's funeral. He was forced to watch from the 4×12 window in the cell door, while his brother lay in a pool of his own blood, fighting for every breath. The attack happened so fast, that by the time the correctional officers made it to the scene, Johnathon had already bled out from the stab wounds to his chest and gut.

I watched as he held back tears, telling me what followed the days after the releasing of my mother's ashes. 3 large men approached him. He recognized some of them from the murder of Johnathon.

He was on the yard, playing a game of basketball with a few dudes that ran the streets for him when they were out. A gut feeling told him to turn around immediately. What he saw was the three guys walking towards him. Their faces grimaced, fixed upon him. He knew he was in danger, so instead of waiting for them, he attacked them first, not giving them the satisfaction of surprising him. That was the first fight. His second altercation, only a few days later, left a man with a broken rib and another with a dislocated jaw. They attempted to jump him in the shower, underestimating his fortitude. The attack was stopped by a guard who overheard the commotion, giving Stephan praise for surviving not only one attack, but two. My dad was then transferred to the general population, the division where he would least likely to be attacked.

I almost cried listening to my dad talk about his life behind bars. Turns out I wasn't having nearly as hard a time as I thought.

"Does Aunt Crystal not know about…?"

"Yeah, absolutely she does. I wrote her a letter telling her I apologized for not being able to keep him safe." He put his hands over his face as he sniffled, stopping himself from crying. "I haven't talked to her since." He put his hands back down on the table. "I got a few niggas on the outside, but I cant have shit to do with them right now. You all I got on the outside."

That statement alone, hit me like a ton of bricks. I felt three times, the amount of guilt I've felt for being so angry and furious with him. Never did it once occur to me that my father was also hurting, right along with me.

"I'm going to go grab a smoke. You two deserve some time alone. It was a pleasure meeting you Mr. Reyes." Sean said, standing.

"Call me, Steph. It was nice to meet you too, lil man. Imma figure out where I know you from too, blood." My dad said, smiling. He stuck his hand out and Sean quickly shook it.

"Hey! No touching!" Yelled the correctional officer. He sounded tired of giving warnings.

"See you in a bit, babe." I said as he kissed my cheek, heading outside. "I'm so sorry, daddy." I said starting to sob into my hands. I quickly reeled the tears in, realizing I just wanted a hug from my daddy, but that it wouldn't happen. "Daddy, I'm sorry I haven't been by to visit...or even write you. It's just been a lot to deal with. You know?"

"No, baby girl. Don't apologize. I get it. You had to grow up pretty much overnight. If only I'd done a better..." he said, stopping himself. A few seconds went by before I reached into my pocket. I pulled out the photograph that was found with Johnathon's body.

"Fuck." He sighed, looking down, hands on his head. "Liam took this picture. He knows. He knows I'm the one that got him locked up."

"What?" I asked, confused. And yet, things were starting to finally make sense.

"Baby girl, you need to leave. You and your brothers need to get the fuck out of here." He whispered loudly. He looked concerned. "Liam is going to use you to get to me, since he can't *get* to me. You understand? You and the twins need to go." He said. The look on his face scared me. Like he knew that I was not safe and that he couldn't help me, what so ever. Suddenly, his eyes shot up to the right, like he had a moment of clarity. "Is the house still in foreclosure?" He asked. I was stuck and had no idea what was going on. Or why.

"I don't know, dad. Maybe. I haven't been there since...I haven't been there in months." I said matter-of-factly.

"Go back to the house. Duct taped to the inside of the mailbox, is a safe deposit key. Bank of San Francisco. Talk to Demetrius."

"Wh-what's Demetrius got to do with anything?" I asked, confused. "Dad, what's in the deposit box?"

"Proof that I didn't kill no-fucking body and a little money to get you and your brothers out of here. Shit maybe even the country. I don't want you involved in this more than you already are. This ain't the life I want for you and the twins."

"What about the money? Is there a way to get that back?" I asked.

Suddenly a loud, almost deafening buzzing noise flooded the room. "Alright, inmates, hours up. Say your goodbyes." Said the CO.

"We gotta go legit, the money we had is gone." He said standing. I stood with him. "It should be enough to get you started. And stay focused. Liam has a son, Phillippe. He's a little older than you, by a couple years, so be careful." He warned. I ran around the table and hugged him. I didn't care about the guards.

"Hey!! No touching! Let's go." Said the officer. He came over and grabbed dad's arm, pulling him away from me.

"Remember, ask for Demetrius. Tell him I said it's time for Plan B. Go as soon as you can." Was all he was able to get out, before the large steel door slammed behind him.

"Love you, dad." I whispered to myself, saddened that our time was so limited. Words couldn't begin to express how heavy my heart was in that moment. All my life, my father had been my black Superman. Maybe that was why me and Johnny didn't work out. I based our entire relationship off of my parents' and their love for each other, and he was nothing like my father.

My dad was always *the* man. The man that couldn't do any wrong, the man that would never fall or fail, and definitely not the man that's being beaten down emotionally or physically. It's not fair. He doesn't deserve to be here in this hell hole.

I was headed to the car, hurrying for some fresh air, when my mind rested on the fact that Liam not only had a son, but he's only a couple years older. I began wondering if I'd met him already. Fucked him already? The thought was so unnerving.

"Hey, baby. How'd it go?" Sean asked once I made it to the car. He had a lap full of orange leaves and a Dutch weed wrap already gutted.

"It was good." I said, slamming the door shut. "He said there may be a chance to lower his sentence. Clearing him of 20 counts of murder. He would still have to do time for the trafficking and shit though." I said. He started the car before igniting the blunt. "I'm so happy you got these tints." I chuckled as he passed the weed over to me. I felt like a piece of the boulder, that's lived on my shoulders, has been chipped off.

"Hopefully they let him out on bail or something." He said.

"I don't know. We gotta go to the City to get it. I think it'll put Liam right back behind bars, where his dog ass belongs." I said. He began reversing the car out of the spot and began speeding out of the lot.

I checked the time on my phone against the bank's hours. I tried not to be too disappointed learning that they are closed on the weekend.

"You ready for your surprise?" He asked, hand on my thigh.

"Yeah, I'm ready, babe." I said, grabbing his hand. It was almost half an hour later, when I noticed we weren't headed in the direction of the hotel room. We looked to be heading Downtown. "What we doing?"

"I made you an appointment to get yo feet and nails did. I'll send a car to take you back to the room." He said, pulling the car over. I barely had time to process everything before he was expecting me to get out.

"You're serious..." I said, wearing the largest smile. I looked to the right, out of the window. The nail salon, Lacquered Nails, was sandwiched between a frozen yogurt spot and a vintage furniture store. In the shops display window, was a set of Chanel bags, from their upcoming Fall line.

"I don't play bout my baby." He said, smiling. I got out of the car and walked over to the window, wondering how to get my hands on one of those bags. "You better take yo sexy ass in there before one of these niggas snatch you up." He yelled out the car window.

"Bye, babe." I said laughing, turning to him to wave. I walked inside the nail shop, the bell chimed, welcoming me inside. That signature scent filled my nose, as I walked over to the cashier counter.

"Hey! Welcome to Lacquered Nails!" Said the lady behind the register. She stood in front of a large, 8' rock waterfall. The salon was decorated somewhat like a yoga studio. The large massage chairs, covered in burgundy leather, lined the far-left wall. Behind the waterfall, lined against the wall to the right, were the nail booths. "Is your name Liyah?" She asked.

"Uhm, yes." I said forcing a chuckle, a little taken back.

"I'm sorry. Your husband called and got you set up with a…" she paused for a second, looking through the computer "massage and a mani-pedi."

"Oh, did he?" I asked smiling from ear-to-ear.

"Yeah, he sure did." She said laughing. "You're all set. Follow me." She said, walking back from behind the register.

I followed her passed the nail stations, to a large, brown wooden door on the back wall. There was a neon sign next to it, that read *Spa*. Passing through the door led us into a hallway, of 6 massage rooms. 3 on each side. At the end of the hallway was the sauna. I made a mental note to make that part of the package next time.

Once inside the vanilla scented room, lit by only candles and a sliver of natural light, she reached up into a cabinet, pulling out a stack of folded towels. She instructed me disrobe and wrap one around my breast and another around my waist, before she left the room. I did as she instructed and laid face down on the table, awaiting my massage.

After an amazing rub down, it was time to get my nails and feet done. I put my clothes back on, before being guided over to the foot bowls and was seated in the plush chair. The hot water was running into the bowl as I sat down. Susan and Karen, the young nail techs, made me feel like I was cheating on my nail lady, Desiree. But this place had her beat.

They started me off by soaking both hands in a warming ginger-peach scented oil bath. Following it up with shaping my nails and my cuticles. Karen massaged my feet with a hot towel, soaked in the lavender oil. Before Susan got to work on my hands, she brought me over a bottle of Dom Perignon champagne. I was surprised they had this here. She showed me the color wheel, filled with tons of different styles. I decided on the coffin shaped nails, matte-black for the color, outlined in little square rhinestones for a bit of a pop.

I tried my best to relax as Susan and Karen rubbed my feet, and another girl by the name of Trista, rubbed my hand as I finished my champagne. My mind wouldn't settle knowing that Liam's son probably knows me, and I have no idea who he is.

I sat at the dryer, bored, doing my best to stay off of my phone, when I saw a black Mercedes SUV pull up to the curb. My phone chimed, sitting face up next to the dryer so I wouldn't miss an important call. Sean texted me with the name and the picture of the driver that was coming to get me. I started to get anxious, wishing this damn thing would hurry up and finish drying my nails.

It was another 15 minutes before the nail dryer automatically shut off. Susan came over as I was standing. "Here's your receipt. Have a great day."

"Thank you. You do the same." I said before going through the shops glass door to exit.

"Hey, Liyah?" The driver asked, holding the back door open. I slid into the truck.

"Hey, yeah. Stan?" I shut the door and rolled the window down a bit to get some air.

"How are you doing, miss?" The driver asked, pulling away from the nail salon.

"I'm well. And you?"

"Can't complain. Enjoying the beautiful May weather." He said smiling through the rearview. I smiled back. He was an attractive older white gentleman, buff with the white boy's version of the fade. He had on a Givenchy muscle T-shirt, a pair of beige cargo shorts and a pair of reflective aviator sunglasses.

We made it to the hotel about half an hour later.

"I'll get that for you." He said before jumping out. He ran around the front to the passenger's side and opened my door. I grabbed his hand, as he helped me step down onto the sidewalk.

"Thank you." I said smiling, before walking into the hotel. The door man opening the door for me.

I made it upstairs to the suite and was all alone. On the bed was a couple of boxes. The first, was long and red. I opened it and pulled out a black, Chanel mesh top. Long sleeved, stopping just under my breasts.

It came with a matching, ankle-length skirt. In the smaller box, was a pair of black, leather Alexander Wang pumps, with a gold-leaf, 5" heel. Everything was the right size. My heart smiled and I'm sure it showed prominently on my face. I reached into my Louis Vuitton duffle and grabbed my strapless, push up bra. I kicked off my pumps and rushed into the bathroom, staring the shower. I was anxious to get the prison's dead atmosphere and stale scent off of me.

Just like I imagined, everything fit like a glove. I quickly straightened my curly, shoulder-length hair. I thought about wearing the jewelry Johnathon bought me, but I decided against it, in case Sean asked me where it came from. I went with a pair of large, diamond hoops, and the matching tennis bracelet. I stepped into a cloud of Dior, then studied my reflection in the mirror. Unable to find any imperfections, I texted Sean a picture of the outfit. He responded almost immediately with, "Yeah, that's my girl. Your driver should be downstairs in less than 10 to bring yo' sexy ass to me." He ended the text message with a kissing emoji. I went over to the nightstand and grabbed the other half of the blunt we smoked this morning. By the time I was finishing it, my phone chimed, letting me know the driver was downstairs. It was the same driver. He stood at the open back door, waiting for me.

"Hello, again." He said.

"Hey." I smiled, sliding behind the passenger's seat. The ride lasted about 10 minutes. Kirk Franklin's *Smile* played softly through the truck's speakers.

"Here we are, Miss Liyah." He said, pulling in front of Firehouse restaurant, located in Old Sacramento. I walked inside, scanning the room for Sean.

"Mrs. Reyes?" The hostess asked. I was caught off guard again, but I thought back on the nail salon. "Your party is here." She said smiling, before guiding me through the high-class restaurant. Everyone was in suits and ties, and cocktail dresses. I couldn't help but notice the atmosphere was predominantly Caucasian and/or rich. I soon laid eyes on Sean, sitting in the center of a large booth, overlooking the entire restaurant. He looked up from his phone and directly at me. He stood up from the booth, with a large pink rose in his hands as I walked over.

"Hey, baby." He said, handing it to me. A hello wasn't enough for me. I placed the rose onto the table and wrapped my arms around his neck, kissing him passionately on the lips.

"Thank you, baby." I said, all smiles, before scooting into the booth.

The restaurant was gorgeously decorated, with themes from 1970s Brooklyn. The walls were an eggshell white, with gold crown and floor molding. Smooth jazz played from speakers in each booth's headrest and from the 6 club speakers suspended from the high ceiling, which was being held up by large black columns, trimmed with gold. The giant, gold and crystal chandeliers matched the big gold mirrors, that hung on the walls, adding an extra touch of grace and elegance.

"Would you guys like to start off with any wines? Maybe a nice spirit?" Asked the hostess.

"Yes, could you bring the bottle of your Screaming Eagle Cabernet?" He asked softly. The look on the hostess' face changed to concern, as she smiled, stumbling over her thought.

"The entire bottle, sir?" She asked. He looked at her, wondering if he was speaking English.

"That's what *whole* means, right?" He asked, closing the menu and setting it in the center of the table.

"Sure, sir. But, that's a $4,500 bottle." I wondered why she was asking so many questions instead of writing it down. She had her pen and notepad out but has yet to write down a single letter.

"Yeah, I know." He said sarcastically. I could see the annoyance making itself known in his face. It happened rather quickly, too. "Bring it to me." He continued. I expected the word *Bitch* to follow.

"Sure thing, sir." She said, rushing off to grab the wine. He shook his head, looking over towards me. I chuckled as he broke out a little half smile.

"Damn, you are beautiful." He said smiling wider, as he bit his bottom lip, leaning in for a kiss. I leaned in, smelling his Armani cologne and kissed him passionately.

"You're looking pretty good, too, babe." He wore a black YSL blazer, over a black Armani button up and a pair of dark blue Gucci jeans with black Chanel loafers.

The two of us flipped through the Chef's Tasting menu; a five-course dinner with a wine pairing for each deliciously crafted entrée.

The servings left just enough room for a great dessert. I ordered the cappuccino mousse, while Sean ordered the Passion Fruit cheesecake, which tasted delicious as well.

I was already feeling a little tipsy before we killed off the bottle of wine. I stood up, feeling a little more than wavy. Sean held my hand, helping me get to the car. We slid into the back seat. It was the same driver I've had my last two trips. I was starting to think Sean personally hired this guy. As soon as the door shut, his hands were lifting up my skirt. Squeezing the inside of my left thigh. He kissed on my neck, playing with the thigh hole in my panties, teasingly rubbing against my clit. I spread my legs wider, sliding down into the seat, giving Sean more access. I kissed him, trying to stop myself from moaning and his long finger slid inside and out of my flower bud. I couldn't hold back any longer. I was about to blow.

"Aahh-" I began moaning. Sean stopped me by kissing me passionately. Adding another finger just as I came, creaming in the palm of his hand. He began moving faster and faster. I parted my legs wider, ready to embrace another orgasm. He stopped, pulling back just as I reached my peak. I opened my eyes, looking at him. He smiled devilishly, before pulling my skirt up to my waist. Ducking under my left thigh, he got down on his knees, burrying his face directly into my pussy, shoving his fingers into my mouth stopping me from screaming. I looked up and seen the driver smiling, turning me on even more.

"Yes, daddy." I moaned softly, lifting my shirt and bra up, exposing my size c cup breasts. I looked the driver in his eyes, riding Sean's mouth, as he sucked the nut out of me.

It wasn't 20 minutes before we were pulling up to the hotel. Sean popped up, digging into his pocket. He tossed a few crumpled large bills onto the empty passenger seat, giving me time to straighten up, before he opened the door. I shot the driver a quick wink before getting out, following Sean into the hotel lobby. In the elevator, I fondled his rock hard dick as we kissed, my back pushed into the corner. It was hard not to stop the elevator and hike this skirt back up.

As soon as we made it up to the suite. Sean pushed me against the wall, face first, snatching down my skirt, leaving on only my shirt and heels. It was an outfit similar to one I wore on stage at the club, one night. I stood there, hands and face against the wall, poking my ass out, anxiously awaiting his entrance. I listened to him unbuckle his belt and drop his pants

"Ooh. Shit this pushy tight." He whispered in my ear, entering from behind. "Look what I got." He said, holding up a bag next to me. It was filled with little pink pills. Ecstasy. I stuck my tongue out for him to give me one. He did. Making me 10 times hornier, and less inhibited than I was before.

A couple of hours later, we were sitting on the couch, on the hotel's patio, smoking a blunt. The sky was starting to change from black, to a dark blue. Our naked bodies completely exposed to the cool breeze. It felt amazing. Sean was between my legs, licking me softly.

"Here, daddy. Hit this." I whispered, barely able to speak after screaming all over the hotel suite. He came up and sat down next to me, his 3rd leg aimed to the sky, tempting me to have another taste. I lost the war against my will and straddled his lap. He slouched down, giving me more of himself. We were back at it again. I rode him slowly, taking my time before making him bust again.

I moved Sean's long hair out of his face as I watched him sleep. He was passed out on the bed, laying on his stomach arms folded under his head. "He doesn't even snore." I whispered to myself. I could feel the attraction to him growing stronger with every kiss of his soft, pillow-like lips. Every stroke, every touch and every glance. The more I got of him, the more I wanted from him. More and more into his heart, as he busted down the walls to mine.

I jumped off of the bed, still feeling wide awake. I grabbed my phone to call Tracey, before walking over to the bar. It was almost 6:30 in the morning and I still unable to fall asleep. After I finished rolling a blunt and pouring myself a glass of whiskey, I headed to the balcony to call her.

"Hey, girl." She answered. "Yo' man know you on the phone this late?" She answered.

"He sleep." I responded, chuckling. I looked back at him, through the patio's glass double doors. He hadn't moved an inch. My heart skipped a beat before telling her, "I think I love him."

"Whaaat?!" She exclaimed. "Hold on, bitch. Let me find something to smoke on real quick. Mmm hmmmm." She said. I heard a lighter flickering in the background. "Now, bitch. Do tell."

I chuckled before telling her about the visit with my dad and how well the meet between him and Sean went. "Daddy's pretty blunt and would've told me *and* Sean that he didn't approve. Although he did try to kill him when he saw my black eye." I told her. I, then went into our date. Told her how everything was set up, all I had to do was be ready. And I absolutely *h*had to tell her about the car ride back to the hotel. I was excited again just thinking about it.

"Wait, so you watched the driver watch you getting ate out?" She asked, completely shocked.

"I'm sure that's the most excitement he's seen in that backseat." I chuckled

"I fucking bet." She laughed along with me.

Towards the end of our conversation, which lasted an hour, I started to finally feel a little sleepy. I hung up the phone, putting it face down on the nightstand. I curled up under Sean, who was now asleep on his side, in a fetal position.

I walked up the stairs to the hotel, out of breath after running all the way from Lake Merrit. I saw my mother standing on the second story railing.

"Mom! What are you doing?" I cried from the parking lot, just below her. She didn't even acknowledge my presence. Her face soaked with black streaks of mascara. She just stood there, on the railing ready to jump. "Mommy! Wait there. Just stay right there." I quickly found the staircase, skipping steps as I did my best to run up to her. It was too late. The moment I was close enough to touch her, she was gone, jumping head first into the cement.

The sound of her body crashing against the pavement, woke me up in a cold sweat. The first thing I wanted to do was call my mother. After realizing it was just a dream, I broke down, sobbing silently into my pillow. I peeled myself from the bed, legs weak as I wobbled into the bathroom to shower. I cried a little more before washing my body.

The two of us decided that were just going to stay in the suite on this rainy Sunday. Extending our stay, just to hold and love on each other.

We both dressed comfortably in T-shirts, sweatpants, and Jordan's.

The ride back to the Bay was spent smoking weed and holding my man's hand. I've learned a lot about him the last few months that we've been together. But you really learn a lot about a person when you spend more than an hour in a car with them. He went with the flow better than the breeze. I loved how much he loved Aaliyah. He could rock the boat to her, then get a little ratchet with some Kevin Gates or Gucci Mane.

"Babe, go here, real quick." I said, keying the address to my childhood home into the GPS, once we dropped down into Oakland. It was now going on two in the afternoon.

"That's where you used to stay at?" He asked. He seemed surprised at the neighborhood I grew up in. I nodded my head, *yes*, as I reached into his glove box, grabbing a blunt.

It was another 15 minutes before making it to what I still called home. It was completely boarded up, with graffiti ridden planks and walls. Getting out of the car, my heart broke once again, staring at the dying behemoth from the outside of the rod iron fence. The gate was locked, by a heavy steel chain.

"What's going on, baby?" Sean asked, walking up behind me.

"I need to get in there." I said, looking at the large pad-lock. He ran back to the car and opened the trunk. I watched as he slammed the trunk down, now with a large, muddy shovel.

"Watch out." He said running back over to me. 3 swift whacks of the shovel, the pad-lock broke, falling to the ground.

"Thank you, babe." I said as I removed the chains from the fence. I wanted to question the shovel in the trunk, but I was too focused with getting onto the property.

Sean parted the gate, just big enough for us to squeeze through the opening. Walking up the long driveway, gave me an eerie sense of being. The house looked dead and the lawn had grown unkempt. It symbolized a moment in my life that was no more. And yet, a remainder of where we were as a family. We stepped onto the porch. I peered through two planks of wood, through the crystal window, in the large, wooden double doors.

"Is this it?" He asked, holding up a key, stuck to a piece of duct tape.

"I think so. Let's go." I said, touching the planks, as a way to say goodbye to home.

"...baby, wake up." Sean said, rubbing my left thigh. I looked at him, then looked around. The first thing I noticed was the chaos in the street next to us. Then to my right. I noticed we were parked in front of a large, glass building. Had to have been about 20 stories into the sky. "This the place. You want me to come inside with you?" He asked.

"Nah, babe. It's okay. I'll be right back." I said before kissing him.

"Alright. Imma go find parking. Just call me when you're heading out." He replied. I nodded and stepped out of the vehicle. I began walking down the short corridor, by all of the men and women in their suits and briefcases. Some on the phone handling business, and some just enjoying a nice coffee with a smoke break.

"Good morning, ma'am." Said the armed security, stationed right near the entrance. I was in awe, stepping foot inside of the bank. It was gorgeously built and meticulously decorated. The high, vaulted-glass ceilings and tall Canary Island palm trees gave you a sense of being outside. Four crystal chandeliers hung from the gold beams of the high ceiling and ran along the width of the large room. The walls were painted a golden-yellow with prints of white flowers. Swarms of people pulled themselves in each direction around me. I looked around, confused and lost, wondering what direction to go into next. The more I observed, I realized there were no teller windows.

"Hi! Welcome to the First Trust St Bank. Is there anything I can help you with?" Asked a young, short Asian girl, couldn't have been older than 23. She wore her hair in a slicked-back ponytail, with a black skirt suit and black Mary Jane slip-ons. She could obviously read the lost expression on my face.

"Hi, yes. I'm looking for Demetrius." I replied.

"Demetrius, Dem-Oh! Yes, Demetrius. Let me go grab him. Just have a seat and he'll be right with you, I'm sure." She said, resting her left hand on my right shoulder as she led me over to the large, burgundy sofa. I sat across from a white man, in a pair of Jean shorts, a Fendi T-shirt and a pair of Hermes sandals. He was reading a Forbes magazine, through his Oliver Peoples shades. I fondled the key in my hands, anxiety growing rampant at what secrets this thing may open up, and how Demetrius fits into all of this.

"Hey, Liyah" A few minutes later, I heard a deep, smooth voice from my right side.

Demetrius was tall, about 6'4 and built like a quarter back. He had hazelnut -brown eyes and a strong jawline. His grey, taylored Tom Ford suit fit him well, giving off just a hint of his bulge. I couldn't believe it's been almost 6 years since I've seen him last.

"You finally here for the box?" He asked, hugging me.

"Yeah it's pretty bad. Johnny, *and* his dad were murdered." I held up the gold-plated key.

"Sure, follow me." He said. We walked deeper into the bank and passed a line of ATMs, then up a narrow flight of stairs. We made it to a marble landing, stopped by a black gate to the room I needed to be in. Next to the gate, on the wall, was a little 8×8 screen, that went from black to illuminated, once touched.

"So, with this is 3 steps of security. First you scroll until you find your name, then enter your box number. Second you sign, then the gate will pop open if your name is on the approved life. And once you're inside, the box will be visible, but you need the key to open it fully."

"Thank you." I said, following his instruction. The gate popped open. "So, how'd you end up here? This where you been all this time?" I asked, holding onto the gate.

"Nah, I've never stopped working for him. Even to this day." He said, letting me know the lady that owns this bank, works with dad. I was surprised by how large my father's reach was. "Yeah, Steph gave us all *very* specific instructions." He chuckled. "He knew this day would come, it seems. He did say you shouldn't know about this. I actually thought it'd be your mom to-" He stopped, looking up at me. "Was she arrested, too?"

"No, she killed herself. I guess she was in too much from the drugs she started shaking...I don't know."

"I'm so fucking sorry, Li." He said, hugging me again. "Seems like shit's going farther just hitting the fan..."

"Yeah...it seems." I chuckled dryly. Feeling the need to break away from his grasp. I turned back and looking at the small box, slightly protruding from the wall. "He said to tell you that it was time for Plan B. What's Plan B?"

"Well, A was getting rid of Liam. B is getting the family out of town, as far as you guys could go of any shit pops off."

"What's Plan C?" I asked, sticking the key into the box.

"If anything happens to his kids. He was going back to the streets, to take all the way over…war." He responded. My father sounded like some military general. Maybe he was in the eyes of his soldiers. "I'll go head and let you rock. If you need anything just wave at that camera in the center of the room and I'll be right up." He said, pointing to the ceiling. There was a large, black bulb, directly in the center of the room, housed over the large marble table. I sat my Birkin bag down on top, walking towards the deposit box, placing the key in the slot. I twisted it, allowing the wall to release. I placed the box on the waist high table, next to my bag, and lifted the top.

I began searching the contents. I found an old-school tape recorder, 10 banded stacks of $100 bills, each with $10,000. I was now $100,000 and a few old pieces of jewelry richer. What really caught my attention, was the manila envelope that was filled to the brim. I lifted the fold, intrigued about what may be on the inside.

"Hi, Miss Reyes?" I suddenly heard a female voice behind me causing me to jump.

"Yes, hi." I said as I spun around, forcing out a nervous chuckle. She was an older white lady, a few years older than my dad. She wore her blonde hair in a pixie cut, showing off large diamond studs. She wore a purple, Christian Dior blouse, a pair of black Lanvin capris, with a pair of Balenciaga pumps.

"Hi, my name is Sandra Geoff." She said, extending her perfectly manicured hand for a shake. "What's your relationship with Mr. and Mrs. Reyes?" She asked.

"They're my parents. My dad asked me to come down and here and grab his things." I responded.

"Ahh. It's so nice to meet you. Me and your father have been doing business for a long time. Very good man. My heart broke when I saw what happened to your family, in the news." She said, wearing a warm smile, gaining my trust.

I began to place the contents into my bag, anxious to go home and comb through all of this.

"Are you sure you wouldn't want to open up your own account here? I think we'd be really beneficial to each other. Maybe pick up where your father and I left off?" She asked, she reached into her pocket and pulled out a silver business card, with her information neatly sketched onto the surface. "Don't answer right away. Give me a call once you make up your mind."

"Sure. I'll consider it. Thank you." I said, tossing the card into my purse.

"Good. Well I'll look forward to hearing from you." She flashed another warm smile and twirled around, heading down the stairs. I locked the box back into the wall, and followed her lead, texting Sean letting him know I was finished. Walking through the lobby me and Demetrius locked eyes again, forcing me to smile. If only we'd ran into each other before Sean...

Making it to the car, I immediately began to go through the envelope, pulling out a few 8×11 sized photographs. There was a few of me and Johnny's parents. They looked to be around our ages, now. The pictures were Innocent, days hanging out at the house or at a party. Then they suddenly began to get dark.

"This must be him." I said, looking at a picture of a man I didn't recognize. He was standing over a dead body, the flash from his gun, forever immortalized in the photo. I studied the pictures further. Him and a woman seemed to rain blood and mayhem. The pictures included stills of slit throats and severed heads. I felt a sudden onslaught of nausea. I opened the door and threw up onto the pavement next to me.

"Baby, you okay?" Sean asked, rubbing my back. I felt better after tossing up the Jack 'N' The Box, we ate on our way to Sacramento.

"Yeah. I can't even finish looking at these." I handed him the photos.

"Damn, this nigga look ugly as fuck. This that Liam dude?" He asked. I nodded my head, leaning back on the head rest, trying to stop feeling sick. He placed the photos back into the envelope and then into my purse, before starting the engine and pulling away from the curb. "I have to go into to work tonight, over see some things. You want to go home or pick up the boys first?" He asked. We were now crossing the bridge into Oakland.

"Home, I'll pick them up a little later."

CHAPTER 11

I kept good on my promise, bringing my brothers with me to visit my dad. Even keeping some type of money on his books so that he could have a semblance of normalcy. Every Saturday and Thursday, for the last two months we were right there, sitting at that table. Even on the 4th of July, just last weekend. Malakhi still harbored some ill feelings towards dad, so he didn't really say much. I asked my dad why. Why'd he set Liam up, instead of just getting rid of him. He responded with the simplest of answers.

"Because if I didn't get him, he would've gotten us. Plus, I like to keep my hands clean. That's why I handed Déjà vu over to Demetrius..." My jaw dropped, learning that he owned the club I danced at, the one I was attacked in. I kept that piece of information from him, for now. Though it was hard to wrap my head around.

"Why not me, dad? We could really use the money now." I said, matter-of-factly.

"Because, I was still running drug money through it." He whispered. "It all looks legit, but if the feds ever found out otherwise...then it'll be you in this ugly ass orange jumpsuit." He explained. "I told you. I don't want you-"

"Anymore involved than I already am. I know, daddy."

Changing the subject, my dad then went into further detail for us, about how he knew Liam was shady, that he didn't care about anything or anybody but himself. He didn't take him out because he still looked at him like a brother, and Liam was the reason they were who they were. Though he still loved his brother, he couldn't ignore the danger that was building up around him. He kept eyes on him after Liam killed a man and woman murdered in cold blood, right in front of him.

Liam had a little cousin in New York, NY, named Fernando, placing him out there so that he could begin to take over the East Coast. He had the money and manpower to do so. If only his sanity was also up to par.

There was a young lady by the name of Rosalita. She was first, Fernando's girl, until cheating on him with Liam. They carried on a relationship, even after Fernando found out, which ate at him day in and out. He decided to steal her back, along with a few kilos of heroine, just to teach his older cousin a lesson. Sadly, though, for Fernando, the lesson that was taught would be learned by him.

His body washed ashore of the Hudson River, after he had been missing for weeks. Rosalita was never seen or heard from again.

My father knew if he was capable of that, there wouldn't be anything…or anybody that Liam wouldn't mow down, if it happened to get in his way.

It's been a rough couple of weeks since the visit, trying to find a lawyer for my father's case. One that didn't cost an arm and a nipple, but still gave a fuck. I found out the original lawyer, would not be able to represent him. Mostly due to the fact no one's seen or heard from him, since my father was initially incarcerated.

It was now the middle of July, 5 months since my dad's been locked up. Sean showed us how much of angel he was. Going out of his way to take care of me and my brothers. I thought about reaching out to Demetrius to see if maybe we can go into a partnership, with the club, but in reality I knew nothing about running an organization. And it's his, my father gave it to him.

I got lucky when I stumbled across Daren Monfrey on Google, located 40 minutes away in Concord. I called him, excited that he was more than willing to take on my father's trial. He admitted that when everything originally went down, that it was a big deal to him. He hated seeing a fellow black man, and his family, going through something like this. He didn't even know the half. I couldn't wait to show him all of this evidence, that proved Liam guilty. I just really hoped it proved my father innocent as well, because it wasn't much proving *him* guilty.

I was anxious pulling onto Stanford St, to the lawyer's given address.

The GPS stopped us in front of a 2-story suburban home. Complete with a 3-car garage and stone décor on the outside wall. I backed into the driveway, next to a brand new 2009 Mercedes AMG. Colored money-green.

"I'll be right back. Let me drop this stuff off and we can head to the suite." I said to Tracey. Officer Jacob reached out to me for his bachelor party. Said he needed me and my finest friend to dance for him. $3,000 a piece to come and whatever we made in tips. This is the 3rd time I've danced for him, and Tracey's second. A couple months ago, in March, was for his 38th birthday. That's was my first dance for him.

I stepped out of the car and approached the front door. "Hello, Liyah?" Darren asked, coming outside.

"Hi, yes." I responded shaking his hand. He was a handsome light skinned guy. A full beard and a wavy fade. He was dressed in a pair of white jeans, and a black button up with a pair of Armani slippers. I followed him into the house. The living room and dining room shared one large, open space. From the front entrance you could see a view of the back yard, and the landscape of the city behind it. "Nice house." I said, looking around at the expensive paintings that hung on the walls along the staircase. I recognized a few pieces from the estate sale the government had. I wasn't allowed to attend.

"Thank you. My wife hates when I work from home, but I prefer it." He said. I followed him into his office, right off of the foyer. "Please have a seat." He said, pointing to one of the two plush chairs across from his large glass desk, with strong steel legs.

"I'm glad you were able to meet me today." I said still a little nervous. I crossed my legs and placed my bag in my lap.

"Of course, like I said, your father's case bothered me since I first heard it. There's a rat in all this cheese. I remember when Liam was first arrested, it was all over the news. Now almost 15 years later, he's free and your dad's pinched for the same crimes? What do you have for me?" He asked, nodding his head, towards my bag.

"Oh, right." I said, letting out a nervous chuckle. I reached into my bag and pulled out the envelope. He opened it up, grabbing the tape recorder.

"Have you listened to this already?" He asked making direct eye contact.

"No," I shook my head. "This would be the first time, today." He nodded and hit play on the side. We listened to it together.

"Sup, Dashon?" Said an unfamiliar voice.

"Hey, Liam. What are you - what's going on?" Said Dashon after a nervous chuckle.

"We're about to take a ride. Just you and me." Responded Liam. Daren looked at me, intrigued.

"Whoa! What's going on? Where's Gisela?" Dashon asked.

"Oh, you wanna see your little bitch?" Liam asked, I could hear the smile in his voice.

"You won't be needing this." Said a third voice. My only guess was that it was my father's.

Three loud gunshots rang from the tape recorder, followed by Dashon screaming, "No!"

"Won't be needing her anymore, either." Liam said. The recorder then cut to Liam yelling, "Go get that nigga!" Followed by another gunshot a few seconds later.

"Aaaaaahh! Fuck!" Dashon cried.

"Get his bitch ass up!" Liam ordered.

"Help! Help me, pl-." The tape recorder then jumped to Liam ordering the car be driven.

"I'm sorry, man. I'm fucking sorry!" Dashon pleaded. The fear in his voice was prominent. I was afraid for him.

"I don't give a fuck. Stick your tongue out!" Liam growled. Just then, Darren flipped open his silver Dell laptop.

"What?" Dashon asked. The next thing we heard, was the sound of a man screaming. Screaming so loud it was almost deafening. Even over the tape. We then heard profuse gagging and coughing. It made me sick to my stomach. Daren saw my reaction and stopped the tape.

"That's a lot. We can stop, if you'd like."

"Uhm, I – No." I wasn't sure if I wanted to hear the rest of the tape, but I knew I had to. "No, let it play. Please." I said, looking him in his eyes. He agreed and hit play. It started with Liam's voice.

"Ew, bitch!" He growled. Then suddenly we heard pounding thuds.

It sounded like a struggle, followed by the sounds of someone hacking away at something, or someone else. Then, the sudden slams of a car door. The tape stopped.

"Wait a minute." He said, rubbing his goatee, still looking at his computer.

"What's going on?" I asked, confused.

"I think I know who the man on the tape was." He said, turning the computer to face me. The first thing I saw was a man's mangled face. He was dressed in his pajamas. His normal photo was next to it, nowhere near recognizable. "His name was Dashon Langston. Beaten then thrown from a moving vehicle on the road next to 580 in Emeryville. Get this," he said turning the computer back around. "his tongue was cut out. *CUT OUT.*" I covered my mouth with my hand, feeling sick to my stomach again. I was able to hold it at bay. "He was stabbed over 20 times with a blade at least 14" long." He shook his head.

He looked through the photos.

"Jesus." He whispered, face screwed up.

"Yeah, those pictures are–"

"Gruesom." He said, taking the word directly out of my mouth. "How the hell did this guy even get out of prison?"

"He has to know somebody."

"Jesus, it's like your dad knew what was going to happen. I'll keep in touch, okay?" He said, stretching out his hand.

"Thank you so much." I said standing, shaking his hand. I made it the porch, and suddenly felt nauseated again, this time violently. My mouth began to suddenly water. Then the next thing I knew, I was vomiting into my lawyer's bushes, unable to hold it in. I wiped my mouth with the back of the sleeve on my sweater, then took it off and tossed it into his brown garbage bin, which sat out on the curb. Tracey was leant against the car, smoking a cigarette, watching me.

"Are you okay?"

"I just felt a little sick. You ready to go?" I asked, hopping into the truck. It took almost an hour to make it to San Jose's Marriott Suites. I was exhausted, ready to get tonight over with and get back in bed with Sean tomorrow morning.

We made it to the suite. There were two beds in the room, right passed the small kitchen area. I dropped all of my stuff on the bed closest to the large window, looking out over Downtown. I looked at the clock, realizing it was almost 4 in the afternoon. We decided to go ahead and get ready.

Tracey pulled out a bottle of Amaretto Cîroc, from her large, black leather Michael Kors bag. Tossing it onto my bed.

"Yes, bitch. I need a drink." I said, as I sat on the bed, opening her bottle as she jumped into the shower. I grabbed a plastic cup, from by the microwave and poured myself 4 shots. Nursing it as I pulled out my outfit for tonight. It was a silver, sequined tube top with beaded tassels, that fell down to my high thigh, with a matching pair of spanks underneath. It gave off the illusion that I was wearing a short dress, until I moved. I paired the outfit with matching, thigh-high Balenciaga boots. I straightened my hair and covered myself in Victoria's Secret glittered-perfume, and beat my face with a full face of Maybelline. Tracey wore black lingerie from Chanel, and a pair of black, Balenciaga pumps, covered by a thigh-length, Gucci trench. She pinned her hair up into a high ponytail, adding another 18 inches of Brazilian. We were officially the baddest bitches in world.

She dug into her bag, and pulled out a small sandwich baggy filled with little ecstasy pills, in the shape of Bart Simpson's head. I grabbed two, she took 3. We then took more shots of her drink, mixed with a bit of Orange juice. I rolled us a blunt, while we threw on some Pandora and had a pre turn up. My stomach began to feel a bit queasy after a few songs. I sat down laughing at the fun we were having, trying to ignore the feeling. Looking at the clock on the nightstand, I realized t was five minutes to 8. I noticed my phone start to ring. The caller ID read Officer Jacob.

"I guess we're taking too long." I said chuckling. "Hey, Officer."

"Hey, beautiful. You and your friend close?"

"Closer than you think. See you soon." I said, hanging up the line. I stood up, tossing the phone onto my bed, and placing the room key in my top.

"Whooo!! Let's hit this shit!" Tracey yelled as we walked out of the door, her smacking my ass before letting the door slam behind her. From the patio, we could see the downstairs lobby, centered with a large fountain, surrounded by fake trees. The smell of weed was strong in the air, though hard to determine it's source. I noticed a white guy, walking towards us, with his girlfriend. His eyes popped out of his head, even as they passed us by. I turned back to see if he was still looking. He was. His girlfriend finally noticed and began to beat him upside his head. Me and Tracey could barely contain our laughter.

"What the fuck are you bitches laughing at? Put on some fucking clothes!" She yelled. I had to stop Tracey from walking up on her.

"Hold on, bitch. Don't get beat-the fuck-up. You better watch who the fuck you're talking to." I said, stepping a little closer. Her boyfriend grew silent, trying to pull her away. "Don't be mad because you're bad built, shaped like SpongeBob, bitch!" Her face fell to the floor. I saw her mouth trying to move, trying to say words, but she was speechless. We laughed more, as we turned and walked away.

Tracey and I got off the elevator, six stories up on the 16th floor. We could hear the music getting louder and louder as we approached the suite.

"Whoo hoo!! Look what we have here, boys!" Officer Jacob yelled, letting us in. He had a Corona in his right hand, hugging us as we walked by him, meeting the other two officers. One of them was the Spanish officer I met at the bar, the first night I met Jake. The other was a mixed guy. He kind of resembled Michael Ealey, even his hair was the same.

The suite was complete with a kitchen, and a bedroom on either side of the large living room. Each with their own bathroom. Without hesitation, we changed the music from the light rock they were listening to, to some new day hip hop. Lil Wayne's *Lollipop* blasted from the stereo system. The guys were nice enough to clear the couches, lounge chairs and the coffee table out of the way. Giving us an immense amount of space to dance with.

The next four hours were like magic, watching money seemingly fall from the ceiling. I wasn't sure just how dirty these cops were, but their money was a clean tint of green, so it didn't matter to us. We danced until our legs were sore and then decided to enjoy some of their weed and alcohol with them. I noticed Jake snorting a line of cocaine, before taking a call in one of the bedrooms.

"So how long you girls been doing this for?" Asked the light-skinned officer, with Tracey on his lap. He had a firm grip on her ass, and I could tell she was rubbing her thigh against his dick, through his khaki shorts.

"I've been doing this since I was 16." Tracey responded. "Me and circumstance kinda dragged my sister into it." We laughed.

"For real. But it's fun, being able to party every night and making money doing it." I added.

"Hey, Li!" Officer Jacob called from behind me suddenly. I turned around to see him standing between the black double sliding French doors. His button up was buttoned down, exposing his strong chest, showcasing his V-Line. "Can we talk for a second?" He asked. I looked over at Tracey. She smiled, nodding and nudging me to go.

"Sure." I said, standing, walking over to him. The room was dark once he slid the door closed. As I felt his arm around my waist, and his lips on the back of my neck, I felt a moistening in my panties as slid his finger into me. "Mmm, you're getting married tomorrow." I moaned, unable to stop him.

"I'm not married, *yet*." He bent me over the bed, yanking down my shorts, and my panties in one swoop, I kicked them off. He dropped to his knees, eating me out from behind, purposely slipping up to my asshole. "Ooh, yes." I moaned, riding his face, before he flipped me over onto my back, eating me like his last meal. "Fuck." I whispered loudly. Trying not to scream. "Goddamn, that shit feel so fucking good." I moaned, running my finger through my hair as he gripped my thighs, locking me onto him. "Aaaahhhh!" I screamed out cumming into his mouth again. I couldn't hold back. He then stood, kissing me all over my neck. I could feel my juice in his beard against my jaw. "Ooooohhhh!!" I moaned as he slowly slid his dick into me. "Fuck."

"You like that?"

"Yes." I whispered as he sped up. He exposed my breasts, sucking on them as he beat my box in, fucking another three orgasms out of me.

"Aahh, shit!" He moaned, pulling out of me and stroking his dick until busting a large nut on my inner thigh, only inches from my kitty. I laid back, elated.

Suddenly a wave of guilt flooded over me, followed by that same nausea from earlier. I ran into the bathroom, throwing up before I embarrassed myself in front of him. Once done, I rinsed my mouth and headed back into the room, wondering what the fuck was going on with me.

"Damn, I've never gotten that reaction before." He said, chuckling. He sat in the edge of the bed, wearing nothing but his calf-high tube socks.

"It's not you. I guess I'm just not really feeling good today." I said, forcing a chuckle.

"You ain't pregnant is you?" He asked, jokingly.

"No, no, no." I said as I jumped back into my shorts. "Birth control." I headed back to the suite's living room. Tracey was coming out of the other bedroom. She looked pissed as she snatched on her coat.

"Girl, let's go." She said in a huff, once laying eyes on me.

"What happened?"

"He tried to put his big ass dick in my ass." She said, grabbing the two envelopes off of the fireplace, filled with our money. I laughed my ass off as we left and headed back downstairs to our room. We took turns showering, then rolled a couple blunts as we sat on our beds, counting the cash making sure it was all there. We made $4,800 each.

"I want to get into music." Tracey said, as we lay on our beds, smoking our blunts relaxing. Looking up at the ceiling. The thought of me being pregnant wouldn't leave me. It made a few things add up. Like wanting to suddenly eat chocolate ice cream, when I hated it, vehemently. Or throwing up everything I ate. She snapped me out of my train of thought. I welcomed the distraction.

"What makes you want to get into music?" I asked sitting up to face her, she did the same.

"My poems I've been writing. I can rap em over a beat, you know?" I had an idea and grabbed my phone off of the nightstand, pulling up the YouTube instrumental to NAS *Hate Me Now.*

Hate me now or love me. Can't put anyone above me. Running shit like these Nikes, ain't none of you bitches like me.

She rapped. I was excited, hearing her rap a couple bars. I then threw on the instrumental to Bobby Valentino's *Slow Down.*

"Ooh, bitch, okay." She said, taking a pull of her blunt. She sat up all the way.

I feel your energy. Your chemistry's so real to me. Really dig your pedigree really hope that you're feeling me. I'm down, for you baby whenever you need me say it. No, I'll never come later. I'm real, all these other bitches faker. I don't know, something like that.

"Bitch, yes!" I said excitedly. She reminding me that through all of this bullshit, I'd forgotten my own dreams of being on the big screen. My stomach started turning again.

"Fuck." I whispered, running to the bathroom to throw up, but nothing came up. After a couple hard heaves, still nothing.

"Damn, bitch you okay?" She asked coming into the bathroom. "Too much drank?" She asked.

"I didn't even drink that much." I said standing, washing my mouth out.

"No..."

"What?" I asked, walking to the bed. She followed and sat down next to me.

"Bitch, you pregnant." She said after a few moments of silence.

"Don't say that." I said, forcing a chuckle, nudging her shoulder. "I'm on birth control."

"Bitch, so was I when I had Casey. When was your last period?" She asked. I thought back as I watched her go over to her bed and get underneath her covers.

I looked at the clock. "Fuck." I said, realizing it was almost three in the morning. I got underneath my covers. "I think it was right before my birthday. I remember being happy that I could fuck again." I responded, staring up at the ceiling. "But, I'm on birth control. It must be the stress."

"Mmmm. I don't know." She said, shutting off her lamp. I did the same and rolled over, looking out of the window. I closed my eyes, falling asleep to the air conditioner. I couldn't shake thinking, "What if I am pregnant?"

"Mommy!" I heard a little girl singing, laughing. I walked through the incredible living room, with high ceilings attached to marble pillars with gold base molding. The cold of the marble floors was none of my concern due to being heated. I turned around and noticed I was being followed by the most beautiful little girl I've ever seen. Her eyes were light brown, and she had long curly locks. "Mommy!" She laughed, as I bent down to pick her up. I poked at her chest, tickling her sides to see her gorgeous smile.

"Liyah." I heard a male voice behind me. I swirled around to face him and woke up to Tracey.

"Liyah, bitch wake up." She said, standing over me. Realizing my eyes were awake, she tossed some boxes onto my bed. I looked down, seeing a bunch of pregnancy tests. "Take these. Then, get dressed. It's almost 11 and we check out in an hour." She said walking towards the bag on her bed. She was pretty much almost done getting dressed and was currently working on her make up. All she had to do now was her hair.

"Why didn't you get me up sooner." I said, sitting up in bed, looking through my eye lashes. The room was bright, maybe too bright. I followed her into the bathroom and started the shower.

"Aye, nah. Take that test real quick." She said, in the midst of applying her eye shadow.

"Why you want me to take this so bad?" I asked chuckling, holding up the test.

"Because, my daughter needs a play mate. And if you have a little girl, too…awww." She said, melting. I smiled, holding back laughter. "I'm ready to be an aunt. You know Kareena and Jovonnie ain't having no kids."

"Fine, bitch, I'll take the test. Get out the bathroom." I said, pushing her out and closing the door. I sat on the toilet, anxiously peeing on the stick. I reframed from chewing on my manicure as I waited. After five minutes, which actually felt like years, my cellphone alarm rang. Tracey came bursting into the bathroom.

"What it say? What it say? What it say?" She asked, jumping up and down. I put the test against the box, so that I could figure out how to read this thing. "Oh, God." I sighed, walking over to the tub and sitting on the edge. I could barely bring myself to say the words out loud, so I just handed her the box and the stick.

"Oh, my God. Bitch, you're fucking pregnant!" She said excitedly, wrapping her arms around me, hugging me. I felt like my life had just gotten that much harder. I placed my face into my hands, elbows anchored into my knees, and sobbed as I thought hard about what pill I could have missed. I took my birth control faithfully. What happened? Tracey sat down next to me. She hugged me as I cried into her shoulder. I felt like my life was officially over. I can't dance with no fucking baby on my hip. "It's okay, boo. And then again, those things could be wrong."

"Not at no damn 99.99%." I said, forcing a chuckle through my tears. She agreed, shrugging her shoulders and nodding her head.

"Think about this, birth control has the same success percentage." She chuckled, but I was no longer in the mood to joke. I just wanted to go home and sleep. "You're going to be okay. You got me and Kareena, and Monica, *when she comes out.*" She chuckled.

"On top of all of this other shit? I don't know."

"Come on. Clean your face and take another test. Let's get home." She said standing, leaving the bathroom, shutting the door behind her. I stood, staring at the test, shaking myself out of it after a few short moments. I took Tracey's advice, and pissed on another 3 tests. They were all positive. I started the shower and shed a few more light tears, before getting out and dressed. I rinsed off the tests and returned them to their caps, tossing them into my bag as a reminder to make myself a doctor's appointment. Soon.

*******************👑THE NIGHT BEFORE👑*******************

Kareena had just gotten off of her 6th overtime shift this week at the Walmart, located on Davis Street, in East Oakland. The store closed at midnight, but she was frequently unable to leave before 2. She'd just punched out, stuffing her blue vest into her over-sized leather purse, excited to go home and relax with her boyfriend, Jovonnie.

"Aye! Kareena!" She heard a loud male voice from behind her, before she could slide the key into her car door. She spun around nervous, then relaxed, recognizing a familiar face. She was no longer startled, but still confused.

"Hey, what's up? What's going on? Is Tracey ok-."

PEW! PEW! PEW! PEW!

Four bullets ripped through her thin, purple BAPE hoodie, and into her chest. All shots aimed at her heart. The pistol was silenced, concealing Kareena's murderer and his escape.

*****************************👑TODAY👑******************************

We made it to Tracey's house around 1:30. Tracey's mom, Yvette was walking up the steps to the porch. Her head hung low, as she held onto the banister railing for support. She looked broken down as she turned her attention to the truck as I pulled into the driveway, behind her white Audi.

"Hey, ma." Tracey said, as we walked along the fence, to the gate. Her eyes were red and puffy, like she'd been crying. "Mom, what's wrong?" She asked, smiling. Her mom rushed over to her, hugging her.

"Have you talked to your sister?" She asked.

"No, why? Is she okay?" Tracey asked, worried, pulling back to see her mother's face.

She began telling us that Kareena's coworker, coincidentally named Corina, came outside, ending her shift just minutes after Kareena. She noticed her car was in the parking lot but, Kareena was nowhere to be found. All she found, was her purse, wallet and keys laying on the ground near the driver's door. The police called Yvette, getting her number from Kareena's application. She's still listed as the emergency contact.

"Something's wrong. I can feel it." Yvette said, breaking down.

Me and Tracey looked at each other, then back at Yvette. She looked like she could barely hold it together. My heart broke for her, wondering where the fuck Kareena could possibly be.

"It's alright, mom." She said hugging her. "We'll find her."

Just then Yvette's phone began to ring in her long-strapped purse. She looked at the screen, answering the call, placing it on speaker. "Hello?" She answered.

"Hello? Mrs. West? This is Sergeant Henry, with the Oakland Police Department. We believe we've found Kareena. Would you mind coming down to the precinct, at your soonest convenience. We'd like to speak in person." The three of us could tell by the tone in his voice, that he had no good news to share. The three of us jumped right back into my truck, and sped Downtown. The station was only about 10 minutes away, with no traffic. I followed behind Tracey and Yvette, as they entered the police station, walking up to the reception desk. A tall, heavy-set black guy came out from the hallway next to the desk. He wore a cheap black suit, and was talking to one of the police officers.

"Sarge." Said the desk clerk. He looked over at us and started walking in our direction.

"Are you, Mrs. West?" He asked, extending his hand.

"Yes." Yvette responded, shaking his hand. "Where's my daughter?"

"I want to first offer my condolences. We found-"

"What?! No!! What are you saying? What happened?!!" Yvette sobbed, breaking down. Tracey rushed over, hugging her to keep from falling to the cold, grungy tile floor below.

"What happened to my sister?" Tracey asked, eyes full of tears. I helped her assist Yvette, with sitting down in one of the hard, blue plastic chairs.

"My officers found her in her own trunk...shot to death."

"No!!" Yvette screamed out in pain as she fell to the linoleum. I cried.

"Take your time. I'll escort you back to identify the body."

"No, take me to her." Yvette said, standing to her feet.

"Mama, are you-"

"Take me to my baby, please." She pleaded, ignoring Tracey.

"You got it. Follow me, please." Said Sergeant Henry. We followed him down the long hallway, then made a right, down another hall, into the morgue. I began having flashbacks of coming down here to identify my mother's body. He led us to a room that looked identical to the one I was in just a few months ago. Yvette took a seat. The shades on the other side, shot up. The coroner standing by the metal slab, removed the blanket from Kareena's face. There was a large collective gasp. I think we all knew it was her, before they drew the blanket. But we wished, hoped even, that it was someone else under there. But, it wasn't, she was gone. Laying on that steel table. I began to wonder, if like Johnny, was Kareena a casualty of war? She had nothing to do with *anything* that my family did. My heart broke with each sob and sniffle I heard from

Tracey and her mother. "Is this my fault? Were those bullets meant for me?" I thought to myself, crying.

"I'm so sorry, guys." I cried, hugging them. We cried harder as the shades came back down, moments later, covering the view of Kareena's body. I couldn't believe she was really gone. The three of us were always really close. She was like a sister to me, as well. We were the same age, her birthday just a few weeks before mine. I missed her already. I couldn't imagine how she was feeling. I wouldn't know how to accept one of my little brother's dying. Especially in such a violent way.

"I got it. Can you just get us home please?" Tracey asked after a few minutes. I tried to help her pick Yvette up out of the chair, but she coldly pushed my hand away.

The ride back to Tracey's was extremely sad and awkward. Her and her mother sat in the back seat, no doubt to console each other. We all got out of the truck, prepared to go into the house.

"Hey, ma. I'll meet you in the house, okay?" Said Tracey. Yvette walked up the steps to get into the house. "We got a problem, sis." Said Tracey as soon as her front door slammed shut.

"What you mean?" I asked, facing her. She was staring me up and down, face full of hurt, pain and confusion.

"I mean, we have a problem!" She exclaimed, pointing between the two of us. I never expected, in a hundred years, what happened next, to ever happen. "Fight me." She said, walking up to me, pushing me against the back of my truck, tears streaming down her face. I could feel Tracey was using me as an outlet for her emotions. Though I couldn't help but feel this was somehow my fault. I decided to remove myself from the situation. I walked back around my truck to the driver's side and opened the door to get in. But before I could lift my right foot to enter, Tracey slammed the door shut, narrowly missing my fingers. She then pushed me again, against the car. The next thing I knew, she swung on me. I grabbed my cheek, resisting the urge to punch her back.

"Fight me, bitch." She yelled, almost sobbing. I hurt for her. Shakenly, I climbed into the driver's seat. I started the engine and sped off towards my house. It's time to find Liam and handle this shit, once and for all.

I pulled into my driveway, unable to shake off what had just took place. I rested my head down on the steering wheel, sobbing. I cried until my face felt puffy and my head began to feel full of pressure. I was finally able to pull myself together and head into the house, suddenly feeling an strange sense of loneliness.

"Khi'?! Malik?! Ya'll in here?" I yelled, like the house was even a fraction of the one we grew up in. I felt myself beginning to panic, calling Malakhi. He answered on the second ring.

"Hey where ya'll at?" I asked, before he could even say hello.

"I...I...I'm at my girl's house. You aight, bruh? You sound a little –"

"I need you guys to get here. *Now*." I said, hanging up to call Malik. He answered and told me he was only around the corner, headed home, which eased my mind. Sean was busy at work and wouldn't be by until later.

I flopped down on the couch, thinking about Kareena and Tracey. I couldn't believe that bitch actually *punched* me. I chuckled a little through my tears, but I wasn't angry, I understood how she felt. I would be the *same* way if something happened to Malik or Malakhi. I just couldn't believe that happened to her. She was one of the sweetest girls anyone's known. To be gunned down and stuffed into her own trunk was just sickening.

I got up and decided to smoke another blunt and take a few shots of Jose Cuervo. It was only about 3:30 in the afternoon, but I didn't give a fuck.

I went into the kitchen and grabbed a glass, after lighting my freshly-rolled blunt. I poured myself a glass then went back into the living room. I stared at the black tv screen, just looking at my reflection. The Tequila had definitely begun to take a hold of me, and I was his willing participant. I wasn't sure how long I'd sat there, staring at myself. But after a few moments, I thought I seen my mom, sitting next to me. I blinked a few times, and there was nothing there. I shook my head in disbelief at myself, looking at the half-empty bottle. I gripped the neck and took another swig.

My head shot to the door as Malik and Malakhi walked into the house.

"Hey, sis." Malakhi said, sitting on the couch, to the right of me. I moved my feet off of the couch, allowing him to sit.

"Yeah, what's wrong? You look stressed." Malik added.

Forcing a chuckle, trying not to start bawling again, I said, "Shit, I am." I could see my vision getting blurry, at the sound of my quaking voice. "Kareena's dead."

"What?? *Kareena*?" Malakhi asked. I nodded my head up and down. Putting my face into my palm after taking a drag of my blunt.

"Fuck. I'm sorry, sis." Malik said, sitting on the couch to the left of me. They both wrapped their arms around me, hugging me. I sobbed harder. "What happened? How did she die?"

"She was shot and thrown into her trunk." I responded.

"Jesus. What the fuck...what was she into? Who did it?" Malakhi asked.

"We don't know. Only thing we *do* know is that Tracey blames *me* for it." I said standing, smacking my teeth, dumping ash, from my blunt onto the carpet. I saw them look at it, then at each other. "My best guess is that it's the dude that set up daddy up."

"What are we going to do?" Malik asked. "Why did he go after her and not after us?"

"I don't know. We need guns. At least, until I figure out a way to get to Liam. We're sitting ducks." I said, turning to face them. I felt like shit, not being able to give them more detailed answers and solutions.

"What if he's going after everyone we know, just to get back at dad?" Malakhi asked.

"Unless we find him first." Malik added. I nodded, feeling defeated. Nowhere to start, nowhere to go or run.

I let them finish off the rest of the blunt I was smoking before I headed into my room. I peeked through the blinds, fearing a militia on my front lawn. Just my neighbor Grace, walking her dog. She was a sweet old lady, with a short pixie cut. She was short and skinny, really petite, walking around a large German Shephard.

The neighborhood was completely different from where I grew up. Littered streets, unkempt and ungated lawns. It just felt different. Definitely not as safe as I'm used to.

I plopped down on my bed and plugged my phone up into the socket next to me. I reached into my purse, grabbing the pregnancy test, staring at it blankly for a few moments, rubbing my stomach at the same time.

I immediately picked up my phone, thinking maybe it wasn't a good idea for daddy to be out of jail just yet. I called Daren.

"Hey, Liyah. Are you okay?" He answered.

"I'm good. Did you pass along the evidence yet?" I asked. Pretty sure that came off as rushing, I tried to smoothen it up a bit. "I was wondering, if you could hold off for a little while?"

"Oh! Really? Why? That means he'll be in jail for something he didn't do. I can't do that."

"Just give me some time." I said sitting up and throwing my legs over the edge of the bed. "It's been this long. I just want to find Liam so that he doesn't get out and end up murdered. Someone killed one of my best friends last night, at her fucking job."

"Wait, wait, wait. Liyah, calm down." He said, the line went silent for a little bit. "Look, the best I can do is a month. Then, I'm turning this evidence in. Let your father know what's going on. And you stay safe, okay? I could be disbarred for this."

"Thank you! Thank you, so much." I said, laying back down. "Now, I just need help with one more thing."

"What's that?"

"I need help finding Liam."

"Wait, that's what the police is for. Are you asking me to sit on evidence, so you can play vigilante? Nah, little girl."

"Please. I'm asking you this, so my father can have a safe homecoming. I can get $10,000 more, in cash for you."

"Make it $15,000 and we can work something out." He said, hanging up the line. I then called the Planned Parenthood, over at Eastmont to schedule an appointment for a pregnancy test. Nearest one I was able to get, was about a week out. I rolled over, onto my back, staring at the ceiling again, thinking about Tracey. I wanted so badly to call her and be there for her, but I knew she needed her space. I felt horrible, not knowing what to do. Reaching into the drawer of my nightstand, I grabbed my weed and another Dutch, rolling another blunt. After lighting it, I laid back down smoking, trying not to break.

"Stay strong, Liyah." I said to myself, rubbing my stomach.

I'm not sure what it was that I was dreaming about, but I awoke to Sean kissing me. The room was dark, with the exception of the TV. He must've gotten bored and started watching it. All I could see was the outline of his face, illuminated by the 60" flat screen.

"Hey, babe." I said, groggily stretching.

"Hey, beautiful." He said, caressing my cheek and my jaw line. "What's *this*?" He asked, holding up the pregnancy test box. My stomach dropped into my ass. How could I possibly be dumb enough to fall asleep without putting the test away.

"Uhmm...." I said, sitting up, against the pillows, unable to speak, becoming super nervous. His smile grew wide and bright as the sun.

"Are you?" He asked, eyes full of hope. He jumped on me, wrapping his arms around me, kissing all over my face.

"I think so." I said laughing. "I have an appointment next week."

"I'm going to be a daddy?!" He said excitedly, grinning from ear to ear. "I love you baby." He said, kissing me again.

"I love you, too." I replied, kissing him on those pillow-soft lips. This relationship was moving fast. Even being 19 I knew that. But, it felt so right that I never had a reason to question it...even when I should have.

He turned and sat on the edge of his bed. After a moment, I could smell the raw weed in the air.

"Babe, I got to tell you something." I said, thinking about Tracey and Kareena.

"What's up, boo?" He said turning around, sealing the blunt.

"Liam's people had Kareena killed."

"Tracey sister, right?" He asked, eyes wide. He put the blunt down on the nightstand and hugged me. "I'm sorry, baby. Are you okay?"

"I don't know. I'm worried about Tracey."

"Let me go make you some food."

"Thank you."

"Let me call my dad, too." He said, grabbing the blunt, and leaving the room. It suddenly occurred to me that I've never even met his parents, or even talked to them. I've never even been to his house, after all of this time. I don't even know where he lives. I shook the thought and decided to call Tracey. I wanted her to know that I was still here for her. Even if she declines the call, at least I know I tried. She answered before the first ring could finish on my end.

"Hi, sis." She answered sobbing. "Can you come to the door please?"

"What? My front door?" I asked, a little confused.

"Babe!" I heard Sean yell, from the front room and in her background.

"What the fuck?" I whispered to myself, scooting to the end of the bed. I walked around the corner, passed the unused dining room table, and into the living room. My front door was wide open, two men in suits, standing in my living room, both with a gun to Tracey and Sean's heads. She looked terrified and so was I.

"Liyah, don't trust-"

BAH!!

"Nooooo!" I screamed, at the top of my lungs, dropping to my knees. The man behind Tracey pulled the trigger. She died instantly, falling to the floor.

"Man, you ain't got to do this." Sean said. "She's pregnant."

"So what?" The man asked. "That's supposed to change anything?" I suddenly felt a presence behind me, then a sharp pain in the back of my head. I collapsed to the floor.

"Dude what the fuck you hit her for?! I told you she was fucking pregnant." I heard Sean yelling out. My vision was blurry in the dark room, but I saw him push one of the suited gunmen. My head throbbed, as I tried to stay awake. I felt my body wanting to shut down. So, I let it.

CHAPTER 12

M y eyes opened slowly, but everything around me was still out of focus. All I could hear were distant voices and a metallic clinking in rhythm. I blinked a few times, trying to get my vision to finally focus. I was in a large airplane hangar, wrists and ankles roped to a steel chair. I noticed on the wall to my right, were towers of wooden crates, stacked at least the height of 3 fully grown men. On the wall to my left were rows of windows, allowing me to see a portion of the airport outside. It was pitch black, with the exception of the lights, that hung from the roofs of the neighboring hangars. I seen a shadow pass by the window.

"Hey! Help!! Help!!" I screamed, struggling to shake the ropes loose. My wrists hurt a lot more than I thought. "Help me, please!!" I screamed, until the back of my throat got a little sore. I then heard a large, steel door slam shut. The sound came right from behind me, causing me to jump. My heart raced, beating out of my chest as the heavy footsteps grew closer.

"*Shut* the fuck up!" A man yelled, causing me to jump again, this time with tears streaming down my face.

"Please, don't do this. Don't kill me, please." I begged. He came around to the front of me, where I could see him.

"*Please, no. Please don't do this.*" He said, in a high pitched tone, mocking me. "Please, you do not have a single clue how many times I've heard that exact same sentence. What's next? You offer me some pussy? Is that it?" He said standing directly in front of me. He was every bit as menacing as he was in the pictures, almost 15 years ago. He was just bald now, face a little wrinkly. His voice sounded horrifically different from the video tape, but a lot can change in that amount of time. He was dressed in a pair of black slacks, a black YSL button down shirt, a pair of gold and black Louboutin loafers and a large brown mink coat. "You better hope I don't put a dick in your mouth, and a bullet in your fuckin brain." He said, walking back around behind me. He yanked my hair, forcing my head back, then jammed a large gun down my throat. The muzzle clicked as it hit my back tooth. I cried in pain as the gun pressed against the inside of my throat. I gagged, which only made it worse. The more I gagged the harder he pushed. He removed the gun, making me throw up all over my shoes and the ground in front of me. I began to taste blood. I spit out. He came back around to my front, squatting and laughing right in my face. I became angry and spit blood into his. I watched as his face went from a scary smile, to an evil grimace. He stood up, tossed his right hand over his shoulder and swung it back into my face.

"Ahh!" I screamed out in pain, spitting more blood onto the floor, to the left of me. He growled looking at me, blood splattered over his face. He grabbed my chin, squeezing my checks until they pressed hard against my back teeth. I had to open my jaw to keep it from hurting. He jammed the gun back into my mouth.

"I should blow your fucking brains out." He said, slowly moving the gun in and out of my mouth. I started gagging again.

"Please, I'm pregnant!" I said muffled. He stepped back.

"What?" He asked, looking at me with his head tilted to his left. "What the fuck did you just say to me, bitch?!"

"I said," holding back tears, "that I'm pregnant. I'm pregnant!" I screamed aloud, beginning to sob. I couldn't help but feel defeated. I just hoped my brothers made it out of that house before Liam's goons showed up.

*********************👑URBAN QUEEN👑*********************

"Babe!" Sean yelled, jarring Malik from his sleep. He'd passed out, fully clothed, after he and his brother smoked the blunt Liyah let them kill. He noticed Malakhi standing in the doorway.

"What the "

"Shh!" Malakhi said, finger to his lips. He was also still dressed from earlier in the day. He was nervous, feeling how thick the atmosphere was. He saw his direct path from their bedroom door, to the guest bathroom window.

BAH!!

"Nooooo!!" They heard Liyah scream.

"We have to go." Malakhi said. He and Malik darted down the hallway, passed the living room, into the bathroom. Malik closed and locked the door behind them, while Malakhi kicked the screen off of the window.

BANG BANG BANG BANG

"Let's go." Khi whispered loudly, he was already halfway out of the window ready to drop to the high, dead grass below.

"What about, Liyah?" Asked Malik, following Malakhi out of the window. "We can't just fucking leave her." Malik said. They were now in the unkempt backyard.

"We have to. We can't help her if we're-"

CRASH!!!!

They looked back through the window, two large men had literally broken the door down and immediately locked their eyes on them. "dead." He continued. "Come on, lets go." He said grabbing Malik's arm. Malik didn't want to leave Liyah, though he knew, there was nothing they could do if Liam decided he didn't need them. They jumped over their neighbor's wooden fence, just inches away from a Pitbull, asleep in the backyard. Quickly getting out of dodge, before the dog decided to fully awake. They looked back and realized no one was chasing them, so they slowed down to catch their breath, in a space between two houses. Malik leaned against an old, brown Cadillac, that hadn't moved in almost a decade. Just then, a line of black SUVs, just like the ones parked in front of their house, drove passed them. Scared, they ducked behind the old car, trying not to be spotted.

But they were too late, hearing an almost deafening screeching nose. The twins looked at each other, then back at the street, seeing one of the SUVs do an immediate reverse, then stop directly in front of them. Two men in expensive black suits, jumped out of the right side of the vehicle, AMP-69s ready to shoot.

They took off in a full sprint, back towards the backyard, dodging hellfire as they jumped over a wooden fence into another backyard. They kept running, not stopping until they made it to International Blvd. The warm mid-July night air, taking a toll on them.

"Come on, bruh. We gotta get to Clarence house." Malakhi said, seeing the bus, just make it to the stop, right out front of the KFC. The street was busy, everyone had someplace to go this Friday night. Malik wished he was someone different for that moment. He looked at everyone, from the homeless to the unbothered and wished he was *anyone* else but himself. He found himself secretly angry with everyone, because they didn't have the problems he had. He knew that no one around him had a drug dealing father with people trying to murder him and the people he loved. He was *jealous*. A foreign concept to a child who has always had everything.

They ran to the bus as fast as possible, just barely making it on. Only one thing, they had no money on them. The bus was packed, barely enough room to stand. Ready to finish his routes and head home, the driver gave them a nod, waving them on back. Malik froze in fear, seeing the group of SUVs shoot right passed them in the opposite direction, as the bus passed by the street they lived on. He took a sigh of relief.

Malakhi and Malik stepped off of the bus across the street from a Walgreens, on the corner of Broadway and 14th street. They had to walk the rest of the way to get Clarence's house.

"We should have someone call the police." Malik said, as they crossed onto the other side of the street.

"They wouldn't get here fast enough. We just go to the West and we should be-"

"What? Why'd you stop?" Malik asked. Malakhi followed his gaze, to a line of black trucks. "Fuck. Run!" He yelled. They made a mad dash to their left just as SUV headlights seemed to turn on simultaneously. They heard screams from around them as the SUVs did little to avoid hitting innocent bystanders, chasing them through Oakland's City Center. "Malik, come on!" Malakhi yelled, noticing his brother was starting to fall behind. Gunshots started up again.

"No!!" A woman screamed, realizing her young daughter was hit by a stray bullet. The scene was horrific. But, they managed to lose the crusade once making it to Clay street. 4 solid poles blocked traffic… in or out.

They turned the corner, sprinting at full speed down 12th street, running passed Jefferson and then Martin Luther King Jr. Way.

"We-we gotta stop for a minute." Malik said, breathing heavy, hands on his knees. He struggled to find his breath.

"We can't, bruh. We're almost there. Come on. We gotta go." Malakhi responded, trying to help his brother up. His years playing football were paying off. Malik was never much for cardio, he was more into the weights. Suddenly a barrage of machine-gun fire rang out from behind them. Luckily, they were able to duck behind the building next to them, avoiding fire. "Fuck!!!!!" He screamed. "Let's go!" He yelled, grabbing Malik's arm. They crossed Clay street, stopping at a fence that blocked pedestrians from freeway traffic. Finding a hole in the gate, Malakhi went through first.

"Hurry up! They're coming." Malik said, looking back and seeing three large dudes, all holding rifles. They made it to the corner, looking around for them.

"There!" One of them shouted, pointing to them. Malik ran through the hole, just as they began to shoot at them. The two made it to the edge of the freeway, cars zooming by them at 80-100 miles per hour. Underneath the over-pass on the shoulder of the freeway, they waited for the best time to cross, more afraid than they have ever been in their short lives.

The opportunity for them to cross came and they took it. Climbing over the center-divide. The machine gun bullets followed them, as they climbed up the embankment on the other side. They climbed the fence, making it to Brush St. After verifying there wasn't another SUV on the other side, they hid behind a parked car. Malakhi, nor Malik could run any further, without a breath. They rested against the car's doors.

"Ah!" He heard Malik exhale. He turned to his left, seeing his brother had collapsed to the pavement, rolling over onto his back.

"Yo! Yo! Are you okay?" He asked, rushing to his side. Malik coughed, spitting up blood. Malakhi sat him up and rested his head against the car. "Where? Where are you hit?" Malik just continued to cough. He pointed towards his side. Malakhi realized he was shot in his back. There was no exit wound, so the bullet had to have been lodged into his left lung. He could see the fear, flooding Malik's eyes. He had no idea what to do. "Fuck! Fuck! Fuck! Fuck! Fuck!" He exclaimed, hands pressed against his clammy forehead as Malik drew his last breath. He couldn't take his eyes off of him, scooting into the brick wall of someone's fence, frozen.

"Hey! What the fucks going on?!" His head shot left. There was an older man, maybe late 40s, coming down the street with his dog. Not knowing what else to do, he ran as hard he could the rest of the way to Clarence, hearing the sounds of gunshots as he got closer.

Malakhi was only a block away from West Oakland BART station. Able to see Clarence's house, clearly from the station's parking lot. There was a group of SUVs, parked outside the front of the house. The gang just finished shooting it up, then suddenly, the living room became engulfed in flames. He watched, eyes full of anger as the fire quickly took over the rest of the house. They all hopped into their SUVs and drove off. Malakhi stayed hidden behind a car, as to not be seen.

"Hey!!" He screamed out in fear, feeling a strong hand grab him by his upper arm. He swung frantically, trying to hit whomever it was. It took Clarence and Lamarr a moment to get Malakhi to realize it was just them.

"It's okay, man. It's just us. It's just us." Clarence said, grabbing him trying to help him calm down. He was finally able to settle.

"I…I shouldn't have left her." Was all that he could say, over and over again, sobbing uncontrollably. His heart felt like a black hole that continued to grow with every tear he cried. After a few moments, he was finally able to pull himself together and tell them about his night.

**********************👑URBAN QUEEN***********************

I sat in the cold, steel chair, staring at the lonely walls of the airplane hangar. I tried my best to free myself, but every effort allowed the thin rope to dig farther into my wrists. Defeated, I dropped my head and sobbed, letting my body get heavy. I sat in that chair, crying, out of options. Body getting stiff from the lack of movement.

I suddenly heard the door creak open, then slam shut. I seen Sean walking up, around to face me. I eyed the .357 Magnum in his left hand.

"Oh, my God. Baby hurry up and undo these ropes!" I said anxiously, struggling, showing him my urgency to get out of this chair. I sat up straight, confident I was finally getting out of here. I could see the solemn look on his face, though he never once looked me in mine. He stood there, tears streaming down his face. "Baby, we got to go. Come on." I said, wondering why he still allowed me to sit in this chair. He turned and walked away, over to the wall and stood there, his left Timberland boot pressed firmly against the crate. He rested his head back, and looked up to the ceiling. Confusion barely explained my current emotion. "Sean, baby, what are you doing? We have to get out of here." I said again, tears still falling from my eyes.

"You aren't going anywhere. But, since you are pregnant with my grandchild, I'll let you live." Liam said, coming around to my field of view. I looked over at Sean, he stood there, silent, trying to hide his face from me.

"Excu- What?" I said, feeling like the ground had dropped from beneath me. "Your- He's your- What?" I couldn't get any words out. My thoughts were moving faster than my mouth could relay the messages. The room began to spin, though I knew I wasn't moving. I started feeling sick to my stomach, looking at the floor, trying to center myself. I found the strength to look up and between the two of them. My eyes paced between Liam and Sean, trying to find the similarities. It wasn't difficult. They shared a complexion, the same flat, wide nose and light green eyes. Sean looked like a younger version of his father. I had no idea how I didn't see this before.

"How about you two talk?" Liam said chuckling, which then turned into outright laughter, like Kevin Hart was hosting a standup right outside in the hall. The steel door slammed shut. My heartbeat was loud enough to cut through the strong, intense silence. Emotions cycled through me like bullets in a revolver; anger, fear, hurt, sadness, vengeance. I felt them all, one after the other, realizing Sean was not here to save me.

"I'm sorry." He whispered. I ignored him, tightly shutting my eyes, trying to convince myself this was all a dream. But the pain I felt, physically and emotionally, was all to real. "Baby, please-" He said. My eyes shot open when I heard his footsteps coming closer in my direction. "You got to believe me. I had no choice." My head cocked to the side in disbelief. He stopped walking once I spit at his feet.

"Just fucking kill me!" I said, full of hate. "What the fuck do you want from me?!" I cried.

"Baby, I'm trying to keep you alive!" He exclaimed. Suddenly, the hangar's door began to roll up, into the ceiling. "I need you to see that." I watched as a small, black jet stopped just in front of the hangar entrance. He turned and began walking towards the plane, just as the doors opened, causing the stairs to drop. Suddenly a female silhouette appeared at the entrance, and walked slowly down the steps. I couldn't see her face just yet, but I felt her looking directly through me.

"Hola, mami." Sean said, hugging her and kissing her on the cheek. They stepped into the light. I recognized her from the photographs. She wore an all black, slim fitting Alexander McQueen pants suit, with an all-white Vera Wang blouse, a white Pucci scarf, and a pair of white Jimmy Chu pumps. She wore her hair done up, in a bun.

"Hola, hijo. ¿Por qué no está muerta esta perra?" She asked. My father didn't speak too much Spanish, around me and my brothers, but I knew she wanted me dead.

"She's pregnant, mommy." He said.

"What?!" She said, slapping him so hard across his face, his bottom lip began to bleed. "Stupiiiiid!!!" She screamed, as loud as she could, fists bawled, ready to pound on him, but she restrained. "How dare you!! How dare you get this bitch pregnant?!!" She said, with a very thick Spanish accent. "You were supposed to trick her and bring her to me. I'm glad I finally sent my men to your house." She said, shooting an intense look towards me.

"Mom, I'm...I'm sorr-"

"Shut the fuck up!" She said, holding her hand up, to his face. She stared at me up and down, walking over towards me. "You cook and clean in Tijuana."

"Bitch, fuck you-" I said. She punched me in my temple, causing me to almost lose consciousness. A splitting headache began to form directly where the punch landed. I hung my head low, hoping *to* lose consciousness…this pain.

"Like I said…you cook for me. You clean for me. In Tijuana. Then, once the babies born, off with your head!" She yelled, followed by a cackle. "Bueno? Good."

"Bitch, if I wasn't tied up in this chair…" I responded. She walked back over to me, hitting me with a powerful left backhand.

"Really? What would you do?" She asked laughing.

"Untie me and find out, you fucking bitch." She began laughing even harder.

"Awww. She's so cute." She responded. Her face went emotionless, as she walked around behind me. I was ready for her to untie me, just so I could beat her ass. I felt the ropes around my wrist loosen then fall. The moment I went to fight, I suddenly saw her silk scarf going over my face, then tightening around my neck. If felt like she was trying to break it as hard as she was squeezing. I struggled to kick out of the makeshift noose, but my feet were still tied to the legs of the chair. I bawled my fist, unable to stop the pain of my lungs burning. I was dying. I sucked hard for any air possible, but it was futile. Nothing was making it away from her manly grip. Everything went silent, minus the deafening sound of my heart beating in my ears. I felt weaker and weaker with each passing moment. I closed my eyes as my toes and finger tips began to tingle. Like that feeling when you wake up in the middle of the night and one of your pinkies are numb. Except, it was all ten fingers and toes. I closed my eyes, feeling my life literally slip away from me.

"Mom, stop!" I could hear Sean yell. He sounded like he was on the other side of a football field. "Hey, hey, hey. Wake up. Breathe!" He yelled, somewhat closer to me. My eyes shot open and directly at him. I gasped for air, coughing as I tried to pull in as much as I could.

"Whatever." She scoffed, tossing her scarf at me. "Where's your father?" She said, turning and walking away. I heard the large door creak open, then slam shut behind her as she left. I began to finally catch the rhythm of my breaths. I began to bawl. Angry that I was so close to being finished. Done with everything in this life, but I'm still here.

"Are you okay?" Sean asked, holding me. I cried into his chest, grabbing onto his leather coat, keeping myself upright. I then realized who he was, and jumped back, crawling backwards trying to get away from him, quickly realizing that the chair was impeding my movement. He jumped up, sitting the chair upright.

"Hey! Calm the fuck down!" He ordered, before standing above me, yanking me up to my feet by my arms. He forced me back into the chair, tightly binding my wrists to the arms. "I love you." He said as he tied the rope.

"Why?" I whispered loudly, as loud as I could without my throat feeling like I swallowed a blade. The pain was almost enough to make me never want to speak again. After he was done he stood there, facing me, staring at me. I yanked away from his hand as he tried to caress my cheek.

"This is the best way." He said, squatting down, right in front of me. "You're not going to spit on me are you?" He forced a smile as he looked up at me, I could see the hurt in his face. He didn't really want to be doing this. I thought maybe I could use that to my advantage.

"Please just let me go. I'll forgive you. We can run away to the Bahamas, with our baby." I pleaded. He smiled. As quickly as his smile came, it went. "Please, baby. I love you, too. We can take our baby and go to...to the Bahamas, or Tahiti. Please baby. I just want to go home." Staring at me, I was starting to think he was considering it.

"I can't." He said after a few moments. "There's nowhere we could go they wouldn't find us. Might as well let, getting out of here, out of your head." He said, standing up. He grabbed my head, kissing me on the forehead, before exiting the area.

I heard the door open. SLAM!!

I hung my head low and sobbed, letting my tears fall to my jeans. My heart was heavy. I have no clue how I'm getting out of this.

***********************♛URBAN QUEEN♛***********************

Sean angrily threw the door shut, as he stepped out into the hallway. He leaned back against it, resting his head, trying to hold in tears. He did his best, but as soon as he opened his eyes, warm streams fell down his cheeks. He grabbed at his heart, wishing he could just rip it out and let Liyah step on it. His guilt had him wanting to put the .357 in his mouth, and swallow a bullet right there.

When his father, hired him for this job, she was nothing more than a pretty face and a paycheck. His job was to keep tabs on Liyah and the people she loved, make her fall for him, while he systematically took out everyone she loved. Then kill her slowly and send the proof to her father. He was never meant to fall in love, but he did. 6 months later, he began to feel the pressure from his parents after taking too long to get the job done, so he killed Kareena, thinking it would buy him more time. But, it was too late. Liam and Esmeralda had already lost their patience.

Sean grabbed his phone out of his blazer pocket, and sent a location pin to Liyah's phone, hoping her brothers survived to see it. It was the least he could do to try and save her. He quickly deleted the transmission, before heading up to his mother's office, up a flight of steel steps. He could see people in the office as he walked by the six, large windows, before making it through the door. He walked into the large office, trying to keep his attention off of the wall to his left, which gave a complete view of the hangar. Esmeralda's feet were kicked up onto her large Cherry wood desk, smoking a thick cigar. She had six of her goons, wearing black suits, standing behind her, in front of an old, 16th Century bookcase. They were there to exaggerate her strength. Liam sat on the couch, nearest the door. His fingers intertwined, hands resting under his chin. His eyes were closed, as the sounds of smooth jazz filled the room. They stared at him, pensively as the office door swung open, then closed again. One of her men came over to him, handing him a large, brown-leather briefcase, before he could step foot on the large, Fendi area rug.

"Well, well, well. Looks like our little cub, fell in love with the gazelle." She sang, smiling. He avoided her intense gaze by looking at the large shark tank that covered the entire wall, to his right.

"Wasn't that my job?" Sean asked, taking the case. The weight of the money tilted his body to the right a bit, but he quickly regained his balance. Esmeralda stood up. Her heels clicking against the bare hardwood floors as she made her way to the front of her desk.

"No, stupid. Your job was to isolate and assassinate. And you end up getting the bitch pregnant." She said, smiling, leaning against the desk. Sean, feeling embarrassed, shot his gaze over to the hangar. He looked down and seen Liyah sobbing. He hated how big his part in causing her pain was. "Don't worry about that little bitch. Take a vacation. Go to Cannes. I'll call you when the babies born." She said, waving for him to leave, while walking back around her desk, sitting in her black and gold throne seat.

"Mom, why don't we just let her-"

"Phillippe, listen to your mother, please. I'm not in the mood to make you bleed tonight." Liam said, looking up at Sean, directly in his eyes. Not wanting to take another one of his father's beat downs, he clenched his jaw, turning and leaving out of the office. He shut the door, finally able to breathe deep, unsure why. He shook off his nerves and headed to his car.

"Find him and kill him. Then bring my fucking money back." Esmeralda ordered. All but two of them ran after Sean, ready to let blood flow.

Once in the driver's seat of his black-on-black 2010 Maserati, Sean locked the doors and opened the briefcase. The aroma of cold hard cash quickly making its presence known. He shook his head, at the fact that Liyah's life was only worth $2.5 million. His phone began to ring in his slim Balmain jeans. He placed the money into his passengers seat, before pulling the phone out of his pocket. His heart sank seeing Liyah's face pop up on the caller ID.

"H-h-hello?" He answered nervously.

"Sean? This you?" It was Clarence. Sean recognized his voice immediately.

"Yeah, please tell me you're on your way. This jet got another 30 minutes before it's full."

"Bruh, what jet? Where the fuck is Tracey and Liyah, bruh?" He asked, scared and angry. He and Lamarr stood in Liyah's living room, while Malakhi sat in his room. He could still see Malik sitting on his bed, on the other side of the room, staring right back at him.

"Just get here before my parents take her to their villa in Tijuana." He said, hanging up the phone, and tossing it out of the window. He pushed the button to start the engine. Throwing the car into gear, he sped to get away from the airport.

Esmeralda watched him as she stood at the window of her office, arms folded. Her heart smiled when she noticed two of her SUVs racing after Sean, trying to catch up. Liam stood beside her, at the mini bar, fixing the two of them a drink.

"Think we went a little far with the hit?" He asked her, handing her a vodka-tonic.

"No. If he survives, he may be stronger. If he dies, then good riddance." She said taking a sip out of her glass. "He betrayed us. He's no son of mine." She continued, watching her men almost catch up to Sean. Then, he did something that intrigued her, which not many people could do. He spun the car around, driving backwards, straight down the run way. He shot the driver of one of the SUVs, causing it to veer to the left, T-Boning the SUV next to it. Sean stopped, making sure there was no movement from within the two piles of mangled steel. Shifting the car into drive, he sped back towards Liyah.

"Get the girl!" Esmeralda yelled, shouting at her remaining two thugs.

**********************👑URBAN QUEEN👑**********************

My heart sank at the thought that this may be my last night on Earth. I sat in the steel chair, freezing. My body felt like I was being stabbed with a thousand pins. I wanted nothing more than to go home. The exhaustion I felt was foreign to me. I still found it hard to take a deep breath after Esmeralda's scarf.

I suddenly began hearing gunshots in the far distance, almost sounding like fireworks. I sat up with confidence. Finally, someone was here to save me. Then what sounded like screeching metal. I got nervous, hoping my saviors were still okay. Just then, that loud screeching sound of the metal door behind me, opened up. Two large, buff Samoans, both wearing ponytails and Georgio Armani suits walked before me. They stared me dead in the eyes, holding AR-15s, aimed at the floor. My stomach dropped, realizing this was it. Whoever was here to save me, was just a few minutes to late. I shut my eyes, hearing gunshots. Confused because I felt no pain. Opening my eyes, I saw one of the men was on the ground, right in front of me. A bloody hole directly between his eyes.

BAH!! BAH!! BAH!!

Someone was shooting at the second thug. He ducked behind me for cover and the bullets stopped. My body clenched up as the thug cut the ropes and lifted me into the air by my forearm, almost yanking it out of its socket. He was now using me as a human shield.

"Help!" I screamed out in pain as I noticed we were heading towards the jet. I tried to pull away from him, hearing the jet's engines roar. I suddenly felt a sharp pain in the back of my head, causing my body to go limp for a moment.

"Get the fuck up there." Esmeralda ordered, pushing me up the steps of the jet. "Sean, I'm taking your little puta with me, now!!" She sang loudly.

Once on the jet, Esmeralda forced me to the right, and onto a beige, leather bench, situated under a set of windows. The gunshots rangout again. I could hear them ricocheting off of the plane. I turned back to see Liam and the thug, turning to head back outside, leaving Esmeralda defenseless. I took my chance, jumping up fast as I could, swinging, like a wild animal. I connected a couple lefts and a rights, kicking her in her stomach. I smiled when she fell to the floor. She moved the hair from her face, exposing an evil grin. She wiped the blood off of her bottom lip and looked at her back hand, laughing.

"What the fuck is so funny, bitch?!" I spat full of hate, waiting for her old ass to try me when I'm not tied down. I decided to run up and start swinging again, suddenly feeling strong hands squeeze my arms to my sides. I struggled to get free as she stood, then slowly walked over.

"My turn now, puta." She punched me in my stomach, knocking all of the wide out of me. Being held made it impossible to double over or ease the pain in any way. I did my best to stay conscious. She then swung a left, then right hook.

"Aahhhh!!" I screamed out in pain, as she dug the heel of her shoe into my bare foot. I was then able to stand on my own feet, but no sooner than her thug released me, she came down on me with a heavy right hook, causing me to fall. Onto the table next to me, then onto the floor. I spit blood onto the plane's floor, struggling to my hands and knees.

"Get this shit in the air. This nigga got friends." I heard Liam yelling from behind me. I continued to cough, spitting up blood onto the floor.

"Lock her up, Bruno." Esmeralda ordered. Last thing I remembered was a heavy boot to top of my back, just below my neck.

Outside of the vessel, was what could have only been described as a war zone. Sean stayed until Clarence and Lamarr showed up with a crew of 8 guys. He knew exactly where his parents, and that jet were going. He thought if he fought against a fraction of his parents' army, a dangerous crew of 20, that he would have been able to almost save Liyah earlier, when he killed one of the two thugs that was in there with her. He hated that he used her as a shield.

"Draw their fire away from the plane. idiots!!" Esmeralda yelled into her gold iPhone. After knocking Liyah out, Bruno tossed her over his shoulder. He walked down the narrow aisle, passed the small bathroom, complete with a standing shower, sink and toilet. He opened the door to the small bedroom, tossing her onto the bed, slamming and locking the door behind them both.

Clarence and Lamarr's small crew, tried to shoot out the engines on the plane, but it was difficult while also defending themselves. They shot at the tires, windows…anything they thought would at least slow the plane.

"Bruh, hit *something*!" Clarence yelled out. He suddenly felt a burning, pressure in his upper right shoulder. He was thrown to the ground behind Sean and Lamarr. They turned around, helping him to his feet, before they all ducked back into the hangar. The plane had just started its descent down the runway. Clarence looked around, realizing the three of them, and 3 others were all that remained. The three of them remained hidden, behind a stack of wooden crates.

"Clarence, you alright, bruh?" Sean asked, trying to see where he was shot at.

"Get the fuck off me, nigga!" Clarence exclaimed, aiming his gun directly at Sean. Lamarr followed and did the same.

"Whoa! What the fuck, bruh?"

"Tell me why I shouldn't just shoot yo ass right fucking here?!" Clarence asked. With the help of Lamarr he slowly stood up, pain emanating from his arm. He was no stranger to the feeling of a fresh bullet, permeating his skin.

"I'll give you four." Sean said, hands up, nodding to the four men that was heading in their direction. They were coming into the hangar, just as the three of them snuck through that large, steel red door. "Follow me, I can take you to the garage. Get ya'll a car." Sean continued as they ran down the hall. Lamarr assisting Clarence up, helping him run. They turned down a short corner, entering the garage through a slim metal door. "Come on, one of my cars is over here."

"Ours is too, nigga. We ain't stupid."

"Clarence, bruh, look-"

"Don't say my mothafuckin name, nigga!" Clarence yelled, grabbing Sean by the collar and pushing him up against the concrete wall. Lamarr had his gun aimed at Sean's head, daring him to make a move. "You never answered my fuckin question. Why shouldn't I just shoot yo ass?"

"Because, I'm the only one that knows where that plane is going."

"He's right, bruh. Let's just get them back and see what they wanna do." Clarence looked at him, knowing he was right, but hating it all the same. He looked back towards Sean, pressing his pistol deeper into his neck. Sean wanted so badly to tell him that Tracey wasn't on that plane, that his parents' men had already put a bullet in her head. But he held off, knowing that Clarence would likely just leave and not help him save Liyah. He needed him.

"Fuck!" Clarence exclaimed, forcing himself to lower his weapon. Sean began straightening his clothes, when Clarence hit him with a right hook, as hard as he could, almost knocking him out. He ignored the fact that he was shot, immediately feeling the pain afterwards. "That's for Liyah. When you get up, meet us at her house." He ordered, kneeling down next to him. "Fucking bitch." He said standing.

"Sit up, lil man." Clarence said as he and Lamarr made it back to his candy-painted Camaro. Malakhi was laying in the back seat, under a dark wool blanket.

"Did you get her?" He asked, hopeful, looking around for his big sister. All he saw was Clarence and Lamarr.

"Not yet. But we *will*." Clarence turned around, trying not to aggravate his arm more than necessary. "We're going to need your help if we are." Clarence said, holding up his pistol. Malakhi looked at him, directly in his eyes.

CHAPTER 13

I woke up feeling dazed and confused. My head throbbed, but my lower parts ached more. The more I noticed, the worse it got. I looked down, pants *and* panties were missing. Thighs sticky from dried blood. I still had on my black sweater, though the collar had been ripped, almost to the sleeve. I looked around the small 8x10 room, space for nothing more than the large bed and a wooden chair. I looked out of the small window, noticing clouds swirling around us. Suddenly the flimsy white door folded open, Esmeralda and Liam peering at me from the other side. My heart began racing, looking at their cynical smiles, eyes locked onto me.

"Well, look who's awake." She said as they walked in towards me. Her large goon followed in behind them, smirking. I scooted against the headboard, trying to put as much distance as possible between us. She sat down on the bed, not too far from where I woke up. "Such pretty legs." She whispered reaching over to me. I couldn't get far enough from away her icy cold hand. She chuckled as I began to sob. "Sorry if you are in pain. Bruno couldn't help himself. I was upset at first, but thinking about it, we can make a pretty little penny off of you."

"Start a whole new business." Liam said, smiling maniacally as he rubbed his hands together.

"Nothing new about human traffic, mi amor." She giggled, reaching into her small black clutch purse. She pulled out a long needle and removed the clear plastic tip.

"What is that?! No!!" I screamed, kicking Liam in his gut as he walked over to hold me down. That's when Bruno walked over, grabbed me by my throat, punching me in my face. The size of his fist, covering my entire face.

"Perfect timing, Bruno." Esmeralda said sarcastically. I felt a sense of defeat as all three of them were now on top of me, holding me down. I was virtually paralyzed.

"Nooooo!!! Please, help me!!" I screamed, unsure of who it was I even screamed out to help from. I suddenly felt a sharp pain in my left hip. First everything went numb, followed by a violent queasiness. It was starting to get hard to form words, even the thoughts behind them. After a few seconds, I felt sleepy, and the more I fought it, the worse it got.

Just opening my eyes left me with an immense nausea. Everything was still blurry. I heard distorted voices surrounding me, children laughing and then a distant voice, announcing flights to America and Guatemala. I found the strength to open my eyes and realized I was being wheeled through an almost empty airport lobby. I looked down and realized I was in a pair of fuzzy, purple pajama pants, feet still bare. My head was heavy as I attempted to lift it once more. I needed to reach out to someone and let them know that I was in danger. "Help." I whispered weakly. Not even my captors heard me. I had to risk being beaten by them, by yelling louder. "Heelllp!" I said a little louder this time. I suddenly felt that sharp pain from the needle, this time it was in the back of my neck. I suddenly felt the sensation of the ground being pulled out from under me. I fell through the darkness, unable to grab onto any one of the million shadows that surrounded me.

"Liyah, you have to fight, baby." I heard my mothers voice coming from somewhere in this abyss.

"Mommy?!" I cried out, looking around.

"You'll know when the time is right. You have to *fight* baby!" She said, voice full of strength. "Fight, baby. Fight!!!" She said louder, forcing me awake. I was on my back looking up at a stone ceiling. My head began pounding as I sat up on the hard, musty cot. I rested my head against the stone wall, trying to nurse the pounding between my ears. I scanned the empty room and found a black, metal door. The stone cell was dark, with the exception of a small sliver of light, coming from an 8x8 square-shaped hole in the wall, directly above me. I tried to stand and look out the hole, but the weight of my body atop my own legs proved to be too much.

"Ahh, shit!" I sighed as I fell off the cot, and onto the cold floor below, landing on my left shoulder. "Fuck." I said to myself, sitting up on the ground, rubbing my shoulder. "Ow." I whispered, feeling a lump form in my throat.

My mind shot to Sean, heart breaking when I began to suddenly think of how he lied to me this whole time. That son of a bitch played me and got me fucking pregnant. I wanted to scream. But I wanted to do more than scream. I wanted fucking revenge. If only I can have my dad reach out and touch him. Touch them all.

I sucked in my tears, trying desperately not to cry. I used my arms to pull myself up onto the cot, minimal feeling in my legs and feet. I sat with my feet on the floor, moving my toes, trying to regain feeling. I could smell the saltiness and hear the sound of the ocean crashing ashore, somewhere near. I also heard the incessant squeals of seagulls, becoming more envious of their God-given freedom, with each passing moment. My mother's voice continued to play in my head. Finally able to stand, on my tip toes, I looked at the scene outside. The morning sun was just starting it's peek over the ocean. I could see the jagged rocks that the waves crashed into, with the beach in between two large formations of stones.

The large metal door slammed open behind me, startling me, causing me to fall back down onto the cot. It was Bruno. He just stared at me, grinning as he undid his black slacks. His mouth turned into a half-grin as he let them fall to the floor. He began walking over towards me.

"Stay the *fuck* away from me." I cried, jumping over the dirty pillow and onto the floor. There was a large space between the bed and wall. I backed into the corner. "No." I whimpered as he walked over to me. He laughed as his left hand disappeared into his white briefs. He already knew what had just begun to settle in for me; there's nowhere to run and that my life is no longer my own.

"Fight! When the time comes, baby girl, fight!" My mother's voice started to scream in my head again.

"Pretty girl like cock, no?" He said in a thick, scratched Russian accent.

"No." I responded. I felt a tear leave my left eye, roll down my cheek and curl under my chin. He laughed even harder, continuing to walk towards me.

"Little girl like *pussy*? Me too!" He sang loudly, dropping his drawers. He swung his flaccid penis back and forth, making it clap against his thigh. Each time it slapped, I could see it become firmer, until it was staring directly at me.

"This man is eight times my size. There's no way I can fight him off of me." I thought to myself. I was afraid and knew I'd lose, but I stood up and held my ground, fists up and ready to go. His smile sent chills through my bones, as he stroked his abnormally large dick, walking over to me. One step at a time until he was towering directly over me. "St-st-stay...stay away from me!" I cried putting my hands against his chest, trying to distance myself away from him.

"Come here, little girl!" He yelled, grabbing a fistful of my hair.

"No!" I screamed as he forced me down to my knees.

"No bitey, bitey." He sang. His fetid dick staring me right in the face, touching the tip of my nose.

"No, no, no, no, no-" I begged, tears flowing down my eyes, as he shoved his wood down my throat, choking me. The taste was like *nothing* I've ever had in my mouth. It tasted like putting my tongue on a D-battery. My hands held tightly together by his free hand. I was defenseless as I threw up, with him still in my mouth. I gagged, throwing up once more. He laughed as he continued to force himself down my throat, causing me to literally choke on my own vomit.

"Fight! Baby girl, fight!" My mother's voice rang out once more. I forced my mouth onto as much of him as possible and bit down as hard as I could. Locking my jaw, shaking like a rabid pitbull. Blood began to gorge over my face, neck, breasts and legs as I ripped his prized possession away from him. It was tougher than I'd expected. I bounced to my feet. The sound of his high-pitched scream was almost deafening. He reached down with both hands, trying to stop the bleeding as he dropped to his knees. I tossed his severed dick at him as he fell to his side, becoming more pale by each passing moment. His eyes trailed off into the corner, as he began to shake and turn blue. I turned around and noticed Bruno had left the door open, just slightly. I peeked out into the narrow, dimly-lit hallway. The stench of urine, feces and death filled my nostrils immediately. I looked in both directions, not sure which way to go. It looked like I was in an underground dungeon. Directly across the hall was another black, steel door. The ground was covered in dirt and little twigs and leaves. I stepped out, wanting to get away before anyone starts running in this direction. I turned to the right, feeling my way along the smooth, bricked wall down the long corridor, lit by only a small torch, housed above the door of every fifth cell door. I felt like I ran forever, hearing soft pounding on the doors as I passed them. "This is a dungeon." I thought to myself.

I reached the end of the hall, that made a left turn. A left turn into pitch black darkness. There were no more torches to lead my way. I decided to keep going, refusing to turn around. I ran down the hallway at full speed, trying to get through the darkness as fast as possible. I suddenly began to see two flickering lights in the distance. I ran towards them, stopping as I realized I had reached the end of the hall, and the beginning of two more. A fork in the path.

"Fuck." I sighed, standing at the opening of a split hallway. I felt myself getting angry and more lost. I'd rather be shot, than die wandering around here for the next few weeks. I had to decide. I ran left, running passed another set of holding cells. 3 on each side of me. The stench got stronger the more I ran, heels digging into the dirt below. I reached a staircase, heading upward to a gated door. The gate was cracked open, with a chain hanging loosely through the iron rods. There was just enough slack in the chain, to allow me to squeeze through. I pushed it open slowly, stepping foot onto a grand, oval-shaped patio, looking out over the ocean.

The patio was unfurnished, and the floor was inundated with dust. I ran over to the half-wall wanting to see if I could survive the fall to the beach. "Oh, shit." I whispered, looking at the 6 story drop to the jagged rocks below. Back against the wall, I slid down, feeling myself wanting to break down and cry. Knees into my chest I felt myself breaking down. I looked up and down a straight path, off of the patio. It led to what seemed to be another portion of the house. I shot to my feet and ran down the short path, along the half-wall. The mist from the ocean gracing the side of my face. I came upon a staircase with a set of 8 steps, leading to an iron fence and iron gate. On the other side was a basketball court, directly next to a set of 4 tennis courts. Beyond the tennis courts, was a large pool, with a black onyx fountain, erected right in the center of the pool. Just beyond the grand pool, was a stone staircase. The stairs looked to lead to the main house. The gate and fence were about 12 inches tall with speared tips. There was no way over. There was a heavy chain keeping it locked, this one too tight to even attempt to squeeze through. I walked down a couple of steps and collapsed. "Fuck!" I sighed as I leaned against the dusty, coral-colored wall dry heaving, feeling emotionally exhausted, too weak to even cry. My head hurt as the lump in my throat seemed to continuously grow in size. Realizing I had to go back the way I came, I clenched my teeth, mad at myself for choosing the wrong hallway in that fork. I tried not to feel defeated. I had no choice but to go back.

"This is not safe." I thought to myself, slowly walking back through that iron gate and back down the steps. I ran down the hallway until I made it to that other hallway, running down that one as I hit the corner. I soon realized that was also a mistake.

The hallway led to a set of steps going down. I stopped at the top, noticing I couldn't see the bottom through the darkness. "Someone could be down there waiting for me." I thought to myself. My heart thumped through my ripped sweater as a knot formed in my gut. I slowly walked down the steps. The light flickered on, like an old car trying to start, once I made it to the last step.

"Oh my, God!" I screamed, quickly rushing my hand to my mouth. There was a large, surgical table, smack dab in the middle of the room. Laying on top, was a large, naked black man, strapped to the table, by his legs and feet. His chest cavity was held open by metal prongs. He looked as if someone had just performed an autopsy, or open heart surgery on him. I tried my best, not to gag.

I looked around. Behind him was a large, black porcelain sink. My eye zoomed in at the mass of rusty and blood-stained surgical tools, that hung directly above it. I began walking closer, suddenly feeling sharp pains in the balls of my feet. I looked down and saw that the floor was grated. It helped me notice there was a bloody machete, resting against the wall to my left. I sighed, knowing someone just lost their life to this thing. I hesitantly reached to pick it up. I looked at the shelves, that lined the other walls. They were stocked to the max with boxes and miscellaneous items. A lot of the items looked bloody, and rotting.

I'd already seen enough to keep me awake at night for years. I started up the stairs, slowly walking back down the hallway I came down the first time. I turned a corner, and down the hall I could see Esmeralda with two of her goons. She wore a pink, Pucci pants suit, with light pink Jimmy Chu pumps. Her hair was down, long, stopping just at her lower back. They were carrying Bruno's body out of my cell, by his arms and legs. My heart nearly jumping through my chest, I ducked back behind the corner, before they had the chance to see me.

"¿Dónde coño pudo haber ido?!!" I heard her yell. She sounded pissed.

"We're not sure, ma'am. But she couldn't have gotten too far." I heard one of her men respond.

"Bring the big lug to dismemberment. Entonces, encuéntrame arriba." She ordered and began walking further down the hallway, as her men walked the opposite direction...my direction. I ran back down to where I assumed *dismemberment* was and ducked behind one of the fully stocked shelves, just to the right of the entrance. I held the machete in hand tightly, ready to fight, or die if caught. My heart began to race as I seen the men's profiles walking passed the empty space between the wall and shelf.

"Why the fuck are these lights on?" One asked the other, in an American accent. They tossed Bruno's large body onto the table, almost crushing the naked Mexican's.

"I don't know, man. Check those gates up there at the tower and make sure she didn't get out." I watched as one of the men did as ordered and headed back up the steps. "Where the fuck did I put that damn-" The goon said, hands on his hips. I looked at the metal-handled, 20" razor-sharp blade in my left hand. "Oh, well." He said, walking over to the sink, grabbing a large hand-saw off the wall. "Bruno, Bruno. You just couldn't keep your fucking dick in your pants, could you?" He asked chuckling. I then seen a set of keys of his waist. They looked like they went to the gates outside, and if they did, then maybe I could get out of here. He was directly in front of me, but there was no way to get them without alerting him I was there. I tried my best to reach, but it was no use. I had to decide.

I slowly turned around to face the wall, making sure he was still behind me. The sounds of him hacking away at Bruno's flesh and bone, playing like a bad movie in the background.

"Ahhhh!" I yelled out, using the wall as leverage, I pushed with every bit of strength I had. The shelf fell over, pinning him to the table, by his shoulders. Knocking Bruno's body to the ground. I climbed over the shelf and onto the grated floor.

"Get the fuck over here, bitch! I'll fucking kill you!" He growled, trying his best to reach out and grab me. I stayed clear of his grasp, walking around to his front, stepping over Bruno. With both hands, I held the machete over my head, and dug it as deep as possible into his skull as I could. He stopped moving instantly. I rested my hands on my knees, trying to catch my breath as my adrenaline subsided. Just then, I began to hear heavy footsteps coming back down the hall. There was no way I could hide behind another shelf, so I ran back to the wall. Trying not to make noise. I was terrified, hearing those foot steps come back down the steps.

"Whoa! What the fuck?!" He lamented, turning to see me. I shoved the tip of the machete into his throat, without thinking. He grabbed at his throat, trying to stop the blood as I snatched it out. He toppled over, falling onto his stomach, the blood poured from his body and down the grate.

"Ahhhh!!" I screamed, seeing red, as I began hacking away at his body. Emotion flooding me, as if the Hoover Dam had just broken down.

I became overcome with debility, dropping the machete as I fell to the floor. Panting, I shakily stood to my feet, body vibrating with an immeasurable infuriation. After snatching the first guy's keys, I quietly walked down the hall and passed my cell, making sure there was no one else down here looking for me.

I kept straight, down the corridor until it made a sharp left turn, leading to a staircase heading upwards. The top of the staircase, blocked by a metal gate. I could smell the strong scent of chlorine and fermented fruits in the air. On the other side, all I could see where large, wooden barrels. They lined all 3 walls, stacked high atop each other.

I began fumbling with the keys, going through 12 of them, nervously, before the gate finally granted me access to the other side. Centered in the room, was a large fountain of a woman standing, holding a large, shimmering black vase in her hands, pouring the water into the shallow pool below her. She looked Spanish by the tone of her skin, with long flowy back hair. She wore nothing but a shimmering, purple sarong around her waist. I walked around the fountain and through a set of large, wooden double-doors on the other side of the room. I entered into a wine tasting room, soft jazz played just above mute's whisper.

The room was split off into two sections. To my right was a long, mirrored bar, with marble counter-tops. There was enough room to sit about 8 people. A large shark tank made up the backdrop of expensive bottles of tequilas, rums and whiskeys. Further down was a large, white grand piano, with the player facing the room. To my left was more of a lounge and hang area. Six love seats; two sectionals, both had three, white leather couches positioned in a U-shape, facing the bar. Filling the wall behind them, were a row of glass cabinets, encased in white wood. They displayed bottles of alcohol. Brands I've never heard of before. I walked down the black and gold Versace rug, heading to a spiral staircase with crystal banisters for stability. I suddenly heard loud Spanish music coming right above my head, as my barefoot touched the cold step. My heart dropped, hearing a woman giggle. Just as my foot touched the first cold, metal step, a heavy door slammed from the top, shutting off the music. I scrambled in the middle of the room, panicking, looking for somewhere to hide.

"Callarse, papi. Someone's going to hear us." I heard a female voice. It wasn't Esmeralda, too young. But still, I didn't want to get caught. I ducked behind the couch, between the display, closest to the stairs. I began hearing steps coming towards me.

"Shhhh. Está bien. Nadie te va a encontrar aquí abajo. No one. Just relax." I heard a guy respond. I heard one of the bar stools scoot across the floor a short distance.

"Mmmm, yes." She moaned. I started to hear the sensual noises of intercourse. I laid flat on my stomach, peeping through the smallest of spaces between the two couches. The bar stools were just short enough for her to sit on the edge, with his tiny dick between her legs, pants down to his ankles. "Fuck me!" She screamed, fabricated moans of pleasure.

"Te gusta este Pito, ¿no perra?" He growled, fucking her harder and harder the longer she took to answer him.

"Si! Si!" She screamed. His body began to jerk, as he growled just a little harder. Just as quickly as it had begun, it was over. He almost collapsed onto her, trying to pull his pants up. They kissed passionately. I saw her pick her black thong up off the floor and stuff it into his face, then his shirt pocket. He smiled, while playfully snapping his jaws at her. He smacked her ass, shoving her panties into his back pocket, as they walked up the stairs. The music blared for a few seconds, and then that same slam. Silence.

I regained my focus and headed up the steps, leading to a brightly lit hallway. Wooden walls adorned with nothing but mid-century Spanish paintings, and a few maps of different parts of the country of Mexico. I could smell an array of different foods and dishes. Turning around, looking out of the large, stained window, I seen that same pool. I continued down the short hallway, to my right, I saw a large wooden door. I slowly opened it, immediately seeing two men inside. I closed the door quickly, but silently, hoping they didn't noticed me.

I turned around and went through a set of silver metal doors, adjacent to the wooden one. I peeked into one of the two small circular windows, making sure no one was on the other side. I walked into the large, industrial kitchen, the heavenly scent growing stronger. I rested my eyes on an abundance of food. Snack, treats, dishes galore. My stomach rumbled violently. I ran over to one of the counters, placing my machete down next to me, before digging my hands into a pan of almost-hot pulled pork. I turned around and grabbed three sweet rolls off of the counter behind me and scarfed them down with the meat. I ran over to another counter, where a whole chicken rested, sitting on a bed of rice pilaf.

I suddenly heard a door close from about 10 feet from my right.

There was a heavy-set Mexican lady, wearing all white, coming out of the freezer, carrying a desert tray.

"Aaaahhhh!!!!!" She screamed, dropping the glass, rectangular dish, taking one look at the blood on my dirty, tattered clothes.

"Fuck." I exhaled, grabbing the machete, then through another set of metal double doors. I found myself in a grand dining room, right in the middle of an all-white party. Luckily, no one's noticed my presence.

I ran passed the 8-foot, marble fireplace and to a large set of double oak doors, in the center of the wall. I peeked through one of the door's large, oval-shaped crystal windows. It was an all-white party, people in the middle of the dance floor, having a good time. I could see two of Esmeralda's goons, guarding both doors. I hated the people out there hanging out, having fun. Enjoying themselves. I wasn't sure if I'd ever be able to do that again. I tried to back out, before the circumstances changed.

"Aye!" I heard a male voice yell from behind me.

"Ahh!" I screamed, realizing he had a gun to my head.

"Drop the fucking machete, puta and don't fucking move." I took my chances, running into the party, hearing the screams of the party goers, as security chased me. I made them run around the room, trying to get them so focused on me, that one of them left a door clear. The party goers were mortified. I ran out of the banquet and into a bright hallway. Almost running into a large pane of glass, separating the hallway from a large botanical garden; filled with plants of all kinds. The wooden hallways wrapped around it like it was on display.

I hurried down the hallway, through a large arch, passed a marble bust of some old man, and into the foyer of the large home. I passed the grand staircase, shooting for the front door.

"Fuck!" I cried, kicking the door, realizing it was dead bolted. Locking with a key from the inside. I began to suddenly hear a set of hands clapping behind me. I spun around to see Esmeralda standing at the landing of the steps. She was backed by 13 of her goons.

"Poor little kitty. So close, yet so far." She cackled. I made a mad dash to the right, into the large sitting room, keeping a tight grip on this machete. The furniture was beautiful. All beige sofas and love-seats, framed in solid gold, with matching coffee and end tables. "There's nowhere for you to go, little girl!" Esmeralda yelled, her voice catching up to me before her goons did. I ran passed another large fireplace, and almost made it through a set of glass-paned, wooden doors, before suddenly feeling a sharp pain in the back of my left shoulder. I spun around, loosing my footing. There were four thugs behind me, each holding rifles. I then felt four simultaneous pains in my chest, causing me to crash through the doors.

"Unhh!!" I sighed as I slapped against the hardwood floor. I looked up at the ceiling, unable to move, feeling the first dart being shoved deeper into my back. I could feel my conscious slipping. The ceiling began to get farther and farther away. My body began to overflow with fear, hearing heavy footsteps approach me. They were now surrounding me. One of them held up his rifle, directly at my face. I thought for sure, I was going to lose an eye, if the dart didn't go deep enough to kill me. The last thing I felt was a sharp pain in my neck.

I woke up some hours later, hearing the seagulls on the beach and the crashing waves. The room was dark, with the exception of a few, well-placed torches. I felt a little woozy, but tried to sit up anyways. I felt so sick I couldn't do anything but rest my head back, falling fast asleep.

My eyes shot open, my body, feeling hot and sweaty. I sat up, feeling the worse headache in my life. I held both hands to my temple, trying to alleviate the pain. It didn't work.

I ripped the thick duvet off of me, realizing my hands had been manicured. My feet were also done. Both with simple French-tips. I also noticed I had been washed, and changed into a black, silk nightgown. "What the fuck?!" I whispered to myself, tossing my feet over the edge of the large King bed. They didn't even hit the floor. I looked around the gorgeously decorated bedroom. The first thing I noticed was the size. It was as large as a 2 bedroom New York apartment. The walls were painted rose pedal red, will gold flowers stenciled all over. I walked over to the stone fireplace, where an incent burned. It smelled like wild jasmine and lavender. A strangely soothing scent for the situation. I turned and looked at the bedroom door, trying to open it. I wasn't surprised that it was locked. I walked to the terraces double doors. The two wooden doors had large glass panes in the center. I parted the silk, white curtains and stepped out.

The smell of the ocean filling my nostrils as the afternoon breeze wrapped itself around me like an expensive coat. I looked to the right, seeing that there was more to the patio. I walked down, seeing there was a Jacuzzi by a large seating area, which came complete with a fully stocked bar, underneath a cabana. I rushed over, almost tripping up the four steps, looking for water or juice, anything to quench my thirst. I wanted to turn around and down one of the bottles of Patron I seen displayed, but feeling like I haven't eaten or drank anything in weeks, made me realize I should stay sober. I turned and sat on the steps, looking out onto the ocean, wishing I had something to drink. I stood and walked back into the room, remembering there was an adjoining bathroom, passed the fireplace.

The bathroom was simply decorated with a few small paintings and portraits. There was a large plant, situated in the corner, right next to the built-in-bench, giving a nice view of the ocean from the terrace's point of view. There was an old, claw-foot tub, directly in the middle of the room. It was situated between the wide, matching shower and double sinks. I walked over to the sink, grabbing handfuls of the water from the faucet unable to stop as I placed my mouth under the stream.

I stood up, seeing my reflection for the first time since I was kidnapped. My left cheek was swollen so bad, the skin had begun to split open. My jaw was bruised in three different places and my left eye brow and left portion of my bottom lip, were cut open. I leaned into the large, gold mirror to inspect my injuries further, removing the nightgown to locate the bruises on my stomach, my side and arms. They felt tender to the touch. I looked at my left shoulder, where the dart was lodged into my muscle. The hole had been cleaned and bandaged, but the blood underneath told me I needed stitches.

I sat on the edge of the tub, sobbing into my hands. I tried to not to breathe in too hard as it aggravated the bruises on my torso.

I jumped at the sound of 3 heavy thuds, coming from the bedroom, before the heavy, wooden door, slowly creeped open. My heart sank into my feet, hearing the ominous sounds of high heels walking slowly towards me.

"Here, Kitty Kitty." She said after clicking her tongue. I could feel my blood boiling in my skin.

"I'm not your fucking *pet*, bitch." I said full of venom as I walked out of the bathroom to meet her. It was her and a couple of her goons, they were both armed, weapons aimed directly at my head. She had on a red gown, with a long, red silk robe draped over. She had in her hand a garment bag.

"Ooh, I like that. *Pet*, why you must keep fighting me?" She asked walking over to the bed to lay the garment bag down. She unzipped it then held up a short, white cocktail dress. The entire stomach was cut out, leaving only a sliver of fabric going down the middle of the back. The top was completely encrusted with diamonds and strapless. While the skirt was decorated with diamonds, forming floral patterns. The dress had to have cost almost a million dollars. She walked over, holding it up to me. I smacked the dress out of her hand, causing it to slide across the floor. She looked down at it, then back up and me. Her left hand came swooping across my left cheek. Before I had time to do or say anything else, I fell to the floor, holding my face to avoid any further bruising, bleeding or splitting of my skin. But looking at my palm, I could tell it was too late.

"Tsk, tsk, tsk. Little kitty. I'm starting to think you don't like me." She walked over and squatted down next me. Grabbing my hair, forcing my head back. "I had a little kitty once, given to me by my mother." She let my hair free before standing up fully. "It never liked me either. I did my best to mother that pussy. She would hiss and hiss and hiss. One night she scratched at me." She said laughing, looking up to the high, vaulted ceilings. "Can you believe that? She actually went to scratch at *me*. So one night, while she was sleeping, I snuck up on her with a pair of garden shears. You know, the long ones." She smiled, thinking back on that night. "Her head was mounted above my bed by the morning." She glared at me, seemingly through my soul. I took a moment to evaluate the situation. I wasn't going to win this one.

I stood up, slowly, careful not to make any sudden movements, watching her and the men with the guns, making sure I wasn't going to get shot. I walked over to the bed, still holding my face as I held back tears. I lifted the dress off the bed.

"W-what shoes should I wear?" I asked, solemnly, holding the dress up to myself, forcing a smile across my face. Her face seemed to perk up a bit.

"Oh, you have your pick." She said, guiding me to a door on the other side of the fireplace. A door that just seemed to appear out of nowhere. It shared the same red paint and golden flower patterns as the wall, aiding in its camouflage. She opened the door, ushering me into a large, walk in closet. It was huge, about the size of my entire bedroom at home. My eyes grew to the size of kiwis as I ran my hands across the designer dresses and shoes. There was an island in the middle of the floor, watches and bracelets littered the island top. Gold, Ruby's and diamonds. My heart fluttered at the sapphire and jade jewelry. This was definitely a woman's dream closet. I rested my hands on a pair of Giuseppe Zanoti pumps. They were an all white, suede material, with an all gold 6-inch stiletto. "*Perfect* choice." She sang. "Be ready in one hour." She ordered leaving the closet. She raised her hands in the air, clapping forcefully, causing her bangles to jingle each time her hands slapped.

Esmeralda and her goons were gone, locking the door from the outside, behind them they left. I held the dress up, looking at it against the light. I smiled a bit, not mad at the dress' design and loved how it paired with the shoes.

"The *fuck* is wrong with you? *None* of this is okay." I said to myself tossing the dress back onto the bed, heading into the bathroom and starting the shower.

The steam from the shower filled the room, gracing against the mirror, blocking out its reflection. I stepped inside, allowing the hot water to caress me. Images of the last few months of my life flooded my cerebellum starting with my mother. I've always remembered her how she was, alive and beautiful. Not the way I last seen her; her body twisted up the way its was. I sobbed as I thought about my brothers hoping they were okay. I thought about my father, probably anxious about me not reaching out to him after my visit with the lawyer, like I said I would. I sobbed harder as flashes from Tracey's murder ran across my mind, and then I thought about Kareena. I played it over and over in my head, still unable to fathom what happened. The fact that someone would shove her body into her trunk and walk away. I absolutely felt responsible.

"Nope." I said to myself, holding back a river of tears. I found my mind wandering over to Sean. My head began to pound as the tears swelled up behind my eyes. I collapsed to the shower floor, holding my knees to my chest. I sobbed hard and loud. "Fuck!" I screamed out in anger and hurt, kicking the porcelain shower wall as hard as I could.

I stepped out of the shower, wrapping the large towel around my breasts as I walked back into the room. I sat on the bed, running my right hand across the diamonds on the top of the dress. Tears still rolling down my face. I *wanted* to keep fighting, but I saw no win for me. "She has this whole place lined up with men that will die and kill for her. I can't fight that. Not by *myself.* I'm so sorry, mommy." I sobbed aloud. Standing to get into the dress. It fit over my body like a glove, squeezing onto all of the right places. I sat on the plush ottoman, pushing my feet into the shoes. "I can't wait to kill this bitch…with these shoes." I thought to myself, loving how sharp the tip of the heel was. I stood and returned to the mirror in the closet. It was long and wide enough to reflect the entire room.

KNOCK! KNOCK! KNOCK!

I walked back into the room, just as the large door was swinging open. It was 3 of Esmeralda's trigger-happy goons. The first one in grabbed my upper right arm.

"Let's go." He grunted, grabbing me like he hated me. He squeezed my arm so tight I began losing the feeling in my fingers before we even left the bedroom. The hallway looked as if we were at a resort. Directly outside the room, was a large, outside sitting area. The grass was fake but the trees seemed to be real. I looked up and studied how tall they went. They stretched up another 3 stories of the house. He yanked me to the right and down the corridor. We made another right, through a large archway, to a set of elevators. One of the goons, used a key card to call for it.

The four of us stood, waiting for the middle elevator to make its presence known. I stood there, staring at my reflection in the elevator doors. Saddened looking at my face, though I couldn't turn away. My reflection then went away, being replaced by the elevators interior. The man pushed me inside, followed by the three of them. The same guy had to use the key card again to send the elevator to the desired floor.

I made a mental note of the floor we started on…#5. Then, got off on floor B1. I was pushed forcefully off the elevator. Unable to maintain my balance, I was snatched up by the goon with the key card, saving me from falling flat on my face. To my left, I seen a dirty man, wearing tattered clothes. He was pushing a mop back and forth over the tiled stone. He had to have been one of her janitors.

I noticed the large dining room table, long enough to fit 40 people, but there were only 8 in attendance. My eyes rested on the enormous spread of food. Everything from chicken, ham, turkey, greens, rolls and more, filled the table. Alongside enchiladas, tacos and more. My nose opened, reacting to the sensational smell of the foods. My stomach growled, reminding me of the last time I'd eaten a full meal. The music was played by a large mariachi band, standing directly across from the table from me. I can see them playing with everything they had. They played from their heart, with passion. There was a dinner party being held, but what was the occasion?

I felt a sharp poke in my back. It was Key Card, rushing me to get down the stairs.

"Yes, ladies and gentlemen!! Please give a warm welcome to our *bride*." Esmeralda shouted, standing with a gold glass of champagne in the air. She wore a silk, egg-white halter-top dress, with a white shawl covering her shoulders. Her hair was done up, into an up do like Dolly Parton. I was met by a storm of applause. I stood there, smiling like an idiot. I couldn't breathe, I couldn't think.

"What the fuck?" Was all that I could say to myself.

CHAPTER 14

"What do you need me to do?" Malakhi asked, full of fear and anger. He was determined to get his sister back, not willing to lose another sibling. He looked at the gun in his hands, like a fish out of water. He had no idea how to eve use one. All he knew was they killed people. He looked up at the plane's lights, as they faded away in the darkness. Feeling guilty, like he should have helped without even knowing *how*.

"You ever shoot a gun before?" Clarence asked him.

"Nah, bruh. He too young." Lamarr said, before Malakhi had the chance to answer for himself.

"My nigga, who else we got?" Clarence said, matter-of-factly.

"We don't!" Lamarr exclaimed, pounding his palms against the car's dashboard. "Everybody we had is on that field, bleeding the-fuck out, bruh."

"I'm not leaving my sis *or* my girl with them crazy mothafuckas." Clarence argued. Malakhi was starting to look at Lamarr suspiciously. He couldn't see the point he was trying to get to.

"Bruh, they got who they wanted. *Liyah and Johnny.* They killed Kareena just because they fucking-could, bruh. I say we forget all this bullshit ever happened." He continued. He lit his Newport 100 cigarette with shaky hands.

"Bruh, What the fuck are you saying?! Nigga, that's my fucking *wife*...the mother of my *child*. Plus, my nigga, you've known Liyah just as long as I have. Her daddy lined yo pockets all cus you was Johnny's potnah."

"Man, I'm sorry, but that's not yo wife. Ya'll common law. And for all we know, Tre could be dead." Lamarr said, puffing on his cigarette.

"Get out, bruh." Clarence ordered, starting the engine. He'd just seen Sean's Maserati ride by.

"What?" Lamarr asked, chuckling in disbelief. Clarence now recognized him as a snake. Someone not to be trusted. He had the car in drive, but wouldn't move, until Lamarr exited the vehicle. Malakhi was now seeing red as well.

"Come on, bruh." Malakhi grabbed the steel bars that held the head rest to the seat for stability. He tightly balled up his left fist and swung, hitting Lamarr directly in the mouth, twice. It happened so fast he didn't have time to think. Lamarr pulled out his .380 and pressed the barrel against Malakhi's forehead, right between the eyes. Clarence grabbed his .9mm and pushed it against Lamarr's temple. Malakhi froze, realizing what he'd just did. "Damn, cus. Like that? *This* lil nigga ain't even blood to you, bruh."

"You looking a little unfamiliar yourself, my dude." Clarence said, pressing the pistol deeper into his skull. "Put yo' fucking gun down." He ordered. "He a fuckin kid, bruh."

"Bruh, just let me off this nigga so our lives can go back to normal." Lamarr said, hands still shakey. His eyes were bugged out. His fear had gotten the best of him.

"Put the fucking gun *down*, Lamarr. I ain't saying it again, bruh." A few tense moments passed. Suddenly, Lamarr tried to quickly turn the gun on Clarence.

BAH!

The bullet went right through Lamarr's temple, exiting on the other side, going right through the back, passenger window. Malakhi ducked as the glass shattered just inches from his face.

"Fuck!!!" Clarence cried, yelling to the top of his lungs, pounding his gun on the dashboard, cracking the radio's LCD screen. Malakhi sat up, once everything quieted down.

"Are you ok-" Malakhi said, tapping Clarence's shoulder. Still in a tense state of being, he turned around, aiming the gun at Malakhi.

"I-I-I-I-....I'm sorry, man. I'm sorry." Malakhi stuttered, throwing himself against the back of the seat. Malakhi could see Clarence come back to reality. He shook his head violently before dropping the gun at Malakhi's feet.

As Malakhi dropped his hands, in his peripheral, he could see Lamarr's face, clear as day through the side view mirror. Lamarr's eyes were rolled back as his head rested on the door in the window frame. Malakhi could see the blood dripping from Lamarr's head. His eyes grew wide with fear.

"I'm so sorry, bruh." Clarence's deep voice caught Malakhi's attention. He watched as Clarence reached over Lamarr's lap, opening the passenger's side door. He pushed Lamarr out of the vehicle, shutting the door as Lamarr's lifeless body slammed to the cold cement. He spun the car around, trying to catch up to Sean's taillights. Malakhi sat frozen in the backseat, unable to take his mind off of the side mirror. He knew Lamarr was long gone, out of the vehicle, but he could still see his face staring back at him, through the mirror. Another life lost to the Reyes legacy.

It's been an hour since they checked into the Motel 6, right near the Oakland Coliseum. He ran into the bathroom, long tired of listening to Sean and Clarence argue about how to get his sister and Tracey back. The crew they had was all but wiped out and they were quickly running out of options and time. Malakhi sat with his back to the flimsy, wooden door, knees to his chest. He sobbed, palms over his ear, thinking about Malik. He ached, feeling a wave of guilt flow over him. He couldn't get over the regret, feeling like he let Malik down. He wished he'd gotten that bullet instead.

"Bruh! I know my way around that mothafucka! Trust me, dude." Sean yelled.

"My nigga," Clarence chuckled. "I *don't* fucking trust you!" His voice roared, shaking the thin walls around them. Malakhi heard a sudden thud, then Clarence grunting in pain. He then heard guns cocking.

He quickly stood to exit the bathroom, eager to see what's going on. He rushed out into the cheap hotel room, making a right. Clarence stood in front of the small, 30" TV, holding onto his shoulder, gun trained on Sean's head. Sean was in between the two beds, gun aimed at Clarence. Both of them were ready to kill. Malakhi realized the heavy burgundy curtains were still drawn back.

"Yo, what the fuck?!" Malakhi yelled, walking between the two of them, closing the curtains. They dropped their guns, putting them back where they'd got them from. He turned back around to face them, tears still streaming down his face. "I can't find Liyah by myself." Malakhi sobbed, fighting a mental and emotional breakdown. A part of him wondered if she was even still alive. He knew she was being tortured and abused somewhere. Somewhere too far out of reach. "And Tracey was killed when they came and took her...took Liyah." He was angry, but even worse, he felt helpless. Not wanting them to see him cry, he ran out of the motel room.

"I swear to God, I didn't know, man." Sean lied.

Clarence sighed, sitting on the edge of the bed, making the decision to trust Sean. A part of him regretted killing Lamarr. Maybe he was right. He thought about Casey, and if this goes wrong, how she'd have lost both parents. He felt a sense of fear, but shook it off. "So, what's the plan?" He asked, trying to hold back tears.

Sean sat on the other bed, facing the window. He pulled his phone from the inside pocket of his leather YSL coat, going through the contacts. "My parents had me keep tabs on Stephan's most important contacts, along with a list of people my family fucked over. We gotta get lil bruh, though." He said, relieved his parents weren't as interested in Steph's associates, as they were his family.

"What you need from me?" Clarence asked. Sean turned around, looking at him over his left shoulder, unsure he was hearing him correctly. He sat silent for a few seconds.

"Just teach him how to shoot." He said. He began thinking about the baby in Liyah's belly, and teared up. Sean shot his gaze towards the curtain, sniffling, so that Clarence wouldn't see his tears. "He's all she got now." Sean continued, sniffling and wiping his face.

Clarence stood and walked over to Sean, resting his right on his left shoulder. "I can't say she'll forgive you, but for now she got us, too. Imma run and grab Khi." He said, before leaving the motel room. Sean reached for his chest, snatching off his Jesus chain. He unscrewed Jesus' head and poured a bump of cocaine out onto the back of his left hand, between his thumb and pointer finger.

"Ahh, shit!" He exclaimed, taking another bump, before starting his phone calls. He contacted everyone with a grudge against his parents, and being the first in line to inherit his family's half a billion dollar fortune, he had one hell of a bargaining chip.

He'd spent hours calling and texting, leaving voicemails to be called back. Malakhi and Clarence were still out, and it was going on 5 in the morning.

Sean was able to get in contact with only 3 people. One of those people was Demetrius.

"Hello?" He answered groggily. He couldn't understand why an unknown number was calling, especially at this time in the morning.

7 AM rolled around quickly. Clarence bursted into the hotel room with Malakhi. "Dude calm the fuck down!" Clarence ordered. Tossing him down to the bed. He jumped back up, looking like he was ready for a fight, then spun around and headed back for the bathroom.

"Remind you of anybody?" Sean laughed slightly.

"Man, for real. What you got?"

"Demetrius, this nigga was like Stephan's son, before the twins. Kid is smart as fuck. Works for the lady who handled their finances. I took Li to the bank she owns a couple months ago. Apparently there was a lot of shit Stephan held back from his family. He knew this day would come. He was ready. Or as ready as he could be."

"Well, let's get ready, then." Clarence said.

Sean and Clarence each spent close to $2,000 at the San Leandro Rifle and Pistol range, teaching Malakhi to shoot and also honing in on their abilities as well at the outside ranges. It was almost 4 hours, before they felt confident that Malakhi could handle himself, buying 4 bulletproof vests, equaling $1,800 more, a piece.

"It's almost time to meet up with, bruh." Sean said. Looking at his Patek watch. It was almost 2:30 PM.

"Aight, I'll follow you." Clarence replied.

"I'm riding with you." Malakhi said, following Clarence to his vehicle. The ride to the Oakland Hills gave Malakhi flashbacks of his family being literally ripped from their beds by the FBI. Luckily for his psyche, they never went near the home.

"Hey, bruh. We outside. Aight." Sean said, pulling up in front of the address that Demetrius gave. It was only 5 minutes away from the Reyes estate. "Good, this dude got money." Sean said to himself, stepping out of his car and walking around to the curb. Clarence pulled up right behind him. "He said to just go to the door." Sean said once with Clarence and Malakhi.

"What's good yall." Demetrius said, opening the door. He wore a pair of grey joggers, a fitted black Givenchy T-Shirt and a pair of black Ferragamo slip on sandals. The frosted glass door hinged in the center, able to swing in a full revolving circle. Sean shut the door behind them, following Demetrius through the foyer, passed the steps, and to the spacious living room. There was a large, red leather couch placed in the middle of the room, facing the fireplace. Above the large, grey-stone fireplace, was a mounted 65" plasma. The large red, leather sectional came complete with a matching ottoman and cup holders in the 2 recliners. Demetrius sat down on the couch. "Have a seat fellas." He said, grabbing a large, black Jordan gym bag from the floor and tossing it onto the ottoman. "This is just a little of what we got." He said as he ripped the zipper back, exposing an artillery of firearms. "After we talked I called some niggas home." He continued, "They said you tried to reach out, but…"

"They don't know me…" Sean continued his sentence.

"We got a crew?" Clarence asked, looking between Sean and Demetrius.

"Hell yeah. The Carters and Reyess made all these niggas rich. Including me." He said, digging into the bag, pulling out a Mac10, slamming the extended clip into the handle. "If we ain't got a crew, they ain't breathing."

"For sure. Let's mob." Sean said, pulling a blunt out of his front coat pocket. Clarence and Malakhi headed to his Chevy, while Demetrius followed Sean to his Maserati.

"Head for the San Leandro Marina. Steph got the majority of his stash in his boat. Hidden under the radar in case he got pinned."

Demetrius said, sending out a mass text message, dropping a location pin for his people to meet them. ASAP.

"What kinda shit he got?" Sean asked, handing Demetrius the blunt. He looked in the rearview mirror, making sure Clarence was still close behind him.

"Shit, an all black Mercedes Benz powerboat, for starters. Bitch go about 200. That thing is loaded with guns, bombs, knives. All types of shit. I just hope the feds didn't get wind of it." Demetrius said, taking another long pull of the weed.

They made it to the Marina in just less than an hour. The early evening sun, shining bright over head. They continued down Mulford Point Drive to reach the solitude of Mulford Point. They had a great view of the Oakland Airport, right across the bay.

"That's them right there." Demetrius said, pointing at a ruby red, 2010 Ferrari 458 and a silver Aston Martin V8 Vantage. Sean stopped the car, facing the Aston Martin. He and Demetrius jumped out, heading to the passenger side of the Ferrari. It was his big brother, Rodney. He stepped out of the car with two of his potnahs; Justice and Christian. James slid out of the Aston with 3 of his; Maurice, Donovan, and Jae.

"This everybody?" Clarence asked, walking up to the group.

"Where Malakhi at?" Sean asked. Demetrius wondered where the other twin was.

"Lil nigga passed out a few minutes ago." Clarence responded.

"Where's Malik?" Demetrius asked.

"They killed him, man. Just last night." Clarence answered. Demetrius put his hands to his face in disbelief. He felt immensely saddened by the news.

"Bruh, the cops been picking up bodies downtown all night. It was a war zone over that mothafucka, G. Tahoe's mobbing through the center, hitting people and shit 'cus." Said Justice. He grabbed the blunt James was handing over to him. Clarence and Sean each sparked one of their own. "They didn't give a fuck, bruh. Kids, old people…who ever." He continued, holding the smoke in his lungs.

"Yeah the news started identifying the victims, but no Malik." James added.

"What about a Tracey West?" Clarence asked. He pulled out his cell and showed James a picture of his wife.

"Nah, she wasn't on there either." James responded, shaking his head. "Who is she?"

"My wife." He said solemnly, placing his cell back into his pocket.

"Liam and Esmeralda must have had their people pick them up. Get rid of the evidence." Sean suggested. "It wouldn't be the first time they caused a war, and *didn't* leave any bodies behind. *Especially*, their victims."

Malakhi woke up, hearing the mention of his brother's name. He looked around, realizing he was at the Marina. His heart ached, thinking about the night before. Looking at the empty seat next to him, he could still feel his brother's energy.

"The fuck?" He said to himself, reaching into the pocket behind the driver's seat. He pulled out a silver, 7-shooter revolver, fully loaded. He reached down, tucking it into his left sock.

"I hit up my nigga, Brian, he should be here soon." Maurice said, taking a hit of his joint.

"Is that them?" James asked, nodding towards the entrance at the other end of the large parking lot. James and Sean, leaning against Rodney's Ferrari, turned around. There was a black 2010, Porsche Panamera followed by a candy apple red Mustang V6.

"Yeah it is." Demetrius responded. They pulled up, joining the group. The cars were now forming a circle, all facing each other, while the fella's stood inside. Demetrius started walking towards the docks, opening the gate, letting the men in. "Straight that way." He said, pointing to one of five boat houses, at the end of the long, wobbly platform.

The breeze kicked up off of the icy bay, dropping the temperature a couple of degrees. Demetrius unlocked the large, weather eaten double doors. Inside, there was a long, slim boat, covered under a dirty, beige tarp. Demetrius ripped it off, exposing the marine beast.

The boat was black, with silver stripes all over it to resemble waves. The roof extended from the bow, curving over the cab, secured by thick, six inch steel rods. There were two levels; the captain's quarters were equipped with a large, round mattress, and it's own small bathroom.

"Damn, bruh." Maurice said. "My yacht ain't even this fuckin fly." He added taking the boat in. Demetrius stepped up and onto the boat, heading to the sleeping quarters. The bed was crowded with crates.

"Rod, bruh come grab this. Strap up." Demetrius said, placing the boxes on the top of the steps, one at a time. He tossed a crowbar upstairs next to one of the boxes. Rodney handed it to James, signaling for him to open them up.

"Fuck, bruh!! Where the fuck all this shit come from!! This bitch mine!" He heard everyone speaking at once, as the first 2 crates were opened up. He walked up the steps with the tenth and final crate. Each one included enough large black gym bags to comfortably carry the items inside each box.

"We gone have to split up. I'll take my boat." Rodney said, pointing to the far side of the docks. His boat was egg white, and used more for leisure than speed, but it was spacious for having only a single level. He named it FYB, *Fucking Your Bitch*.

The group of men headed back to their exotic vehicles, in the parking lot. Armed tooth and nail to save Liyah. Sean begged that time *and* the universe, were on their side, knowing the longer it took to save her, the least likely it would become.

******************👑URBAN QUEEN👑*********************

I sat at the long table, feeling sick to my stomach. Liam and Esmeralda sat on the sides at the other end. All of the mysterious guests, wearing different masquerade costumes, made me feel that much more uneasy. Suddenly, Esmeralda stood up and walked over to the elevators. The bell dinged and the light above the center one lit up.

"Please everyone, welcome my son, Eduardo, the groom." Esmeralda said, walking him over to the table. Once seated, at the opposite side, she placed a gold crown on his head.

"What's going on?" I asked, voice cracking. The atmosphere thick with danger and surprise.

"Today's your wedding child! Be merry and marry." She laughed, followed by everyone else in the room. "My grandchild will *not* be born into sin." She continued, lifting her gold champagne glass to her lips.

I'd say this bitch has totally lost it, but I'm not sure she ever had it to begin with.

"And…you…expect…me to…marry a-a child?"

"Oh, sweetie. He's not much younger than you. I can maybe tell by the wrinkles in your face, but I'll help with that. You did just turned 19, in February, right?"

"How'd you know how-"

"Let's not fret over the irrelevant details, darling." She said waving me off. She turned to Eduardo fixing his crooked tie. I continued looking around for an exit, an escape. The only way out was through the elevators, and the only doors seemed to lead to another terrace. I suddenly stood to make a break for the outside, hoping I was far enough down to take my chances with the shore below. My ass wasn't able to lift from the seat before I felt a heavy hand on my right shoulder, slamming me back down. I felt the sharp ridges of a steak knife, being held at my jugular. "Please, for your sake, don't do that again. No ones coming to save you. Phillippe's dead, honey." She said, callously.

"Wait, what?" Eduardo asked. Esmeralda just hushed him. This must be the first of the news he has heard of his brother's death. My heart ached for him, but the sadness was completely and quickly wiped away by rage. I could feel my heart beating in my chest, wishing I'd killed him myself.

Suddenly two doors flung open from behind Eduardo. Two lines of servers, 8 each, came out in single files. Each one held in her hand a large silver platter. One was placed in front of me, lifting the lid before moving away. Baked duck with orange sauce, sitting on a bed of rice pilaf with a side of broccoli and a baked potato. I didn't realize how hungry I was until I tasted the food. The duck seemed to spread apart before any teeth were able to chew. I didn't worry about appearances as I dug into the meal. Stuffing my face with food, faster than I was able to get it down. Esmeralda and Liam barely touched their plates. They mostly watched me eat, which struck me as odd, but didn't deter me from gaining some nourishment. Eddie barely even looked at his plate, after news of his brother.

"Alright, ladies and germs. Who's ready for the ceremony?!" She sang, standing holding her arms in the air, less than an hour later, once everyone was done with their meals. Eddie stood up while at the same time I was being hoisted out of the chair, to my feet. "Jacky, go clean the bride off. She eats like a fucking pig. The rest of you, follow me." While being tugged through the silver double doors, into another industrial kitchen, I watched as everyone headed out to the terrace. Jacky grabbed a large white towel right out of one of the kitchen workers hands and began roughly wiping my face, then hands. The women in the kitchen looked mortified. I watched as their judging eyes tore through me like a hot steak knife through butter. They covered their mouths as they whispered in each other's ears. They were of Pilipino descent, I wouldn't have understood what they were saying anyways. Though, it didn't ease the discomfort of embarrassment.

I was walked through the terrace's doors, escorted by the arm, passed a seating area, filled with more tropical plants than probably needed. We then came upon a set of stairs.

"Watch your step." Ordered Jacky, never loosening his grip on me. We made it down to the beautiful white-sand beach below. Everything in me wanted to make a run for the water, but the sharks might get me before Esmeralda and Liam did. Honestly, it might have been better than anything they could've planned.

I was standing on a blue, silk rug. The Spanish band from dinner, began to play 'Here Comes the Bride'. There were four rows of plush white love seats on either side, leading to a large white arch, covered with white roses. Eddie was standing under the arch, with Liam and Esmeralda standing directly behind him. There was a priest standing before them wearing a black robe. I stopped in the middle of the aisle, immediately feeling a gun pointed into my back. The priest signaled for me to take up the empty space in front of Eddie. Esmeralda forced us to hold hands. I stood there, stomach in knots. I couldn't believe she was actually going through with this.

Esmeralda walked up to me and whispered into my ear, "The next year of your life won't be easy. But you'll be *alive*. Play nice you might get to see motherhood before I chop your head off." She chuckled. "My handsome little man." She squealed, brimming with joy. "Father?" She said, eyebrows raised, ready for him to start.

"Mom. I don't want to do this." He said, finally speaking. His English was quite impressive. "We don't even know each other."

"Shh!" She snapped. "Young men your age wish they were you! Be grateful. You're fucking *lucky*!" She barked.

"Father!" She said, turning back to the priest. I was beside myself, standing there like a deer in headlights, staring at everyone, stare at me through their masks. Liam sat in the front row, holding a silver Beretta, while Esmeralda stood behind me, smiling with a pistol in my back.

The priest completed the ceremony. "I now pronounce you man and wife. You may now kiss your bride." He said after we both reluctantly said our 'I Do's'. We stared at each other for a little while. He still had his baby-face, with the exception of what looked to be a few hairs where his goatee will be. My heart ached as I got glimpses of a young Sean, or Phillippe. Even down to the brown eyes.

"Ahem." Esmeralda said, forcefully clearing her throat. "Get it over with, the sun is starting to set." I couldn't believe she really expected us to kiss. He looked barely older than 16, the same age as my little brothers. I looked around at the party, the creepy people in attendance, aside from the goons and their rifles, to Esmeralda and Liam.

"God, I hope they are okay." I thought to myself, shutting my eyes tight, puckering my lips. Everyone clapped for our unholy matrimony, after Eddie reluctantly placed the gold band on my finger, and I placed one on his.

"Whoooo!!!" She squealed loudly, stepping between us two. She grabbed us by our wrists, holding our hands up like we just won a championship fight. "Who's ready to party, huh?" Esmeralda said before cackling. I was happy this wedding was over. My feet had already started to get sore, from standing on them for almost an hour straight.

The party was held in the same room as dinner, only the table was now gone, and the room was completely decorated for the ceremony. There where large, white silk sheets covered by haunting photos of the wedding, on large canvases. Two large, gold thrones were placed against the wall, where the kitchen door would be, blocking them shut. "How the fuck-?" I couldn't understand

Suddenly, Mariachi music began playing and all of the guests in masquerade costumes began dancing. It was choreographed, all for us. Esmeralda tapped me on the shoulder, placing me back into the moment. I had somehow been teleported from a horror movie to a Spanish musical. I looked at her. Her arm was stretched out towards the gold thrones. Eddie was already sitting down. I unwillingly walked over and took my seat next to him as the dance continued. I noticed Liam had gone up the elevator alone, while Esmeralda gave a few of her goons some instructions, then followed behind him. I noticed two of her goons, lock up the doors to the terrace and stand right in front of them and another 2 standing in front of the elevators.

Eddie rested with his head in his palm and his elbow on the arm rest. He looked like he was ready to get over with this, but he didn't seem too surprised.

"Do…do your parents do this often?" I asked, trying to connect with Eddie, maybe get him to see I was human as well.

"Bitch don't talk to me. You're just another one of my mother's play-things." He said as he looked at me and turned up his lip, then returned back to his previous position. The look on his face, daring me to say something else to him. I was terrified, feeling utterly helpless.

The dancers went on for what seemed like hours. I found myself getting naturally drowsy, a feeling I hadn't realized I'd missed until now. I noticed the sun began it's daily descent. Liam and Esmeralda returned to the hall, both wearing all black pant suits. Her hair was straight, as a bone. Both their hands, wrists and necks shining like Christmas tree ornaments.

"Oh my, God." She said, face full of pride. Liam stood next to her, glaring at me like he couldn't wait to see me bleed. "Wasn't that just… just *wonderful?*" She said, starting a round of applause. But instead of applauding the dancers, everyone looked at us as they clapped. I couldn't describe the immense amount of fear and sadness I felt. The pain running through my wrists. I contemplated the rest of my natural life here, knowing as soon as I had this baby I'd never see it again. I would either be killed immediately upon the baby drawing its first breath, or I would simply become the help, and only be able to watch my child grow up from afar. I clenched my jaw, bawling my fists, trying to keep the tears at bay, as my heart broke all over again. I looked at the stained-glass windows. Jesus hung on the cross. I looked him in his face and asked *why me?* "He let's good people go through things like this. And for what?" I asked myself.

Esmeralda began walking over to us. I felt a bowling ball of anger grow in my gut and I wanted to hurl it at her. I looked out the window again and it was now close to getting dark. The band seemingly playing the same song on-end. She walked between us and grabbed our wrists again, tugging, signaling us to stand.

"Well! Looks like my children are a little bit sleepy, eh?" She said touching her chin to her right shoulder with a wink. Everyone laughed like she was holding a Saturday Night Live show right in her...*whatever* this room is."

"Vámonos." She ordered, looking between both of us with a half-smile. I was in a completely different world. Eddie looked at me in my eyes, almost snarling. He seemed personally angry with me. He resembled the son of Satan and it scared me.

She led us to the elevator, with three of her heavily-armed guards. Ave Maria was the song that played as we rode up to the 3rd floor. We stepped off. The silence was loud, as we walked down the long, white corridor, with only the loud thumps of Esmeralda's Manolo Blahnik's to keep us company, as we walked passed a fortune's worth of porcelain and gold sculptures, artifacts and paintings. I turned around to get a view of the thugs behind us. The one in the middle just held his rifle up higher, directly to my face.

"Come, come dears." She said as we walked through a large archway, leading to a seating area. The décor suddenly became homey: going from white porcelain floors and walls to wooden. The fireplace was lit and was the centerpiece for three loveseats, connected to form a "U". I noticed a staircase going down, on the other side of the room, before we turned left down a dark hallway. Lights came on in sections as we continued. It felt like we were in a completely different house. She suddenly stopped at a large, black wooden door.

"Mom." Eddie said, whining. He's been standing next to me the entire time, silent.

"Shut up." She said. Looking at him, as she unlocked the door. "Hm." She smiled as the door crept open. "Chop chop. Let's make it official." She said, motioning for us to go inside.

"Moth-" She slammed the door, locking it from the other side as he once again tried to talk to her. I turned around, looking for a way out of the room. There was a large, king-sized bed in the middle of the room with a short head and foot-board. It faced the fireplace, sitting on a large, black area rug, protecting the shiny hardwood floor below. His large plasma screen was mounted directly over the fireplace. Behind the bed was a couple of couches, centered before a fully-stocked bookcase. I walked over to the window. We were so high up, I couldn't see the ocean on the other side of the terrace ledge. "Fucking bitch!" He yelled, kicking the long, 9-drawer, oak dresser next to the door.

I walked around the bed and sat on the large, black sofa, that rested against the large window.

"I'm *not* fucking you." I said, sitting down. He sat down on the bed, chuckling, trying to hide his true feelings. I could tell he was almost as afraid as I was. "Why is she like this? What's wrong with her?" I asked.

He spun around, shooting an evil glare at me. "What do you mean, *'what's wrong with her'*?" He stood up on the bed, walking over it and to me, jumping off once he made it to the other side. I found myself trying to scoot farther into the couch, away from him. "Huh?! My father spent my whole life behind bars, because of your father! Que es lo que está mal con ella!" He yelled at me.

"Whoa! Okay. I'm sorry." I chuckled dryly, with my hands up. He stood in front of me, hands on his waists. "I didn't mean to offend you. I want us to be friends." He began laughing, wholeheartedly.

"Friends? But, but why?" He said, barely able to catch his breath. "You're not getting off of this island. Even if you do survive it'll just be to clean. So get over it, please! Nothing happens without my mother saying so." He sat down on the bed, looking at me, kicking off his shoes. And in any case, I'm taking the baby, so…" Flustered, I stood and walked over to the terrace doors. I looked back at him before opening them. He was removing his shirt, sitting against his headboard, on a pile of pillows. I turned and continued through the door, feeling the evening breeze rush to my cheeks, blowing my hair back. The sun had set rather quickly. The moon casting a haunting reflection on the ocean surface. I stepped out onto the balcony, becoming dizzy at the height as I leaned over the ledge, contemplating leaping off.

"So…." He said, from inside the room.

"Uh, y….yeah?" I called back nervously, before walking back into the room.

"Let's fuck and get this over with." He said, looking at me from the bed.

"Excuse me little-." I found myself getting ready to say something disrespectful. I stopped in my tracks. He looked up at me. "Listen, how old *are* you?" I asked, walking over to him. I sat on the bed.

"I'm 16." He responded coyly.

"I figured. Your mother-" I began, remembering how protective of her he was. "Your mother raised a smart boy. But, you couldn't possibly think for one second that this is normal. *None* of this is-"

We were suddenly shaken by a heavy quake, following a very loud explosion. Strong enough to shake the windows and knock the mounted TV clean off the wall, while throwing the both of us to the floor. The room went completely dark, then was filled with a flood of red lighting. The door made a loud buzzing noise, then cracked open.

"What the fuck was that?" I asked, terrified, hearing automatic gun shots ring out shortly after. We looked at each other in the face.

"We must be under attack." He said glancing over at the sliver of light that appeared through the crack in the door. I think we were both surprised a swarm of goons didn't rush into the room. They must've had more important things to tend to.

"Can you help me get out of here? I *don't* want to die here." I pleaded to him, grabbing his hand, hoping he could tell in my eyes that I was sincere, and most importantly, human. He snatched my hand as we made a mad dash for the door, then the stairs just beyond that seating area. Suddenly there was another explosion. This one seemed closer, much closer than the first. Eddie was able to hold onto the banister. I couldn't get a good grip, and fell down the remaining few steps, slamming my shoulders against the floor. I looked around, seeing pieces of the roof start to fall around me. I was laying behind a brown leather couch, in another sitting area. Eddie rushed over and helped me up, to my feet. I noticed the lit fireplace, allowed a small spark to escape and hit the white carpet.

"We got to go." He said. We ran through the door that was in front of us, making it to a balcony, looking down another 2 stories. I could see men running around the first floor, large guns drawn. We ran down the corridor, passed the elevators and entered the service stairwell going down. "This way. We can make it to the main house, then out to the boat house from there. You trust me, *wife?*" He asked. The question made me sick to my stomach, him calling me his wife. But I gave him my hand and let him lead me down the stairwell. I found myself urged to duck at the sound of each gunshot. And there seemed to be thousands. "Come on, through here!" He said, reaching for the door. It suddenly shot open and I was staring down the barrel of a rifle. Time slowed and I could hear my heart beating in my ears. Eddie dropped my hand.

"Liyah?" The rifle went down to the man's side. It was Sean. I ran into his arms, hugging him tight. I felt almost safe, seeing a familiar face. As he wrapped his left arm around me, holding me so tight he lifted me off the floor. He put me back down, and even though I was a little apprehensive kissing him, I was still glad to see him. He dug into his waist band and handed me a pistol.

"You know how to use this?" He asked.

"You know exactly who my dad is." I said, sarcastically.

"But, mom said you were- She said she killed you." Eddie said as we followed him back up the stairs. "*And* we're going the wrong way."

"Have you seen the ground floor?" Sean asked. "*That's* the wrong way. Follow me." Eddie ran up passed me and hugged him, tears rolling down his face. I couldn't wait to finally lay eyes on my little brothers. "Are you guys okay?" He said gently gripping my chin, looking at my face. "I'm gone kill them my fuckin self."

"I'm fine. I'm fine." I replied, pushing his hand away.

"She's still our mom, Phillippe!" Eddie lamented.

"She ain't no mother of mine." He said, leading us up two flights, through the stairwell. We entered through the kitchen area, where her thug Jacky, forcefully wiped me down after eating.

BAH!!

"Ahhhh!!" Sean screamed, being thrown to the floor. I tried to stop him from falling, almost throwing myself down with him. He dropped the rifle he was carrying. I got up, and spun around, seeing Esmeralda right behind us, with a gun still aimed. I pointed the rifle at her head, ready to take it off.

"Mom!" Eddie yelled, jumping in front of us.

"Mover, llegar aquí. Now Eddie. Get the fuck over here. That was a real touching moment you guys had in the staircase." Sean stood up and got behind us. I shot at her head. Eddie grabbed the muzzle of the rifle, causing me to miss. We ran for the terrace doors, heading outside, barely missing her bullets. I shot back a little for cover. We ran down the steep steps, my right heel breaking, almost twisting my ankle in the process. Sean caught me. I realized his arm was dripping blood, running down his hand.

"I'm okay. Just keep going. Get to the beach." He ordered. I kicked off the other shoe and continued down the steps, finally making it to the beach, where I saw four boats. One of them was my father's boat. We continued running towards it. Malakhi's head popped up over the side.

"Liyah!!" He screamed when he seen me, jumping out to meet me. I grabbed him and held him close, sobbing tears of joy, happy to see him.

"Where's Malik??" I asked, looking behind him, into the boat for his twin. "Where…where's your brother??" I asked, looking him in the face. His eyebrows raised and tears began to swell in his eyes. "No…." I whispered, covering my mouth, in disbelief. My heart began to ache, as I hugged Malakhi, just happy they both weren't gone.

Suddenly, bullets began to ricochet off the side of the boat and into the sand around us. The 2 of us jumped onto the boat, dodging the bullets. I realized Sean wasn't ducking with us. There were three of Esmeralda's guys that surprised us on the beach. Sean was able to knock down one of them, but the other two were able to get him to the ground. One of them was about to blow his face off. I aimed Sean's rifle at the two thugs and began pulling the trigger. I didn't stop shooting until they were both laid out.

"Help me get him onto the boat and put some pressure on his wounds." I looked up and seen Esmeralda standing at the top of the steps, ducking when I pointed the gun in her direction. "Hey!" I yelled, before running after her back into the house.

The gun fire had yet to cease. Suddenly there was another explosion. The sound scaring me to the ground. I got up and made it back inside, from the terrace. Those silver doors were still swinging. I ran back to the staircase, immediately hearing a male scream, followed by metallic clings. There was a large blur, then a loud thud to the 1st floor beneath me. I looked over the railing. "Fuck." I whispered to myself. My heart broke seeing Clarence laying there, in a pool of his own blood. My heart also broke for Casey, now having to grow up without *either* of her parents, all due to my family drama. I vowed that if I made it out of this, that she would never need for *anything*.

I moved quietly up the staircase, wondering where Esmeralda went to. I then heard a door open and shut, right above me.

"I cannot believe, my own son! Get to the chopper." Esmeralda ordered. I froze right in my tracks, gun ready to shoot. I listened as they went up another flight and through the door. I hurried behind her, making sure no one was coming back out of the door labeled Roof Access. I was barely able to open the door before being shot at. Bullets bounced off of the steel door, almost hitting me in my ear. I slammed the door, trying to remember what daddy taught me about guns. I removed the clip, checking to see how many bullets there were. 10.

"Fuck." I cried, hand on the cold door handle, hoping their aim hasn't gotten better. I shot outside, knowing I'd be met by a barrage of bullets, but I was determined not to let that helicopter off of this roof. There was an air vent, thankfully, right next to the door. I ducked behind it, pinned down, unable to get a shot off. The shots stopped, giving me the ability to move. I snuck around the wall after seeing one of her goons jump off of the chopper, no doubt in an attempt to get rid of me personally. I made it to the other side, as he was walking to my last location, helicopter almost in the air. I knew as soon as I started shooting, that he'd know where I was, but I'd rather die than let Liam and Esmeralda escape. I aimed the gun, repeatedly shooting at the body and the tail propeller of the chopper. I spun to face the goon. His gun was raised to me, and he smiled, scarily. Suddenly the rooftop door opened, obstructing my view.

BAH!! BAH!! BAH!!

The door shut.

"D-Demetrius? What are you doing-" The helicopter crashed behind me. I dropped to the floor, making sure no shrapnel backfired towards the roof. He rushed over, helping me to my feet. I walked over to the edge. I wanted to see the red and black flames. I peeked over, thinking I'd feel a sense of satisfaction. I didn't. I still felt empty. Esmeralda and Liam's death wouldn't bring back my mother *or* my brother. I shed a tear. "So, what's going on? Why are you here?" I asked confused. "Not saying that I'm *not happy* you are. But-".

"Cus, you family." He smiled. "Come on, we have to find Liam." The bottom seemed to drop from under me.

"What? Wait. He wasn't on that-?"

"No. Son of a bitch snuck off the first floor. We thought we had him pinned, but..." He said as we headed back to the stairwell. I stopped dead in my tracks, feeling my heart drop, like I was afraid to step on it. I couldn't breathe. I tried to stop the air from leaving me, but it was like having my lips to a vacuum.

"Don't trip. Don't trip." He said. "He's not getting off of this fucking island. I promise you that." He said, looking me square in my face. I believed him. "We got our dudes combing this place. Let's just get you out." He continued. We walked down the steps, making it back down to the beach.

"There's a lot to comb. That could take a while, right?" I said to him.

"Liyah!" I heard Malakhi yell. Liam took advantage of Sean being too weak to fight back. He had two revolvers pulled up. One at Malakhi and the other at Sean. Eddie was laying face down in the sand. I heard Demetrius' gun cock next to me.

"Tell him to drop it or they both die!!" Liam barked.

"Please!" I cried, falling to my knees. "He's *all* I have left!" I motioned for Demetrius to drop his gun. He refused.

Liam laughed. "You just shot down all that I have. It's quiet poetic if you ask me." He moved his fingers closer to the triggers.

"Please!!!" I screamed, begging. "You'd really kill your own son?" I asked

"What son? This waste of sperm became disowned when he chose someone over family...like he's doing now." Liam said before hitting Sean in his head with the butt of his gun. Liam chuckled, "Choose one!! Malakhi or Sean."

"How am I supposed to-"

BAH!! BAH!! BAH!! BAH!! BAH!!

He fell backwards, crashing onto the body of my father's boat as, Demetrius filled Liam's chest with led. I rushed to my feet and to Malakhi. He had a broken nose, and a split lip, but nothing too bad. I held him, crying.

"Is it over?" He asked, trying not to cry.

"It's over, brother. We're okay." I turned around, hearing Sean cough behind me.

I went to his side. My heart hurt seeing him lying there, barely able to keep his eyes open. Blood pulled from his mouth and onto the sand beneath him.

"I'm...I'm s....I'm sorry." He coughed.

"Shh, shh, shh. Don't say anything. I love you." I said, kissing him on his forehead. I leaned back and looked him on the forehead. His eyes suddenly focused on...nothing. He was gone.

I kissed him on his forehead again, genuinely feeling horrible for him. He was in a position of kill and be killed later, or not kill and be killed now. It had to have been a lot for him to turn on his family and come help save me.

"Is it over?" Malakhi asked, peeking up from over the side of the boat.

"Yeah, kid, it's over. *Finally.*" Demetrius responded. He placed his hand on the nape of my back, urging me to get onto the boat. Once I was on, he pushed the boat back into the water and jumped on with us.

Just as he started the engine, a satellite phone housed next to the steering wheel, began to ring.

"Yup." He answered. "Yeah, I got her. We finna head back to the Bay. Ya'll cool in there?" He continued his conversation. I turned to Malakhi as we pulled away from shore.

"Are you okay?" I asked.

"I don't know." He said, face full of hurt. "I don't know how I feel. I don't think I feel anything, really." He responded. I completely understood where he was coming from. All of this Could've been avoided if my dad just put a bullet into Liam's skull. On the same token I can understand why he didn't. He's not a murderer.

I stared as the mansion got smaller and smaller, unable to shake the feeling that at any moment, I'd start to see emissaries coming after us on jet skis and speedboats. I attempted to shake the feeling, looking over at Malakhi. He rested his head on his arms, on the edge of the boat. His long dreads, flying in the wind as he stared at the waves with the most blank of expressions. I grabbed the gold band off my wedding finger, throwing it into the sea. I wiped the silent tears I cried for Malik, that hole in my heart growing bigger and bigger. I looked over, glancing at Demetrius as he steered the boat back home.

*********************♕URBAN QUEEN♕*********************

Eddie woke up, face down on the beach, the back of his head throbbing. The last thing he remembered was Malakhi knocking him out. He rolled over onto his back, staring at the dim blue morning sky. He began to freeze as he realized the sun was about to get ready to rise. He sat up, looking around seeing a body laying only a few feet away from him. He stood, realizing that two body was Liam's.

"No! Papa!" He yelled, rushing to Liam's side.

CHAPTER 15

I woke up freezing, curled up on the bench of the boat. The morning July sun did little to provide me with much heat, in the middle of the ocean. I immediately began to regret not making the decision to sleep on that dusty mattress, down in the captain's quarters. I looked down and realized Malakhi was laying at my feet, in the opposite direction. I looked over at Demetrius steering the boat. I could finally see the dog towers, of the Port of Oakland, just about a mile out. I stood up from the bench and walked over to him, cold air making the sore parts of my body much more noticeable.

"Hey." I said, reaching up and resting my right hand on his shoulder. "Thank you guys for coming to save me. I really thought I was gonna die there." I said, chuckling dryly, taking a seat in the co-captain's chair.

It seemed like hours before the boat had finally made it to the docks. I was elated to look up and see the Oakland Tribune tower. I struggled to maintain my balance, as the boat tapped the wood slightly, waking up Malakhi. Demetrius secured the boat, into the boathouse before helping me and Malakhi off, he threw a tarp over the boat. Before we headed up the dock, he locked the large, wooden doors.

The three of us walked through the parking lot, seeing a set of foreign cars. I noticed Sean's Maserati and Clarence's Chevy. Demetrius rushed over to Clarence's car, luckily, he left it unlocked.

"Hop in." Demetrius said. Me and Malakhi did just that. He went under the steering wheel and pulled out the fuse box, exposing wires. After splitting one, he touched the two ends together, causing them to spark, until the cars engine began to roar, starting within seconds. Me and Malakhi looked at each other, then back at him.

"Who is this dude?" I asked myself, as he hopped into the driver's seat, slamming the door shut behind him.

I couldn't help but notice how attractive Demetrius has become; his chiseled jaw-line and the veins in his muscles as he gripped the wood-grained steering wheel. I used to always think of him as this ugly older boy who my parents took in, with his little brother. He was out by the time I turned 12, and we never seen him again…at least I didn't.

Demetrius smelled like Egyptian Musk. I had to roll down the window to get some air. Looking out of the window, I noticed we were going down a familiar street after getting off of the freeway. We were around the corner from our home. I watched as we passed directly down the street I grew up on. A lump formed in my throat, thinking of all of the memories I've had.

Four blocks down we made a left turn, and pulled up in front of a house that was almost as nice as the one I grew up in. He shut off the engine and opened the driver's door. "This your house?" I asked, stepping out of the car, looking upward three stories, impressed.

"Yeah. I own this bad boy." He said excited. "Let's get you guys cleaned up." We walked through his front door. The grey hardwood looked so clean and shiny. I was almost ashamed to walk on it as we made it to the spacious living room.

"Make yourselves at home. I'll grab some clothes for you. Go ahead and find a room that's right for you. It's just me now and I got hella space. I got a feeling you're going to be here for a little while." He said before shooting up the stairs. Everything was so neat, I stood at the bottom of the steps, really not wanting to dirty anything up. I had Malakhi do the same. He'd been wearing the same clothes since Esmeralda and Liam took me.

I noticed, on top of the fireplace, were a few framed photos. Being nosey, I walked over. Making sure to avoid the coke-white shag rug, that sat under his glass coffee table. The pictures were mostly of him and beautiful little light-skinned girl with wildly curly hair and light brown eyes. With them next to each other I could see the resemblance. In another few of the pictures, was him kissing a woman who looked like the exact older version of the little girl. There was a photo of the three of them, at the beach, next to their obituaries. It didn't take much to realize who they were. I felt bad for looking, so I quickly turned away and moved out of the seating area. Almost stubbing my toe on the feet of his large, black sofa. "Okay, I got these for you." He said rushing back down to the first floor, handing us clothes.

"There's two bedrooms on the second floor and three on the third. Other than mine, take your pick." He said with a smile, before heading into the kitchen.

"I really don't know what to say. I don't feel like thank-"

"It's okay." He chuckled. "Anybody would have done it, plus *your* family, is family to *me*. Which makes you family." I nodded, smiling and headed upstairs. The first bedroom to right of the second story landing seemed perfect for me. I shut the bedroom door, placing the clothes onto the hardwood dresser next to it. The bed was tall and wide, with a white, fabricated frame, and plush, egg-white bedding. There was a gold, rectangular lamp on either side of the bed, which sat on a glass end table with gold legs. I walked by two large mirrors and into the bathroom, shutting the door behind me. I peeked out of the curtains, to the patio. My breath was taken away by the view of San Francisco. I spun around and looked in one of the light-framed mirrors above the his/her sinks. I shuddered at the sight of my own face in the mirror, almost feeling bad for myself.

I caught a glimpse of my skin as I reached out and turned on the shower. My skin was grimy with debris and soot from the rescue. Scenes of the ordeal began to flash through my head as I removed the dress from my body. I looked down at my bruised torso, thinking about being slapped around and beaten. I jumped into the shower, watching as the dirt poured down the drain like a dark cloud.

"Oh my, God." I sobbed, falling to my knees in the large shower. I sat with my knees to my chest, until my nose ran, and the pressure began to fill my head until the sound from the four overhead nozzles became nonexistent.

A piece of me was also still a little afraid. I felt like someone was still coming to kill me. It kept me from shutting my eyes, even while washing my hair. Every sound in this large bathroom, caught my attention and had my spine crawling, with a knot growing in my tummy.

KNOCK! KNOCK! KNOCK! KNOCK! KNOCK!

I jumped, almost screaming, but feeling silly knowing it was only Demetrius or Khi. I cleared my throat, before turning the water down to hear better. "Yeah?" I asked.

"You hungry?" It was Demetrius. "Lil man want *In N Out*."

"Yeah, that's fine. I'm on my way out now."

"Okay. I'm going to have a doctor come by a little later to look at you, too. I've known her for years, you ain't got nothing to worry about anything."

"Thank you. I appreciate that." I said, feeling like a broken record.

"No problem." He said, before closing the door.

I stepped out a few minutes later, feeling a hundred times better, at least on the outside. I still had to figure out how I was going to get my life back together and my father's as well. I wiped off a little bit of the steam, before I looked in the mirror once more, touching the cuts and bruises on my face. The bruises on my stomach were so dark, I wondered if the baby could have even survived that. Did I have a miscarriage while unconscious?

After throwing on a pair of black basketball shorts and an oversized black T Shirt, I headed back downstairs. They already left to go grab food. I sat down on the leather sectional-sofa, noticing a Jamaican-themed ashtray near the remote, filled with half-smoked blunts, wrapped in gold. There was a light blue sticky note, next to the ashtray that read "*Go ahead and distress.*" I grabbed one and the burgundy throw blanket that rested on the back of the couch. He even had a little green lighter sitting there for me. I flipped through channels, looking for something to watch, something that would take my mind off Esmeralda and Liam's faces. I lit one of the blunts, my body immediately flooding with ecstasy as I took a couple pills, back-to-back. I coughed, unable to hold the smoke in as it filled and tickled the insides of my lungs. The sudden jerking of my body, reminding me where my bruises were. I could see some of my stress float away in smoke and disappear through the ceiling. I stood up, walking around the living room, noticing the pro-black posters that hung around the room. His #WOKE and

#BLACKLIVESMATTER posters hung on either sides of an African queen poster. I walked into the kitchen wanting some juice, and noticed there hung pictures of Martin Luther King, Malcom X and Rosa Parks. I poured myself a glass of Minute Made Fruit Punch, and headed back to the couch, careful not to spill any on his rug. I felt like I was learning a little bit more about Sir Demetrius.

I suddenly heard the front door swivel open. "Yeah, she found it." I heard Demetrius say.

"Told you." Khi responded. They walked into the living room and Khi went right to the kitchen stools, digging into his bag. I began to think about Sean and immediately got saddened.

"Is it...okay if I eat upstairs?"

"Yeah that's fine. Doctor said she'll be here in a less than an hour." He replied. I could see the concern etched across his face. The sadness began to travel through my entire body. I hurried to the bedroom and sat on the plush black leather sofa that sat at the foot of the bed. There was a small glass coffee table, that matched the end tables, for me to put my bag down onto. I turned the TV on and watched a little bit of Gumball on Cartoon Network, still trying to lift my spirits.

KNOCK! KNOCK!

"Yeah?" I said, with a mouthful of bacon double cheeseburger. Demetrius walked in and stood against the doorframe, crossing his arms and his ankles.

"Are you okay?" He said, looking like he just wanted to wrap those large arms around me and make me feel safe.

"Not yet." I said, putting my burger down. "I just keep thinking about...everybody. Tracey, Clarence...Sean. Everybody I'll..." I wanted to cry, thinking back. "never see again." I could feel my throat beginning to close up. He came and sat in the empty seat to the left of me, wrapping his left arm around my shoulder.

"Let me help you. I've been through a lot of shit, just like last night. My brothers gone clean that mansion. It shouldn't be nothing to come up once they get back. Apparently, they lived on a fucking goldmine. I'm here for you. And when we get yo pops out, ya'll gone rebuild, stronger and bigger than ever before." He said smiling. I felt the hope that he tried to convey.

"Thank you." I said hugging him, excited to get some semblance of my life back. I sat back, wiping the tears from my eyes.

"Don't trip. I got you." He said softly, before standing to leave.

"How's he doing down there?" I asked. A part of me didn't want him to leave, but I knew I had no right to ask him to stay.

"He fucking his food up." He chuckled, flashing a smile.

DING!! DONG!! DING!! DONG!!

"I'll be back. I think that's Dr. Malia." He continued, then headed out of the room, returning less than a minute later with the doctor.

"Hi, you must be Liyah." The older, Indian doctor said, extending her hand with a warm smile, as she walked into the bedroom.

"I'll leave you ladies alone." He said, shutting the door behind him.

Dr. Malia looked me over from top to bottom. She checked out my bruises and ruled out any internal bleeding, and gave me stitches where they were needed: just the cuts on my cheek, above my right brow and also behind my left shoulder. She looked at my vaginal area, some tearing and scar tissue, but it should heal within days. I also requested her to give me a pregnancy test on top of all of the STD tests she was conducting. She drew some blood and also had me piss into a cup, advising me she'd be in touch with the results in just a couple of days before she exited.

I didn't really want to go sleep as of yet, so after the doctor left, I stayed awake watching tv, laying on the bed. Suddenly, Esmeralda burst into the room, causing the door handle to smash against the large mirror behind it. She wore all white, covered in blood, carrying Malakhi's head in her hand. She stood there laughing as she aimed her silver revolver in my face.

"Ahhhh!" I screamed in fear, waking up in a cold sweat. I was staring directly at the ceiling fan. It took a few seconds for me to realize I was now awake. Sitting up, I looked around the bedroom. The door was still shut and the mirror remained flawless. I plopped back down onto the pillow, removing the drool from my lips. The smell of bacon suddenly filled the room and then my nostrils. I got off of the now, messy bed and headed downstairs. Malakhi was sitting on the stool, at the kitchen counter, talking to Demetrius. He was in the kitchen cooking. Wearing a white wife beater and a pair of silver basketball shorts.

"Hey, sleepy-head. Welcome back." He said, seeing me come down the steps.

"How long have I been out?" I asked, still feeling exhausted.

"Well, it's almost 11 in the morning now. You was sleep by 1:30, 2 o'clock." He said, handing Malakhi a plate. "I figured we'd let you sleep."

"Thank you." I said, sitting in the empty seat next to Malakhi. He had a plate of bacon, eggs, sausages, and cheese potatoes covered with sour cream, and a side of wheat toast.

"Hey, Liyah!!" He exclaimed, as I snatched a piece of bacon off his plate. Demetrius sat a plate down in front of me, but I wasn't sure if I even had the energy to finish all of this.

"Ya'll go ahead and eat up. Then we can go get ya'll some clothes." He said, skipping steps as he ran up the stairs.

The three of us pulled up to my house on 98th, less than 2 hours later.

"Oh my, God." Malakhi said as Demetrius pulled his egg-white, 2009 Rolls Royce drop top coupe into the driveway. The *first* thing I noticed was that my truck was gone.

"What the fuck?!" I shouted, jumping out of the vehicle, before it had the chance to stop fully. I then noticed all our clothes and shoes, strewn across the front lawn. I walked up to the porch. There was a dried puddle of blood, where Tracey's body fell. That was when I saw the front door was wide open. "No, no, no, no!!" I cried, realizing *every* piece of furniture was gone, I ran to my bedroom closet. "No!!!!!" I cried out in anguish. A lump formed in my throat as I saw the safe that was bolted to the floor, had been ripped up and stolen. "Fuck!!" I wailed, punching the wall repeatedly.

"You okay?" I looked up. Demetrius ran in, gun drawn. Malakhi was right behind him. Demetrius, seeing there was no danger, put his gun back into his waistband. I fell off of my knees, onto my ass, sitting flat on the floor.

"No." I sobbed, shaking my head. "That was literally *everything* I had." I cried harder. "My fuckin safe! That was all of our money in there!" I exclaimed, punching the closet door with the back of my right fist. "That was all the money that daddy left us. To survive and pay the lawyer to get his charges dropped." Demetrius fell to his knees, hugging me tightly. Allowing me to cry into his beige cashmere sweater. I tried to pull away but he only squeezed me harder.

"Hey, hey. Listen to me." He said, pulling away so that he could look me in the face. He grabbed my chin. "I got you. Both of ya'll. I *been* tellin you that. You don't got to worry about *shit*. Okay?" He said, smiling. I reluctantly nodded my head in understanding. "Good. Now stop all that crying." He said, hugging me once more. "How much did you have in there?" He asked, helping me stand.

"$250,000." I replied, hurting to repeat that number out loud. His eyes grew wide as saucers.

"Fuck," he chuckled. "I can loan you the money. I'm sure I'll get it back from the mansion. It should be cleaned out by the end of this week."

"Wow. Really? That's a lot of money."

"You don't believe me when I say I got you, huh?" I began to wonder why he was being so nice. Like there was an ulterior motive somewhere I hadn't quite seen yet. "I like you…guys. I want to help." He responded. I was comfortable with his answer…for now.

DING!! DING!! DONG!!

The doorbell began chiming through the house. My anxiety went through the roof, as he pulled his gun out of his waistband. The three of us slowly walked to the front of the house. Demetrius ordered us to stay behind him and his pistol.

DING!! DING!! DONG!!

It rang again. I knew death was just on the other side of that hardwood door.

KNOCK!! KNOCK!! KNOCK!!

Demetrius reached for the handle, while motioning for us to move back. He snatched the door open, pistol at his eye level. It was just my landlord, Jerry. He looked as though he was getting ready to piss himself. I walked over and put my hand on the gun, quietly telling Demetrius to put it down.

"Jerry, I'm so sorry. Are you here about the mess?" I asked, doing my best to smooth over the situation.

"No, not anymore. I need you out of here, by the end of the week." He said, sounding pissed, yet still shaky. I could hear him mutter something about the lawn and then he said something about the pistol. He hurried back to his black, 2008 Jeep and rolled the window down. "I mean it, Liyah. You got 4 days. Or I'm calling the cops." He said, before pulling off away from the curb.

"Ya'll good to go?" He asked. "Let's go buy ya'll some stuff." We packed up what we were able to salvage, and tossed everything that they destroyed. I walked over the blood stain, saying goodbye to the house. My blood boiled as we walked by the spot my car should have been, and into his. I tried my best not to feel defeated, knowing he had my back. But, it was still hard to tell if his intentions were genuine or not.

"Can I use your phone? My lawyer's been waiting to hear from me." He reached into his pocket and handed me his iPhone 3, after unlocking it.

The line rang a few times, then the voicemail came on. "This is Darren. Please leave me a message." I left him a message, letting him know that everything is okay, for the most part. I had Demetrius leave his phone number, then hang up the line.

"Reach in the glove box for me and grab that Dutch." I did as he asked, reaching into the nearly empty glove box. Next to a silenced pistol, were a few packs of opened Dutch cigars. I grabbed one and handed it to him. He took one out. I could see it was packed, weed stuck out of both ends. He sparked it, the strong scent of Afghan Kush filling the car. He took a few pulls and handed it to me. The underside of my tongue began to tingle as the weed began to relax me.

"Whoa, wait-" Demetrius said as I turned around to hand the blunt to Malakhi.

"It's okay. He's been smoking for a while now. Plus he needs it as much as I do now."

"Oh, shit. My bad. I ain't know." Demetrius said chuckling. He put the car into drive, and pulled out of the driveway.

Demetrius' phone began to ring, vibrating wildly in the center cup holder. He picked it up, answering. "Yeah?" He paused for a few seconds, then handing it over to me, saying, "Here, It's your lawyer."

"Hey, Darren?" I answered, grabbing the phone from him.

"Oh my, God! Liyah, are you okay?"

"Yeah, I'm okay, now. It's been a hellacious couple of days." I said, before letting him know about Liam and Esmeralda.

"I had my guys track Liam down. We found an Island in the middle of Tijuana waters. But, I'm guessing that's where you just came from?" He asked, matter-of-factly. "*Fuck*, this guys slippery, like an eel." He sighed, frustrated. I didn't want to tell him that we killed Liam. That could possibly stop my dad from being let out, so I left that little bit of information out. "Here, I'll just go ahead and have a team go out to the mansion."

"Actually. You think you can give it just a *few* days?" I asked, thinking about what Demetrius told me. He still has people cleaning that house of everything of value. If the feds were to go, they'd just take everything. I just want them to find the bodies. Evidence of the mutilation. That's all the authorities needed. The riches that lay in that mansion, are now my families. And I wanted as much as humanly possible.

"What are you up to, Miss Reyes?" He asked. I grew quiet for a second.

"How long until my dad get his retrial?"

"It's tough to say. We need all the evidence we can get before presenting it to a judge, or it looks sloppy. And a case like *this*, there's no room for error. We are currently still at square one. I have the evidence you gave me locked I'm my drawer so it's a start. But we *have* to get into that house."

"Two days." Demetrius whispered.

"Give me four days. Just four days from right now and you guys can swarm the mansion."

"Most I can do is 72 hours from midnight. Just…keep me posted. Okay?"

"Thanks Darren. I will." I said, hanging up the phone.

CHAPTER 16

D emetrius stayed true to his word and leant me the entire $250,000. It was hard taking the money from him, but I had to get me and Malakhi back on our feet. He surprised me with another other $50,000 to pay Darren the remaining legal fees to get my dad out of prison.

Darren proved himself as a loyal little worker bee. After giving him the okay to send the FBI to Esmeralda and Liam's mansion, he was able to find enough evidence to get my father a retrial in just a couple of weeks from now. The final bail amount wouldn't be settled until the end of the trial, but so far, everything was good to go.

It's now been a month, to the day that Demetrius, Clarence and Sean got together to come and save me, and 5 since my family was torn apart. My relationship with Demetrius had begun to blossom into something a little more than friends. I tried to fight the attraction towards him but, the moment we kissed, was when I realized it was something not worth fighting.

It was just a couple weeks ago, during Independence Day. Rodney and James came over to enjoy some festivities and BBQ. I was still shaken up after finding out Sean's baby had survived. All the other tests the doctor ran came back that I was healthy as a horse. Still overwhelmed with emotion, I decided to head upstairs and get some quiet time, not knowing how to even bring up me being pregnant by Sean. I walked into the room and shut the door, sitting on the edge of the bed preparing to roll myself a blunt.

KNOCK!! KNOCK!! KNOCK!!

"Come in." I responded, placing a few large nugs of weed into a small silver grinder, with a picture of Marilyn Monroe on the top. Demetrius walked in and shut the door behind him, sitting at the foot of the bed.

"You okay?" He asked, looking me dead in my face. I nodded, looking up at him, lying. I could tell by the expression on his face that he didn't fully believe me.

"I'm fine, I just still have a lot on my mind." I said starting to roll the weed in it's wrap.

"If you want to talk, just let me know." He said, standing to leave.

"You want to smoke one with me?" I asked, stopping him from walking out the room.

"For sure." He said, retaking his place on the bed. "You gone tell me what's really on your mind?" He asked as I passed him the blunt. He looked right through me with those large brown eyes. I smiled passively, as I was used to doing my whole life. Using my looks and charm to get me out of situations I didn't want to be in. I continuously had to remind myself not to say the words, "I'm pregnant with my dead ex's baby, and I want to keep it, but I really like the way I feel around you and I know this baby will cause a problem. Leaving me to be a single parent, *inevitably*."

"You ever just want to say something, but you're not sure how they'll look at you afterwards? Like there's a load on your chest…you're embarrassed to get off?"

"You're fucking beautiful yo. And I know you just been through a lot, but you ain't gotta worry no more." He said, looking me in my eyes, handing me the blunt.

Demetrius looked at me, with those gorgeous brown eyes. Neither of us saying a word, he leaned in, kissing me. I wrapped my arms around his shoulders, kissing him back. He pulled me closer to him as he wrapped his arms around my waist. I stopped myself, suddenly, having flash backs of Bruno and waking up in a pool of blood, sore. I buried my face into the pillows as my thoughts brought me to tears.

"Hey. Don't do that crying shit, ma." He said with a half-smile. He laid down on the bed next to me. Holding my face with both hands, he used his thumbs to wipe away my tears. I grabbed his forearm, trying not to cry more. We kissed again. This time a little more passionately "I'm sorry. Am I doing to much right now or-" He started. I answered his question by grabbing his face and planting a kiss right on his lips.

The two of us decided to go up to Sacramento and pay my dad a visit James had to stay back. I looked up as movement from behind the glass, caught my attention. My father was looking directly at me, well at us. He'd caught us kissing.

"Who is that?" He asked. I read his lips as he pointed at us, his face twisted up like he'd just swallowed a lemon slice.

"Turn around..." I said smiling. I watched my father's face light up like the Christmas tree in the middle of Rockefeller Center as the COs let the prisoners file in.

"My man! My son before sons! How are you?! I hope Sandra's treating you right." Dad said excitedly as he sat down. "Boy, is it good to see you!" He said excitedly.

"Hi dad." I said waving.

"I'm sorry, baby girl. How are you. How you been? You been fighting?" He asked.

"Have I been – Dad, have you gotten the letter I sent?"

"No, not yet. Why what's up?"

"Should I leave you guys alone?" Demetrius asked.

"What? No. Why?" My dad asked confused. "What's going on?" He continued. Tears filled my eyes, as it began to get hard to look at him. "Liyah, what's up, baby girl. Talk to me." My father pleaded. I could see his heart breaking as I fought breaking down in front of him. A tear fell out of his left eye and dropped onto his red jumpsuit. "Where are my sons?"

"Dad, I can't go over that. It's too hard to even imagine what-." Just thinking about what Malakhi told me had happened was difficult. How did he expect me to just casually tell him, like something I did over the weekend? "It's in the letter I sent to you-"

"I don't!!" he yelled, pounding his heavy fists on the table. He looked around, seeing the correctional officers notice his outburst. He looked back over to me. "I don't want to read about it in no fucking letter, Liyah. What happened to my sons?" He whispered, which scared me more than him yelling.

"Malik was killed." I said, blurting out, before telling him what Malakhi told me, word for word.

He sat back in his chair, shaking his head. "No. Nah, man." He continued, shaking his head in disbelief.

"They killed Tracey right in front of me, then took me to fuckin Mexico." I said, feeling a knot grow in my throat. It felt so big I thought it was going to suffocate me. It was hard to breathe for a little bit. Feeling Demetrius' hand on my back helped me to find my rhythm.

I've never seen my father cry. Even when my mother died. He didn't even shed a tear at the releasing of her ashes. He looked destroyed. I could see the light fleeing from the colors in his eyes, as the news all but broke him down. The cracks in my heart began to reopen, like fresh wounds. I thought about Malakhi and how hurt he is. Our brother, his best friend before birth, was savagely taken away from us.

"Sean was the reason they knew more than we thought."

"What did he have to do with -?" His eyes squinted, as he seemed to look directly through me. "No...that was Liam's son?" He stated. I nodded my head yes. "Wow that explains so much."

"What? Did something happen in here I asked?"

He nodded his head, "Yeah. Not three days after I met Sean, we got a new inmate on our block – tried to shank me in the shower."

"What happened to him?" Demetrius asked?"

"Hell, you already know young blood. He ended up stabbing himself in the neck that night." He let a smile cross his face, then almost immediately wiped it away.

"Now what's going on with ya'll two? Where James?"

"What you mean, Dad?"

"I seen ya'll suckin face, girl. Don't play wit me?"

"She deserves a man with the same hustle and mindset as her father. Someone who will appreciate her strengths and accept her flaws. I like her a lot. I haven't...felt this way since I lost Mallory and Alicia.

"You mean that?" My dad asked, after a few tense moments of silence. "If I trust my babies in anyone's hands, its yours. You guys are what, six years apart? I guess that's cool. Ya'll grown! You just better treat her right man. I don't wanna have to reach out from inside here and extend my sentence." My dad said, trying to force himself to wear a smile. Though we all knew he was serious. I could tell the news of Malik gutted him.

"Oh for sure! Nothing but. It was good seeing you. I feel like you guys should have some alone time. Ima get up with you a little later." Him and Demetrius shook hands quickly.

"Aye!" The CO shouted.

"Sorry blood." Demetrius said "I'll see you outside."

I nodded my head yes as he kissed my cheek. "Dad, I have a problem." I said with my head hung low.

"What's up? Something I don't know about?" He asked.

"I'm pregnant." I said solemnly. He paused for a few seconds, staring me dead in the eyes.

He was confused as he asked, "How long have you and D. been fuckin' wit each other? Last time I saw you, you was wit Sean."

"We haven't done that yet! But the baby *is* Sean's." He sat still, staring at me.

"And you're still pregnant?" He asked. His expression seemed to change to anger. "Does *he* know?" He continued.

"Yes…" I said timidly, "and, no…he doesn't."

"Go kill that fuckin' baby. I don't want that nigga's bloodline nowhere near mine. Fuck no! Fuck that! You *better* not be pregnant the next time I see you." He said as he stood up from the steel bench. "You should have known better than to tell me that shit." He turned to leave, then looked back at me over his right shoulder. "I love you girl!" He said as he turned and walked away.

"Love you too Daddy." I replied heartbroken, too low for him to hear. I watched as he returned back to the secured area, escorted by the COs.

I sat there, tearing up, taking a moment to pull myself together before meeting Demetrius outside. My father was right. I couldn't keep this baby knowing his father was the son of the person who literally brought my family to its knees. But this baby is also an extension of me and doesn't *have* to have anything to do with Sean. In any case, there was a decision to be made and Demetrius has a right to know, especially if anything he told my father was true. I felt like, once again, a weight was on my shoulders. Not to mention my brother's funeral in a few days. I really hope they let my Dad out so that he can make it like he did my Mom's.

I managed to hold back tears as I climbed into Demetrius's black Range Rover. He had a blunt lit and was playing Nas on low. "Are you okay?" He asked

"Yeah, why wouldn't I be?" I said, grabbing the blunt from him.

"I don't know, you look sad walking up to the car." He started the engine and put the car in gear.

I spent most of the car ride staring out the car window, compelled by my thoughts. I looked up with a smile, suddenly feeling his hand on my knee.

"You want to go away this weekend?" He asked. "After the funeral, the three of us should get out of here for a while. What do you think?" He asked

"I would like that." I responded.

"Come here, beautiful." He said biting that bottom lip. I leaned in and kissed him.

Demetrius dropped me off at my new, money-green Charger SRT8. I looked at my phone to check the time and realized I was almost 10 minutes late to meet my realtor, Karen. I shot her a quick text message, lying that I was stuck in traffic. I felt bad because, for the last few days, she's been helping me find another place. Today, she's showing me a gorgeous condominium in Jack London Square.

I turned left onto 4th street and stopped in front of the 4th Street Condos, parking right behind Karen's C 300. She got out of the car once she seen me walking up to the stairs.

Karen was short, about 5'. She tossed her long, elbow-length brunette locks, over her left shoulder. She was hanging up a call, trying to juggle what seemed to be a heavy manila folder.

"Hi, Karen, I'm so sorry I'm late."

"No, no, no. Don't worry about it! It's really okay. I had the chance to dot some T's and cross some I's." She joked. We shared a chuckle before walking up the steps behind me. There was an older man standing there, holding the door open for us. He wore a black uniform, with a black top hat.

"Hey, Rich." She said, as we passed.

"Hey, ladies. Nice day." He responded. We walked straight to the elevator. Luckily, someone was already getting off as we approached. The lobby was gorgeous, so I *knew* the unit was even better. Directly to the right of the entrance, was the security desk, made of polished hardwood, with a charcoal counter top. It was manned by two officers at all times. 24/7. The walls were made of singed, polished hardwood, matching the floors. Cascading down the entire left wall, was a waterfall, with lights that changed calming blues, greens and yellows.

We continued to the shiny elevators, passed the plush, brown chairs in the waiting area. "You are going to *love* this place. The unit we'll be viewing has three bedrooms, 3 and a half baths, with hardwood floors throughout *and* state-of-the-art appliances. The unit also comes with a washer and a dryer in the unit." She said, excitedly as I waited for the elevator to finish its ascent, so that we could get off.

My anxiety only seemed to worsen as we walked down the long, silent hallway. I noticed as we passed by the other three units, that they all had a small light near the door and apartment number. She turned the key, opening the door.

I was immediately blown away by the entry. The kitchen was large for an apartment. It was almost the size of the one in my family's home, with granite counter tops and black, wooden cabinets. All of the appliances were silver, including the brand-new Samsung fridge. I walked up a couple of steps leading, into the large living room. There was a large Sony flat-screen, housed above a black, stone fireplace. The entire wall adjacent from the entrance, was 3 great windows, giving an amazing view of the Bay and the Oakland docks. I stepped up to the window, placing my hand on the glass. I could see the exact spot I stepped off of my father's boat. My mind showed me images of the late night/early morning that I escaped with my life.

I turned around. Karen stood behind me, just at the bottom of the steps, smiling at me. I smiled back as I walked down the hallway, passed the laundry room, with counters to match to kitchen, and a brand-new washer and dryer. Black and silver like the rest of the appliances. I peeked into the 2 guest bedrooms, impressed by the layouts and sizes. I loved that each bedroom had it's own bath. I was really blown away when I walked into the master. The bed rested against the entry wall.

Like the living room, there was a flat screen, housed above a fireplace, which was built into a small, solid sliver of wall, surrounded by windows. Providing a breathtaking view of the city below.

"Also, remember, no one can see into these windows. *All* of these windows are one-sided." Karen said as we walked into the closet, which was about the same size as the kitchen. This place had my name written all over it.

"What next? I want it." I said, looking her in her eyes. "Does it come with the furniture?"

"I-i-it can." She said, nodding her head fervently. "It will be another $6,000 on the deposit."

"Will you take cash?" I asked.

"Uhm," she said, bewildered. "We can only take money order, check or cashier's check. But once we file the paperwork, with the down of 20%, she's all yours. Meet me at my office?" She asked.

"See you there. Just have to head to the bank first."

I was clicking in my seat belt to head over to the bank when my phone started to ring. The caller I.D. read Rebecca Thourghtly, Malik and Malakhi's social worker. Child protective services have been trying to take Malakhi from me since Malik died, adding to my list of worries.

"Hey Rebecca." I answered dryly.

"Hey Liyah. I spoke with the CPS workers. Things are not looking too good. With all that has happened with you guys, they are not sure that Malakhi is safe. They want him in the system, for his own safety."

"What?! No. There is no one that will hurt him. Please he will be 18 in less than 2 years."

"That was a point I wanted to bring up. If you let them take him, he will age out December and be back with you, *or* we can push for emancipation." I told her to start that process. I don't even know why she didn't start that shit to begin with.

After securing the gorgeous condo with Karen, I headed back to the house to relax a little bit, before my doctor's appointment. I kicked off my pumps and propped my feet up on the sofa, flipping through channels. I heard the grinding noise of the garage door opening, then closing again. I found myself excited to see him. So excited, that when a few moments had passed and he hadn't walked in, I became disappointed.

I got up from the couch and went over to the garage door, noticing that the hatch to Demetrius' Range was opened. I noticed that his brothers Rodney and James were standing in the garage with him, surrounding four large wooden crates.

"Hey Baby!" He said reaching for me to come over. I did.

"is this the rest of the stuff from Liam's mansion?" I asked.

"Yup. Just came through this morning. I got my bitches getting that powder together to hit the streets." Rodney said. "Shit we almost at a million profit, already."

"It will be a hell of a lot more if we got rid of the competition." I said as I walked over to one of the boxes. I grabbed one of the automatic rifles, a pistol and a large machete. "Can you get these painted for me." I asked setting them aside from the others. "Pink."

"Pink?" They all asked in union.

"And…black." I said before kissing him on the cheek and heading back into the house.

"Damn bro! She fine." Rodney said.

"For Real! I had a crush on her since we was in diapers. How'd she pick yo ugly ass?" James added, laughing.

"Bruh shut the fuck up and get back to work!" I heard Demetrius laughing. "Alyssa gone kick Rod ass. I ain't gotta do it." I noticed it was almost time for me to go. I slipped back into my Giuseppe pumps and grabbed my car keys. I let Demetrius know I would be back in a little while. Leaving before we had the opportunity to inquire about where I was going.

I sat in Planned Parenthood, scanning the room. There were kids running around playing in all directions. One of them were moving so fast he almost tripped over my feet. I looked around at the mixed emotions on the pregnant women's faces. Some of them looked happy, the majority however, looked like they were making the worst mistake of their lives. I, myself felt somewhere in between.

"Liyah! Liyah Reyes!" A nurse asked coming out of a large wooden door. She was an older frumpy little white lady with brown curly hair wearing Pink Scooby Doo scrubs. I took deep breaths through my anxiety as I followed her into the exam room. "The doctor will be with you in just a moment." The nurse said after handing me a gown.

I sat on the table, legs in stirrups as Dr. Malia and the nurse prepped me for the procedure. The nurse gave me a small white cup, with two little pink pills inside. Said it's supposed to make *any* pain manageable.

"Ok. You ready?" She asked. I lied, nodding my head, *yes*. I was terrified, not knowing what to expect. I laid back, staring at the ceiling. I suddenly began to feel a great pressure, followed by, what could only be described, as my worse period to date. The pills they gave me, seemed to do nothing to aid the pain. I gripped onto the arms of the chair, clenching my jaw, trying to brace through it. I focused on the sound of the vacuum, trying to distract myself from what was going on between my legs. Just when too much was becoming enough, "Alright, your all done." She said unexpectedly.

"What? Really?" I asked, sitting up to face her. She was popping off her bloody gloves. I laid back down, still in shock, wiping the tears from my eyes.

I sat in the car, bawling onto my steering wheel. The guilt of killing an innocent human life starting to hit me like a ton of bricks.

I walked through the front door and was immediately met by the smell of taco meat. Khi was sitting at the kitchen island, his favorite place to eat. "Hey, Big Head." I said hugging him. I did my best to remain upbeat, when deep down inside, I truly felt like shit. I wanted nothing more than to just curl up and die.

"Where you been at?" He asked, as I took a seat on the couch next to Demetrius.

"Being grown, nigga." I said chuckling, giving D. a kiss on the cheek. "Oh, babe, I got the condo."

"That's what's up. So ya'll really just gone up and leave me, huh?" He asked, sounding disappointed. I couldn't help but to smile.

"I'm not leaving you." I responded with a kiss on his lips, softly caressing the back of his neck.

"You bet' not." He said smiling. "You hungry?"

"No, not right now." I patted his shoulder, before standing to my feet, bending down to pick up my shoes. "I want to take a bath and relax a bit." I said as I headed up the stairs. I filled the tub, with Tokyo Milk, Bon-Bon bubbling bath. Erupting the bathroom in a vanilla and cinnamon scent. The water stung my skin a bit, as I stepped in, but I was able to quickly adjust to it.

I rubbed my belly, as tears came to my eyes. I knew deep down in my heart, that I had to get rid of that baby. But I couldn't seem to shake the immense amount of guilt that I felt.

KNOCK!! KNOCK!! KNOCK!!

I ducked underneath the water, so that I could disguise my tears, with a soaked face.

"Hey, baby." Demetrius said as the bathroom door began to slowly swing open. I watched him peek his head around the corner.

"Hey, what's up?" I smiled.

"My dudes, got those keys sold." He walked in with a large, fire engine-red Gucci gym bag.

"Really? How many?" I asked as he dropped the bag next to the tub. He knelt down, snatching the zipper back. All I could see were large, $100 bills in yellow straps. My eyes grew wide as the bag, thumbing through one of the stacks.

"All 80 of them muhfuckas." He said, standing up straight, clapping his hands in front of him. "It's $13 million in that bag."

"How…how'd they sale all of that so fast?" I said through a chuckle.

"We got some buyers who buy in bulk. *BULK BULK.*" He said, spreading his arms wide. "Don't worry about paying me back. And don't worry about the guys. They been paid already, too."

"Are you telling me…"

"It's all yours, baby." He said smiling.

"Thank you so much, baby." I said running my hand through the bag of money.

"And there's a lot more just waiting to be picked up." He said, sitting on the toilet, lighting a blunt. I looked at him, in awe of how beautiful he was, inside and out.

We spent the rest of the evening cuddled up in Demetrius' large California King bed, under his burgundy chiffon comforter. We smoked almost 6 blunts as we watched Netflix movies. It felt amazing to just be held. Once I heard him snoring, I sobbed silently into my pillow until I dozed off myself.

I woke up alone in the middle of Demetrius' large, custom-made, double-king bed. I heard the sounds of cooing from the baby monitor on my nightstand, with the sound of Demetrius humming softly. I snatched the covers back, and grabbed my large, pink Versace robe from off of the couch in the corner of the room. I walked down the hall to the nursery and peeked through the crack in door, peering in at Demetrius, holding our newborn baby girl. I couldn't help but think how happy I was that Sean's seed was ejected to make room for his. He looked up at me, smiling, putting his finger to his lips, telling me to stay quiet. I nodded my head and went down the stairs for a glass of cold water.

As my foot was getting ready to leave the bottom step, I heard a loud crash, coming from the kitchen. Intrigued, I continued. I wanted to find the source of the crash. I heard a gun clock from behind me. I spun around in a cold fear, only to see Esmeralda holding a large, silver pistol to my face.

CHAPTER 17

I shot up in bed, looking around the bedroom. Demetrius was next to me, in a dead sleep. I realized the sun was up again, shining through the silk curtains. I shook my head, realizing it was only a dream. It felt more real than actual life. I laid back down, trying to soothe my spirit, looking over at Demetrius, running my hand over his large back tattoo of *The Lord's Prayer*.

I rolled onto my back, thinking about how cute he looked with that baby, in my dream. I felt guilty for not feeling guilty, in the dream, about this abortion.

Slowly rolling out of bed, as to not wake Demetrius, I went downstairs to my bedroom and walked into the bathroom, looking at myself in the mirror. A flood of tears began to rush down my cheeks as I sobbed, stepping over the bag of money to get into the shower. I started the over head faucets, letting the water wash away my tears as they came, trying to let the baby go. I was amazed that little fucker even survived after Esmeralda and Liam's house of horrors.

"Whoa! Shit!" I screamed, feeling Demetrius' cold hands around my waist and his hard dick pressed firmly above my ass cheeks. I was so into my thoughts, I hadn't even noticed him get into the shower with me, let alone come in the bathroom.

"I'm sorry, boo." He chuckled. "I didn't mean to scare you." I spun around kissing him, not wanting him to even have the chance to notice I'd been crying.

A couple of hard rounds in the shower, started getting my mind in the correct place.

"Imma see you later." He said, holding my chin kissing me.

"Where you going?" I asked.

"It's time to make some moves. Get Stephan's territory back before he gets out." He kissed me on the forehead, then stepped out of the shower. I watched his booty jiggle as he walked away.

"Wait. Can I go?" I asked, following him into the bathroom, still dripping wet. He walked into the bedroom closet and handed me a fresh towel.

"Hell nah, you can't go." He said as the two of us dried off. "Ain't no way you're coming with me. Shit can go real left, real fast." He said, shaking his head.

"Baby, you're giving my father a foundation to stand on when he gets out. I want to help."

"Girl, if something happened to you, your pops would skin me alive. I've *seen* it happen."

"Seriously?"

"Don't tell him I said shit." He replied, chuckling. He sat on the edge of the bed after sliding back into his basketball shorts, then sliding jeans on over them.

"Nothing's going to happen. I'll just sit in the car. Watch from afar." He bit his lip, looking at my naked body up and down. I walked over and straddled him, wrapping my arms around his neck. "Please, babe. Let me come." I whined. He sat quietly for a few moments.

"Baby, me and Khi need to know what's going on if we gone be in this life. We want to help our dad, babe. If I fall, I want it to be on my back, kicking and screaming. Not on my stomach because I couldn't fight."

"Alright, alright." He said a moment later, scratching the bridge of his nose. "But ya'll two niggas stay in the car. For real." He ordered. "Now if it came down to it, can you shoot?"

I tilted my head to the right in disbelief. "My dad's Stephan Reyes, baby. Come on." I responded, standing. He stood up as well.

"Aight. Be ready in ten." He smacked my ass before exiting the room and closing the door.

I sat in the backseat of Demetrius' black Denali, next to Khi. Rodney sat in the passenger seat, and James sat in the empty seat behind him. I was dressed in all black; a slim Givenchy sweater and some skinny True Religion jeans, with a pair of black on black forces. I pulled my hair up into a high, slicked-back ponytail. We led the line of four other large, black SUVs, filled with men armed to the teeth. Demetrius handed me a small, pink PX4 pistol, shortly before we left the house. I was already in love. I called her peaches.

My anxiety began to shoot through the roof as we rode right by the house Clarence and Tracey lived in. My chest began to pound as I noticed it had been burned down and boarded up. I focused my eyes forward, trying to hold back the pain from the past. We rode further down the street and parked outside of an abandoned building.

"Aight, we here." D. said shifting the car into park.

"What you want us to do?" Malakhi asked, taking his seat belt off.

"*Stay* here." He responded, turning around, looking me directly in my eyes. Malakhi slowly buckled his seat belt. Demetrius then jumped out of the car, followed by Rodney and James. I watched as they backtracked, about 4 houses down, catching up with the other 16 guys behind us. I was unable to look away, as they ran into a two-story, burgundy duplex. The gun fire ensued no sooner than they crossed the threshold for the front yard, storming in like swat.

The bullets seemed like they lasted forever, when in reality it was only a few seconds. Demetrius and James came running out of the bottom unit, arms filled with bags. Rodney followed behind them, less than a second later, with a few guys from the top unit. After D. and his brother, dropped their bags into the back and jumped into the truck, they sped off, burning rubber.

"Whoooo!! Fuck yeah! I missed this shit, bruh." James said excitedly pounding the butt of his pistol against the driver's headrest.

"Calm down, nigga. We still gotta find they fuckin' boss." Rodney interjected.

"No need. We already know where he is." Demetrius said. "All we got to do is take a trip down to San Jose." He added as we hit the on ramp to the 580.

"Yeah, you gone like this one." James said, smiling, looking at me and Khi

"Dude, shut the fuck up." Rodney insisted. James sucked his teeth, waving him off as he gazed out of his window, smoking his blunt. I leaned forward, looking at him from around Malakhi, whom was just staring out of the window as well, seemingly just enjoying the ride.

"Why? Who is he?" I asked.

"See, I was planning on telling her after so that she don't do no stupid shit." Demetrius argued. "He's your mom's brother, babe." He blamed your dad for leaving him to die. He was the reason Liam and Esmeralda knew everything he needed to know about you guys."

"Wait, what? Our *Uncle*? We…" Malakhi stammered, unable to formulate his own thoughts. "Why would mom not tell us *we had… have a uncle?*"

"Are you really surprised. We thought Grandma Felisha was dead until mom died." I said. My mind began to swirl. It slowly became more and more difficult to grasp the simplest of concepts once Demetrius broke the news. I started getting hot, under the collar, rolling the window all the way down, to take in as much air as I possibly could. I needed to see this for my self. "Is that where we headed to now?" I asked.

"Nah, I'm dropping ya'll off. You're done." Demetrius responded.

"What? No. We need to be with you every step of the way. How did you even know he was our uncle?" I asked.

He looked at me through the rearview. "At your dad's trial. I recognized him from a few pictures."

"He actually went?" Malakhi asked.

"Sure did. And reported everything to Liam ever since. Hiring Phil…well, Sean, was *his* idea."

I felt myself once again getting sad. I shook the feeling and turned it into anger. "Fuck that. We're coming with you. I want to be the one to put a bullet in this bitch's face."

"Fuck." He sighed out of frustration. "Why can't I say no to you?"

"Because you know she right. It's *her* blood. She got the right to spill it." Rodney replied.

The ride was long, almost 2 hours. I couldn't wait to lay eyes on the son of a bitch that turned his back on his family. We stopped in front of the gate, of a gorgeous, ranch-styled, three-story home. Each iron Rod was about 8' tall, with sharp arrowheads at the tip of each, discouraging anyone from trying to climb it. The house sat on a large lot, with a front yard the size of an acre. The place looked quiet. Too quiet. I looked around, noticing there were no neighbors near.

"Where all the security at?" James asked.

"I don't give a fuck. We going in." Demetrius said before they exited the truck, large, armor-piercing rifles in hand. A couple of the guys from the other SUVs were already working on getting the fence open. I suddenly heard a loud bang, accompanied by a bright spark, coming from the fence. It swung open like it was never locked. Suddenly 3 men, wearing baggy street clothes, rushed out of the front entrance of the house, guns drawn, like an action movie. They never left the porch. Our eyes were glued to the window, as the men filed into the house. The gunshots rang out immediately.

"We should go in." I said to Malakhi. He dug into the pouch of his black hoodie, and retrieved a silver .380. "Where did you get that from?" I asked shocked. "Did Deme-"

"No, sis. Let's go." He said, cutting me off. He reached for the door, jumping down to the tan gravel below. He began walking towards the sounds of gunfire, ducking against the fences 4ft, stone foundation.

"Fuck." I whispered, following him into the yard. Every bone in my body wanted to run back to the safety of the vehicle. But, I fought passed the urge of cowardice.

We stepped around the three goons that were bleeding out onto the front porch, and into the house. There were bodies scattered all over the foyer, and up the staircase leading to the second floor. We saw 4 of our guys, checking bodies, making sure no one would wake up.

"This nigga still breathing." One of the goons said. He put his rifle to the back of the mans head and pulled the trigger. Out of fear and surprise, I let out a yelp, trying not to scream. Still on edge, all four of them spun to face us, guns drawn.

"Aye, ya'll need to go back to the car!" One of them said.

"Where's Demetrius?" I asked, walking up to him.

"Nah, it's not safe yet for ya'll in here." He said, stopping me.

"Get out...of my way." I said, pushing him as hard as I could. I used the entire weight of my 5'6 frame to displace him, but it did nothing to his 6'6 stature. He stepped back and gestured for me to pass him.

"Watch they back, bruh." He ordered one of the others. "They in the basement." He added as we began walking, passing even more bodies. We walked down a flight of steps, to the lower floor. It was a basement that had been completely converted into an entertainment space. About the size of a 1 bedroom apartment.

"Fuck you!" I heard a male voice yell at the top of his lungs, followed by a metallic thud.

"Nah, fuck you. Why'd you sell out?" Demetrius said, standing before a man, tied to a wooden chair. He was accompanied by Rodney and James, and a few other of our crew. Suddenly, the man turned his attention to me, looking me directly in the eyes.

"Damn, you've grown." He said, locking eyes with me.

Demetrius spun around, looking at me. "Dude, what the fuck?!" He yelled at the guy who brought us down.

"My bad, boss. Tariq told me bring her to you." The guy responded. He stood there glaring at him. For a second I thought he was going to turn his gun to him.

"Fuck, man. Whatever." He said, looking back at me. He forced a smile across his face as he looked to me. "Well, babe, meet your good old uncle Andy." I looked at him. He was still glaring at me. I'd just met him and I hated him already.

"You got my brother and my mother killed." I said, walking up to him.

"Which one? Khi or Malik?" He asked nonchalantly, smiling.

"What the *fuck* does that matter? You piece of shit!" Malakhi yelled.

"Well, it matters because *all* of you should be dead by now. Come to think about it, Esmeralda has been quiet for a few weeks."

"Why?" I asked. It seemed like a moot point now, but something in me needed to know *why*? He answered the question, saying dad and Johnny left him for dead during one of their run-throughs. He was able to crawl out before the police flooded the scene, forcing him to get himself back to health. Once he had gotten back to 100%, he first went after Liam, but Stephan had already gotten him locked up, and Esmeralda thought he'd be perfect for her plan to bring Steph down.

"She asked if I wanted to sell you to the highest bidder, but I wanted to watch each of you suffer, by having you watch your *loved ones* die." He began to chuckle. Now I wish I would've just cut your fucking tongue out myself!" He screamed full of hate. I snatched the gun from Demetrius.

BAH!!! BAH!!!!

"Ahhhh!!!!" He screamed, after I put a bullet in each of his kneecaps. "You fucking bitch! I'll kill you! I swear to fucking God I'm going to skin you ali-"

BAH!! BAH!! BAH!! BAH!!

Blood poured out of his mouth as smoke rose from the four shots placed into his heart. His head slumped down, chin into his chest. His eyes were wide open. I looked around, trying to see who it was that fired the shot. Malakhi had his gun raised, still smoking, trained on our Uncle, well Andrew. I walked over to him, lowering the gun, then taking it from him.

"Aaaaaahh!! Let me go!" All of our attention suddenly shot to the steps of the basement.

"Look what we found upstairs, hiding under the bed." Tariq said, holding a busty blonde wearing nothing but a thin, silk robe, by the hair. He had a large hunting knife to her jugular.

"Is there anyone else in the house?" I asked him. She began frantically shaking her head, no.

"Just a dog." Responded Tariq.

"Good, let me see the knife." I ordered, with the palm of my hand out. He looked over at Demetrius for approval, then handed it over. Without a second thought, I ran the blade deep into the left side of her neck, until it protruded from the other side. Tariq let her drop to the floor, bleeding out. "Get *anything* valuable, and burn this bitch down. Take all those foreigns, too." I ordered, handing Tariq back his knife, and Demetrius back his gun. "Let's go." I said, grabbing Malakhi by the breasts of his coat.

I held my breath as we walked up the steps and through the foyer. Our guys already started to clear out the dead thugs from the house, piling them up outside the front lawn. There was a guy near them, dousing them in gasoline. I couldn't wait to watch the aftermath unfold on the news tonight.

"Oh my God!" Malakhi exclaimed. "You almost chopped her fucking head off!" He continued once we made it to the SUV. I grabbed the half of blunt that was located in the ashtray and sparked it. The guys followed to the car soon after.

"Like taking candy from a baby." James said, sliding into the backseat, next to Khi. Demetrius slammed the hatch shut, then hopped into the driver's seat.

"Yeah, that was too easy, B." Rodney replied.

"I expected the nigga to have more heat than that." Demetrius added, digging into his glove box to light a pre-rolled blunt.

"He was *mad* cocky, though." James said, lighting one of his own.

"That's prolly all he thought he needed." Demetrius said, choking on the blunt.

It was an awkward ride back to Oakland. I could tell by Demetrius stealing glances at me from the rearview, that he was a little less than happy about me and Malakhi going in there today. I jumped down from the SUV and headed to the front door, once we made it to the house.

"We gone talk a little later." Demetrius said, heading to the garage with all the guys. They each carrying a few duffels of all different colors.

"Is he mad at us, Li?" Khi asked, sitting down on the couch. I headed into the kitchen to warm up some taco ingredients from the night before.

"I know he better-fucking-not be." I said, stopping what I was doing, coming out of the kitchen. "But, you don't worry about him. I got this." I said before returning to my food.

"You going to dad's retrial?" He asked. He was full of interesting questions today.

"Of course I am. Why *wouldn't* I go?"

"Maybe he should stay in there." He said, coming into the kitchen with me. My eyebrows raised.

"Why do you feel like that? Why don't you want him out?" I asked handing him a quickly-thrown together beef taco with shredded cheddar, cheese and lettuce.

"I lost-, *we* lost a brother. All fuckin because he couldn't *figure* out when to *get* out. He couldn't make money the right way. Couldn't even fuckin kill Liam when he *should've*. That could've avoided all of this shit!" He said, frustrated. "Now Malik is dead and we're going to join him. I know it." I sat my plate down on the kitchen island, rushing over to him.

"Don't say that. Him and mom just wanted a better life for us. They loved us. Plus, Liam is dead. His crazy ass wife is dead and so is Sean. *No one's* coming after us." I said, trying to reassure him.

"Man…" He said, sucking his teeth, snatching away from me, then replied, "I got friends whose parents are lawyers, restaurant and casino owners. They actually made sure their kids had *good* lives. I'd rather be safe and broke, than in danger and rich, and worrying about shit like this." He took his food and headed up the stairs. I had no idea what to even say to that. He was right, but we're in *this* situation now. We can't go back and tell daddy not to sell drugs with Uncle Johnny.

"Babe!" I heard Demetrius yell, just a few moments later. "What the fuck was that?" He asked, once making it into the living room. I was sitting on the couch, just about to start eating my tacos. He walked over and stood next to me, looking legitimately pissed off, but I couldn't understand why.

"What are you talking about?"

"Seriously?! Bruh, you was supposed to stay in the fuckin truck with your brother!" He yelled, genuinely upset. I couldn't help but feel like I did something wrong. Though I know there was nothing I've done wrong.

"Whoa!" I said standing. "We had the right to see what was going on! That's *our* blood, *not* yours!" I yelled, frustrated, rushing up the stairs. I turned back to make sure he wasn't following me. He wasn't, which actually pissed me off more. He sat there on the couch, shaking his head, watching me run up the stairs.

I sat on top of the comforter, trying to watch reruns of *Charmed*, but I was too upset to even focus. I was seething, wondering where the hell he got off, telling me I couldn't fight for my family.

KNOCK!! KNOCK!! KNOCK!! – It was almost an hour later.

"What?" I asked, knowing who it was. I wasn't in the mood for his company at the moment.

"Can I come in?" He asked, cracking the door open, peeking through at me.

I rolled my eyes. *"This yo' house."* I said sarcastically.

"Baby, don't be like that." He said after forcing a chuckle. "Please?" He asked, opening the door wider, leaning in the doorway, never really coming in. He looked at me smirking for a moment, before repeating his question. "Can I?"

"Yes." I said obviously annoyed. He came in and sat on the bed, next to me. "I'm sorry." He said. "I hear you. I just want to keep you safe. I wasn't playing when I said yo pops will fucking kill me if *anything* happened to either of you." He said, resting his hand on my thigh. "But you're right. We need to be a team and for that you gotta be involved."

"Thank you." I responded, feeling a little better that he decided to come to his senses. I felt that magnetic force, starting to pull me closer to him. I leaned in and kissed him on those soft lips. "I accept your apology." We smiled at each other, realizing we had just survived our first conflict as a...*a couple*. "Guess I should get packing, huh.?" I said, getting ready to stand up.

"Nah, we rich baby. We got people to do shit like that for us. They'll have you packed by the morning." He leaned into me, laying me down. "I got something special planned for you tonight." He kissed me passionately. I got wet, thinking he was about to dick me up. Suddenly he retreated, standing to his feet. "Follow me." He said, holding out his left hand. I grabbed it. He led me up to the third story, down the long hallway, to the master suite. He swung open the large, cream-colored double doors. Every time I walked into the living area, my breath was taken away by the stunning nighttime view of Downtown Oakland and the California mountains.

"What the-." I said, looking down, seeing a trail of pink rose pedals, leading to his bed. On top of the comforter, were more pedals, arranged into the shape of a heart.

"Nope." He said as I started walking over to the bed. He grabbed my hips, guiding me to his large bathroom. I noticed more rose pedals scattered across the floor, of the candle-lit room. In the large Jacuzzi tub, was a strawberry-scented bubble bath, also full of pink rose pedals.

"This is amazing." I said, leaning into his strong chest. He kissed me on my neck, undoing my pajama pants. I let then fall to the floor, before he helped me remove my sweater. I could feel myself folding into him, as he softly kissed the back of my neck and shoulders. Before I knew it, my bra and panties were also on the floor.

"Step inside." He ordered softly, helping me get into the bubbles. I noticed on the bathroom counter, was a silver bucket of ice. Stuffed inside was a bottle of Moet. He walked over, pouring me a glass over a sliced strawberry. "Let me know when you're ready for your massage." He said, smiling, slowly backing out of the bathroom.

"This nigga up to something." I said to myself, unable to stop grinning. I relaxed and took a sip of my wine. Butterflies filled my stomach as I blew rose pedals out of the palm of my hand.

The water was starting to get cold and the wine was starting to get me a little wavy. "Baby." I called. He came in a few seconds later, with a large, brown loofah and a bottle of exfoliating body wash. I watched as he rolled up his jeans to above his calves, before stepping into the tub and sitting on the edge. He kissed the back of my neck and shoulders, as he slowly scrubbed me down.

Once he was done, he helped me out of the tub wrapping a towel around my body.

"What you up to?" I asked, as he led me by my hand to the bed.

"You'll find out soon. Take that off and lay down." He ordered in a whisper. I did just as he instructed.

"Mmmm." I moaned, as his large, strong hands dug into my muscles. I didn't even realize how much I needed it until now. Using his knuckles and elbows, he massaged away my tenses and stresses. I began to think about how fast I grew up. I missed my mother and little brother immensely. It wasn't fucking fair. I buried my face into the bed's comforter and sobbed softly, trying to release my stress. The pain of hurt and loss. I wanted to let it go.

I was so relaxed, that I frequently caught myself dozing off as Demetrius made love to my body. I felt a few times, that his hands grazed against my ass, squeezing ever-so-softly. He had me excited. I was no longer sad, but extremely horny.

"All done. You ready for some fun?" He asked. I turned around, expecting him to bury his face into my bare pussy and devour me. He just simply leaned in over me, kissing me.

"I want to take you out somewhere."

"Where?" I asked, wrapping my legs around his waist.

He chuckled and sat up straight before responding, "Go get dressed." I looked at him confused, sitting up on my elbows. He bit his bottoms lip, looking down between my legs. "Hurry up before I change my mind." He ordered, helping me up as I giggled. "Dress comfortable." He said smacking my ass as I wrapped the towel around myself and sauntered out of the room. I hurried to my bedroom to get ready. It was already the end of August, home to the warmest Summer nights of the year. I found a pair of light-blue Gucci jean short-shorts, a black Givenchy tank top, and a pair of black, leather thigh-high Balenciaga boots. I accessorized with 6 gold chains, assorted sizes, with 6 gold bangles and large gold hoop earrings. I tossed my hair into a slick, high bun. I grabbed a few pre-rolled blunts from my stash, and placed them into my crimson red Hermes clutch purse.

I walked down the stairs after perfecting my reflection. "Where you going?" Asked Malakhi.

"On a date." I chuckled.

"Ooh, I knew it! Ya'll fuckin!" He chuckled.

"Shut up. Mind yo business." I said, heading out of the front door. Demetrius was outside, standing against his ruby-red, Continental Gt, smoking a cigar. He had already dropped the roof.

"What's up, sexy?" He asked, wrapping his arms around my waist, gripping my ass, tight.

"Hey, daddy." I said, hugging him back. He had on a pair of ripped Saint Laurent jeans, a Versace t-shirt, under a vintage Versace button up, with a pair of black Versace high-top sneakers.

"You ready to ride?" He asked, opening the door for me. I sat down, sinking into the blood-red leather, bucket seats. I reached into my clutch and grabbed a blunt, sparking it. Demetrius handed me an ecstasy pill, in the shape of a jumping dolphin.

The two of us rode through Oakland, feeling good and worry-free. The pill mixed in with the weed and had me feeling soft and fluffy on the inside. I reminisced as we rode down Bancroft Avenue, passed Frick Middle School, where me and Tracey first met. Also the first school I've ever attended, outside of my home. I was sad at the memory, but instead I smiled. I thought about the happy times we shared, focusing on the smiles and laughs.

Demetrius made a right down 65th, and parked in a driveway of a small family home, behind a black 2000 Lexus Gs 800. The house was painted white, with blue trim over the bricks, with a sizable front porch, and slanted front lawn. The porch was painted white to match the walls of the house and the driveway. We stepped out of the car and approached the porch. The house was quiet, but every light in the house seemed to be on.

"Who lives here?" I asked, tempted to whisper as he opened the door, letting us inside. I was hit by the sweet smell of candied-yams.

"A friend of mine." He responded, shutting the screen door behind me.

"Who is that?!!" Yelled an older female voice, from another room.

"It's me Mama Belle." Demetrius called back. I stood in the foyer of the home, just at the bottom of the steps, which separated the living room from the dining area. Demetrius continued around the large table, and through a breakfast nook. I followed, only a few short steps behind.

"Demetrius! Hi son!" She exclaimed, excited to see him. Hugging him, kissing both cheeks. She was a little taller than me, 5'7, really fair-skinned with long, curly hair. "Who's this beauty?" She asked, looking at me with those large, brown almond-shaped eyes

"Her name is Liyah." He replied, introducing me to her. "Baby, meet my 3rd mom, Mrs. Baker."

"Hey, baby." She said, pulling me in for a hug. She hugged me tight, like a mother would that missed her child. There was no denying she was the mother of Alicia, Demetrius' deceased wife. "Nice to meet you, sweetheart."

"Nice to meet you, too." I said smiling. It was awkward. I knew she was comparing me to her daughter. But I was wrong. She was accepting of me like I was her own. She was open about her daughter and granddaughter. Telling me stories, more than the short answers Demetrius gave me. I assumed he was still hurting and never pressed any further.

After a nice meal of yams, buttered rolls, mac-n-cheese and fried chicken, we were on our way out. "It was lovely to meet you. You two don't be strangers and I better be invited to the wedding." She said.

"You already know. You're my flower girl, mama." Demetrius said, kissing her on the cheek, as she walked us out to the front porch. She waved and watched as we got into the car.

I didn't think it was possible, but I left her house feeling better than I have all night so far. Being around her was like being around my mother. I didn't even find myself getting sad at the fact she wasn't.

I held onto Demetrius' bicep as we rode down MacArthur Boulevard, smoking a blunt the size of a Cuban cigar, full of strawberry Kush. Suddenly, Demetrius pulled into a small parking lot, behind Club 2101, a dive bar on the corner of Dimond and MacArthur. There were some people in the parking lot, all holding drinks and having a good time in each other's company.

Before getting out of the car, Demetrius replaced the roof, securing our belongings inside. He could already see the attention his car was getting us. We held hands, walking inside. It was packed to say the least. There was a banner at the far-end of the room, wishing a happy birthday to James.

"What's good, brother?" Demetrius said, approaching Rodney at the bar. They slapped hands and hugged.

It was an amazing night, meeting more if their friends and family, but I couldn't wait to *really* put this pill to use. I had a deep itch that needed scratching and Demetrius was the only one who could reach it. He wanted to see the views from my new condo, but once the front door slammed shut, the only thing he had a view of, were my pussy lips.

CHAPTER 18

The day had finally come when I would see my father out of prison. It took us three and a half years longer than it should have, due to Darren continuously getting the run-around when it came to my father's retrial. Even with the newly presented evidence.

Turns out the judge was also in Esmeralda's back pocket. Judge Shanahan, an old white man who grew up in an era where blacks were looked down upon. He wasn't to fond of *any* minorities. Until Esmeralda needed him to get Liam out. His only options were to take a bribe, or a bullet. He was also the same judge that put my father away.

For the last three years, my father's case was handled by him, continuously denying my father's retrial, then his appeals. That's when me and Demetrius took matters into our own hands. With an extra $100,000, Darren was more than willing to get us the judges personal information. He was long divorced and never had any children.

Demetrius and his brothers, Rodney and James, rode through the El Dorado Hills looking for Da Vinci Dr. I decided to tag along. This shit was personal.

The house was nice. It was 2 stories and looked over the city below the hill. The face of the house had the same cobblestone bricks on the surface as the driveway and the steps leading up to the front porch.

Rodney parked the truck a couple houses down and killed the lights, leaving the engine running. The four of us stepped out and approached the home, tiptoeing down the long, bricked driveway we passed the Judge's three car garage and a brand new, red 2013 Mercedes E-Class.

"Shit!" Rodney sighed in frustration. We reached a gate with a large chain keeping it shut.

"Watch out." James said, screwing on the silencer of his pistol. He shot the large, rusted padlock twice causing it to break, falling to the cement below. We quietly removed the chain. I held onto it, wrapping it around my waist in case I needed it later.

Guns ready, we crept through the backyard, careful to avoid the large windows. We passed his waterfall pool and party area, making it onto the back porch. James jiggled the handle.

"Hold up." Demetrius said, stopping James from smashing the glass. "Cops'll be here in minutes. Let me find something." He said, starting to looking around for a spare key. I looked down, and next to my leg, was a plant with a small grey rock inside the soil, which was obviously out of place. It was a hide-a-key.

"This *might* help." I whispered sliding the key into the door, allowing us to walk into the dark kitchen, suddenly met by a large Rottweiler. My heart dropped to the floor as it growled at us, begging anyone of us to move a muscle. It began barking loudly as it ran towards us. James put three bullets into his head, dropping him to the tile floor, just inches away from our feet.

"Rocko, what the *hell* is wrong with you?" We heard a heavy, smokey voice yell from upstairs. Me and Demetrius hid behind the center counter as the heavy footsteps entered into the kitchen. "Rocko? Here boy." The judge said. Demetrius peeked around the counter, to where Rodney and James were hiding, and nodded his head *yes*, then suddenly springing into action. "Whoa! Who-what do you want?" I heard him ask. I stood up after calming my nerves. Rodney and James were holding him in place. James held his left arm and a gun to his head, while Rodney held him in a choke hold. "I have money, you want money? I have $1 Million in cash upstairs, just please dont-"

"Shut the fuck up!" Demetrius ordered. "We wasn't here for money, but since you offered..." he continued. He nodded his head towards the stairs. The judge led us upstairs, through an expensively decorated home.

"All this space for one man." James said.

"Nigga, yo' house just as big." Rodney replied. "This bitch nice though. I can't wait until it goes up for sale."

"What do you mean, *'Goes up for sale'*?" Judge Shanahan asked, turning around to face us.

"Turn around again and I'll blast yo brains all over this Picasso!" Rodney yelled, hitting the judge in the back of his head with the butt of his gun. "Where the fucks the safe, bruh?" Rodney asked as we made it into the judges master bedroom. The judge hurried over to a painting on the wall and swung it open, like a door, exposing a black safe. He keyed in the 8-digit code.

"Please, take it. There's a duffle in the closet." He said pointing. "Just don't kill-"

"Oh, don't worry we will. Give Liam and Esmeralda our regards in Hell." Demetrius said. The judges eyes grew wide as Demetrius put 4 bullets into his brain. I jumped at the thuds from the silenced gunshot, but frozen watching his body fall to the floor.

"Come on. Let's get this and be out." Demetrius said. The three of them scattered, looking for anything of value they can carry out with their hands. I couldn't take my eyes off of him, as he lay there, bleeding out onto the floor. "Baby, you okay?" He asked me, taking me out of my trance. "Come on, let's be out." He said, grabbing me by my upper-arm.

Demetrius, Khi and I, stepped out of the limousine and onto the curb. I stared up at the courthouse, in hope that God had his eyes on us, *especially* today. It was exhausting going to see my dad get out of prison, only to see...and feel the disappointment of the bailiff throwing those cuffs back onto him.

It was extremely devastating not have him there for the holidays like Christmas and Thanksgiving. Khi just turned 19 yesterday and another Christmas was only 6 days away. We hoped the judge would be easy on dad. We *needed* him home. You'd think that this case would've been open and shut, but the people that worked for those psychopaths who put him in here; cops, lawyers, fake witnesses, they were all in here. We continued through the courtroom, to the front row, behind the defendant's table. I smiled as the bailiff brought my father from the back and sat him down in front of us. I hated not being able to hug him yet.

The courtroom was divided in half; them on one side, and us on the other. All of our remaining family, was just *us*. Our party was mostly those who worked for my father.

They tried their hardest to pin him for the murders, but everything they witnessed, were Liam's doing. Darren made sure that the new judge combed through the case with a fine comb twice. Made sure he fully thought about the evidence that surfaced, clearing him of all murder charges. Though the evidence for the weapon trafficking, and money laundering charges against him, was still too strong. The judge wanted to hit him with a 10 year sentence, on top of the 3 that he's served so far. If Darren wanted every cent of this $5 Million, he's going to have to do better than that.

After about 3 hours, it was time for a recess. Things were not looking good and I was starting to get a little heated. I pushed through the courtroom doors and into the hallway.

"Baby, baby. Slow down." Demetrius said as I stepped outside into the cold. The wind wasting no time coming to meet face-to-face. I immediately felt a chill go up my blue, knee-length Fendi skirt, and tap dance around my thighs. I folded my arms for protection. "Where you going, babe? The car's not out here." He said, wrapping his arms around me, trying to keep me warm.

"I…I know, I'm just…pissed off. Like, what the fuck?"

"I feel you. C'mon." He said turning me back around, and walking me back inside the hall.

"There you are." Darren said walking over to us. "I've been looking for you."

"Man, what's going on? He don't sound like he's coming home." Demetrius said, rubbing my shoulder for warmth. My arms were still folded.

"It's okay. I'm going to push for bail, while we fight for a lower sentence. I know this judge. He's tough, but *not* unreasonable."

"He could be on their payroll, too." I said, looking around, noticing it wasn't said discretely.

"No, no, no. You don't have to worry about that. Trust me."

"Aight man, we trust you." Demetrius replied. I looked at him, unsure if I agreed with him. I looked at Darren, speechless, then down at my Giuseppe knee-high boots. It would really suck if Darren turned out to be a waist of money, because I found this lawyer.

The break was now over and it was once again time to locate our seats, that we were all on the edges of, while Darren came through. The judge let my father out on bail, as they fought for a lower sentence.

I skipped out of the courtroom, ready to speed to the bank. Demetrius called Sandra, then had one of his boys drop off the cash for the bail. $1.2 Million to be exact. Khi and I, sat in the limousine waiting for him to return, after paying the court.

We waited A total of about 2 hours, eyes fixated heavily on the center door of the courthouse. My heart palpitated every time it opened, thinking it was my daddy.

Finally, at 7:36 on Dec. 19th 2012, he was released. He wore a pair of black Dolce and Gabbana sweats and a dingy white, Fendi wife beater, barely able to contain his large, new muscles. His beard had grown tremendously, almost covering up his neck.

Malakhi and I all but trampled over each other, trying to run up the stairs to meet him. It felt good to finally be able to hug him without having to worry about one of those lonely COs, yelling at us to break it up. Even at Malik's funeral, we still had to keep our distance.

"My children." He sobbed, kissing each of us on the forehead. He looked up. "Get over here, man." He said to Demetrius, who was standing just a few steps down. He seemed almost just as happy to hug him as well. "Please tell me, *one* of ya'll got some weed." He said wiping the tears from his face. Demetrius chuckled, while reaching into his pocket. He pulled out an open Dutch packet, with three blunts already inside.

"Come on. Let's get out of here." Demetrius said as we headed to the limo. He went to the trunk, grabbing a suitcase and a red duffel bag before we slid back into the car. He handed the items to my dad.

"What's this?" He asked, ripping the zipper of the duffel back, exposing the mounds of large bills.

"$13 Million. You can officially retake your seat on the throne." I said, excited to have him back. I couldn't wipe the smile from my face, as hard as I tried.

"I've been keeping things afloat for you. The crew is excited to lay eyes on you again." Demetrius added. He sounded as excited as I was.

"Nah, I can't go back to that life. I just want to live the rest of my days in peace, young blood." He said, taking a hit of the freshly lit blunt.

"Are you sure, dad? I mean, we're a lot stronger than we used to be…"

"No, Liyah. I'm using this money to buy another club. A clean club. I'm going legit." He said, looking at Khi. Khi smiled and mouthed the words '*Thank you.*'

We finally made it to Demetrius' house, almost an hour later. I walked over to the waist-high, glass bar near the kitchen's sitting area, and poured my dad a glass of Henny Jack. Little did my dad know, we spent $3 Million on a house for him in the Hills, just a mile or two from the home I grew up in. It was almost done with renovations, needing just the last finishing touches. I wanted to tell him, but Demetrius said we should keep it a secret. That it would be a great present for Christmas.

"Hey, Li, Imma head over to Amari's." Malakhi said. We hadn't even been inside more than 10 minutes.

"But, dad *just* got home. You don't want to chill, spend some time with him?"

He looked him in the eyes and said, "We will. I just got to make a run real quick."

"I guess. Just drive safe." I said, before he shot for the door. I handed dad his glass, before he plopped down on the leather sectional.

"Hey, D. I need you to hit up them Jamaicans for me. See what they got for a OG." He stretched his arms across the back of the couch, getting used to being out.

"Got it, boss…I mean, pops." He replied, grabbing his cell out of his white, Armani jeans.

"Dad, you want a shower?" I asked, ready to Febreze the prison off of him. He followed me up the stairs, and to the guest bedroom, right across the hall from mine. Luckily, I didn't spend much time at that house. And even when I did, I slept in Demetrius' room, in his bed. "The suitcase is filled with clothes, that you *might* still be able to fit. You definitely grew since you've been out. I said sitting on the bed, showing him his new room.

"I don't see no toddlers running around here, so I'm guessing that means you did as I asked." I'd put the abortion so far into the recesses of my brain that I nearly had forgotten I had one. My mind had to register what it was, that he was talking about.

"I did. And in my mind it *never* happened…so…" I said standing. "Can we never bring it up again? Please?" I smiled so that my attitude wouldn't be picked up by him so easily.

"Are you going to yell D.? What if ya'll actually try to have kids one day and you can't."

"Dad, please-"

"I didn't raise no liars, Liyah. You better tell that man. He deserves to know."

"Dad, fucking drop it! Please! If he needs to know, he will." I said as I walked out of the room. "Besides, you and mom lied to us our entire lives. Don't spend all of your millions on a moral compass now." I continued, then closing the door behind me. Tears began to fall down my face as I started to remember that guilt of giving up my child.

I walked down stairs and into the living room. Malakhi was laying on the floor with headphones on, drawing something in his notepad. I didn't expect him back so soon. Demetrius was on the patio, still on the phone. I looked at him for a second and it seemed like he was smiling and biting his lip. Like he was flirting. He'd noticed me walking over and waived for me to come outside.

"Hey, man. Let me hit you back." He said, hanging up his phone. Something didn't feel right, like he was hiding something from me. I tried my best to shake it feeling paranoid, but I couldn't for some reason.

"Hey, babe. Who was that?" I asked, hugging him from behind, trying not to sound like I was suspicious.

"Just one of our investors. I ordered a shipment to get things going again." He said, spinning around.

"But, dad's not going back to hustling."

"I feel like he'll change his mind once he sees how much money we're bringing in."

The two of us walked back into the house. I sat on the couch, mind flooded with thought. I figured I'd pick Khi's brain. "How you doing, little bro?"

"Fine, I guess." He responded, looking up at me. He removed one of his earbuds.

"You haven't said much today."

"What is there to say? I just really hope he gets his shit straight this time. And we got enough money, so you and Demetrius won't have to do it either." He said standing. "Check it out…" He brought me over his pad, showing me the drawing of a tennis shoe, with smaller variations, circling it. "This is something my art professor has us doing. It's a mock clothing line…" He began. He sounded excited and it made me happy, proud even. The shoe was dope. It caught me off guard when he told me he thinks he knows what he wants to be; a designer.

I couldn't help but to replay his words over and over again in my head. He was 200% right. I was speechless. My father has the money he needs to go legit, like he wants. I was done. I can go back to being a daughter and a sister, instead of a mother and sister. But, I grew up with certain tastes and luxuries. I have expensive habits that I'm *not* willing to let go. Yeah I could fully focus on me and my dreams of being on the big screen. But that could take years to be successful, and we're making money now.

I had some thinking to do and it was nearly impossible with everyone around me. I grabbed the keys to Demetrius' red 458 Spider and took a drive around Oakland, lighting a blunt of Strawberry Kush, knowing it would aid me in getting my mind right.

I found myself parked outside of the Planned Parenthood where Dr. Malia performed my abortion just 3 long years ago. I was overwhelmed with grief as I thought back on that day.

I wound up smoking my entire blunt, watching the building. I saw a young girl walking out, holding herself closely as tears silently streamed down her face. I remembered that pain she carried. Myself breaking down in this exact same parking lot. It was like living it all over again. I sat in the car, smoking, trying to shake away the guilt from that day. I let a tear leave each eye as I mourned my baby. And the only person who knows is my Dad.

My phone began ringing in my Pink Chloe' clutch bag. The caller I.D. read a local 510 number that wasn't programmed. I was indifferent about picking it up. "Hello?" I answered anxiously.

"Hey, baby girl." It was my dad. "This my new number, lock me in."

"Okay, I will." I said after sniffling. Why did I do that?

"You okay?" He asked.

"Yeah dad, I'm cool." I lied, before forcing a chuckle. I started the engine and got ready to head back to the house.

"Liyah, don't lie to me."

"I'm leaving the place where I had my abortion. Just reminiscing." I spat out.

"Are you okay?"

"Yeah dad. I said I'm fine." I could feel myself getting annoyed again.

"Have you told Demetrius about it yet?"

"No, I *haven't*...And I'm not going to. It had nothing to do with him."

"Bullshit. You need to tell him."

"Fine! I will, okay? I will."

"Liyah, you need to do that shit soon-"

"Dad! I got it!" I said before hitting the call-end button. I decided to go home instead of Demetrius'. I just wanted to be left alone. On top of murdering my first child, I now had to deal with the guilt of keeping it a secret...all over again.

I ran up to my room after stopping at the kitchen. I grabbed me a glass of ice and the entire bottle of Grey Goose VX. I locked the bedroom door and ran me a hot bubble bath. Tears streaming down my face as I fought sobbing. I hoped this hot soapy water, would wash away this guilt, but it was like it had a hold on me. A death grip. I covered my mouth crying, not wanting to hear myself breakdown.

I noticed the sun was no longer coming in through the bathroom window. I put the bottle back, up to my lips, drinking it down to the halfway mark, of what was just a brand new bottle. I didn't even realize the water wasn't cold anymore, I was too into my thoughts. After stumbling out of the tub. I grabbed my fuzzy, Versace robe and collapsed onto my bed, feeling like the room was still spinning. I sat up, just enough to put the bottle to my lips, and took a large swig. I rolled over onto my side, crying as I watched people walk around Jack London square.

BANG!! BANG!! BANG!! BANG!!

I woke up a few hours later. The alcohol still running wild in my bloodstream, as I lay atop my messy pink Chanel comforter.

BANG!! BANG!! BANG!!

"Oh my, God." I said groggily, rolling over onto my back to sit up. I was definitely still drunk and it was nauseating.

BANG!! BANG!! BANG!!

"What the fuck?" I asked myself, closing my robe as I slowly walked down the hallway, to the front door. I peered through the peephole. It was Demetrius and he looked pissed. I took a deep breath before opening the door.

"Bruh, what the fuck? I been calling you all night!" He yelled, following me as I walked back to my room and got under the covers. "Baby, what's going on?" He asked, looking me in my face. "Have you been crying?" He sat down on the bed next me after taking a look at the half-drunken bottle of vodka. I felt myself wanting to cry again. "Baby, talk to me."

I couldn't bring myself to tell him about the abortion. I just couldn't. What if he feels some way about me being careless enough to get pregnant by someone I barely knew. Or what if he hates me for being selfish enough to just get rid of it and keep it a secret all of this time? I weighed my options as he looked at me, studying and waiting for an answer. I decided to shed light on other things that's been bothering me. It hurt my feelings how cold Khi was being to dad, just being bailed from prison. He may still have to go back for another 8-10 years, depending on what the judge says in a few days. I opened up about my mother and how much I missed her. Unable to get the visual of her jumping, out of my head. I sobbed harder opening up to him about Malik. I could only imagine what Khi was still going through, and how he's dealing with it. They were thick as thieves, best friends. They rarely fought each other, only double teamed me.

"I miss my friends, babe. They all died for no reason. *No reason!* Monica won't even talk to me, neither will Tracey's mom." I could feel my heart really breaking all over again. He leaned over and held me as I sobbed into my pillow.

"I'm so sorry, baby." He whispered in my ear over and over as he rubbed my back. "It's going to be okay. I'm here for you, boo. I nodded my head, *yes*. He kissed me on the forehead before kicking off his shoes and laying behind me. He held me tight, making me feel safe and that there was nothing to worry about anymore.

After a few moments, I felt myself dozing back to sleep. I could feel him slowly diving underneath the sheets. He crawled between my legs, immediately sucking on my clit. I was nowhere near the mood to have sex, but it felt so good I couldn't stop him. I decided to let him help me release my anger and sadness, crying through my orgasms. He licked on my sweet, sticky center until I had to physically push him off of me. He came back up smiling, chin full of moisture. We held each other as we drifted off to sleep. I woke up again, this time in a bright room. The sun took advantage of the fact I had left the curtains open. I sat up, my head still wavy.

My attention focused on the bathroom door, hearing the toilet flush. Demetrius walked out, buckling up his pants.

"Morning, baby." He said, smiling. Walking over to kiss me.

"Good morning."

"That shipment came in through Richmond. I'll be back around 2, aight?" I looked up, at the silver digital clock that rested on my nightstand. The time read 9:48 am.

"That's cool, babe." I said, tossing the covers back, craving a glass of water.

"Cool. See you later." He leaned down to kiss me. "Love yo pretty ass." He said, smiling.

"Love you, too. Be safe." I said before he left the room, then the condo.

I made it to the kitchen without incident, and made some steak, eggs and toast. Sitting on the couch, I could feel life coming back into me with every bite. I placed the plate into the sink and headed into the bedroom for a shower. I grabbed my phone first, realizing I had 28 missed calls, all from Demetrius. My dad and Khi called me about 10 times a piece.

I was starting to feel a lot better. It was crazy how talking to him about mourning my family, gave way for me to expressly mourn my baby and the guilt that came with giving her up, without telling him there even was one.

I stepped out of the shower and rolled me a nice blunt. I poured me a mimosa, after sliding into some fuzzy pajama pants and Demetrius' grey, Jordan hoodie. I sat on my bedroom patio with a thin blanket to protect me from the cold.

I relaxed for a bit, then headed to the couch to try and get some more sleep, interrupted by a sudden knocking on my door, just as I felt myself falling. I pulled myself up off the sectional and opened the door.

"I knew you stole my sweater."

"Remind me to get you a key." I said turning around to sit back down.

"I wasn't gone press it, but why you ain't do that shit already?" Demetrius asked, following me into living room after locking the door behind him. "You feel like riding today?" He asked.

"Yeah, where to?" I asked him, sitting on the couch, relighting my Backwood from earlier

"Time to introduce these niggas to they new boss." He said, taking the roach out of my hand and taking a pull.

"Well, you're my man. So you, technically are their boss."

"Nah, I still work for you. I know pops is out, but that just means it's still up to us to run these streets." He said, handing me back the weed. "Throw some clothes on real quick. And you gotta listen to everything I say."

"I do listen, babe." I said, following him into the bedroom.

"Shit you do. You're Stephan's daughter." He chuckled, going into his section of the closet and pulling down a black hoodie. I thought back on going to Déjà vu as an owner, and no longer and employee.

Demetrius and I pulled up to the club just a few hours before opening. The sun was still high in the sky. Images from the night of my attack began to paralyze me as I laid eyes at the big block letters. It was, at the time, an entire year since the night of the attack. And that was the last time I stepped foot inside.

"You okay?" Demetrius asked.

"Yeah, I'm fine. Let's go."

"You ready to take this off my hands, soon?" He asked as we walked into the club's main event room. Even after all of this time, the place still looked the same. I scanned the bar, looking for Trixie. There was a short woman, with a bright purple pixie cut. She looked to be Trixie's build. As she turned around to put some glasses down, I recognized her.

"Hey, Trixie!" I said. She looked up at me, dropping the glass that was in her hand.

"I'm sorry, can you grab that for me please?" She said to one of the two girls behind the bar with her. "Liyah? Jesus Christ!" She said excitedly, as she walked up to me. I went to give a hug, but Demetrius held his hand out, pressing it against her chest, stopping her from coming to me. Her excitement turned to confusion.

"How…how ya'll know each other?" He asked, looking at me.

"She was my boss before…before I was attacked." I said, moving his hand out of the way, hugging her. "She saved my life." I added, feeling a knot in my throat. I shed a tear and quickly wiped it away. Her bottom lip curled.

"I'm sorry darling." She said, hugging me again. "You're still beautiful." She said after grabbing my chin, looking my face over. "How you and my boss know each other?"

"Well actually, *she's* your boss." Demetrius chuckled.

"Wow, so you're Stephan's little girl. Small world." She said, shaking her head. "Let me go grab your money." Me and Demetrius walked over to the bar for a quick drink.

"Yeah it's for sure a small world." I said, before ordering 4 shots of Henny.

"Oooh, you want a dance big daddy." I turned around, it was Zipporah. She looked at me, laughing. "Wow. Bitch, you can't come back to work." She said. She had a long, high pony that flung, almost hitting me when she stood between us turning to him. He pushed her out of the way. "Whoa! Rude ass nigga." She said as she looked him up and down.

"Bitch, you're fired." I said. She looked at me sideways, before chuckling.

"Hoe, who do you think you are?" She asked, trying to get in my face. Demetrius jumped up, creating a barrier.

"Hoe, I owe the building. And prolly the next one you finna work at, you bum ass bitch. Custom Valentino sneaks, bitch. Stay broke and get the fuck out my club!" I yelled. She looked at Demetrius, who had a hand in his coat pocket. I never left my seat. "Three minutes, bitch." I said, looking at my Cartier watch.

"Damn, babe." He laughed. "You cold." He continued as she walked away.

"Fuck that bitch. She think just cus I'm smaller, she won't get fucked up."

"I'm so happy you did that." Said the girl behind the bar. "That bitch is a bully. Can I buy *you* a drink?"

"Sure. What's your name?" I asked.

"Fancy. My real names Lexie. I'm Tick's little sister." We shook hands.

"I like you Lexie. How about a 10% raise?"

"What the fuck? A raise?!" I heard Zipporah yell from behind me.

"Shit, that was fast. That means you know I'm serious." I smiled. "And with you being cut, we can more than afford her raise." I turned back to Rebecca. "Make it 20%. I'll let Trixie know myself." I looked back to Zipporah, who was so angry, she looked like she was on the verge of tears. It made me feel good, striking down another villain. I was 3 for 3. She stormed out just as Trixie was coming downstairs with a black case. "Yo, Zip, where the hell you going?"

"Ask *that* bitch!" She screamed. She spun around, rushing out of the club, bags in tow. Trixie looked at me laughing. She walked over to where we were.

"I'm sure it was for good reason." She said, handing me the case.

"Yeah it definitely was. So, I want to give Ms. Lexie here a 20% raise, and double your salary. You deserve it."

"What?!! Really??!! Thank you so much!" She squealed, jumping up and down, then hugging me.

"You're welcome. You deserve it." I said again. We said our goodbyes, and headed out of the club.

"Bitch." I heard, before seeing Zipporah lunge at me, from around Demetrius. She swung and almost hit me but missed. Demetrius swung her over his shoulder, slamming her to the ground. I walked over and put my foot onto her neck.

"Bitch, you tried to sneak me?" I laughed putting more weight on her throat. She gagged, scratching at my calf. "Get the fuck up." I said letting her up. "If I see you on this block again I'll fuckin kill you, bitch." I said through my teeth, pulling my pistol from the pouch of my black hoodie. She sprung to her feet, trying to catch her breath. Once she did, she quickly hurried down the street, walking as fast as she could to get away.

"Damn, baby. What did that girl do to you?" Demetrius laughed as we got into the car. "Don't worry, babe. I'll never slam you like that. But that big bitch wasn't gone touch you." He said, leaning over to kiss me.

I walked back into the living room, hearing my phone ring. I realized the phone was Demetrius', not mine. On his caller ID, was a picture of a girl blowing a kiss. She was a gorgeous, Spanish girl with light brown eyes, and long, wild curly hair. The caller ID read *Isabella*. I went to answer it, but he had already missed the call. "Who the *fuck* is this?" I asked myself, sitting down on the couch and opening his phone, then his missed calls, realizing Isabella was calling from a Florida number. I went through the texts, feeling my anger start to seize my brain. Flirty messages going back and forth.

"That's *my* man's dick." I said to myself, wanting to cry as I looked at a sent picture. I placed the phone back onto the coffee table, hearing the toilet flush. I wasn't sure why I was afraid of getting caught, when *I* hadn't done *anything* wrong.

I pushed my suspicion to the recesses of my brain, as I tied my hair into a bun and grabbed my pink pistol out of my underwear drawer. Business came first, but rest assured he'd be answering some questions about this. I followed him downstairs to the parking garage. Once in his black Yukon, we were off.

We parked in front of a blue, 2-story house on Dover St. in North Oakland, Liam's old turf. Demetrius has been running things behind the scenes for the last three years, but I'm 22 now. Time to step up to the plate and get my family's business off the ground.

After walking up the three steps to the front porch. Demetrius opened the black screen door, then placed his key into the white, wooden door, pushing it open. I was suddenly hit with the aroma of weed, burned plastic and ammonia. I covered my nose with my sleeve, trying to block the fumes, as we walked through the living room. The sofa and the loveseat, sat across the drug littered coffee table from the 40" floor-set television. There were old, 90's era hip hop music videos playing on BET. The glass coffee table was cluttered with mounds of a white powder, a couple of stacks of hundreds and some rocky, almost clear substance. There were eight girls, around my age or younger, filling little black vials up with the white powder, wearing nothing but bras, no panties. They looked up at me, studying me as we walked through.

"Just stick with me, baby." Demetrius said, grabbing my other hand, leading me through the kitchen and up a flight of steps, through some loose trash and some random articles of clothing. The hallway was dark, with a little light coming from one of the rooms. The two off us passed by a closed door to the right and into the lit room next to it. There were two guys sitting at a naked mattress. One with his back to the door. They were both doing the same thing the naked girls were doing down stairs, also placing those black vials into small sandwich bags.

"My nigga, G." Demetrius said, excited. G turned around to face us, looking away from his work. His eyes lit up when he laid them on Demetrius. G, was tall and slim, same height as Demetrius, about 6'4 and had dark skin and chiseled cheek bones, with light brown eyes. He was Gucci'd down; with the sneakers, the joggers and windbreaker. He also wore a Gucci head band and a Gucci fanny pack, hanging off of his shoulder.

"What's good with you, boss?" He said, shaking his hand and hugging him. "Who the *fuck* is this?" He asked, locking eyes with me. "One of your little groupies."

"Aye, nigga, watch yo' mouth." Demetrius ordered, slapping G's chest with the back of his hand. "That's yo fuckin boss, nigga." He said, sternly, without having to ever raise his voice. "You answer to her, before me."

"My boss?" G. asked, holding both palms to his chest. His eyes grew wide as saucers. "Bruh, this bitch is only-" Demetrius quickly removed his berretta from the inside of his pea coat, smacking G. right in the mouth. He fell against the bed, then to the floor. He looked up, holding his now bloody bottom lip.

"What the fuck did I *just* say?" Demetrius asked, gun aimed right at G.'s face. I was impressed that he stood up for me like that. Even more impressed that he helped him up afterwards. "I'm sorry, *boss*. Like for real. I apologize." He said smiling, holding his hand out.

"We're good." I said shaking his hand. "But if *ANY* of you-"

"It won't happen again. I promise." He said looking me in the eyes, then back at Demetrius. "My bad. So you must be Steph's lil girl." He said, walking over to the closet. He opened the door and reached into the back, grabbing 3 silver briefcases, then handing them all over to Demetrius.

"Yup, that's me." I responded.

"Nice to meet you." He said, heading to the other side of the bed. He picked up a large duffle bag and handed it to me. After the other guy, put all the bags of vials into a black Jansport backpack he tapped G. to let him know that his job was done, and headed out of the room. He was young, maybe about 16 and couldn't really look either me or Demetrius in the face. "The product is ready to go out." G. said, lifting the mattress off of the floor, exposing a small arsenal of weapons. Grenades and firearms of all kinds. I was tempted to grab the sawed-off, until I thought about the kick it carried. "I'll shoot you a text when they come pick it up." He said. Demetrius nodded his head.

Demetrius then turned to me, "Tonight our footmen come and get their stash, bring us the cash in the morning and start all over again that same night. We every night all night to get rid of as much as possible."

"What's in these briefcases?" I asked him as we walked to the car.

"Last weeks profits." He explained, tossing them into the backseat. "Every Monday I come and get these three cases. $2.5 Million a piece." He explained in depth once he jumped into the car. "The bag is my favorite." He said plopping it down onto his lap and ripping the zipper back. My eyes grew wide when I saw all of the different colors of the different types of weed. I saw a couple kilos of powder as well. He handed me one of the cases after closing the bag and tossing it also in the backseat.

"This the cash that goes through the shop?" I asked. He nodded his head while sparking a blunt and throwing the car into gear. I managed to open a hair shop in Atlanta the Black Hair Capitol, as another way to clean our money. It's only been open for a few months and has already became one of the most successful in the Downtown area.

"Yup, keep the circle going." He said. I sat back and relaxed as he handed me the weed, grabbing my phone to send a text message to my new friend and shop manager, Rochelle.

I had her order $35,000 in Remy and Brazilian bundles from Ceni, my bundle connect.

Demetrius started the engine and we pulled away from the curb, holding hands. We headed to another one of our clubs, called *The Penthouse*, also located in The City. It was an upscale restaurant downstairs, with a booming nightclub upstairs. The tables were covered with black and gold tablecloths accompanied by gold-clothed chairs. The walls were painted a matte black, with gold roses painted all over for elegance. The large circular bar was the centerpiece of the room, filled with only high-quality liquors. There were stairs on each side, leading up to the nightclub. There was a wrap-around patio upstairs, which gave 360 degree views of the Downtown area. The dance floor was black, wooden slats with tall tables and booths surrounding it. The place cost a fortune and it looked to match.

We walked passed the second bar upstairs, by the dance floor, and through a set of swinging doors, down a short hallway. There was a wooden door to the right. Demetrius knocked, then walked in.

"Hey. My man. How's it going?" Said a younger, white man in a very expensive Versace suit. His office was decked out as well with Van Gogh's and Picasso's. Immediately upon entry, you're met by two brown, leather sofas facing each other, with a glass waist high bar against the wall. His back was to the large floor-to-ceiling window as he sat his desk. I'm sure that added for a ton of natural light while filing paper work. He had a few different sculptures around the room, and quite a few paintings on the walls. I was truly impressed, by the interior design.

He stood up, coming over to greet us. In his hands was a silver briefcase, which he sat on the leather sofa before they shook hands, then embraced.

"And who's this lovely lady?" He asked, holding out his hand.

"I'm Liyah." I said, shaking his hand. His grip was firm, yet warm.

"Nice to meet you, Liyah. I'm Oliver."

"Olly, meet your new boss." Demetrius introduced.

"Oh, wow. Okay. Nice to meet you miss. What happened to Stephan?"

"That's my dad. He's retiring, so I'm taking over." I said. "It's nice to meet you, too."

"Let me grab you guys a drink?" He asked, walking over to the bar. "What'll it be?"

"Maybe next time. We got a few more stops to make."

"It was a pleasure." He said, smiling at us then returning to behind his desk.

We got back to the truck and were on our way to securing a few more bags. I decided to stay in the car at the next location, Louisiana BBQ close to Treasure Island. I stared at ten bags in the backseat, full of clean money. All of it, with the exception of the cases we got from the trap house on Dover. I suddenly felt my phone in my back pocket. It was my dad. We haven't spoken since yesterday, when he tried to force me to tell Demetrius about the abortion. I didn't want to answer, but knew this wasn't the time to be spiteful or petty. He's out on bail and can still be facing a decade behind bars.

"Hey, Daddy." I answered, lighting another blunt to prepare for the conversation.

"Hey, Baby girl. How are you? I'm sorry about yesterday. You're an adult and I need to start treating you like one. It just sucks because I missed it happen. You turned 18 and then 22 overnight." I understood where he was coming from. The last thing he remembered was being my father and I was his little girl. Now I'm a woman. A *grown woman.*

"I accept your apology, dad. Don't worry about it."

"Thank you. Have you talked to your brother? He didn't come back to the house."

"He *did*, he must've left again."

"He bet not be out there fuckin."

"Ewww, dad. Gross!" We laughed.

"Whatever, ya'll both grown as fuck." He said laughing, followed by a vigorous cough. He must've gotten his weed from the Jamaicans. "Call your brother and have him come home. We gone eat dinner together as a family."

"What time? I'll track him down. He probably still out apartment shopping."

"Apartment shopping? He's only…17?"

"He's 19, dad. And he wants his own space."

"Damn, so am I just getting old?" He asked, laughing. "Well, you and D. try to track down your little brother. Imma call a cab and go get some groceries."

"Just wait until we get back." I said, "We can just take you. Or I can call our limo driver."

"You have your own limo driver? Damn, you spoiled."

"Of course!" I laughed. "You spoiled me. I'll find Khi, dad. Love you."

"You, too." He said, hanging up the line. Demetrius was walking back to the truck with two more duffle bags in hand. He opened the hatch, and tossed it into the back, with the dirty trap house money.

"Was that not clean?" I asked. He nodded, jumping into the driver's seat.

"That's why I fuck wit' you: You smart and sexy as fuck." He smiled, leaning in to kiss me.

We were back on the road again. I called Khi and was sent to voicemail after only two rings *and* the voicemail was full. I called back once more, and it didn't even ring. I found myself getting worried. I checked his Facebook, relieved that he posted about needing space from family almost 5 minutes ago. Convenient.

It was almost 2 in the afternoon, when we made it back to Oakland and the sun was so done providing warmth. The truck pulled up in front a large warehouse on 5th ave, surrounded by industrial warehouses, just like it. Mostly abandoned. We stepped out of the vehicle and walked through the front door, into the main lobby. Frank was sitting behind the long grey desk, dressed in a Securitas uniform. "What's up with you, Frank?" Frank was an older gentleman, about the same age as my father. His head was shiny-bald, with a thick black and grey beard. He was tall, with a slim, muscular physique.

"What's good, boss? How's your pops?" He asked.

"He's good. Out on bail yesterday."

"Tell that old ass nigga to come see about a playa!" He said, excited. I followed Demetrius up the steps, to a small, square landing, with just enough room for a couch, a coffee table and an Alhambra water machine. I put the key into the flimsy white door and walked inside the large office. The office was huge. Adjacent from the entrance was a large window, making up the entire wall. There was a catwalk on the other side, looking over the belly of the warehouse. To the right was a large bookshelf, covering the entire wall. Before it was a large, glass desk with sturdy steel legs. The office chair was white and platinum, plush with a high back. The back rest and arms were encrusted in Swarovski crystals. To the left, was a black propane fireplace. The fire sat behind a thick glass for safety. Mounted on the wall, above it was a large 60" plasma screen.

He walked over to the sofa and plopped down, grabbing the remote off the coffee table, that looked exactly like a smaller version of the desk. I sat down next to him as he turned on the fire and the tv. There was an episode of Scandal playing. He ran outside for a little bit, returning with the remaining bags from our pickups, tossing them into a pile on the floor. I could tell he was getting tired of moving around. He walked over to the bar, that stood against the large warehouse window, pouring us each a glass of rum. "So, how much *did* we make today?" I asked, taking a sip. I stood and walked over to the window, looking down at all of the business as I began to hear a massive amount of activity coming from the warehouse. I looked down at the trucks; one from NY and the other from MIAMI. Both full of drugs and weapons. They were wrapped and loaded under regular everyday products like wrapping paper, cleaning supplies etc. For an extra sense of security, we had 2-3 paid officers at every check point, fake-checking the trucks, then letting them go.

"We made almost $4 million in clean money. And 12 in dirt. But we can't count that yet, though."

"Fuck." I whispered taking another sip.

He wrapped his arms around my waist from behind, pulling us closer together. One hand then went up into my hoodie, then my bra. He slowly slid his other hand into the front of my jeans, separating my thighs with his large hands. I spread my legs giving him more access.

"Mmmm." I moaned as he rubbed his finger against my clit. He swirled his finger around my button, making me hate that I wore these pants. He threw the rest of his drink back and put the glass onto the bar. Kneeling down, he ripped my pants to my ankles, with my thong, in one swift movement. He spun me around, standing up with the backs of my knees on his shoulders, his face buried into me. "Fuck." I moaned, holding onto the back of his head. He was standing up all the way, pressing my back against the glass with his face. "Yes!!" I screamed out in ecstasy. Palms to the ceiling now, for better support. I began hearing him undo his belt, getting more excited with each passing second. He dropped me into his arms. I could feel his hard dick trying to separate my ass cheeks as my thighs rested comfortably in his forearms. He smiled, pressing me back against the glass. "Damn, girl." He whined, gripping my ass cheeks, sliding his long dick into me. I clenched my jaws, bracing to acclimate him.

"Oooohhh." I moaned as he slowly slid in and out of me, kissing me passionately as he dug deeper, keeping his same slow and steady rhythm. I wanted him to start pounding, I was ready for it, but he kept steady, teasing me. I felt like I was on the edge of a Liam, and no matter how hard I tried, I couldn't jump. God I wanted to jump so bad. He secured my back as he moved me away from the window, and onto the couch.

"Fuck, damn girl." He moaned, picking up his pace a bit. Then a bit more. I finally felt him allowing me to fall, and I fell hard, repeatedly.

"Ooooohhh, yes daddy! Get yo pussy, nigga!!" I screamed, as a wave of pleasure rushed over and through me. He lifted my legs, pinning my ankles together as he dove deep, his balls smacking against my ass as he sped up dramatically. I gripped onto the back of the couch, unsure just how much more I'd be able to handle, as he pinned my knees to my chest, pounding himself into me. I could feel him in my stomach. "Aah, fuck!!!!" I screamed, surrendering all control to him. "Oh my, God!!" I screamed out as another orgasm made itself well known, crippling my lower body.

"He can't help you!" He growled, pounding me harder. I felt him grow almost double in size before his seed shot into me. He slowly long stroked me while we kissed. He sat back smiling at me, wiping his sweat off on his arm, letting my legs fall flat. He stood, grinning at me, twisting his body back and forth, causing his semi-hard dick to thwack against his muscled thighs. He stopped, walking over to his desk, and sitting down, still naked. I could not take my eyes off of him. Watching in awe as he rolled a blunt for us, looking up periodically to smile or blow me kisses. He was uniquely beautiful. The embodiment of an Urban King.

His phone began ringing, next to him. "What's good, Miyoko? Yeah, they just got in today. I'll be in contact with you about the buy. Yup, gone." He said before hanging up. He lit the blunt and came back to join me on the sofa. We cuddled while smoking. "Is he cheating on me?" Was all that I could think, while laying in his arms.

CHAPTER 19

I woke up some hours later, under a thin, mink blanket. I stood and realized my legs were still a little wobbly as I looked around, studying the situation. It was quiet. I walked over to the window, not seeing anything down there but those two empty trucks with the back doors still raised. I bent down, grabbing my clothes. I was slipping back into my jeans when I noticed a cream-colored, Chanel backpack sitting on the desk, next to a gold envelope. My name written on the front in an immaculate cursive. I looked inside the bag, learning it was filled with bundles of 20s and 50s, with a few bags of that colorful weed.

I opened the envelope and pulled out the letter inside.

"Hey Baby,

I had an emergency meeting with our connect in New York. One of the products in our shipment came up a little short. Get dressed and head downstairs to the car. Stacey will bring you to the airport to get to me. I can't wait to see you. I got something special planned for you when I do.

P.S.

You got the best pussy on the fucking planet! Got a nigga thinking about marriage and kids again.
I fucking love you, girl........

Sincerely,
Demetrius Halsey

My heart smiled at the letter, but then I got angry thinking about Isabella. Confusing me further. I rolled a blunt and sat on the couch. After getting dressed, I grabbed my phone and did a Facebook search for an Isabella in Florida. I wasn't able to dump my first round of ashes before her profile appeared. I recognized her page immediately. I scrolled through her photos, finding one, from a few months ago. He was sitting in a chair with her on his lap. Demetrius had a stack of money, fanned out in his hands. I kept looking, feeling my anger rise. I found more, taken about a month prior to the first one. They seemed like they were at a party, having the time of their lives. I was ready to toss my phone through the large window, when I seen a picture of them kissing, but I decided against it. I snagged the bag off of the desk and furiously flung open the office door.

"Hey, Liyah. Your car's out front." Frank said, standing to open the front door for me.

"Thank you." I said, dryly, before walking out to the Lincoln truck. The driver was standing next to the door, with a glass of champagne. I looked at my phone at the screenshots I took of her page, wanting to call him and ask about her right now, but I needed to see his face while he answered my questions.

I read the letter over and again, trying to decipher his sincerity. I hoped he had a good explanation for flirting and exchanging pictures with Isabella. I rolled the window down for air, taking in my beautiful city. I couldn't wait to take over, following in my father's footsteps, just with a twist. I reached out to my dad, letting him know the situation and that we would have to reschedule. He said he understood.

I made it to the private sector of Oakland's airport, almost an hour later. We pulled along side a long, black private jet. A Gulfstream G200. My father bought it brand-new back in 2002. He was so proud of it, he painted it black, and in gold, painted *Reyes's* written on the tail, in a whimsical font. I was happy the feds didn't get their hands on this, or the boat for that matter. Maybe because he paid cash and used an alias, Vyrhin Devoe to purchase them.

I stepped out of the truck, with the help of the driver and approached the plane. The pilot was standing near the steps, ready to welcome me aboard. "Ma'am, your plane is almost full. We should be in the air in no less than 20."

"Thank you, sir." I said, stepping onto the plane. I was always impressed by the peanut butter colored interior. There were four rows of double seats. The first 2 rows facing each other, the other 2 facing the nose of the plane. There was a dining table planted between the two seats that faced each other. The walls of the plane were decorated like a Burberry fit. The carpet was plush, a darker beige than the seats. My jaw dropped as I seen the front, seating area littered with designer bags from all of my favorite stores; Monte Blanc, Burberry, Ferragamo and Lagerfeld. I dropped Chanel bag onto the bench seating, next to the entrance. "What the…" I seen a couple bags from Louboutin and started there. I felt like a little girl in a candy store trying on heels from their pre-spring collection. I fell in love with a pair of peach-colored pumps that spelled out *SEX* across the toes when the shoes were together. My phone began to ring in the bag. It was Demetrius. Seeing his name on my screen still put a smile on my face.

"Hey, babe." I answered, trying to sound upset, but I couldn't be hearing his voice.

"You on the plane, boo?" He asked.

"Yeah, I just sat down, looking at all these bags." I said excitedly. I couldn't help but feel like something was missing, even with all of these fancy clothes, shoes and jewelry, I still felt empty. It didn't fill the void that was my mom or little brother.

"Get sexy for me, baby." He ordered. "I love you."

"Yes, baby. I love you, too. I'll see you in a few hours."

"Have a good flight." He said before hanging up. I returned back to the plethora of designer bags, looking for something sexy to put on with these heels.

Once the pilot let me know that we have reached cruising altitude, I jumped up, heading for the bathroom, which came complete with a toilet, a small shower and a sink with pretty decent counter space. I removed my shoes, feeling the warm tile under my feet, stepping into the shower after disrobing. The water was hot as soon as I started it, caressing my body.

I stepped out of the bathroom after drying off and wrapping the towel around my breasts. I reached into the Fendi bag, and pulled out a crimson dress, that tied around the neck and stopped just above the knee. There was even a black YSL leather coat to wear over it. The stewardess emerged from the cockpit pushing a silver cart. On the cart was some tequila, some wine and champagne. There were even a few bottles of Jack, Fireball and Bacardi.

"Would you like a refreshment, miss?" She asked, using tongs to place a couple ice cubes into the clear plastic cup.

"Let's do some tequila. Why the hell not right?" I said, laughing. She smiled handing me cup after filling it with Deleon Tequila. I took a sip of the brown liquor and relaxed, reaching into my bag to test out some more of that colorful weed. It paired nicely with the tequila. I drank about 3 shots worth and put it down as I put the blunt out, to begin getting dressed. I went all out for him today with a full face of makeup. Letting my curly locks flow. The dress fit me like a glove, going perfectly with the pumps.

I stood in front of the bedroom door, staring at my completed reflection in the floor-length mirror. I spun around, checking my backside. Thongs were definitely the way to go. I sat back down in my seat, feeling the need to take some much needed selfies. It's been so long, that I almost forgot what my angles were. Being abused left me with a scar on my left cheek and above my right brow. I didn't feel beautiful for a long time after escaping Esmeralda and Liam.

I sent him a pic with a kissy-face. He responded with a pic of him biting his lips. I sent him another one, this time of the underside of my dress. Just as I was finishing, the co pilot came out, letting me know we'd be back on the ground within 20 minutes. I gazed out of the window, as we descended into the New York skyline. It was even more breathtaking in person, all of the lights. I couldn't wait to experience it up close.

"You better stop before you get pregnant, fucking with me." He said in his text response. That word hit me like the flu. Causing my stomach to do cartwheels. But the question of who and why is Isabella, was still burning in my brain.

I was able to finally step off the plane, breathing in the New York air. It smelled different. The atmosphere was thicker. Demetrius was leaning against a black Rolls Royce wraith, wearing a black Versace button up, a blue pair of Fendi men's skinny jeans and a pair of black and silver Ferragamo loafers. He covered up his outfit with a leather, Fendi coat.

"Hey, baby." He said, hugging me once I made it over to him. "How was your flight?" He asked, walking me to the passenger's side and opened the door. I was excited to get out of the cold, crisp air.

"It wasn't bad at all." I said as he helped me into the car, then ran around to his side.

"Come here." He said, grabbing my chin. "Missed you." He guided my face to his, kissing me. I found myself wanting to pull away. But since we were here for business, I figured he should be at 100%, because I'm going to need that same energy tonight.

"How'd the meeting go?" I asked changing topics as he made our way out of the airport.

"Shit, look at this." He reached into the backseat and handed me a zip lock bag, full of little pink ecstasy pills.

"What's wrong with them?" I asked, suspiciously.

"Nothing. Pablo's just feeling like shit about his employee." A guy working under Pablo, made off with a kilo of cocaine, before the truck left NY. The detective work was easy. He was the only person missing at the meet up last week. Pablo told Demetrius not to worry, and that he was handling it personally. He gave us the pills, and other drugs as an apology, from his own *personal* stash. All he should be worried about is that $26,000 or he himself would be handled personally as well.

"Can I have one?"

"Yeah these ours. They quadruple stacked, so be careful." He said. I dug into the bag and pulled out two pink wonder women's. "You about to take both?" He asked. Without response I chugged them, tossing my head back. I wanted to be in a better mood already.

"You actin like you trynna get that hair pulled tonight." He said smiling.

"Maybe I am." I said, hiking up my dress, showing him my black thong. I slid them over to the side.

"Fuck, babe." He whispered. He couldn't take his eyes off of my bare pussy. "You about to make me head straight to the suite." He threatened.

I ran my finger up and down between my lips, getting my finger wet, before rubbing my juices across his mustache.

"Be patient, daddy." I moaned, rubbing my clit again. It felt too good to stop.

"Ooh, shit. Let me taste." He begged. I rubbed my finger between his lips until he started sucking on my finger.

"I love that shit." I said, taking his right hand and squeezing it between my thighs. "Mmmm." I moaned as he rubbed my clit for me. I kicked my heel up on the dashboard.

It was quite a fun 45 minutes in bumper to bumper traffic as we rode through Downtown Manhattan. We finally pulled over. I looked out of the window and seen one of the longest lines there ever were. Looking up, I noticed the big *40/40 sign*. Demetrius stepped out of the car, coming around to open my door for me, helping me step onto the high curb.

"Come on, baby." He said as we walked into the lounge, receiving 40/40 stamps on our wrists.

The inside was absolutely stunning. The beige three-story walls were decorated with spaced out, wooden slats, framed in gold. There were three, large crystal chandeliers that hung from the mirrored ceiling. The entire wall adjacent from the entrance, was covered with 6, large plasma screens, each playing a different sports game.

We walked passed the first level seating area and down the stairs to the next story. The couches were brown, made of soft leather. The coffee tables that sat in front of each of the couches, had gold plated, X-shaped legs, with a white-marble top and had a large glass vase sitting on them, holding 4 white Rose's each. We took our seats, in the rich atmosphere. Everyone looked gorgeous, dressed to the nines in their best evening wear. I could tell everybody in here had money or was fucking someone with it. If this building collapsed, the world's economy would surely plummet.

"I'll go grab some drinks." He said, smiling.

"Thank you, baby." I said, letting go of his hand as he trotted down the steps. I looked down at the bar he was headed to. The centerpiece of the room. The bar walls behind the bartender, were decorated with golden chalices, stacked top to bottom, in a pyramid fashion. All of the alcohol displayed was top shelf, at least $100 in stores, for any given one.

I watched him as he waved his black card at the bartender, gaining his attention. He was a tall, slim white boy, dressed in an all-black form-fitting uniform. He walked over to Demetrius, taking his drink order, and making them without breaking conversation.

I seen a light skinned chick, with thick thighs and a slim waist, walk over to Demetrius. She had to have seen that card he was toting around. She wore a long, blonde wig, with a flamingo-pink, spandex mini dress, with pink Fendi heels. I laughed as he looked her up and down and curved her without saying a word. He just continued, heading up the stairs to me, with a couple of menus between his arm and his side.

The pills were really starting to kick in and I was in the mood to dance. A hip-hop song I was not familiar with came on, but it made me want to shake my ass, so I did. I looked back at Demetrius and he loved what he was seeing. I was really about to start getting into it, when he began pulling on my left hand. I looked back at him as he looked upstairs. I followed his gaze over to a few men in expensive minks and blazers over their suits. They carried themselves like they thought they were bosses, with a team of bad bitches with them. Honestly, to me, they looked like clowns. But they did look like they knew how to handle business. So I played my part; just sit back and be pretty and let Demetrius be the man. I watched as they scanned the seats, while Demetrius waved for them to come over.

"What's good, my man." The guy said as Demetrius stood to embrace him. He was taller than Demetrius by a couple feet and a little darker. He had full lips and wide brown eyes, with short, neck-length dread locks. His mink was brown and he had a girl on each arm. One of the girls looked like she never grew up, wearing her blonde hair in pigtails and knockers, and a short skirt with a silver bustier. The other was a black girl, wearing an all black, ankle-length, leather pantsuit.

The friends he brought with them looked similar to him. One of them was light-skinned, with hoop readings and face tattoos. He wore his hair like Terrance Howard in Hustle & Flow. The other was short and dark. His skin was shiny and eyes yellow, like he didn't get enough water.

"What's good wit you, bruh?" Demetrius said. "Torey, this my baby, Liyah. Babe, this my nigga Torey. He running shit in New York."

"Nice to meet you." I said, shaking his hand. He leaned down and kissed it.

"Bruh." Demetrius said, grilling him.

"My bad, man. She's beautiful." He said chuckling, grabbing his girls closer to him by the waist.

"Yeah, this wifey right here." Demetrius said as they all sat down, making me feel a little flush. I noticed three bottle girls walking up to us, each carrying an ice bucket, with a different type of liquor. All of the bottles had sparklers attached giving them more celebratory flare. I couldn't understand what the show was for as they placed the buckets in front of us. Two of them left, back downstairs, while one stayed and began to pour everyone a glass.

"Happy birthday, Torey." She said, winking.

"Oh, happy birthday." I said, looking at him from around Demetrius. The other two guys he came with didn't really give me too good of a vibe. I wasn't really sure what it was, but all three of them seemed a little fishy. I did my best to not converse with them, *while also* not being rude. I just sat back, enjoying my Vodka Cranberry. I was happy when they started talking about business.

I was able to finally dance and enjoy myself. I wasn't the only one either. I looked around the room and there were a lot of girls dancing. Either their man was watching, dancing with them, or doing what Demetrius was doing: handling business.

My ears got wind of what sounded like Torey trying to convince Demetrius to move to New York and work for him. I could tell, by the way Demetrius responded, this wasn't his first time declining the invitation. "Nah, bruh. I got my balls rolling in Cali. Let's just, keep it a partnership and keep making money...together? Cheers?" He said, raising his glass.

"Bet. Cheers, nigga. You need anything...I mean *anything*, just holla. You the quality dope man in my book, B." Torey lifted his glass and they cheered. The two guys Torey came with, Chris and Benny, had some other work to do. They left, taking their girls with them.

"Baby, can we go dance?" I asked, finding myself starting to get bored. The pills were now in full effect and the alcohol no longer had a hold on me. I needed to move my body. Coincidentally Jay-Z and Beyoncé's *Bonnie and Clyde* began to blast through the speakers, as I dragged Demetrius down the stairs to the dancefloor. I was completely outside of myself, twerking and grinding on him. He held my waist, trying his best to keep up with my movements. I noticed the dance floor filling up as we urged more and more people to come down and have fun. It quickly became crowded after just a couple songs.

"You hungry?" He asked, trying to keep up with his breath.

"Hell yeah. I could eat." I said, following him by the hand back up to our seats. Torey and his girls were already ordering their food with the waitress. I grabbed the 40/40 tacos, and Demetrius grabbed an order of the 40/40 style wing selections.

"You want to get out of here?" I asked, after a while of watching the crowd.

"Fasho." We turned to Torey, who had his tongue halfway down one of his girls throats. "Aye, bruh!" Demetrius yelled, getting his attention. "We finna head out."

"Bet, it's a new shipment coming in next Friday. You in on that?"

"Hell yeah, nigga. You already know." Demetrius said as they slapped hands.

I felt like royalty as we rode slowly through Manhattan, taken back by the surge of people that walked the streets at any given time. Looking at the large, brightly-lit billboards, made me want to go out and buy something. I imagined my face on one of the large billboards, star of an up and coming movie. I held onto my dreams of being an actress, winning a Golden Glob or Emmy. I rolled the window down, letting the crisp December air come through the window. It suddenly began to snow. "My, God." I said falling in love with this city. I was ready to get an apartment out here, right now. We then began crossing the Brooklyn Bridge, over the East River.

"Welcome to Brooklyn, baby." He said excitedly.

I suddenly felt Demetrius' hand on my left thigh. I parted them, just slightly, to see what it was that he'd do. His hand began to creep up my dress, then sliding my thong to the side and his finger into my panty pie.

"Mmm." I moaned, reclining my seat, propping my feet up on the dash after removing my heels. "Yes." I whispered, untying the back of my dress, letting my bare titties pop out. I bit my lip, playing with my breasts as his middle finger became two, moving faster ever so slightly. "Shit, baby." I moaned, coming on his fingers. He took them out of me sticking his fingers into his mouth, sucking me off of him.

"Mmmmm. Damn I can't wait to fuck the shit out of you, tonight." He whispered, reaching back down under my dress, pulling my thong down to my knees. I decided to take them off completely, letting them fall to the floor.

I was able to get an underside look at the Brooklyn bridge, as we rode down Cranberry St. Demetrius suddenly stopped the car, in front of an original Brooklyn Brownstone. Demetrius helped me tie my dress before, the two of us walked up the steps, to the front door. I could hear the doorbell ringing from the porch, then seen Rodney jogging down the stairs through the large, thick glass in the wooden door. He had on a Fendi T-Shirt, a pair of grey Jordan joggers with a pair of black Gucci flip flops. Following closely behind him, was a cute, little curly haired girl. She tried to keep up with him, coming down the stairs with a stuffed bunny in her arms. He turned around and picked her up, once he made it to the bottom.

"Fuck. Tell him I said I'll be back." Demetrius said, before running back to the car. He popped the trunk, taking out two large bags.

"Hey, sis." Rodney said, hugging me.

"Hey, what's good, bro."

"This for me?" He asked Demetrius as we walked into the living room, passed the staircase. To the right of the entrance, was a large, navy-blue, U-shaped sectional sofa, behind a white leather ottoman. There was a large, bricked fireplace, with a huge vanity mirror hanging above it. The 60" SONY television sat in front of the window, with a couple lounge chairs placed in front of it to our left. Further to the right, through the doorway was the dining room, and further through there was the kitchen. I sat down, crossing my legs. Remembering my thongs were still in the car. Rodney walked over and placed his daughter in one of the navy-blue lounge chairs.

"Yeah, bruh." Demetrius said. He sounded disappointed as he looked at Rodney, taking a seat on the other side of the sofa. He snatched open one of the duffle bags, thumbing through 50s and 100s. He opened the other one and started pulling out bricks and kilos of weed and cocaine. He reached into his pocket, pulling out a black switchblade. He dug the knife into a corner of one of the bricks of cocaine and created a pile on the tip of his blade.

"Yeah, boy!" He yelled, snorting it. "Straight from Columbia!"

"Nothing but the best. You already know." Demetrius sat down to my left, on the other end of the couch, facing his brother Rodney.

"How much I owe you, B?" He said, taking out a couple stacks of 100s.

"Nothing, man. Get back on yo' feet, and the fuck out from under Torey. Bruh, his last two distributors just got shot the fuck up, nigga."

"Wait, so that's why you ain't really been around lately?" I asked, never really even thinking to wonder where he's been until now. "You been working out here?"

"Yeah. Fell in love with some bitch and gave her my seed. Took everything I had clean."

"She had his baby, married him, then divorced him. No prenuptial agreement or none of that." Demetrius said, smacking his teeth. "I told yo ass Alyssa was foul."

"Damn, man. It wasn't all that simple either though!" Rodney said, standing.

"But it wasn't that difficult either, though. This nigga finna kill you, bruh." Demetrius said, grabbing my hand. I could feel the tension growing in the room as we stood to leave.

"I know, man. I know. I'm sorry. Everything was all good until a year ago." Rodney said shaking his head back and forth. "What ya'll got planned for the night?" He asked, plopping back down on the sofa, doing his best to shift moods in the room.

"Nothing much. Just finna kick back at the suite."

"Aight, bruh." He said standing again, walking over to us. "Ya'll be safe, man." He said, hugging us.

"Nah, nigga, you be safe. Cali always got a spot for you. Just let me know." Demetrius said. Rodney nodded, agreeing, before we headed back out to the car.

"Bye, gorgeous!" I exclaimed, not wanting to leave. Malaysia was so adorable with all that curly hair and those big brown eyes. She made me think of the baby I've given up just a few short years ago. A part of me wanted to cry, thinking about how the hell someone could make something so precious, and just turn around and walk away from it. For some fucking money. I realized I was missing something in my life. I wanted a baby.

Demetrius pulled up to the curb of the Plaza Suites, located in Midtown West NY, NY. The hotel looked just like a medieval castle on the outside, with the drab, out dated grey on the bricks, and the many towers on the roof. I looked up and seen 5 American flags hanging proudly from the entrance awning, barely able to get my seat belt off before the eager valet rushed over to help me out.

"Welcome to Plaza at Midtown." Said the Latin man, helping me onto the curb. The cold air was really starting to bite at me and my thighs. I looked down at the checkered cement, thankful to the awning above for keeping the snow at bay. Me and Demetrius hurried up the steps and inside the hotel. The doors were glass, framed in gold, leading to the spectacular lobby. I instantly thought about the movie *Home Alone*. There were people moving in a million different directions. We headed straight for the elevators. I couldn't wait to get upstairs and… relax.

Finally, were going to be all alone. I was excited to spend some alone time with him, but even more excited to get some questions answered.

We walked into the suite, on the 16th floor. It was like a small apartment the way it was layed out. Upon entry, to the left, was a full-sized kitchen area, complete with stove, microwave and a full-sized refrigerator. All new, black appliances, with charcoal black counters and cabinets. The kitchen came complete with a fully-stocked bar area, looking into the living room, which was furnished with a black, top-of-the-line leather sectional and matching love seats on either side. The TV was about 42" and sat on top a black, wooden entertainment center.

I plopped down on the couch, removing my shoes, instantly happy to wiggle my toes. I looked around at all of the bags that littered the front room and recognized most of them as the ones that were on the plane.

"Babe, can I talk to you about something?" I asked, scrolling through my phone's gallery. He was sitting at the bar, enjoying himself a glass of Belvedere liquor. I turned to look at him, once I located the screenshots, I had questions about. He just looked at me, face full of confusion.

"What's up, boo?" He asked, taking another sip of his drink. He walked over and sat on the couch with me. He leaned in to kiss me, but I just stuck my phone screen in his face. He sat there looking between me and Isabella. "What's up, babe?" He asked again, with a nervous half-smile.

"Don't do that. Don't play stupid." I said calmly. I could tell by the look on his face that he knew he was busted.

"It's nothing like you probably thinking, baby."

"I'm thinking I should show my dad and see what *he* thinks. See what happens." I said, scrolling through the photos. I remembered I'd found one of them together, she was on his lap. "Did you fuck her?" I asked, a little less calm this time.

"No, baby. *Never.* One of our biggest connects agreed that if I'm in town I'd take his daughter out and show her around, and he'd make sure he could get me product at the wholesale rate."

"One of our biggest connects? She don't look like she needs help being shown around anywhere, unless you gave her a tour of your dick? Yeah I seen that picture too. I would've took a screenshot, but you know what your dick looks like." I said, tossing the phone down onto the couch.

"You know that tour won't ever end." He said. Smiling as he placed his drink down onto the coffee table.

"Don't fucking play with me, Demetrius?" I said, arms folded, legs under my ass for warmth. I was no longer in the mood for jokes.

"Let me call her. I'll tell her the only reason we went out is because of her dad."

"She don't know that already?" I asked. He hunched his shoulders, placing the phone on speaker. Once, she answered, he told her the same, verbatim.

"What the fuck do you mean? Is that why you wouldn't fuck me?!!!" She answered, screaming. Her voice was a little distorted as it came through the speaker phone, she was so loud.

"Whoa, whoa, Bella, chill the fuck out. You knew I had a girl and wasn't trippin then." Demetrius looked like he was ready to start arguing with her, which in my book is too much energy already. I cleared my throat, letting him know to keep it short and sweet. "Look, my girl knows about you and we can't be cool no more."

"Excuse me?! Who the fuck do you think you are? My father will *never* do business with you again."

"I'm not sure I want to do business with someone who would pimp out his daughter for a piece of bread anyways. Ya'll all weird as fuck."

"You will *never* fuck me. You understand? If I wanted it before, I don't now. Fuck you, for this one!" She yelled, before the line went dead.

"See, baby. Just business." He said, tossing his phone onto the couch. "She can't touch you, baby." He said, leaning in to kiss me.

"Eh." I said, stopping him. The confusion spread across his face once more. "Rub my feet." I placed my foot in his lap.

"Oh, imma rub a foot, alright." He said looking at me, biting his lip, rubbing on his dick through his jeans. He smiled, laying me down and hovering over me. "I'm sorry, baby." He whispered, looking me in my eyes. "I should've told you, but I really didn't even give a fuck about that bitch. It was all business." He said, as I was just about to ask him why he didn't tell me.

"I need you to tell me everything, *always*." I said, grabbing on the collar of his shirt.

"I will, baby." He said, kissing me. "I will, I promise." His hand was now under my dress. I gave into him. I knew he was sincere, and it was time for us to…make up.

I woke up the next morning feeling like a new woman. Except, I was in the bed alone. I peeled the covers back. Cold air immediately hitting my naked body. I began to smile thinking about how the room got as messy as it was. I stood, smelling the aroma of a fat blunt. I walked over to the blue, lounge chaise in the corner of the room, that rested next to the patio door and grabbed the thick black robe, given to us by the hotel.

"Morning, baby." I said, walking to the open patio door. Demetrius was smoking a blunt, looking down on all of the NY morning traffic. He only wore a pair of sweats and a white wife-beater.

"Hey, look whose up. Good morning, boo." He said turning around smiling wide, walking over hugging me. He kissed me, laying me down on the bed. He handed me the blunt as he snatched me to the edge of the bed and stood between my legs, before dropping down to his knees.

"Aaah!" I moaned as he put my pussy in his mouth. He was going to work for so long, I couldn't think straight. He stood up, with a face full of cum and a fist full of hard dick. I quivered. "Yes!!" I screamed as he pounded my back out, again, until I fell fast asleep.

"Babe... baby, wake up." I heard Demetrius whispering as I felt him kissing all over my face. "Babe..." I heard him whine. "wake up. I want to show you something."

"It better not be your dick." I said, stretching, rolling over to face him.

"Shit, it can if you want it to be. Girl, you know me." He said standing. I opened my eyes finally. He was fully dressed in an all-black Nike track suit. I sat up.

"What you up to, D.?"

"Come find out." He said, with his hand out. I grabbed it. He led me out of the bedroom and into the living-area.

"What?!" I screamed out in excitement. The ottoman was flooded with little black jewelry boxes. I couldn't believe what I was seeing.

"I had Rod's jeweler stop by. I couldn't pick just one for you, so I had him leave 'em all."

"You...bought all....of this for...*me*?"

"You sound surprised." He said chuckling. I sat down at the sofa, going through the boxes. "Pick out something and get dressed." He said, coming from behind me, kissing me on the cheek. "Imma go do the same."

"Where the hell you going?" I asked, looking over my shoulder.

"I'm in the room, right above us." He said pointing upwards. "I figured you'd want all the space you could get to throw shit around until you piece together the perfect outfit for daddy." He said before kissing me on the cheek. I couldn't think of anything to say to him reading me before leaving the room.

Something in me couldn't fight the feeling that he had something planned for me today. The room was silent, with exception of a ticking right behind me. I turned around, above the doorway to the kitchen, was a gold wall-clock. It was almost 4:30 in the evening.

Finding something to wear was a task. By the time I was done, the room was exactly how he said it'd look. I decided on a simple pair of Rag & Bone jeans, a pair of black Alexander McQueen pumps and a tight-fitting Burberry sweater. I tossed on a diamond tennis bracelet with the matching 2" hoop earrings. I let my curly hair wild and free, with a fresh face. Minus a bold red lipstick to match my crimson leather crop jacket. I looked in the mirror, giving myself a once over. "Damn, she bad." I said to myself, chuckling before I grabbed the room key and my phone. I started heading to his room, but he was on the elevator coming down, on the one I waited for to go up. He wore a brown Valentino turtle neck, a pair of black Balenciaga jeans, with a pair of brown Timberland boots.

Demetrius held my hand as he whipped through traffic on the I-495, in route to the Queens/Midtown tunnel. I couldn't take my eyes off of him. The way his fresh fade blended with his side burns and his goatee, turned me on. I'd barely noticed it had stopped snowing, before it started again. He suddenly turned right, into an underground garage. We walked hand in hand up the steps to the street level, where the deafening sounds of car horns filled the atmosphere. But it was music to my ears. Demetrius gripped my hand tighter as we ran across the street. I loved every minute of this experience. I looked up, barely able see the top of the Empire State building without breaking my neck.

"Is…is that where we're going?" I asked, feeling anxious about being up that high.

"Stop being nosey." He chuckled. "Come on." He gripped my hand again as we walked along the side of the building, and into the lobby.

"Wow." I said, looking around at the grand, golden walls. They were at least 3 stories tall, with golden portraits of the different boroughs of New York. It was like walking through a mural. My heels clicked against the black and gold tiled floor. We approached a large, black desk where an overweight security guard sat. His uniform was blue and black, with a little white. He was middle-aged, white with brown hair that was starting to go grey. He handed Demetrius two passes. On the wall behind the desk, was arguably one of the most famous images of New York; the Empire State building, impressed into the 24-karat gold and aluminum leaf wall, with beams of golden-light, radiating from the mast.

We walked passed the desk, through a sea of people. It was crazy how busy it was just a couple of days before Christmas. Demetrius held my hand as we waited in line for the elevators. It was finally our turn to get on. Squeezed into place like sardines in a can, or clowns in a car.

"I know you hate heights, but you're going to *love* this." He said as we squeezed to the back of the elevator, until our backs were against the wall. We started heading upward. I turned around and my stomach dropped, noticing the elevator get suddenly brighter. It felt like I was flying. I could see the Brooklyn Bridge and the Hudson River. The back wall acted as it's own observation deck. I was nervous with this height, but there was *nothing* that could take away from this view.

"*Floor 80...Dare to Dream.*" Said a mechanical female voice over the intercom.

We all stepped off of the elevator, meeting up with another group of tourists, in a dimly lit museum. The *Dare to Dream* exhibit captured and encapsulated the buildings history, from design to construction. This museum played tribute to the pioneering work of the builders and architects of the day. The exhibit, just recently added a year ago, included original documents, along with period photographs. It was like walking through a timeline of the buildings beginnings. Like the crash of 1948. Heavy fog caused a U.S. military plane to fly into the face of the skyscraper, killing 14 people, including the two pilots.

We made it to back to the elevators, thankful there was no wait to get onto this one, *and* it was empty, minus the people getting off.

"*Floor 102...Top Deck.*" Said that same robotic voice, before those two silver and black doors opened to a large room. The room was a large seating area, filled with large black lounge sofas, facing each other with a round, glass coffee table between them. Demetrius led me through a set of metal double doors with a large glass square in both of them. We reached the deck, the wind whipped and whistled into my ear. I began to freeze instantly. That went over the edge when I saw the 360° views of New York.

"Oh my, God." I said to myself looking at the city around us.

"Liyah Angel Reyes?" I heard him ask from behind me. I was confused as to why he was calling me by my full name.

I spun around. "Why are you...oh, my God. Babe, what are you doing?" He was on his knees, holding open a black, velvet box. Inside was a ring with a diamond almost the size of my knuckle.

"Will you be my forever and always and marry me?" He asked, smiling. He couldn't keep his teeth from chattering either. I stood there staring at him, smiling, unable to say actual words. I stuck my left hand out, nodding my head up and down. I could feel a lump growing in my throat and my eyes beginning to water.

"Yes." My voice was choking up. "Yes." I said louder. "Yes, I'll marry you." His grin stretched from ear to ear as he slid the ring onto my finger. He hoisted me off of my feet, kissing me and spinning me in tight circles.

"She said yes! New York, she said yes!" He said, running over to the roofs gated-edge, screaming to the top of his lungs, through the suicide barrier. I giggled as he ran back to me, kissing me. I felt like I was the luckiest girl in the world.

The two of us sat on the sofa of the suite, wrapped in our fluffy, coke white robes. I sat between his legs, as we smoked a fat Backwood, stuffed with Key Lime OG. I sat between his legs, staring at my new diamond ring.

"How you feeling, Mrs. Halsey?" He asked, hugging onto me, and kissing the side of my neck.

"Like I'm…on cloud 80." I giggled. I looked back and kissed him on the lips.

"As you should. And our kids are going to feel the same way." He said as he passed me the weed. Butterflies fluttered around in my stomach, as the prospect of a life growing inside of me reared it's ugly head again. I grabbed his large hand, playing with it in my own. His hand was twice the size as mine. Something about that, gave me a strong sense of security.

"You want me to have your…your baby? Even after what happened with Mallory and Alicia?" I asked, wanting to see his expression to my question. He never flinched.

"I do, baby. It took meeting you to finally be able to let them go and I realize that means something….." He said, looking me square in the face. I reached up, grabbing the back of his head to bring myself closer to him, kissing him amorously. I turned around facing him, not wanting to keep my lips off of him. I could feel his manhood quickly growing, pressing against my stomach. Vying for my undivided attention. I looked down, seeing it peek through the opening of his robe. Biting his bottom lip, he looked down on me. I took him into my mouth. I played with his balls as I took him down my throat. I severely wanted him inside me. After a few minutes, I climbed on top of him, kissing him as I slid down onto him. My toes curled as I tried to sit all the way down.

"Damn, girl." He moaned. "Fuck. Baby..." He smiled. His eyes were closed as he gently thrust back. "You finna make me....ah, shit!" He yelled thrusting deeper into me. I clenched my walls around him, feeling him shoot his seed into me. He was biting on his bottom lip so hard, I thought he was gonna bite it off.

"Fuuuuck. Nah." He said, shaking his head. "You got me fucked up." He continued, laying me down on my back. He was still hard as a brick, inside me. "I'm not going out like that." I wrapped my legs around his waist, losing all sense of control and sanity as he fell deeper into me.

"Yes, yes, yes, yes!!!!" I screamed out, holding my legs up so that he could focus on making me drip.

The next morning, we got on the plane, headed back to California. Demetrius was on the phone, with a notepad, talking about business. I could barely keep my eyes off of my ring. I was excited to become his wife. I couldn't wait to start planning. I felt a sudden twinge of sadness thinking about Tracey. She would have forced me to let her plan this shit for me. I missed my girls. Even to this day, Monica still wants shit to do with me. In retrospect, I can't blame her. Lamarr was killed and she has to raise her daughter by herself. "Damn." I thought to myself, realizing I couldn't even remember her daughter's name.

"You good, babe?" Demetrius asked, with his hand covering his phone.

"Yeah, babe. I'm good. Just...in my head." I said, grabbing my mimosa from the cup holder under the window. I took a sip.

Demetrius hung up his phone, putting it back into his blazer pocket, staring at me lovingly. It made me feel wanted, yet awkward. Horny, but inhabited.

"What's up, babe?" I asked, smiling, taking another sip.

"You ready to get to work?" He asked.

"You already *know* I am." I responded taking another sip.

It was almost an hour before hitting the runway at Oakland's Executive Airport and stepped off. There was a black, stretch limousine parked, waiting on us. The driver and pilot worked together to get all of our bags into the trunk as we enjoyed a nice blunt while we waited. Once all of our bags were secure, we were off.

"What's good, G.?" Demetrius said, answering his phone. I handed him the weed before rolling down my window more. I loved New York, but it was great to be home. "Wait! Nigga, stop talking so fast." He added. He handed me back the weed, before reaching into his pocket and lighting up another blunt. He rolled up the partition between us and the driver. I looked at him pensively, wondering what was going on, with the other side of that phone call. "Bruh, don't do shit. We in the Town, bruh. Just wait." He said, hanging up his phone.

"Babe, what's wrong?" I asked. He looked at me, then out of the window.

"Shit's going out of whack. Niggas know Stephan is out. They starting to fight back. A few of our D-boys was shot up. Like 6 of them." He said, breaking his attention away from his phone, looking up at me.

"How much?" I asked, a little afraid of the answer.

"About five to 8 thousand in powder a piece." He said. I could tell, in his face, he was pissed off. I found myself not as upset, as much as I seen an opportunity.

"So, why don't we get that shit back?" I asked. "We got the manpower and firepower."

He bit the inside of his cheek. "You trynna go to war, baby? You know we ain't the only niggas running shit now. Yo pops. and Johnny getting rid of Liam alone, gave niggas the chance to really come up." Damn, didn't know it was like that. "They trynna push us out." He reached over to the limousine bar and poured us each a glass of whiskey.

"Whatever it takes." I said, taking one of the glasses from him. "What if…what if we buy a house, in Vegas or Tahoe. Somewhere far enough away from the action, but we can still get there quickly." He picked up the phone smiling, as I took a sip of the drink, at the thought of what I'd just suggested.

"Aye, G. Have everybody meet me at the warehouse in 30 minutes.

Everybody on my fucking payroll. Cops, too, yup. Yeah, nigga, who ever these new niggas working for, is about to be handled. Send up the Bat signal." He said hanging up. "You got balls, baby. You know shit is about to get real bloody, right?"

"Whatever it takes." I said, taking another sip out of my glass.

We pulled up behind the warehouse. I've never *seen* it this full before. The driver opened our door and we headed inside through the side door. "Fuck." I said, unexpectedly. I never realized we had this many people working for us. It was about 100, 110 men and women. I followed Demetrius up the stairs, to the catwalk just outside of the office. Luckily they were right next to the door.

"I'm pretty sure you guys know why I called you here today. Some of these new dudes on the block think it's cool to just come and take our shit. Almost $50,000 gone. Just like that." He said clapping. His voice really carried through the large room. "Now, I'm not about to waste time to get that back. Yeah it's eating in our pockets, but we bout to get that back and more." The crowd uproariously began to cheer. He used his hands to motion for them to calm down. It was amazing, like watching the President give a speech. "Now, instead of just hunting them down, we going after *everything* that ain't already ours. They either get down or get laid down, you understand me? And if they decide to get down, then bring em to us." He said, pointing to me.

"Some of you may not be here when the smoke clears. We understand if you wanna leave. Go now." I said, watching the crowd, looking around at each other. I noticed one guy, moving through the crowd, towards the door. I grabbed at Demetrius' waist, for his gun.

BAH!! BAH!!

Two shots to his neck, just as he opened the door.

"Take him downstairs." I ordered. "Only way out is through a bag. Ya'll know too fucking much."

Murmurs of, "Fuck hims," and "fuck that niggas," rang through the crowd.

"Anyone else object?" I asked.

"G., take them downstairs and get them geared up to hit the streets. We combing through the West come tomorrow night. Meeting adjourned." Demetrius said. I followed him into the office, closing the door behind me. I turned and stared at the crew filing down the stairs.

"Will they be enough?" I asked, turning around to him.

"They have to be. Usually, the incentive of getting paid more, or dying...makes a person hustle harder." He said, wrapping his arms around my waist. I leaned back, resting my head against his chest.

"Mrs. Halsey." I thought to myself. "I love you, babe."

"I love you, too." He whispered, squeezing me tighter for a few moments. "I'm gone go have Frank take me to get some clothes. I'll be back." He said, kissing my shoulder, before exiting the office. I sat down, grabbing the remote off of the coffee table. The fireplace shot on right with the TV. The movie *Paid in Full*, had just started on HBO.

CHAPTER 20

It was finally Christmas morning. I woke hearing an incessant buzzing noise. I grabbed my phone, just a picture of me and Demetrius on the front screen, but the noise continued. I rolled over onto Demetrius' side and grabbed his phone, vibrating violently on the nightstand.

"Head Dr.?" I asked aloud, confused. I swiped the green button to the right side of the phone. "Hello?" I answered, unable to contain my attitude. The line suddenly dropped, beeping twice as the screen shut off. I waited a few moments, fuming before calling the number back.

"Hey, daddy. Merry Christmas." Said a sultry, lustful female voice.

"Bitch, who the fuck is *this*?" I growled. The line hung up once more. I shot up, snatching the covers back. Walking down the steps, I wrapped my thick robe around my pajamas, ready to spend the rest of my life in the same place I'm fighting to keep my dad out of.

"Oh, looks who's finally awake." My dad said as I sat down on the couch next to Khi. I'd noticed they had a round of hot chocolate, waiting for me to wake up.

"Merry Christmas, dad." I said, reaching under the tree, handing him a small box, wrapped in metallic blue paper. I swallowed my attitude so that everyone could have a good day. Except Demetrius, I still plan on fucking him up.

"Merry Christmas, baby girl." He replied, smiling.

"Hey, baby." I said, looking over to Demetrius, saying Merry Christmas to him, and then to Khi. Dad opened his present, and pulled out a set of keys. He looked confused.

"It's done?" Demetrius asked.

I nodded my head up and down. "They called me last night and said they're done. They may not be the only one's, either." I said.

"What are ya'll talking about? And what does this go to?" Dad asked smiling.

"To your new house, dad!" I said, excitedly. His left brow went up. I pulled my phone out of my pocket and showed him pictures of the house we bought him a few miles away from here. A very modern, 5 bedroom 4.5 bathroom house. 6 fireplaces, a pool, and an entertaining basement with a full kitchen. He was excited now and I couldn't wait to see the look on his face, when he finally saw the house in person.

I reached under the tree and tossed Demetrius a small box, wrapped in silver paper.

"Hmm. What's this?" He asked, shredding the paper.

"That is the key, to your present, in the garage." I said. He jumped off of the floor to his feet, and to the garage.

"Holy shit!" He yelled out, excited. He sat on it, starting it up. "Whooo!!" He yelled into the helmet. It was nice to have a normal Christmas again. Even if it was only temporary.

The two of is were back in the bedroom, getting dressed to go out and show dad his new house. I was in the shower, fuming, unable to take my mind off of this morning. I thought back on Isabella.

"Can I join you?" He asked, opening the glass shower door. He dropped his towel.

"Nah, I'm almost done." I lied. "There's 8 showers in the house." I said. He frowned up, as he backed away, closing the door. I watched him as he exited the bathroom, looking at me over his shoulder.

I stayed in the shower a little longer than planned, to get the message across that I *wasn't* almost done, I just didn't want him in there with me. I stepped out the bathroom and into the bedroom. Demetrius was sitting on the edge of the bed. He only had on a pair of Levi Jeans and his black and white Jordan Concords. He had on his face, a confused look as I walked around him, going into the closet.

"Baby, you okay?" He asked following me into the walk-in. He grabbed onto my right upper arm, stopping me from moving forward.

"What?" I asked, snatching away from him. I was already over his presence. His brows crinkled, feeling my energy.

"What's up?" He asked. I liked seeing the hurt and confusion on his face. It was all I had to mask my own.

"*What's up*'?! Why don't you go and ask that bitch what's up." I said, snapping. It took everything in me not to swing on him.

"What bitch, babe?" He asked, forcing a chuckle.

"The bitch, that's been blowing you up all fucking morning." I said, walking over to the black ankle-length dress than hung from one of the mirrored doors.

"Babe, that's was my neurologist. She's calling me about-?" he said looking through his call log.

"And you gone sit here, and fucking lie about it? Fucking really?! Really, Demetrius. I called her back. Why is she calling you *'Daddy'*." I asked. I was so pissed I grabbed one of my high heeled boots and tossed it at his head, missing as it flew into the bedroom, smashing the lamp on his nightstand. I was thankful, yet disappointed that it didn't fly through the large window. "You know what? Don't answer that." I said, taking off his ring.

"Babe-" His voice was stricken with heartache and qualm.

"No! Get the fuck away from me!" I yelled, throwing the ring into the bedroom. He ducked, avoiding contact. As he turned and walked into the room to grab it, I slammed the closet door shut, locking myself in. I sat at the bay window, looking at the swirled garden on the side of the house. I wanted to break everything in sight, starting with Demetrius. I thought hard, fighting myself with not telling my dad about Demetrius' lying and cheating. I decided against it. This is our first Christmas together as a family since we were ripped down from our pedestal. I wanted dad and Khi to enjoy their day.

My dad loved the house. It came with furniture for each of the 5 bedrooms, 4.5 bathrooms and 3 dens. I gifted Khi with furniture for his new apartment and another semester at UC Berkeley.

Later on that night, Demetrius dragged me along with him, to a business dinner out in Napa Valley, to meet up with Pablo. Him admitting to me that he's cheated was no better than finding out on my own. I went to the dinner because this is *my* business now and I'm going to remain involved, no matter my emotions. I straightened my hair and did my face up. I put on my black Gucci leather pants, with gold Swarovski Crystal's on the outside of the leg and a gold blazer with red buttons and a red bra underneath. I completed the outfit with a gold Saint Laurent pump, a gold chain, gold hoop earrings, bracelet and Rolex watch.

The two of us pulled up to the front of La Toque, a high-end restaurant in the Napa Valley. I spent most of the ride silent and awkward looking out the window of my black 2012 Ferrari Spider, avoiding his gaze.

"Baby, can you forgive me, please?" He asked, as two valets approached the car.

"Welcome. First time?" The young valet asked. I nodded my head, smiling as I stepped onto the curb.

"Welcome back Mr. Halsey." I heard the other valet ask him. All I could think was, *What bitch were you here with?* I wanted nothing more than to be sitting in my decked-out condo, smoking a fat blunt listening to some Sevyn Streeter. I stayed quiet and forced myself to smile as we met with our party. The restaurant was dimly lit by small chandeliers that hung above each table. The soft carpet looked like wooden slats. I sat down at the large table, with enough room to seat 8 people comfortably. Centered on the table was a large bowl of water, the bottom covered with blue and turquoise flat-marbles. Floating on top of the water, were 10 white, tea lit candles. The table was covered with a gold tablecloth, and turquoise place mats with matching silverware and napkins.

"Hey guys!" Pablo said, sitting next to his wife Alania. Pablo was short, 5'7 and slim. His shoulder-length hair, a shiny black and grey, was balding at the crown. It gave me an idea to start a male wig line as well. Alania was tall, slim as well, with a thick head of long brown hair. She had a nice shape, and I could tell she came from wealth. She carried herself like money means nothing to her. It put me off, but I ignored it, chalking it up to my personal issues.

I grabbed the drink menu, looking for something strong to deal with the man sitting next to me. I had to keep my mind off of grabbing the steak knife, to the left of me, and jamming it into his thigh. I'd absolutely be the next Reyes behind bars.

"Demetrius? Oh, so you're here without me?" I heard a female voice from behind us. I turned around….it was her, Isabella. I looked at Demetrius who was already looking at me like I went through with my steak knife plans. Busted, he jumped from his seat.

"Whoa! Whoa! What's good wit' you?" He asked, forcing a chuckle as he dodged her hug. "Not really a good time." He tried to whisper.

"Oh, I see what's going on. I thought you said this was our place?" I began to reach for the knife, when suddenly I felt a warm hand on top of mine, stopping me. I shot my gaze to Alania, holding back tears. She took the knife from under my hand and tucked it under her burgundy, Gucci shawl.

Isabella was beautiful. Full figured with C-cup breast and long black hair. She stood 5'6, 6' with her heels. But so did I. She had on an olive-green, tight, thigh-high Alexander McQueen cocktail dress with one spaghetti strap going across her chest and left shoulder.

She shot her gaze to me, saying, "You're not even worth the case." She turned and walked away. Pablo had gotten up and walked off with Demetrius. Which was a good idea because I was going to waist a $1,300 manicure, punching him repeatedly in his head. I noticed people looking at us, catching just a glimpse of the drama. I couldn't take it and ran outside, to the curb. The cold air rushing into my lungs, soothed the anger, but it allowed the hurt to sleep in.

"Aaaaaahh!!!!" I screamed out at the top of my lungs, not caring who heard. I watched as the cars passed by me on the lonely street.

"Baby!!" I heard Demetrius yell from behind me.

"Oh, hell no." I sighed, turning to face him. He was jogging over towards me. "Fuck." I sighed, feeling anxious and short of breath. I rested my body against the chain link fence, trying to ground myself when I felt his arm wrap around me.

"Get….off!! Get the fuck!...off of me!!" I screamed, slapping him as hard as I could. So hard, my right hand stung. "Please, just get off of me." I said exhausted, starting to cry.

"Baby, please. I'm sorry. She don't mean shit to me. I swear to God."

"Apparently I don't either. Get my fucking car out here, then find your own way fucking home. Tomorrow. I don't want to see you tonight." I said, walking back into the restaurant. I rushed into the women's restroom. There was a large, baby blue couch centered in the room. I plopped down, holding back my tears, sniffling.

"He's really not worth it. You should just let him go. I'm sure both of you would be happy." I heard a familiar voice from behind me once more. It was her...again. I felt the left corner of my top lip snarl. "I mean, the dick is okay. But aren't you tired of how quick the head is. Like where's the jaw strength?" She chuckled standing at the sink popping open her Chloe clutch bag, pulling out a pink, matte MAC lip gloss. I jumped up, losing all sense of reason.

I grabbed her by her hair, and smashed her face against the mirror. She tried to fight back, but not hard enough. She slipped in her heels, falling onto her back, making it easier to pick up a shard of glass and slice her right cheek from earlobe to lip. "Goodbye beauty." After two quick kicks to the face, I headed out of the restroom. Alania was standing by the door arms folded smiling. I nodded and continued to the front of the establishment, where I seen my car waiting for me. Demetrius must have already gotten an Uber, because he was nowhere to be found. I started the engine and sped off, back towards the bay.

It's been almost 3 weeks solid since I've stepped foot into my condo. The place was freezing. After turning on the heat, I kicked off my heels and grabbed a bottle Bacardi Gold from my bar. I then headed to my bedroom, slamming the door shut behind me. I flopped down on my Chanel duvet. "Merry fucking Christmas, Liyah!" I said into the darkness before turning the bottle upside down to my lips. I ignored my phone ringing in the living room. I knew exactly who it was. My hand still hurt from beating Isabella upside her head. "Fuck that bitch. Fuck both those bitches!" I said, taking another swig.

A few hours later, Demetrius was bold enough to use his key to get in. I was sitting on the sofa, in my pajamas, finishing off the bottle. I was on my laptop, looking at shoes, doing a little retail therapy. I looked up at him as the door shut.

"*Why* are you here?" I asked, slamming the laptop shut. I grabbed the bottle and took a sip. He was walking over to me slowly, like a dog that knew he was in trouble and was about to be beat. He never looked up from the floor, stopping before walking up the 3 steps. He still hadn't answered my question. "Why?!! Why are you here?!" I asked again, louder. He looked up at me, with the nerve to allow tears to fall. "How... *dare* you!!" I screamed, throwing the bottle at him. In my drunken state, I missed completely...again. He didn't even flinch.

"Baby...I'm so sorry." He said, voice cracking. I backed away, keeping my distance. "Please forgive me." He pleaded, reaching into his pocket, and grabbing the ring. He held it out for me to take.

"Get the fuck out! I'm not taking that shit back. I should've never taken it in the first place." I said, folding my arms. After a moment, he sat it down on the glass coffee table and silently turned away, leaving the condo.

******************👑URBAN QUEEN👑********************

Demetrius sped down 580, heading to San Francisco. After 37 stitches, Isabella was sent home. He raced to go and see her, his heart beating faster than his wheels spun as he put distance between him and Liyah. He dialed her number, being sent to voicemail.

He'd finally made it to Hilltop Condos, in Richmond, almost 30 minutes later, keying the gate code to get inside her apartments.

"Bella!! Open up!" He yelled, banging on the door. It was now almost 3 in the morning. The liquor in his system made him not care that she had neighbors. He only pounded harder, until she opened up, finally. But just as far as the security chain would allow. She looked messed up, with a large white bandage covering her entire right cheek. He could see the blood showing through the bandage. Her mascara had run a mile down her face.

"What do you want Demetrius?" She sobbed. He regretted having her get an apartment in the bay area, just so she could be closer to him. Now, due to his own selfishness, her modeling career could be over.

"Why would you do that? You knew I had a girl." He asked. She scoffed and shut the door, only opening it within a few seconds to let him in.

"Maybe I was getting tired of being the side bitch!" She yelled. He burst into her apartment, kissing her on the lips, angrily, but careful not to touch her bandages. She was wearing a pair of dark blue, silk pajama pants and a matching T-Shirt, with no bra.

Demetrius used her to ease a bit of his stress momentarily. He wished it was Liyah he was making scream into the darkness. After an hour of non-stop pounding he stood to get dressed and begun doing so. Isabella's smile faded from her face.

"Where...where are you going?" She asked, sitting up in bed. "Just sleep here. She already knows about us. Just leave her already." She said. Her heart dropped when he took off the condom and threw it onto the comforter of her bed. He turned facing her, leaning against the bed with his fists.

"Don't call me no more. Don't fuckin email, text...none of that shit." He snarled before sitting up and tossing on his leather Gucci jacket. He pulled his wallet out of his pocket and tossed onto the bed, at her, 7 $100 bills. "If I ever see you again," he said, stopping just at the bedroom door. "even on your own turf I'll fucking kill you, bitch. Go back to where you came from." He finished, leaving her naked atop the comforter, heartbroken.

CHAPTER 21

The last 4 months have been a true battle of will. I took Demetrius back, tentatively, leaving his ring in my jewelry box. I've been trying to learn to trust him again, but so far, I've only gotten around to letting him make me nut, this passing New Years of 2013.

It was hard getting myself able to even talk to him again. I listened to him explain how he's fucked bitch left right, since the loss of his daughter and wife. He went on to explain that Isabella was the last of it. He swore on his mother's grave she was the only one, as he broke down into my arms. He cried I was the only girl for him and that he just wants me. He begged me to take him back.

The 130 goons we had working for us, just wasn't enough. Recruiting was even harder, because these young niggas out here would rather die than make a check. They called it *loyalty*. Mutual losses, on all sides, had the streets running red with blood, making very little progress. We were able to hit up some stash houses, but the men we had to man them were thin because we still needed them on the streets.

Until Demetrius swallowed his pride and reached out to Torey. We paid him $8 million in cash for 10 of his best dudes. They had to be big, but fast. Know how to handle a gun and their fists. We got them all apartments in Piedmont, right between East and West Oakland, and Berkeley. They can get anywhere quickly. All they had to do, was hop into one of the black Yukons we provided. Rent, utilities and groceries were taken care of for the first 6 months. More than enough time for them to start maintaining on their own. It was a good deal, but it wasn't enough.

Demetrius and I went shopping, heading to Atlanta to hire some more hands. I sat on the plane, staring out of the window, sipping a glass of champagne as I rubbed on my 5-month-old belly.

"What you thinking about? The girls?" Demetrius asked. I hadn't even noticed he was awake. He sat in the chair across from me. The wooden table between us was folded down and put away for leg room. He got up and sat in the empty seat next to the left of me. As soon as he put his arms around my shoulders, I began to tear up. I rested my head on his right shoulder and cried softly. "It's okay, baby." He whispered, kissing the top of my head. I missed my mom and little brother so much, my friends. It was like losing them all over again, *every year.*

I sat up, sniffing, trying to suck back my tears. "So, you think the guys are doing okay?"

"Yeah. I put em all on first-class flights. They *better* be okay." He said, forcing a chuckle. "I'm worried about you though."

"I'll be fine. I promise."

"Baby, every year it's the same. You start getting sad, then distant. Then you get mad depressed for weeks straight." He said, the concern in his voice unavoidable. I knew in my gut he was right, but the hurt was crippling. There was nothing I could do about it. "What if you talked to somebody?"

"Fuck *that.*" I scoffed. "Babe, I'll be fine. I'm starting to feel a little better." I said smiling, wiping my tears. I really just wanted to fall to my knees and bawl. Bawl until my hurt no longer bled and my tears ran dry.

The two of us stepped off of the plane, and slid into the black, brand new 2013 Navigator truck. I rolled down the window to get some fresh air. We've been here so many times, we decided to buy us a house in Brookhaven, sitting on 2 acres and cost about $4.5 million, but was worth every penny. Plus, I could stay closer to my hair salon a little longer.

The house was 4,500 square feet with 7 beds and 8 baths. It came with 4 master suites and 2 swimming pools: a large resort-like pool in the spacious backyard, and another, more private pool in the basement, next to the fully loaded gym and in-home theater.

The driver rode up the limestone driveway and parked the truck just before the front porch. The humidity was already getting to me, and I couldn't wait to relax in the sun by the pool. It was already 88° at 2 in the afternoon.

Demetrius and I walked into the all-white foyer with marble floors, leading up to the double staircase, separated by the entrance into the kitchen and family room. "Baby, go ahead and relax, I'll handle the boys." He said, kissing me on the forehead. I headed upstairs to the second story to put on my swimwear. Looking at myself in the mirror, I noticed I had gained a little extra weight, and tossed a sarong over my waist. It was jet black, just like my bikini.

The sun was blazing as I stepped out onto the back patio, with a fresh mimosa. Courtesy of Alara, our daytime maid. She was here since this morning, making sure everything was ready for us. The sun rays danced on the surface of the water like ballerinas, yelling, motioning for me to jump in.

I walked over to the steps and dipped my toe into the water. It was warm to the touch, yet immensely refreshing as I fully immersed myself. I swam over to the deep end, sunk myself to the bottom, thinking. I came back up, swimming over to the steps, wanting another sip of my mimosa.

"Hey, baby!" Demetrius said, from our bedroom balcony, with a glass of champagne in one hand, and a blunt in the other. I was walking back up the steps.

"Hey! How long you've been up there for?"

"A minute. I'm coming down." He said, smiling. I sat on one of the 5 steel, black lounge chairs, with plush red cushions. I suddenly heard Mary J. Blige's *My Life* playing through the outside surround sound speakers. He emerged a couple moments later, in a pair of swimming trunks. Alara was following behind him with a glass of champagne on a silver food tray.

"Thank you, Alara." He said, taking the glass away from her. Demetrius sat down on the lounge chair, next to me, laying on his side, looking at me, cheesing. "What's up?" I chuckled, sipping my glass.

"You're fuckin fine, yo." His smile widened, before he jumped up and did a cannonball into the pools deep end.

*********************♕**URBAN QUEEN**♕*********************

6 of Liyah and Demetrius hired guns, were on the prowl, looking for people to join the family. Michael, Charley, Timothy, Jordan and Angel, and Sidney.

Michael was 6'4 and 220 pounds of pure, tattooed, chocolatey muscle and a bald head. Charley, Michael's big brother and best friend was short, 5'9, with a lighter complexion. He was always underestimated for his small stature but was known for putting even gorillas on their backs. Liyah was extremely excited to have them on their team. Brooklyn bred. Timothy was big and tall, hailing from Harlem. He stood at 6'8 and weighed 360, before the holidays. He was dark skinned with a row full of white teeth. His specialty was guns and damn was he a trigger happy son of a bitch. Jordan and Angel De Leon were twins and the youngest of the group, at only 18 years old. They stood at 6'5, 220 and 235, with basketball player builds. Hailing from the Bronx, their Dominican blood always ran red hot, and their enemies were quick to find out. For those who didn't know them, it was impossible to tell them apart.

Sidney was large, almost big as Timothy. He stood at 6'6 with a solid 290 pounds of muscles. He was from Russia. Only lived in Manhattan for the last decade of his life. He was one white guy you didn't want to fuck with. He would've made Michael Myers piss down his leg, no mask necessary.

They were dressed in tailored, black velvet Tom Ford blazers with a red Armani button up underneath. They wore a pair of All Saints jeans, with black and red velvet Louboutin loafers. Their uniform was money. Liyah and Demetrius sent them out on the streets, with $10,000 in their pockets each to give as an incentive for their newcomers. Michael, Charley and Timothy headed up the two-truck caravan. Sidney drove the second truck, with Angel and Jordan.

They rode down 1st ave, looking for anyone that looked like they were posted up, selling…anything. Then 2nd ave, still nothing. They made a left onto College, then a right onto Olympic Pl, stopping in front of a grey, one-story house, with a busted down, dark green Astro Van parked in the driveway. There was a 2011, navy blue BMW parked out front, with chrome spinning rims.

"Look at those niggas, G." Charley said, stopping the truck in the street. They laid eyes on a group of young thugs, posted on the porch, playing a game of craps. They wore their pants baggy. Some had long dreads, most had short fades. Some of them wore long t-shirts or wife beaters, while the rest of them were bare-chested, showing off the artillery in their waistbands.

"I got this." Michael said, tucking his semiautomatic pistol into the inside of his blazer pocket, then stepping out of the truck. Angel sat in the second trunk with a high-powered rifle, in case things went south. He had the window rolled down partially to conceal the weapon. "How are you gentlemen doing today?" He asked, walking up the way, stopping just before the first step. They were so into their game, they barely noticed him approach. All 8 of them spun around once his deep voice broke through like thunder through their game.

"Fuck you want, bruh?" One of them asked. He started to tug at his waist as he approached Michael, stepping down a couple steps, trying to make himself seem bigger.

"Whoa, whoa, whoa young blood." Michael chuckled, hands in the air. Jordan rolled the window down a bit more. Michael looked back to be sure the dude seem him. He knew Jordan's AR-22 would clean off the entire porch in a matter of seconds. "We didn't come for no trouble." He said, reaching his coat pocket, pulling out a long, white envelope. "Just wanted to present you with an opportunity."

"This nigga gay, blood." One of the guys on the porch behind him yelled out.

The first one looked at Michael, "Nah, Uncle Tom. We straight. Go…gay for pay, one of them niggas around the block, homey." He said laughing, turning around.

"Last chance. Or I'm leaving you bummy ass niggas on yo grannies porch playing dice." He was already getting annoyed by the group's immaturity. He dug into the envelope, and tossed out 6 $100 Bill's onto the stairs, before he turned around, getting ready to head back to the truck.

"Wait, wait…this real?" The first dude asked. Michael turned around. He finally had the attention of everyone in attendance. At least, almost everyone.

"Yeah, this shit real?" Said one of the other guys in the group.

"There's *way* more where that came from, bruh." He said, turning back around.

"Well these my homies. I'm Trey. We down to make some real

bread." He said, holding out his hand. Michael shook it, surprised the young man had a firm handshake.

"Good, meet us at the Constitution building on Alabama."

"We gone be there, if you got more than $600 when we show up." Trey stated.

"You got yourself a deal, young sir." Michael said, heading back into the car.

"You didn't give them the money?" Charles said, starting the engine.

"Why would they come, if I did that?" He replied, reaching into the center console to grab some items to roll a blunt.

"Demetrius said, *'Come back broke. Cashless.'*" Charley said, looking at him with his head tilted to the left. Michael chuckled. He grabbed the envelope and rolled down the window. Trey was still peeping out the two trucks, while his friends went back to their game.

"Come here, bruh." Michael said, waving for him to come closer. Trey trotted down the steps and passed the BMW. "Is that gone be enough?" He said, handing him the envelope with the remaining $9,400. Trey thumbed through the cash, eyes wide.

"Man, I ain't never seen this much…Hell yeah this enough. What time, man?" He asked. He and Michael shook hands.

"Midnight, bruh." Michael responded. "You just make sure you bring yo *most* loyal. Homey back there," He said, nodding to the second guy that spoke up. He was still on the porch looking at Trey, talking to Michael, trying to hear what they were saying. He became even more interested when Trey and Michael both turned to look at him. "he a snake. I can already tell." Trey looked down, chuckling. He nodded his head, understandably. "You knew that though. You gotta keep better company, bruh. You gone be working for me now, aight? Play yo cards right and you can get access to the bank that came from." Charley started the engine. "Stay up, man." Michael rolled the window up as Charley began to drive off. Trey tried to see into the second truck, but the limo tints were too dark.

"Think he'll come?" Sidney asked, rolling the window down, about to smoke a Camel cigarette. Charley grabbed a Cuban cigar from the center console.

In the other car, Jordan wanted to get out and see what bitches he could snatch up. Angel and Timothy just wanted some shooters. "Lock and load, boys." Angel said, as they followed the first truck, crossing over Joseph E. Boone, into what was known as Da Bluff, one of Atlanta's harder neighborhoods. Corner boys everywhere. There were even a few girls dressed in cheap whore costumes, and nappy wigs. Most of them strung out, but a few of them looked like they didn't belong there. Jordan pulled out his phone and called Michael as they pulled up on four of the girls, who looked like they were waiting for a leg-up in life.

"Sup?" He answered.

"Lemme handle these bitches, bruh. I look better than you, anyways." He responded. He heard the entire other car erupt in laughter, including Michael.

"Ya'll young niggas, blood." He said laughing. "Go ahead, bruh. Knock yourself out." He replied before hanging up the line.

"These bitches look mad dusty, B." Angel said examining the girls through the tinted window.

Jordan turned to face him replying, "Bruh, sometimes you ain't ugly, you just broke."

"Yeah, nigga, and sometimes you just fuckin ugly." Angel laughed. Jordan mocked his brother's laughter, silently as he got out of the truck. The girls had been trying to see through the tints since the two SUVs pulled up. They wanted a glimpse of who was inside. Their faces relaxed in approval as Jordan stepped out and slammed the passenger door behind him.

"Nice night we're having, aren't we?" He asked, approaching the group of girls. They all had on different colored wigs, and their outfits just as tacky as the rest. But their skin was smooth, even toned and still young-looking. They figured, "if this is the job they're used to, then let's get em paid."

"Nigga, if you ain't trynna get no pussy, you need to bounce the fuck out." Said one of the girls. Her wig was blonde and pulled back into a loose ponytail. She wore a sequin, baby blue skirt that barely covered her red panties, pairing it with a red halter top, and a pair of black, high-top Converse on her feet. The other three girls didn't really look much better. Another one of the girls wore a bright green wig, with inches that ran passed her thigh. Her hair was maintained, only slightly more than the others. She wore a black, Gucci jumpsuit with a pair of black Air Forces. The next girl wore her hair short, in a fire engine-red, pixie-cut. She had on a black pair of sequin joggers and a black leather jacket. Jordan could tell she didn't have a shirt or bra on underneath. The last girl was heavier set, with her red curls out and wild. She had on a black sequin halter-dress, that was just as short as the first girl's skirt. He wanted to shake his head. Angel was right. These bitches were busted, but he was already out of the vehicle.

"It ain't even like that, Shorty." He said, reaching into the inside of his coat pocket. Grabbing the thick envelope, he pulled out a small stack of cash. "It's way more out there than that little couch change you're used to. You like Prada, La Perla, Balmain? Just come to Cali. Doing the same shit you doing now. Just actually making bread." He said, fanning himself with the cash. "What's ya'll names?"

"Hmmm, you gone take all of us?" The first girl asked. "I'm Cherish." She said, now flirting, shaking Jordan's hand. She played with her blonde ponytail, unable to peel her eyes away from Jordan and the stack of cash.

"Nah, bitch. Speak for yourself. Manuel crazy as fuck, bruh." Said the heavier set girl.

"That's Charmaine, don't listen to her. I'm Tanisha." Said the girl with the long green wig. "And that's our girl Eve." She continued, pointing to the girl with the red pixie cut.

"Hey." Said Eve, smiling and waving.

"What exactly is the job?" Asked Cherish.

"Like I said, the same shit you doing now…just no more corners, and way more money. Ya'll not hoes no more. Ya'll independent workers who see *all* your money."

"Aye!! Cherish!" Jordan heard a male voice coming from behind him. He turned around, seeing three men walking in his direction. Charley, Michael and Sidney, were watching from the front truck. Charley hit a button, lowering the hatch window just slightly. Sidney positioned his gun, aiming at the men. Angel did the same for Timothy. No one even knew how much firepower was on them. "This nigga bothering ya'll?" The shorter guy asked once making it to Jordan and the girls. They never even looked at the SUVs. "Huh? This nigga fuckin wit' my bitches?" This time in Jordan's face.

"Just tell me when.'" Timothy growled with his raspy voice. His finger was on the trigger and the safety was off.

"Be cool, my nigga. Just wait for his signal." Angel replied.

"You must be *Manny*." Said Jordan, looking down on the 5'9 punk, dressed in a long, red T-shirt and a pair of long, beige shorts. He had on a pair of white Nikes, with a matching A's team baseball cap. "Actually, Manny, these girls will be coming with us," He said, snapping his finger, giving the signal. Angel, Charley and Michael all stepped out of the trucks. Timothy and Sidney kept the heat on. "We feel like they're... not living to their fullest potential." He continued.

"Oh, so ya'll 007 niggas, think you can just ride up in this bitch and take mine? Nah bitch-ass nigga." He said reaching into his waist band.

PEW! PEW! PEW!

A clean headshot for all 3 of them. Manny and his two dudes simultaneously dropped like flies. The girls screamed, holding onto each other.

"Come on, bruh. We need to be out." Angel said. Jordan put up his index finger, telling him to let him work.

"So, ya'll ready to make some *real* money?" He asked, turning back to them. They were still terrified, and he knew that any chance he had on baiting them was just lost. "Take this, baby girl." He said, handing Cherish the entire envelope.

"Twin, what you-"

"Shut up, bruh." Jordan said, with his finger up. "What's good, sexy. You coming wit' daddy, or nah?"

"Hell yeah." She said, running to the truck she'd seen Jordan get out of. She wanted to do a little more than make money with him.

"I'm coming, too." Eve said, following Cherish to the truck.

"What about you?" Tanisha asked Charmaine, as she followed Cherish and Eve.

"Nah, I ain't fucking wit' you flip-flopping-ass bitches. You don't even know these niggas. What if they end up doing ya'll just like they did Manny? Huh? Fucking stupid!" She yelled, tears streaming down her face.

"Bitch fuck him! He beat our asses!" Tanisha yelled back, before realizing Angel. "Hi." She said smiling.

"Whoa! We respect the ladies. Any beatin' going down is between the sheets." Angel said, looking at Tanisha.

"I ain't asking again bitch." Jordan said, turning around to walk back to the truck.

"They gone fuckin kill ya'll dumb-ass bitches!" She yelled. Everyone was now back inside the 2 SUVs. She saw the two windows roll up, and the passenger to the second one roll down.

"Aye, bruh. What the fuck 10 racks come up to split 3 ways!" Jordan yelled out of the window, before he mockingly cackled at Charmaine. "Let's dip, B." He said, rolling his window back up.

The crew made a few more stops handing out some more donations to the young gangsters of Atlanta. The girls ended up forming their own little clique, called Mona Lisa. That's a different story in its self. All three of the girls agreed that there was nothing back at Manny's house that they needed. Instead, the guys dropped them off at the Westin, while they continued to recruit.

*******************👑URBAN QUEEN👑*******************

Later that night, around midnight, Demetrius went out to some old building to meet our new recruits. With the baby in my tummy, I really didn't feel like being out and around the thugs right now. Plus, I had better, more entertaining things planned for the remainder of my evening.

I'd just stepped out of the bath and lathered up with strawberry kiwi body oils. I slipped into my peach-colored, La Perla lingerie 2-piece set, my peach-colored red bottoms, the ones that spelled out *SEX*, and grabbed a glass of red wine after stepping into a mist of *TEASE* from Victoria's Secret.

DING! DONG! Ding! Dong!

"What's up, wit' you sexy?" Michael asked, wrapping his arms around my waist, pulling me closer to him. He took an entire handful of my left ass-cheek. And God were they big hands, fingers, feet... Dropping my glass, I jumped up into his strong arms as he slammed the door shut with his foot. He kissed me passionately, carrying me into the living area. The only light showing into the room, were the lights from the pool out in the backyard. I was mesmerized. He laid me down on the sofa, and went straight for my thighs, then ripping my clothes off, tossing them across the room. I rubbed the back of his bald head, as his tongue drove me wild.

"Ahh. Yes." I whispered, listening to him slip and slurp. "Fuck. Mmmm. Michael." I was getting ready to burst and I couldn't hold it in much longer. "Fuck!!!!!" I screamed, uninhibited into the darkness.

CHAPTER 22

T he last few years of my life have been more than what I could have ever asked for. I was married to the man of my dreams, with the most precious daughter in the world. And hell, with $600 million in the bank, we weren't needing or wanting for anything under the sun. Asia just turned 4 a couple weeks ago, at the end of August. I was able to get out of my affair with Michael, without any catastrophic results. Though, the love I have for that Adonis, will never secede. I looked at my protruding belly in the mirror. It's time to get out the game while we still can. 2018 was right around the corner and I had already begun making plans to move to Atlanta full-time to open more shops. Queen was doing quite well, and there was no need to keep doing this. I've learned from my father's mistakes. Not getting out in time was one of them.

I looked at Demetrius in bed, behind me through the mirror's reflection. He was sitting up in bed, scrolling through his phone. He was in the middle of getting dressed when he stopped to look at new articles. Every time our dudes took over a city block, he checked for casualties setting them up for a normal life out of the game. We've only had a couple of instances, when our guys were named. They had to be put to rest, so that they weren't questioned. Keeping our organization, and more importantly our family, way out of reach. By now, my family ran all of Oakland. Not just a side. All of Richmond, Berkeley and was now working on Vallejo. He tossed his phone onto the bed and continued getting dressed. So, did I once he left.

Me and Asia were done getting dressed and had just made it

downstairs to the foyer before my phone started ringing in my back pocket. I let go of Asia's hand, realizing it was a picture message from Khi.

"No." I whispered, tearing up, voice cracking. It was a video message from Khi, in the living room of his apartment. His fiancée and soon to be mother of his child, Amari, was laying face up in a pool of her own blood. Four men surrounded him, each towering him by at least a foot. They had beat him so badly, the entire left side of his face was visibly swollen, with a few lumps on his right. He was bruised and bloodied. The video was silent and only lasted for 8 seconds. I called Demetrius, shaking as I put the phone to my ear. It went straight to voicemail.

"Are you okay, mommy?" Asia asked, clutching onto her life-sized Barbie doll. I realized I had been pacing.

"Mommy needs you to sit on the couch, okay. Go to the living room and don't move." I said, calling Demetrius again. Same thing, straight to voicemail. I ran upstairs, going into survival mode, packing a bag for Asia. I, then ran into our bedroom and changed out of my pumps and into my Timbs, before running up to the 3rd floor, which acted as our entertainment lounge, complete with a full bar. I ran behind it, taking out the false wall, from under the sink. It was where we kept emergency money, food, and weapons, in case any of our enemies found out where we laid our heads. There were two bags; one filled with weapons, and the other filled with $3.5 million in $100 bills.

I realized I was moving a mile a minute, without a second to spare. I sat on my heels, trying to keep it all together. I shut the wall, grabbing the bags and ran back downstairs. "Asia, come on, babes! Where you at?" I called, placing the bags down on the foyer floor. I walked into the family room after not getting a response as soon as I thought I should have. My heart sank when I realized she was not on the couch. Just her Barbie doll, where she sat. "Asia! Oh, my-Asia!" I screamed, trying not to panic. I hurried upstairs, thinking maybe I missed her, passing by her bedroom. I ran inside, nothing. Her room was as quiet as the moment I left it. I ran back downstairs, starting to *really* to freak out, thinking maybe she ran outside. But she couldn't have. The door was still locked. "Asia!" I cried. "Oh, God. Not again."

CRASH!!

My heart sank, hearing a glass shatter in the kitchen.

"Oops!" I heard her sweet voice saying from the kitchen. I ran back into the living room. Looking left I seen her standing on a chair, at the counter. I was proud of my little girl, growing up so fast. She was attempting to pour herself a glass of Minute Made fruit punch. "I'm sorry, Mommy." She said, looking up at me as I approached her. I could hear the shards of glass crushing underneath my feet as I picked her up by her sides.

"It's okay, baby. We'll get some on the way." I said, setting her down in the foyer, grabbing the bags. We made it out to my navy-blue, Tesla sport. I strapped Asia into her car seat, then ran around to the driver's side, dropping the bags into the passenger's seat.

While on the road, I called Demetrius. Once again, it went straight to voicemail. "Fuck!" I screamed out, pounding on the steering wheel.

"Oooh, mommy owes a dollar to the swear-jar." She sang from the backseat.

"I know, baby. I'm sorry. You're right." I said, smiling at her from the rearview mirror. I smiled, holding back tears, trying my best not to worry her. All I could think to myself was, "Not again."

I made it to Fremont, where Monica moved after the death of Lamarr. She lived in a simple beige, 2 story, 4 bedroom 4.5 bathroom home. It was quiet and, for the most part, out of the way for her daughter, Kamiyah. She was sitting on the porch, scrolling through her phone and smoking a blunt, while watching her daughter, play with her dolls on the front lawn. It was hard for me to ask her for help. We had only gotten close again a few months ago. She looked up at me as I pulled up behind her money-green Lexus SUV.

"Mommy, look. It's Kami!" Asia said, excited. Monica stepped off of the porch, coming to meet me. She helped Asia out of the car, allowing her to run over to go play with Kamiyah. I handed Monica the bag of money as I stepped out. I told her to use it to raise Asia, in the event I didn't come back.

"It's Liam and Esmeralda again isn't it?" She asked as I showed her the video of Khi, that was sent to me.

"No, it can't be. I *watched* them die. Like with my own eyes." I replied, starting to question what I saw. "No, Liam's neck was broken after being gunned down and Esmeralda's helicopter crashed. There's *no* way."

"It's going to be okay. I'll watch Asia. Go save your brother." She said, hugging me.

"Thank you." I smiled, trying to stop myself from crying. I ran back around to the driver's side and jumped into the car.

"Hey, you be careful." She said, through the passenger's side window, after hoisting the bag of money over her shoulder. "I'll see you soon."

"Thank you. Please kiss her again for me. Please." I tossed the car into reverse and began backing out of the driveway. I stopped for a second, watching Asia play. This could be the last time that I ever see her.

I sped off down the street, heading back to Oakland as quick as possible, to get to Khi. I grabbed my phone, getting ready to call Michael, when another video came through on my phone from Khi. I forced myself to hit the play button.

"Let me go!!" He sobbed, yelling at the top of his lungs. He struggled against the ropes, that restrained him to the chair. One of the men came across the screen, he was about 4 times bigger than Khi. He suddenly punched him in his face repeatedly, then a few times directly in the gut, causing him to spit out blood onto this hardwood floor. I called Michael.

"I want *everybody* on my payroll to meet up at the warehouse. But I need you and Charley to meet me at Khi's."

"You got it, baby." He replied. I dropped the call.

I made it to Higby, off of Folgers Ave in Berkeley and parked my car right in front of the entrance. I fought the urge to run right upstairs, incase those men were still there. I reached into the other black duffle and pulled out 2 silver .45's, making sure they were loaded. As I was putting them into the inside pockets of my leather coat, I saw a black Denali pull up right behind me. It was Michael and Charley. I got out just as they did, running full speed to meet Michael. I ran into his arms as he wrapped them around me, allowing me to sob into his chest.

"Hey, look at me." He said, lifting my chin. "We're going to get him. Everything's going to be fine." He said before kissing me on the forehead. I followed them up the stairs.

"40-E." I said, wiping my tears, bracing my self for what was on the other side of that door. They broke it down and I rushed over to Khi, who was still sitting in one of his dining chairs, head slumped, with a blade sticking out of his stomach. Blood dripped from his mouth, onto his white Ralph Lauren polo and black jeans. He had been turned, staged to face the door. To my left, laying on the floor near the couch, was Amari's lifeless body.

"Oh, God. What did they do to you?" I asked, dropping to my knees, at Khi's feet. I sobbed, noticing he was bleeding from four of his fingernails.

(COUGH!!) (COUGH!!) (COUGH!!)

"Liyah..." He said, weakly floating in and out of consciousness.

"Shhh, shhh. Don't speak. It's me. We're going to get you out of here." I looked up at Michael.

"No." (COUGH!!) "There's no time. I'm done, sis. (COUGH!!) I'm done."

"Stop." I said, standing, untying the ropes. "Help me get him out of this chair guys! What are you-"

"No! Listen to me. (COUGH!!) Liam's son, the younger one. He's here. I heard them say something..." (COUGH!!) (COUGH!!) (COUGH!!) (COUGH!!) More blood came out of his mouth and onto the floor. I couldn't believe I was watching my brother die before my eyes. I could feel my heart being literally ripped out of my chest. "They said something about a Yatch. Santa Mariella. That's gotta be where they are. Please...don't let..." He said, trailing off, eyes focused on the corner of the room.

"Khi? Khi!" I shouted, dropping back down to my knees. "Please, Khi! Wake up!" I shouted, shaking him. Begging him to wake up. I broke down in his lap. Suddenly, I felt a hand on my right shoulder.

"Baby, we gotta go." I heard Michael whisper. "Come on. We got work to do." He said, helping to my feet, and out of the apartment. It was hard to walk out on my own. I didn't want to leave him there. I could hardly take my eyes off of him.

"Call the police. Apartment 40-E." Charley said to the doorman on our way out. "You never saw us here today." He continued, handing him a large stack of cash.

"Here, B. Take these." Michael said, handing Charley the keys to the Denali. He helped me into the passenger seat of my car. He hit the push start and sped away from the curb.

Back at the warehouse, Jordan and Angel held down the fort. It seemed like everyone got the distress signal. And, just like soldiers, they all came dressed in black, weapons in tow, ready for war. I held back tears, trying to remain strong as I looked at them through the office glass. It had to have been more than 200 people in that room right now. I had to go out there and face them, tell them what happened. So, I did.

The response I got from them was nothing less than supportive. I was glad that we had the people we did on our team. The true definition of *Ride or Die.*

After talking to them, I realized my dad had been blowing up my phone. He was now calling me again. Afraid of what would be on the other side, I answered.

"Hey, baby girl." (COUGH!!) My dad sounded weak. Tears streaming down my face again.

"Daddy? Are you okay?" I asked.

"Not as of this morn-ahhhh!!!" I heard a loud, metallic thud before he cried out in pain.

"Stick to the fucking script." I heard a loud male voice in the background. He had a thick Mexican accent.

"Leave him fuck alone!" I screamed out. Michael heard me yelling and burst into the office. "What do you fucking want?!" I shouted.

"Your life." I heard the man respond.

BAH! BAH! BAH! BAH! BAH! BAH! BAH! BAH! BAH! BAH! BAH! BAH! BAH!

"Your next." He said, before hanging up the line. My phone fell to my feet. I was starting to fall, but Michael caught me, holding me tight.

"They...killed him. They fucking killed him!!" I sobbed into his shirt. He just continued to hold me.

"Stay strong, ma." He said softly. "Don't give up just yet. Not yet."

"I'm sorry I hurt you." I cried. Not even sure why.

"Stop, you're married. I knew what I was getting into when I told you I loved you." Him saying those words, urged me to reach up and kiss him. He gave me the strength I needed to see this through. Frank was able to locate the yacht, Santa Mariella, docked at the Alameda

Marina. Everyone was split up into teams of six. We headed out, a 20 SUV caravan in broad daylight. I had a group of 50 stay behind, in case that was the next place that was attacked. Speeding through the Alameda tunnel, I called Demetrius again, seriously hoping that he'd just gotten caught up and couldn't pick up his phone earlier.

"Please be okay." I whispered, full of hope, that he'd answer. Someone did and turned it into a video call. Demetrius was roped and bound to a chair, just the same as Malakhi. His face was bruised and completely battered. His left eye swollen shut. I could barely recognize him. Someone recorded as 4 large men took turns beating my husband. One of them took a sledge hammer to his right knee-cap. "No!!" I exclaimed, unsure how much more of this I was going to be able to handle. "Fuck!! Drive faster!" I screamed at Charley, pounding on the back of his seat. I wanted so badly to cry, but I couldn't. My tears seemed to have dried up.

We made a right onto Clement Ave, speeding down the street until we made it to the empty lot. I was ready to wage an all-out war. We exited the vehicle, careful not to be spotted until we were ready. Though it was hard to hide 120 niggas all dressed in black, with military-grade weapons, and armor piercing rounds.

We finally laid eyes on the boat. It was exactly where Frank said it'd be: parked on the far side of the docks.

"Check this out." Jordan said, handing me a pair of binoculars. Through them I was able to see just how guarded and protected the boat was.

On the docks were three men sitting at a fold-up table, listening to something on the radio, drinking bears and smoking what looked like Cuban cigars. On the large yacht, it had to have been about 50-60 guards on that boat. We had guys spread out all over the Marina looking for Eddie and Demetrius.

"Watch out boss." Michael said, as he, Angel and Timothy came up, front and center.

"Shoot when you're ready." I said, never taking my eyes off of the boat's guards. My heart smiled as I witnessed them begin to fall simultaneously. The commotion alerted the boats remaining guards, causing them to scatter. We split up into 3 different directions, blocking their routes to dry land. The gun fire rang out, bullets ricocheting off of the boats and surrounding yachts. I had nowhere to go, but to dive into one of the speedboats that were also docked there. I kept my head covered as bullets bounced all around me. I heard the water from the cold Bay splash, as some of us dove in for cover.

I started wondering if I was in over my head. I shook it off and moved forward, sitting up slightly to get a view of the action, just in time to see Angel take at least a dozen bullets to his upper torso. My heart broke when I seen Rodney, holding his gut, scooting backwards for cover, shooting back the best that he could. Michael was on his way over, to help him get to cover, but one of Eddie's goons beat Michael to the spot, shooting Rodney twice in the head. My people were starting to fall and Eddie's men were moving closer to us.

"Get on that fucking boat!" I yelled to the top of my lungs. Everyone began to fight harder, making a way onto the yacht. The gunfire suddenly ceased, leaving an eerie silence behind. Jordan went up first, followed by Michael. The rest of us stayed outside, to make sure no one else came and joined the fight. Michael emerged back onto the dock a few moments later, shaking his head.

"What's going on? Where is he?" I asked.

"Ain't nobody else on there. Alive anyways. He's not on that boat–" Just as soon as it had stopped, the gun fire started again from somewhere in the distance. We ran off in the direction we thought it was coming from, but it stopped before we could pinpoint its exact location. All we could tell was that it was coming from one of the dry-docks; a large space, that housed 80-85 boats, keeping them safe and away from the elements, when not in use.

"Fuck." Michael said, frustrated. We rushed into the building, stunned at how many bodies littered the ground. Losses on both sides. It looked as if Timothy's entire team was wiped out. Charley, Michael's brother, was among the deceased. I saw him holding back tears, turning and walking back outside.

"Ahhh, shit!" I heard a man yelling out in pain. I followed the noise and seen Trey, one of our Atlanta guys sitting against a boat, left on the ground for later loading. He looked like he was beat, then shot in the gut a couple times.

"Hey, did you see? Did you see where they took him?" I asked, running to kneel by his side. He didn't look like he was gonna last too much longer. He just shook his head *no* at my question.

"Tell my mama I tried...I wanted out the game." He said before laughing and coughing up more blood. "I really did." He said, looking at me square in the eyes. He rested his head against the boat, drawing his last breath. I grabbed the automatic rifle out of his hands.

"Come on. We gotta find Demetrius before they get away." Jordan said. The hellfire began once more, in a dry dock just next door. We ran out as quickly as we could to help the rest of our people. I ducked behind a boat, just by the entrance. From my cover, I could see Demetrius, and he was in horrible shape. His body limp and lifeless. It broke my heart I couldn't just go and take him out of all of this, like he did for me in Mexico.

"Let him go!!!" I screamed, feeling a surge of adrenaline. I started shooting, dropping one of the guys holding Demetrius, but his men gave the other guy cover. We watched helpless as they dragged Demetrius through a door, protected by a hail of gunfire.

"We'll be in touch, bitch!" I heard a male voice say. I looked up in the rafters, it was Eddie.

"Give him back." I growled before shooting at them until the rifle began to click. I tried to run after them, suddenly feeling a force pulling me in the opposite direction. Looking back, I realized it was Michael holding me. I fought hard, to get out of his grasp, but it was worthless, to no avail. "Michael, fucking put me down!" I screamed, still trying to fight him off. He simply hauled me over his shoulder. All I could see was the distance he and our remaining men, were putting between us and the Marina. "What the fuck?! Why are we leaving?!" I yelled as Michael tossed me into the back of the SUV like a kidnap victim.

"We gotta go. Go! Go! Go!" Michael yelled. Jordan threw the car into drive and sped off, the force pinning me to my seat. Just as we hit the corner, I could see tons of cop cars approaching the Marina from the opposite direction. Some of them kept going, chasing us. "Monty grabbed Eddie, before he could get on the chopper. Don't tell me how, but we got our own leverage now. We just gotta get out the cops way, Jae!" Michael said, turning from me to Jordan.

"Working on it!" Jordan exclaimed, focusing on dodging in and out of traffic. I looked back and he was doing a good job. I noticed we only had 3 trucks following behind us, and about 5 police cars. If we made it out of this, I had to know how Monty snuck Eddie away. We made it back to the warehouse after doing circles around Oakland, trying to loose the cops. It was quiet just as the moment we left. Frank and his team had no trouble. Maybe I should've had them come along. This might be over already.

"The trucks." I said, worrying if there could be anything in there to lead back to us. We only came back with 4 trucks out of 20.

"OPD got them, baby." Michael said. "Hopefully, if anybody made it, they can get here without dragging the heat behind them." The warehouse door suddenly opened, allowing 3 more trucks to enter, just a couple moments later.

Montrell hopped out of the backseat of the first truck, with Eddie in tow. He had a black sack over his face and tied around his neck.

"Take this little bitch downstairs." I said, almost excited to start torturing him, just as he did my father, my brother and my husband.

"Yes ma'am." Montrell said, grinning from ear to ear. "My pleasure."

I couldn't wait to find out how he did it. How he managed to steal Eddie, but not Demetrius.

Montrell snuck off, watching them as they exited the dry docks with Demetrius. They already made it to chopper and was waiting on Eddie and a couple more men. There was no way he could get to Demetrius, so he went with the next best thing. He killed the 2 guys that guarded Eddie, then knocked Eddie unconscious, as the chopper lifted in the air, leaving him behind.

CHAPTER 23

I sat in a metallic, folding chair, directly across from Eddie. He was tightly roped to a wooden chair, laughing softly with a burlap sack over his head. Michael stood by the door of the basement, making sure I wasn't interrupted. This was my first time down here, usually one of our goons would be down here doing the torturing, or Demetrius in case they became ineffective. But, this was personal. I wanted to see him beg, plead and bleed with my own eyes. The blood-stained cement below, told a hundred stories, and I was ready to add a few more chapters. I pulled my phone and hit record, tired of waiting for him to answer my question.

"One more time…where is Demetrius?" I asked, full of hate. "Fuck it. Beat his ass." I ordered. I watched as Michael came between us smiling, giving him a powerful right jab, and an equally powerful left hook. *My* face started hurting when I heard his jaw break.

"That was for my brother, *bitch*." He said, before connecting a right cross. "That's for my girl." Seeing his muscles swell in my name was definitely a turn on.

"Okay." I said standing, placing my arm on his large left shoulder. I could see blood seeping through the pores of the burlap sack. I removed it, seeing his face turning blue and lumpy.

"You fucking bitch!" He yelled, no doubt scathing with pain, as he spit blood onto my boots. I held onto Michael's shoulder, kicking Eddie in his chest as hard as I could, causing him to fall backwards. I watched as his head bounced off of the concrete. Wasting no time, I rushed over and forced my foot onto his throat, pushing down on his Adam's Apple. I took great pleasure watching him gasp for air.

"Baby," Michael said, clearing his throat and getting my attention. "don't kill him. We still need him alive." I looked back down at Eddie, unable to take my foot off of him. I kept telling myself to move, but the hate made my leg heavy. "Babe!" He said, with more force and bass in his voice.

"Fine." I said, rolling my eyes. Michael was right. If I killed Eddie now, there would be no reason for his men to keep Demetrius alive. I stepped off of him. Eddie began gagging, sucking in as much air as his lungs could. He choked, trying to catch his breathing rhythm. "Get this little bitch up, please." I said taking a hit of my blunt, then scratching my eyebrows.

"Aaaaahhh!!!" He screamed out in pain, as I put my blunt out in one of the cuts in his cheek. I sat in his lap facing him. I wanted to be up close.

"I'm not going to keep asking." I said, looking him square in the eyes. I shot my gaze up to Michael, who was now standing behind the chair. "I'm getting ready to start cutting off body parts." I said. He handed me his large hunting knife, then whipped Eddie's head back by his hair. I held the knife against Eddie's throat, wanting so badly to slice him from mouth to asshole, but I fought the urge.

"You don't get it do you?" He asked, smirking. "Grab my phone."

"Excuse me?" I asked confused. I stood, going through his pockets, until I found his cell phone.

"6895." He said as I turned it on. I unlocked the phone. There was a message from *Mommy*. My anxiety began to go through the roof as my legs started to go weak. My mouth started to dry as I opened the message, playing another video. "This is *all* part of her plan, you stupid cunt! You can't w-" Michael punched Eddie in his mouth, shutting him up.

The video started with me dropping Asia off at Monica's house this morning. It played up to me leaving, then cutting over to 5 men with assault rifles busting down her front door.

"No!!" I screamed, but I couldn't cry. I was too afraid. The video cut again, only getting worse. I could hear Asia and Kamiyah in the background, screaming for their mothers.

"Which ones the Reyes?" A man asked.

"The younger one." Another man answered off of camera.

BAH!! BAH!!

I heard a couple shots off of camera. As the cameraman approached Monica. She was laying on the floor, near the couch, dying from a single gunshot to the chest.

"Please, no." she whispered, faintly. "Please!" She begged before the cameraman put two bullets into her brain. I could still hear Asia screaming for me. I tossed Eddie's phone at him, hitting him in the forehead. I jumped back into his lap whit my knees in his gut, causing the chair to fail backwards again.

"Where are they!!" I screamed, punching him in his face, trying to loosen his jaw completely. I grabbed the sides of his head, gripping his hair, "Where...are...they!" I screamed, slamming his head against the pavement. "Where...are they!!" I growled.

"Okay, come on." I heard Michael say, lifting me into the air.

"Stop!!!" I screamed. "Fucking put me down!!" I yelled, unable to hold my temper. The moment my feet touched the ground, I swung, punching him in his jaw, as hard as I could. "Stop doing that shit!" I yelled, attempting to save face, realizing what I'd just done. He held his face to the right, not wanting to look at me.

"You know what? Fuck it. Kill his ass if you want to. I don't give a fuck anymore." He said, hands out backing away from me, headed for the door.

"Get the water bucket." I said, softening my tone.

"Nah, fuck all that. You got this right? Get it then." He said, hand on the doorknob, getting ready to leave. I didn't remember saying we were done down here

"I *might* be love you, but nigga I'm *still* your boss. Grab the fucking bucket." I ordered, fully aware of my attitude and actions.

"Damn." He said, forcing a chuckle. He bit the inside of his cheek, trying to stay quiet as he walked over to the corner of the room, grabbing a bucket and grimy towel from under the sink. He filled the dusty bucket up with water, and stood over Eddie, placing the towel over his face. "Tell me when, *boss*." He said sarcastically, still not wanting to look at me. As bad and guilty as I felt, there was still work to do. I didn't have time to cater to his ego, and damn sure his emotions.

"*When...*" I responded. He started pouring the water over Eddie's mouth and nose. I held his head straight, forcing him to look at the ceiling. It wasn't long before he was fighting to get out of my grip. "Aight." I ordered him to stop.

"O….K…OKAY!!" Eddie choked, gasping for air.

"That was easy." I said, looking at Michael. He nodded, agreeing with me. I them heard a cell phone ringing. I looked around, thinking it was mine or Michael's. Nothing. Black screen. I looked over, seeing Eddie's phone vibrate and light up. I rushed over, seeing *Mommy* displayed across the ID. I stepped out of myself, watching myself scroll the green button to the middle of the screen.

"Eddie! Que pasa? Where are you?" I heard her voice. After a few moments of me not being able to respond, she sang, "Hola, little puta!!" The phone slipped out of my hand and crashed to the floor, shattering the phone's screen, and ending the call.

"She's alive. She's fucking alive?" I said in disbelief. "I *watched* her die. I fucking *watched* her die."

"No, you watched the helicopter crash. She was able to jump out, just as it was getting ready to hit the rocks. She's been telling me the story every day for the last few years, plotting her revenge." Eddie said, laughing.

"Where are they!!" I said now almost afraid. I grabbed the knife and punched the handle onto his chest, ready to stab him in his heart over 100 times.

"Te llevare!! Te llevare! I'll take you. I'll take you to her." He begged.

"Good." I said, standing. "Get him up and ready to go. I ordered, heading back upstairs to the office. Jordan was smoking a blunt, sitting on the couch with his hands to his head.

"Hey, we're getting ready to move out. Michael needs your help downstairs." I said, going under the desk, where we kept a safe of weapons and money. I realized he hadn't moved and looked back up at him. "You good?" I said, opening the safe, pulling out a black backpack.

"I can't get Angel out of my head. I feel like he's screaming for help and I can't get to him." Jordan said, sniffling, trying to stop crying. I felt for him.

"I feel you. I remember when Malik died. It ate me up! I felt even worse for Khi, cus just like ya'll, they were twins. After he died, he all but shut down. The only advice I can give you, that I should've given to Khi is, if you don't want to join him…fight. Fight like you're fighting to get him back." I said, stuffing the backpack with grenades and pistols. He was still sitting on the couch. I needed him to start moving, but I didn't want to seem insensitive. "You gotta make a choice. If you sit here, he died for nothing. You gotta survive for him." I said, bag in tow, ready to leave the office. "What do you say?" I asked, holding my hand out for him.

"Make a right on Rockridge." Eddie said as we led a caravan through the Oakland Hills. Montrell held a gun to his temple in case he tried anything he shouldn't. "You should recognize this place." He said. Michael killed the lights, as we parked up the street from my childhood home. It looked completely different from where I grew up. I watched as Esmeralda's guys posted outside of the main gate. It was four of them, all carrying assault weapons. On the other side of the fence, where guards, lining the driveway. It was about 20 of them, 10 on either side.

"Aye, Mike, let's us go in first." Jordan said over the CB, from the truck behind us.

"That could work." Montrell said.

"Is my daughter in there?" I asked, turning back to face Eddie. He nodded his head yes. Michael looked at me, waiting for an answer for him to give to Jordan. I grabbed my phone out of my pocket, calling Demetrius, hoping she would answer. I really didn't want my daughter in all of this. I wanted to get her to safety first.

"Aww, little puta." She answered. "Why did you...hang up on me??!" She screamed, distorting the phone's speaker.

"Let's meet, somewhere neutral. Where are you?" I asked. Not sure if she knew that I already know where to find her. "You have my kid. And I yours. Let's trade and just finish this like...women." It was hard for me to even say that. She didn't deserve the title.

"No." She replied. I was stunned. "No. My son and $800 Million. And I may give this sweet little girl back, before I bleed her."

"You lay a finger on her and–"

"Que? What will you do? Dime."

"Try me and find out." I said, she just broke into laughter.

"Tonight. Downtown. Ogawa Plaza. 10 o'clock." She ordered, hanging up the line. My brain went through all the different ways she could have survived that helicopter crash, none of them made sense. But it didn't matter. I was going to end this shit tonight.

We sat there, parked for almost 2 hours waiting for the time when we would meet. It was 9:45 when the gates opened. 4 Lexus trucks drove out, with a 2017 red Lexus Rx between them.

"Follow them." I said to Michael. I had Jordan and 2 of the other trucks hang back to storm the house. "She has to be holding him there." I said as we rode away from the house, following Esmeralda. We made it to the plaza, rested and engines killed before they even hit the corner, driving right by us. "Let's go." I said, getting out of the back of the truck. Montrell followed closely behind me with Eddie at gun point. We walked up the short block, not wanting them to see where we left the vehicles. I watched as Esmeralda stepped out of the car. Once she did, 3 doors from all of her trucks opened up. Leaving the drivers of those vehicles behind the wheel. "Where's my daughter?" I yelled out at the hooded figure. I snatching Eddie from Monty, putting my pistol to his head. I knew Asia was still in the car, but she was still too heavenly guarded. I had no plans of letting her *or* Eddie walk out of here alive. Though, I still had to get Asia out without a ton of gun fire. Then it dawned on me, "That's not possible."

"Monty, go get Asia. Me and this bitch need to have a conversation." I ordered. She probably thought that leaving the driver's in the cars were a good idea, but it just made them easier targets.

It was now a standoff between me, and a handful of my remaining guys against her and 20-25 of her best men. The odds were not in our favor.

********************👑**URBAN QUEEN**👑********************

Jordan and Sid led 20 men into the house less than 5 minutes after Liyah and Michael began to follow Esmeralda. The darkness gave them cover, as they ran up the U-Shaped driveway, getting rid of the guards that remained. Most of her Forces that stayed behind were on the inside, with only 4 men on the front terrace of the mansion. They snuck in, still undetected after sniping the four scouts. Debris and dust filled the house with a haunting vibe. The air was thick with loud music, cigar and cigarette smoke and urine. The 20 of them split up. 5 going down to the basement and the rest moving through the house. Divide and conquer. The guys stepped over weak spots in the floor, and portions of the ceiling that fell to the weakened floorboards.

Jordan and the rest continued upstairs, trying their best to stay silent. Hoping the music lasted and continued to play. The stairs squeaked with each step they took, heading to the second story. They ran into 6 guys once they made it to the second level of the home. Two of the guys were sitting at a table, playing cards, laughing, and joking in Spanish. Jordan could understand that they were talking about the man in the basement. It had to have been Demetrius. There were a few other guys, getting lap dances to the Spanish rap that played. The entire floor was covered with Esmeralda's goons. There was no way a sneak and escape was going to happen. Jordan began backing up, down the stairs, realizing they were outnumbered. He hoped no one had spotted them before the other group could get Demetrius out safely.

BAH!! BAH!! BAH!!

One of Esmeralda's women, saw them skulking back downstairs as she was on her way up. Jermaine, another one of Liyah's goons caught one to the back of his head, while she missed the other two shots. Everyone spun around, putting her down instantly, while also alerting everyone in the house. All Jordan could hope was that this wasn't all for nothing. They rushed down the stairs, dodging the bullets, trying to fight back.

Down in the basement, Franklin found Demetrius, bloody and laying on a dirty mattress, behind a locked chain link fence. One of the four guys Frank was with, shot the lock off the gate with his silenced pistol.

"Come on, son." Frank said, as two of them grabbed Demetrius and started up the stairs.

BAH!! BAH!! BAH!!

"Shit. We gotta get out of here." Frank said. The five of them resisted the urge to help the others in the fight, knowing if they did, they'd never make it out with Demetrius alive.

Everyone soon realized they had greatly underestimated the force of power Esmeralda left behind. All of Liyah's men, who reminded inside, were gunned down. But before officer Jacob took his last breath, he set off a series of grenades, almost leveling the *entire* estate.

Franklin sped down Broadway, passed Liyah and the others as he raced to the old warehouse, where a handful of doctors on payroll where waiting.

Demetrius was barely clinging to life as he bled onto the white leather sofa and shag rug.

"Aight, Frank, back up. Let us work." One of the male doctors ordered as they laid Demetrius flat onto the floor. Demetrius didn't care whether he lived or died. All he could think about was, where is his wife and daughter?

*********************♛URBAN QUEEN♛**********************

"I want my daughter, Esmeralda!" I screamed at the hooded figure. She had on a black, ankle-length trench coat, with a large hood, that shadowed her face. Her men outnumbered us 4-1 easily. I was nervous, terrified, but I refused to let that be seen. Especially by this evil bitch. "Where's my child?" I asked again, cocking the gun I held to Eddie's head. "I won't ask again."

"Mommy!!" I heard Asia yelling. One of the hardest things I've ever done, was to resists the God-like call to run to her side. She stepped forward and out of the shadows, grabbing her hood, letting it fall to the back of her neck. The entire left side of her head was covered in 2–3-degree burns. The other side of her face looked perfectly fine, like nothing had ever happened. Her long black locks flowing freely over her shoulder. Suddenly, gunshots began to ring out from one of the SUVs protecting Esmeralda. I ducked behind the wall of one of the shops in the small area. Esmeralda and her men began shooting at us, trying to separate us from Eddie. And it worked. But not for long. I attempted to raise my gun to put him down, but one of my guys beat me to it.

"Please save my baby, Monty." I thought to myself. I couldn't see him. All I could see, was that my men were starting to fall. I rushed over to get a different view. I could see Monty sitting on the ground, head against the back tire of the Lexus. The driver stood over him, putting two bullets into his chest and one in his head, finishing the job. He leaned into the car, staring in at Asia, tapping on the glass with the muzzle of his pistol. I could hear her screaming for me, terrified. I shot him in the back twice, dropping him instantly. "Mommy's coming, baby." I said to myself, slowly creeping over to the car. I suddenly felt someone tackle me to the ground. I fought back, stopping once I realized I wasn't being attacked. I pulled myself out from under the weight and noticed it was Michael. He'd taken a ton of bullets to his back, tackling me so I wouldn't get hit by them.

The gun fire had me frozen with fear, surrounded by mayhem. My attention was caught by Esmeralda running across the dark field, trying to vanish again. I wanted to go after her, but Asia came first. I couldn't pass up the chance at saving her.

"Mommy!!!" She cried; face drenched with tears of fear.

"Get back, baby. Cover your head. Just like when we're playing hide and seek. Hide and seek." I said. She crouched onto the floor behind the passenger's seat and covered her head with both arms. I broke out the window with my gun, before reaching in and unlocking the door to snatch her out, just as another bullet was heading for us. I fell to the ground as the driver's window shattered. I was staring at the shooter when out of the shadows, 3 of my guys came over beating him to a bloody pulp.

"You okay, boss?" One of them asked approaching me, as the other two filled the shooter with lead. "We got this. You get out of here." He said, urging me to run towards the truck.

"No, I still got business here. Get her to Frank." I said, looking around for Esmeralda. I know she'd be long gone by now. But as I scanned the park's shadows, I could see a figure hiding behind a tree. He took Asia out of my hands and ran a full sprint to one of our trucks. My heart ached, hearing Asia call for me as I took off running after Esmeralda.

I began hearing sirens. As I stopped to turn back, I saw that blue and white lights had quickly joined the fight. "Fuck!" I yelled angrily, once again being tackled to the ground. It was her. We rolled around on the ground, trading blows, punching and kicking each other. She wasn't so tough when I wasn't drugged up or tied to a chair. I was about to start taking out all of my frustration and hurt onto her face. Punching her repeatedly once I was able to get her on her back.

"Oakland PD!! Freeze!!" We heard a man yell. We looked in that direction and seen 3 cops running towards us. She punched me, using the cops as a distraction before she took off running. I got up in enough time, chasing her. I had her turning tail. It was a nice change. Staying on her heels. The cops couldn't keep up.

I chased Esmeralda passed the greyhound station, and right onto San Pablo, into Skid Row: a place where the majority of Oakland's homeless population pitched their tents, for shelter. She continued down San Pablo Ave, cutting a left onto Athens, once again trying to lose me.

"What the fuck?" I heard a female voice exclaim. There was a group of girls on one of the porches. One of the girls, stood in the doorway, like she'd been pushed out of the way. "She went this way!" She said to me, allowing me into her home to find Esmeralda.

"What the fuck, bitch?!!" I heard someone yell from the kitchen. I ran through, almost running into her. "Oh Lord." She cried as we barely missed each other. I continued chasing her into the backyard, where she was trying to climb to the other side of the fence.

BAH!!

I shot a bullet into her leg, causing her to fall back onto the dirty ground. She stood up, facing me, holding her upper thigh. "What are you going to do? Kill a poor, defenseless woman." I began walking up on her, closing the 20' gap that separated us. "God, I enjoyed gutting your brother, and that whore of his?..." She chuckled. She was feeding my anger. I raised my pistol to her face. I turned around, realizing we had an audience. I turned back around to see Esmeralda trying to snatch the gun from me. I suddenly heard sirens screaming in the distance. And they were getting closer. Out of the corner of my eye, I saw her trying to inch closer to me.

"Nah, bitch." I said, cocking the pistol. She stood up straight, her hands in the air.

"What are you waiting for? Do it, little puta! Kill me!!" She screamed. Here it was, the moment I've been waiting for, but I couldn't bring myself to pull the trigger. "Do it, bitch! Your brother begged for his life I won't. He begged me not to gut-"

BAH!! BAH!! BAH!! BAH!! BAH!! BAH!! BAH!! Click!! Click!! Click!!

"I'll see you in hell." I said, before stomping on her head a few times. Without looking back, I jumped over the fence, into the neighboring yard. Continuing to hop over fences, until I made it to Market St, tossing my leather YSL coat into the dumpster behind All Stars Donuts. I needed to get to my family. I felt the keys to one of the trucks in my pants. There was *no way* I could go back Downtown, especially that close to the action. I made it to a bus stop, happy that I saw someone waiting.

"'Scuse me? How much is the bus?" I asked him. The guy couldn't have been much older than me. He was tall, built like a basketball player and dark skinned, with corn rolls in his hair.

"It's...$1.75." He responded, confused.

"I'm sorry, I've never caught the bus and I have to get to my daughter, would you mind-"

"Sure, no problem." He said, digging into his pocket and pulling out 2 $1 bills. I felt like an alien looking at the money. Even when I stripped, I've never seen currency so low.

"Thank you." I said as the bus approached the curb. I took my seat in the front, seeing a group of guys and girls in the back that didn't look like they had a problem starting anything. I felt vulnerable without my team or a loaded weapon.

The bus ended up going Downtown, right passed the war scene. I saw news vans from all over the Bay Area and more police cars and yellow tape than ever. I felt the urge to hide, but resisted as it would only arouse suspicion. As the bus rode by, I couldn't help but stare at all of the dead bodies that littered the plaza, before we crossed over the freeway, and into West Oakland. I got off the bus near the Acorn projects, taking the long way, often looking back to make sure I wasn't being followed.

Walking the dark streets, I've never felt so alone. There were so many people just out and about. I felt out of place, and even more vulnerable as I passed by creepy men...and women on the street. I recognized an area close to the old warehouse, and ran the rest of the way, until I made it, busting through the side door. Everyone was nursing their wounds, but it was only about 20 of my people left.

"Li!!" I heard someone yell. I looked up at the catwalk, running across the room to get to the staircase. Frank was waiting outside of the office door. He was covered in blood, but he looked healthy as a horse. "He's inside." He said as I made it to the top of the steps. I walked in and saw Demetrius laying on the couch. The doctors had done all they could and left. The rest of the battle was up to him.

"Oh, my God!!" I cried, dropping down next to him. The scene was horrific and it didn't look like he was going to make it. He was covered in bandages, most of which already needing to he changed. His leg was in a sling, and he also had an IV drip, more than likely for all of the pain. And all due from my family.

"Ba..." He whispered. He tried his best to turn his head towards me, but it stopped midway.

"Shhhh." I said. "Don't speak. Just rest." I sobbed. Wanting badly to just hold him. "Where's Asia?" I asked, looking up at Frank. He nodded his head towards the office door. I kissed Demetrius on his forehead and stood to follow Frank.

"She's right outside, watching TV." He said, opening the main door to the office. Asia was on the sofa, passed out under a brown leather Fendi coat. She looked terrified and scared, even in her slumber. I rushed over to her. Hugging and kissing her awake, happy that we were all finally safe.

"Mommy!!" She cried, just as soon as her eyelids parted ways. She held onto my neck so tight I could barely breathe. I could tell she was still terrified.

"I'm so sorry." I sobbed, hugging her back. I was so happy to see her make it out of this alive.

"I wanna go home, mommy." She cried

"I know, baby. Let's go home." I said, picking her up, holding back tears. I held her close as she rested on my right shoulder. "Frank, call Sandra and tell her I want our accounts under new names. If she asks what happened...tell her. I'm taking Asia home. Watch over Demetrius, please. You and them doctors keep him alive. Call me *if* you need me."

"Will do, boss."

The two of us stepped outside. I froze in my tracks seeing Eddie standing right in front of me, holding a silver .380, pointing right at me.

"But, you're de-" I began.

BAH! BAH! BAH!

"My baby!" I screamed, feeling hot pressure in my chest as I began falling to the ground.

Printed in the United States
by Baker & Taylor Publisher Services